PRAISE FOR *DE*

'Riveting stuff'—*Tehelka*

'Compelling characters . . . and observations'—*Indian Express*

'Gives you an image of Delhi that takes a while to shake off'—*Mail Today*

'A page turner in every sense . . . uncovers the real character of Delhi'—*Pioneer*

'Private-eye Arjun Arora is the star of this crackling thriller'—*Eclectic Northeast*

'*Dead Meat* makes Delhi come alive'—*Assam Tribune*

PRAISE FOR *THE GIRL FROM NONGRIM HILLS*

'Packs a punch'—*Telegraph*

'A gripping thriller'—*Time Out*

'Dark and detailed'—*Deccan Chronicle*

'The first noir thriller from India's North East'—*Mint*

'Unputdownable'—ibnlive.com

PENGUIN BOOKS
REMEMBER DEATH

Ankush Saikia was born in Tezpur, Assam. He worked in journalism and publishing in New Delhi for over a decade and was shortlisted for the Outlook–Picador India non-fiction writing award (2005). He is the author of *The Girl from Nongrim Hills* (2013) and *Dead Meat* (2015), among others.

ANKUSH SAIKIA

REMEMBER DEATH

PENGUIN BOOKS

PENGUIN BOOKS

USA | Canada | UK | Ireland | Australia
New Zealand | India | South Africa | China

Penguin Books is part of the Penguin Random House group of companies
whose addresses can be found at global.penguinrandomhouse.com

Published by Penguin Random House India Pvt. Ltd
7th Floor, Infinity Tower C, DLF Cyber City,
Gurgaon 122 002, Haryana, India

Penguin
Random House
India

First published in Penguin Books by Penguin Random House India 2016

ISBN 9780143424895

Typeset in Adobe Garamond Pro by Manipal Digital Systems, Manipal
Printed at Replika Press Pvt. Ltd, India

www.penguinbooksindia.com

For my aunt,
Dr Lakshmi Goswami of Tezpur

PROLOGUE

Shimla, Himachal Pradesh
October 1962

THE ROADS WERE DESERTED IN this small British-era hill station in the north of India. A cold, wet night: nearly everyone was indoors. The mood here, as elsewhere in the country, was one of despair; fifteen years after winning her independence, India had been brought down to earth.

At the Oldfield Sanatorium on the outskirts of town the lights shone weakly on the deserted verandas, while in their common room a handful of nurses were listening in glum silence to the All India Radio news on the heavy Grundig. Chinese troops were advancing in the North-East Frontier Agency and in Ladakh. Indian soldiers were in retreat, and Prime Minister Nehru had appealed to his countrymen for courage and sacrifice in this hour of national crisis. The slogan he had earlier come up with—'*Hindi–Chini bhai bhai*', or 'Indians and Chinese are brothers'—now seemed like a cruel joke.

A woman in a sari and a thin pullover hurried out of the sanatorium's deserted reception area to the porch. In her arms was a day-old infant swaddled in blankets, its piteous cry similar to the mewing of a kitten. Behind the woman was a man in a dhoti and a coat, a frown upon his brow as he chewed on the stem of his pipe. They were followed by a nurse, a fair, stocky Anglo-Indian woman in her mid-thirties.

The nurse stood on the porch and watched them hurry through the thin rain to the car waiting in the parking area. They got in, the driver started the engine and she saw the headlights of the vehicle disappear past the gates into the night. An immense sorrow gripped her heart. What would become of that poor child?

She turned and went back inside. Walking towards her was a tall figure in a black salwar kameez: the patient's mother. It was rumoured that she had once been a highly paid dancing girl in Lucknow, performing for the nawabs and the British. She looked the same as usual—cold and haughty, her kohl-rimmed eyes unblinking, though signs of age were beginning to show beneath the stony reserve.

'Nurse,' the woman said in her high voice, 'a pair of my daughter's earrings is missing. Have you seen it?'

The nurse's features could have been set in stone. 'No, I haven't.'

'My daughter wore those earrings in her last film. They were given to me by someone, and I had gifted them to her.'

'I'll ask the other nurses to look for them.'

'Please. Also, can you get another blanket? My daughter might feel cold tonight.'

'I'll get one in a while,' the nurse said.

There was an uncomfortable silence as they observed the steadily increasing rain.

'Why did you tell her it was a girl?' the older woman suddenly asked. 'I told you not to say anything to her.'

'They should have taken *your* daughter away from you at birth!' the nurse burst out at the patient's mother, who for a moment was too surprised to reply.

Then the woman said, 'Anyway, when she wakes up tomorrow we have to tell her the baby didn't survive.'

The nurse glared at the woman, then went into the common room and slammed the door shut behind her.

'A witch,' she muttered to herself, 'that woman is a real witch.'

None of the other nurses dared ask her what had happened.

1

Delhi
October 2012

A WHITE INDICA WITH TWO turbaned sardars inside it bumped along a potholed road running through a dismal-looking colony on the outskirts of north-east Delhi, not far from the highway running to Loni in Ghaziabad. Half-dressed children and scrawny goats loitered beside open drains, young men lounged in the doorways of brick hovels eyeing the women who walked past, and cows rummaged through piles of rubbish.

'You know the address, don't you?' the driver asked his passenger yet again.

The driver was a big, fat sardar who ran a taxi depot in south Delhi; he used this private car of his to ferry people past the city limits.

'Just keep driving, I'll tell you when to stop,' his passenger replied.

The taxi depot owner glanced at his rear-view mirror. The shiny grey suit, the sunglasses, the beard, the tight black turban—there was something about his passenger that didn't seem right. But his job was to drive, not to ask questions.

A short distance ahead, the passenger asked him to stop in front of a whitewashed building with a godown beside it.

'Wait here, I'll be out in a while,' the man said, and got down with his briefcase.

'Jo hukum, maharaj,' the driver muttered and turned on his car's FM radio.

The passenger looked up and down the road, then went and knocked on the door. From the godown came the whine of metal being worked. The door was opened by a thickset, dark-complexioned man in a denim shirt, sporting a few days of stubble, and thick, greasy hair. He looked the passenger up and down, and let him in. The room was bare save for a Sunmica-topped steel table with a telephone in the middle and a couple of plastic chairs around it. There was a smell of damp and fried food, and a colourful calendar on a wall. The man in the denim shirt disappeared, and the passenger put his briefcase on the table and sat down. He took a deep breath and then exhaled, trying to relax his tense muscles. The metallic whining from next door set his teeth on edge.

The first man reappeared with two others in tow: a short, thin man wearing a white shirt and a gold chain, and a curly-haired man in a faded red T-shirt that said 'Hot Chicks'.

'Mr Singh!' the short man exclaimed. 'Good to see you. Is that the money?'

The passenger nodded. 'Where are the samples?'

Gold Chain raised a hand in a gesture of placation, and told Denim Shirt to go get the samples. Hot Chicks came around the table and sat by the visitor.

'Nice sunglasses you're wearing,' the man said, laying a hand on the visitor's tie-knot. 'Anything else you're wearing? Anything hidden?'

The visitor took off his sunglasses and stared back coldly at the man. 'Get your hands off me, you sisterfucker,' he said in a low tone.

Hot Chicks withdrew his hands warily, while Gold Chain let out a nervous laugh and said, 'Arré, Mr Singh, please don't mind. We had a motherfucker journalist come in once wearing a spy camera. Just checking, just checking.'

The visitor pulled the briefcase towards him, opened the locks and threw the cover back to reveal stacks of crisp, new five-hundred-rupee notes.

'Let's talk business, Gullu,' he said. 'I need to be back in Kolkata tonight.'

'Certainly, Mr Singh. Ah, here are the samples.'

Denim Shirt had returned with a large metal tray which he placed on the table. In it were several automobile spare parts: clutch plates, ball bearings, brake linings. They were all stamped with the logo of a well-known auto-parts brand. The visitor picked up a brake lining and examined it closely.

'Looks good,' he said. 'The parts in the shipments will be identical, won't they?'

'Don't worry about that, Mr Singh. We guarantee you genuine articles.'

'Genuine fakes, you mean,' the visitor said.

'Arré, it's the same thing, Mr Singh,' Gullu said. 'Even if we told people these were fake they would still buy them because they're cheaper. So what's the harm in selling them as originals at the original price? It makes the customer feel good.'

'This is half of the payment,' the visitor said. 'Get it counted. The other half on delivery.'

Gullu told Denim Shirt to take the briefcase and feed the notes through the counting machine.

'Delivery at the shop address in Kolkata, right?' he asked the visitor.

'Yes, the Dum Dum address.'

'Did you have someone go there and inquire?' Gullu asked Hot Chicks.

The other man nodded. 'He said it seemed okay. They told him Mr Singh was in Delhi.'

'Just checking, just checking,' Gullu said to the visitor with a smile. 'And what about our next consignment?'

'Let me get back and talk to my partner. We can open up the north-east market for you: Guwahati, Shillong, Dimapur. Nobody checks these things there, you just have to pay.'

'*Sahi hai*. Let me know. For larger orders, I'll have to talk to my boss in Mumbai.'

'Who's that?'

'Place your order first, then we'll talk. What will you have, Mr Singh—tea, cold drink, water?'

'Thank you, but it's okay.'

'We have stronger stuff, if you want,' Gullu said with a wink. 'Whisky, grass, hash.'

'Maybe next time,' the visitor said with a tight smile.

'Next time you come we'll go out at night, okay?' Gullu said to the visitor, and then to Hot Chicks, 'We'll take him to our nearby *kotha*, *kyun*? Ha ha!'

Hot Chicks took out a large touchscreen phone and showed the visitor a photo: a plump, made-up girl dressed in glittering pink. He said with a wink, 'First-class *maal*!'

Denim Shirt returned with the empty briefcase and told Gullu that the amount added up, at which the latter stood up and shook hands with the visitor.

'You don't worry, Mr Singh, your stuff will reach in a week's time.' He thumped his chest. 'Gullu takes personal responsibility for it.'

'We'll meet again,' the visitor said, opening the briefcase on the table once more. 'And I'm taking these samples to show my partner.'

He stopped at the door as if struck by a sudden thought and, without turning around, asked, 'What happened to that journalist?'

Gullu gave a snort. 'We broke his spy camera, and then we broke one of his arms. He never came back.'

Outside, the visitor put the newly loaded briefcase into the car before turning to look back at the building, as if trying to imprint it on his mind. He got in and asked the driver to take him back to south Delhi.

2

THE WHITE INDICA TURNED OFF the Outer Ring Road and cut through the old Bengali colonies of Kalkaji and Chittaranjan Park. The fat sardar halted on the left of the road, in front of a footwear showroom situated above a Chinese restaurant called Kolkata Hot Pot. The building next to it housed the office of the detective agency Nexus Security; in the basement was a computer and cell phone outlet, while the owners had the two flats above. The passenger paid the fare and got down, briefcase in hand. He had asked the driver to take him to the restaurant, but once the car left, he walked up to the ground floor of the adjoining building and pushed open the tinted-glass door of the agency.

A dusky, bespectacled woman in a red-and-blue salwar kameez looked up from her computer. She looked south Indian, in her late twenties.

'Yes?' she said. 'May I help you?'

The man didn't answer, but looked around without taking his sunglasses off. Another dark-glass wall partitioned off an inner room. Across from the woman's desk were a sofa and a table, a filing cabinet and a small wall-mounted television. It was tuned to a Hindi news channel being watched by a bored-looking youth perched on a stool in the corner.

'Can I help you, sir?' the woman asked again in a louder voice.

'Is this Arjun Arora's office?' the man said by way of reply, stepping up to her table.

'Can you tell me what you're here for?' the woman asked, a little flustered now.

'This is the office of Nexus Security, isn't it?'

'Yes, it is. But—'

'Mr Arjun Arora is the owner of this agency, isn't he? It opened two or three months ago?'

'Yes, he's the owner—'

The man cut her short, put his briefcase on the floor, placed his hands on the table and leaned over her computer.

'What's your name, miss?'

'What? Liza, I'm Liza Thomas. Can you please take a seat over there until Mr Arora is back?'

She cast a nervous glance at the youth, but the man paid no attention to that.

'Where's Arjun Arora? I need to see him. It's urgent.'

'Arjun sir is out handling a case.'

'What case is that? Something to do with fake automobile parts?'

The woman's eyes widened. She stood up and said loudly, 'Listen, I don't know who you are, but if you want to discuss something, wait till Mr Arora is back, okay?'

The young man had got to his feet now. Was there going to be a problem? The visitor took a step back, smiled, took off his sunglasses and peeled off his beard. There was a gasp of surprise from the woman. Next, the man pulled off his one-piece turban—in the place of the sardar, now stood Arjun Arora.

'How did you . . . ?' Liza couldn't complete her question and just stood there.

'Did you like my disguise?' Arjun asked, grinning. 'Thought I was a sardar, didn't you?'

'I suspected something was wrong,' she said.

'Now you say so,' Arjun said. 'And by the way, what did I say about giving people information about me?'

'I'm sorry, sir. I was taken by surprise . . .'

'It's okay, but in the future, you only discuss the client's case, all right?'

'Right, sir,' his secretary said, sitting down. 'You know, you were like Dharmendra in that old movie *Jeevan Mrityu*,' she added sheepishly.

'The one where he is in disguise, wearing a turban and a beard?'

'Yes, sir, that one.'

'Maybe I have a future in Bollywood.'

His secretary rolled her eyes; he knew she didn't particularly appreciate his occasional attempts at humour. Arjun asked the youth, whose name was Chandu, to take the thermos and get some tea from Market No. 1, and told Liza he would type out a report which she would then have to send to their client, along with the preliminary report, the address of the factory, the phone numbers of the people involved, and photographs of the fake spare parts in his briefcase.

'All right, sir,' she said, opening a drawer to look for the digital camera.

Arjun stood there a while looking at her, then turned to face the television. The police were still looking, the newsreader was saying, for the dead girl's female companion, who had disappeared from the Bharat Lodge in Mumbai's Santacruz that morning, after the murder. He listened for a moment to the morning's events from a reporter before stepping into his office where he switched on the tube light and the air conditioner and opened his laptop. He took off his tie and jacket, and stepped into the small bathroom to wash his face. A female companion—that was strange. In such cases it was usually a boyfriend or husband. When he came out he stood under the AC vent for a while. It

11

was humid; outside, the sky had turned dark grey, threatening to rain. He then sat at his desk and mentally outlined the points for his report.

Chandu returned with the thermos and poured out three cups of tea, one of which he brought to the detective. He went back out to help Liza arrange the auto parts on the table to photograph them. Arjun leaned back in his chair, sipped the hot tea, and winced—too much sugar again. The whole place still had an air of make-believe for him. Nexus Security was barely three months old—less than a hundred days. Further down the road was the restaurant he had started with his ex-wife and then let go; this place had been fixed for him by the same broker. When the sign painter had turned up, he didn't even have a name ready. In the end he picked the name off a phone box he had seen in the window of the cell phone store below them.

Arjun put down the tea cup and started typing: 'The National Capital Region of Delhi is home to countless operations that churn out all manner of fake goods, from cosmetics to designer luggage, electronics to soft drinks and alcohol. One such unit—'

He paused and read what he had written, then deleted the words. It had sounded more like a newspaper story. He started typing again: 'Upon the request of our esteemed clients, the Automobile Parts Manufacturers Association of India, we began investigating an operation that was manufacturing low-grade duplicate spare parts and using well-known brand names for the same. A fake profile of a Kolkata-based trader was created, and Nexus Security approached a person known as Gullu, a former resident of Gurgaon.' Here Arjun paused for a moment. Much better, but there was still something wrong with it. Now it read like a police report. He sighed and picked up the tea cup. Sheer exhaustion was making him drowsy, even though he hadn't had a particularly hectic day by his standards. Impersonating a sardar

12

from Kolkata—what would his father have to say about that? Thinking about his father, Arjun resolved to call his mother later and ask about him. And he had to call his daughter as well. He drained his cup and resumed typing.

Twenty-five minutes later, he was done with the report. He attached it to an email where he itemized the agency's bill, and sent it to Liza in the outer room. He was getting used to the conveniences of an office, of a secretary and an assistant, and the place wasn't too far from his flat. From the landline on his desk he called Arun George, an official of the automobile association, and informed him that the results of the investigation would be with him shortly. George thanked him and said he would send across the rest of the payment in a day or two. He said they would ask the police to conduct a raid by the next day. Arjun said he hoped they recovered the money, and then remembered something.

'They mentioned their boss was in Mumbai. Who could that be?'

'I'm not sure, Arjun. Could be a chap called Sanjay Walekar. You want to go have a look?'

'I'm based in Delhi. To operate out of Mumbai would . . .'

'Just go meet him. Phone number, description, that's all. I'll handle it from there.'

'But if you have that raid tomorrow . . .'

'I can defer it by a day or two. Till you meet this guy. I'll make it worth your while.'

'I'll think about it,' Arjun said, and hung up.

He spent a further twenty minutes checking mail and surfing some news stories before shutting down his laptop and putting it into his backpack. He switched off the lights and the air conditioner, picked up his tie, jacket and backpack, and told Liza and Chandu to stick around till 6.30 p.m. and shut shop after that.

Once he was outside, he lit a cigarette and savoured the rush of the tobacco smoke. He hadn't smoked while he had been undercover, and he tried not to smoke in the office. At his age, he knew he should quit smoking. He walked ahead to where he had parked his car. The sky was turning black, and a rough breeze ruffled the roadside trees. As he flicked the cigarette into the gutter and got into his silver-grey Swift, the first fat drops of rain fell on the car's bonnet and on the road.

3

BY THE TIME HE SLOTTED the car into his parking space beside the park wall in CR Park's B Block, the rain was pelting down. The roads would soon be flooded due to all the blocked drains. Arjun turned off the ignition and sat listening to the rain drumming on the car roof. He remembers an old, red Assam State Transport Corporation bus slowly winding up the road from Guwahati to Shillong in heavy rain, water leaking through the sliding window beside which he sits. Next to him on the bench-like seat is his mother, then his father. When the bus stops at Nongpoh they run into the 'hotel' where his father gets tea, a packet of orange-cream biscuits and 'egg devil' chops for them. He eats the breadcrumb-coated boiled egg and potato chop slowly, relishing its taste. Such simple pleasures! He could almost see the steam rising from their tea glasses, his mother looking at the other passengers and his father staring out at the rain, a faraway look on his face.

Arjun felt a sense of sorrow for his lost younger self, but something made him snap out of his reverie—a vague sense of foreboding came over him. He glanced up and down the deserted lane weakly lit by street lights, and then up at his darkened flat. He was still wary after the events of a few months ago when an investigation into the disappearance of an accountant had led to his getting tangled up with a cricket match-fixing ring. One of the main bookies had gone to jail because of Arjun, and had also ended up killing a psychopathic butcher. He told himself to get a grip on his nerves. His profession was such that it coloured everything in shades of grey. He got out of the car and ran across to the entrance.

On the first-floor landing, he switched on the light and unlocked his front door. He stepped inside his flat and stood still for a moment, trying to detect any foreign odours. Then he turned on the lights, shut the door and inspected the items on the table by the door. The trinkets and notepad and desk calendar he had arranged in a precise pattern. Nothing appeared to have been moved. He went to his bedroom where he took off his clothes and stepped into the bathroom. After a long shower he stood before the wide mirror above the washbasin, looking at himself.

Three months short of his forty-second birthday, he was still naturally lean and muscular. Around his midriff were the scars left by a bullet wound and a knife stab, souvenirs of his present trade, but the real scars were inside his head, born of his kidnapping and near-death experience in Iraq. He could make out a slight thinning of his arms and thighs, and a thickening around his gut. Bringing his face closer to the mirror he could see fine lines on his forehead and below his eyes and flecks of grey in his close-cropped hair. He was growing old. He went out into the bedroom and put on a pair of shorts and a T-shirt.

He turned on the table lamp in the sitting room and opened the balcony door. The rain was still coming down hard; the air growing chilly. I need to start exercising, he told himself, and also cut down on the alcohol. His doctor had warned him that his occasional swollen toe joints and painful knees could progress to full-scale gout, arthritis or even avascular necrosis or osteonecrosis—bone cell death caused by interrupted blood supply—which would freeze his joints and cripple him. But he knew he would keep putting it off—next week, next month, next year. He went and took out a bottle of Blenders Pride from the cabinet near the dining table and poured himself a drink. That he had a drinking problem, he had known for years now, but had somehow managed to keep things under control. But for how much longer? And yet, the thought of being without a glass of whisky as night fell when he was alone in his flat was terrifying.

To distract himself, Arjun got busy preparing dinner. Comfort food on a cold, wet evening: rice, dal, small potatoes fried with garlic the way his mother cooked them and some fish, already smeared with salt and turmeric, which he took out from the freezer to defrost. He was trying to cut down on red meat too, on his doctor's orders. He switched on the television news as he cooked, just to hear some voices in the empty flat, and poured himself a second and then a third peg. Once the potatoes were done, he went out to the balcony for a smoke. The fish he would fry just before he ate.

One of the legs of the chair on the balcony had broken, and it wobbled as he sat down. The flowers in the pots, uncared for after his wife had left, were dead; just one or two of the shrubs were still growing. But I don't mind, he thought, I like it this way. He lit a cigarette and looked out at a solitary orange street light at the entrance to the park shining through the rain. How many people had come to the flat after Sonali had left? Just two, he realized: his friend Bunty and his daughter, Rhea. Three if you counted the maid.

I should call someone, he thought. But Yamini Gupta hadn't called him since she had moved to Mumbai, just forwarded him her new number one day in what seemed like a group text message. Who else was there? The newspaper editor Poppy Barua. She had given him a few hints. But he decided against it. She was too useful to his work for him to risk things going wrong. Arjun knew he had to call his father and his daughter, but he felt a reluctance to pick up the phone now. It had been a long day and he was tired. Maybe tomorrow. He sat on the darkened balcony with the raindrops splashing at his feet, thinking about the time he had spent with the army in the north-east, and with the security contractor on the dry, dusty streets of Iraq. What did a man's life add up to in the end?

4

THE SUDDEN CHIRPING OF THE doorbell startled Arjun. He had been lost in his remembrance of times past and hadn't noticed if anyone had stopped their car down below and approached the building. Leaving his glass on the wobbly chair he went to the front door and looked through the peephole. It was a man in a black overcoat with his back turned to the door, patting his pale, bald head with a crumpled handkerchief. Arjun hesitated, and the man turned around and pressed the doorbell again. A pale face with round eyes, a look of annoyance upon it. What did he want, and why was he wearing an overcoat at this time of the year? Arjun opened the door.

'Detective Arjun Arora?' the man inquired in a soft voice, hands held together and bending forward from the waist. His manner had changed from a moment ago; he was meek and submissive now.

'Yes, you're talking to him.'

'Can I come in, please?' The man took a step forward. 'I got wet in the rain.'

'If you have a case for me, I think you should come to my office tomorrow morning.'

'Oh, but it's an emergency, and I've come a long way.'

An unpleasant false humility radiated from the man's wet face, but Arjun found himself unable to shut the door on him.

In his profession, he had all types of clients. He stepped aside to let the visitor in, and closed the door.

The man took off his overcoat in the sitting room and extracted from within it a long envelope. He was wearing grey trousers and a white shirt, and his large body had a shapeless quality about it.

'Where can I keep this?' he asked, holding up the wet overcoat.

Arjun took it from him and draped the heavy coat over one of the dining table chairs.

'My name is Vikas,' the man said, bending forward again and extending a hand. 'I have come from Bombay.'

The hand was soft and damp. Arjun asked the man to take a seat. 'Bombay', he noted, as people from that city would say, and not 'Mumbai'. The man looked to be in his fifties. But there didn't seem to be anything Mumbai-like about him.

'What can I do for you?' Arjun asked, turning down the volume of the news channel.

'Can you turn it off, please?' the visitor said in his soft voice. 'The television.'

Arjun felt a stab of irritation, but did as he was requested and put the remote down on the coffee table. 'How can I help you, Mr Vikas?'

The man held out the envelope and said, 'I have been sent to give this to you.'

Arjun took the envelope and turned it around in his hands. It was an unmarked brown-paper envelope of the sort available at any stationery shop.

'How did you find my house?' he asked.

'You were referred to us.'

'By whom? And who is "us"?'

'Please, first look at what is inside the envelope.'

Arjun opened the flap and shook the contents out on the table: a bundle of thousand-rupee notes, a folded sheet of paper and a slip with the typewritten words LOBBY OF HOTEL SUNSET VIEW, 4 P.M. Did someone not want their handwriting to be recognized?

He looked up at Mr Vikas. 'Who has sent you?'

The man placed a thick forefinger on the bundle of notes. 'One lakh rupees in cash,' he said. The light from the table lamp threw a yellow glow on the man's damp, bald head. He spread out the folded sheet of paper. 'One business-class flight ticket to Bombay in the name of Arjun Arora.' He put his finger on the typewritten note. 'One appointment slip.'

'Tell me what this is about,' Arjun said, his irritation returning.

'This is a ticket to Bombay for tomorrow,' the man said, moving his thighs to come forward on the chair, 'and this slip of paper has the time and place of your appointment with the person who wants to hire you. Plus one lakh rupees for immediate expenses.'

Arjun looked into the man's large, watery eyes, half-believing what he was hearing.

'Who wants to hire me? And why didn't he come himself?'

'He's a busy man, so he sent me instead.'

'Listen, I can't fly to Mumbai just like that. I need to know about the case. I need to discuss my payment. I need to—'

'You'll be told everything in Bombay,' the man interrupted. 'And as for your payment, we'll pay you twice your normal fee.'

Arjun considered this for a moment, and then asked, 'What is the case about?'

'You'll find out everything in Bombay,' Mr Vikas repeated, and got to his feet in an ungainly manner. 'Remember, twice your normal fee. It's just a short flight to Bombay.'

'This case . . . I'll be working in Mumbai?'

'You could be working anywhere. I hope you'll be present for the appointment.'

'If I get to the hotel, who do I look for?'

'Just get there on time. Your client will be waiting.'

The man put on his coat, said goodnight and let himself out of the flat. Arjun latched the door and went out to the balcony where he gulped down the rest of his whisky. He could see the stocky figure in the overcoat disappear around the bend in the lane. Arjun had forgotten to hand over his visiting card, but the man hadn't asked for his number. About a minute later, at the far end of the park, a vehicle started. Its headlights came on, and it drove off. Was that Mr Vikas's car? If yes, why had he parked it so far away? So that Arjun couldn't see it? And Vikas what—what was the man's last name? Who was the potential client in Mumbai? Who could have referred him—was it Bunty?

He went back inside, switched on the tube light and picked up the slip. He tried to remember where the Sunset View was located. Was it someplace new? The ticket confirmed the business-class seat on a 9 a.m. flight out of Delhi. He flicked through the thousand-rupee notes; they seemed genuine enough. He put the items back into the envelope and pushed it to the centre of the table. He went and poured himself another drink in the kitchen. The fish in the plastic container had defrosted by then. He came back to the sitting room, turned off the light and sank into the sofa.

There was something odd about the whole business: the bald man, the envelope, the appointment in another city. Why did they need *him*, weren't there detectives in Mumbai? Some sixth sense told him to stay away from it. But he was curious about the case. Maybe something involving a Bollywood star? Then he remembered his conversation with Arun George, and immediately thought: Yamini, she was in Mumbai. He shook his head. That couldn't be a factor with him. Still, he could fly first class to Mumbai, turn down the offer and keep the cash and also finish off the auto spare parts case. He groaned when he realized he would have to be up by 5 a.m. to make the flight. He switched on the television—not so much to watch, but because he had been asked to switch it off. Mr Vikas—there had been something fraudulent about the character. Arjun watched a story on a rape and murder case in an Uttar Pradesh village with his thoughts elsewhere. Then he got up to fry the fish.

5

AT FIVE MINUTES TO FOUR the next evening, Arjun walked past Hotel Sunset View on Mumbai's Marine Drive. He went some distance ahead, stopped near the gates of a residential building and lit a cigarette. He shaded his eyes against the afternoon sun and looked around—pedestrians, traffic, the haze over the sea and the high-rises at the other end of Marine Drive. A few isolated individuals sat hunched on the sea wall staring into the distance. Mumbai was hot and muggy as always. A white Mercedes entered through the hotel gates, and Arjun swept his gaze over the people moving leisurely along the promenade.

He had woken up at 4.30 a.m. knowing that he would be going to Mumbai. He would make the appointment and then take care of the spare parts business. It had nothing to do with Yamini, he told himself. After the taxi ride in the early-morning coolness, there had been the plush comfort of business class and the extra attention from the air hostesses. At the airport he had kept an eye out for Mr Vikas, if that was his name, but there was no sign of him. Maybe he was staying on in Delhi, *if* he had come from Mumbai at all. He had called Arun George and told him that he was on his way to Mumbai. Arjun had slept after they served breakfast, and woken up as the plane was about to land, with Mumbai and the Arabian Sea lying in a white haze below them. From the airport he had taken a taxi to Hotel Diplomat, located along one of the roads off Marine Drive.

It was an old hotel where he had once stayed years ago, and an Internet search at Delhi airport had shown him that the Sunset View, a new hotel, was within walking distance.

Arjun crushed his half-smoked cigarette and retraced his footsteps. There didn't seem to be anyone watching the hotel from the outside. The Sunset View had come up in the place of one of those immense Mumbai residential buildings which always seemed to have 'Mahal' after their names. On either side of it were the older art deco buildings. He went up the black-marble steps and past the metal detector and the glass door held open by a doorman, and the air conditioning hit him like a wave. Looking around, his eye was caught by a tall, middle-aged man sitting in one of the lobby chairs and going through a document. The man looked up at the same moment, saw Arjun and got up on his feet. Both of them advanced a few feet, and the man rasped, 'Arjun Arora?' He was taller than Arjun, with wide shoulders and a slight stoop, a prominent nose and thinning hair.

'Yes,' Arjun said, holding out his hand. 'And you?'

'Vishwanathan. Come, let's sit.' He had a strong grip.

They sat down. The man was wearing brown chinos, worn leather moccasins, a white polo shirt and an expensive chronometer. There was something forceful and intimidating about him, a hint of violence behind the polished exterior. He put the document in a yellow folder, and Arjun looked out at the haze over the sea through the glass panes of the lobby.

'So my man met you last night?' Vishwanathan asked, fixing his gaze on Arjun.

'Yes. That's why I'm here. What's this about?'

The other man looked away and pursed his lips, as if he were having second thoughts. He opened the folder and took out a photograph which he handed to Arjun. It was a square, glossy-paper print of a young girl in a sleeveless dress standing in front of a glass door. The slightly grainy image, taken from above and to the side, seemed to have been captured off a CCTV camera. Arjun found himself getting curious.

'Who is she?' he asked.

'The person you have to find. Agnes Pereira. The phone number she was using is on the back of the photo.'

Arjun turned the photo around and saw a number scrawled in red. 'Was?'

'It's most probably switched off now. We were told you're good at phone tracing?'

'Depends on who you've been talking to.'

'Someone who recommended you highly.'

'Really? This someone must have a name.'

'How does it matter, Mr Arora? I'm willing to pay twice your normal fee.'

Arjun studied the photo again. She was tall, maybe close to 5' 8". He asked, 'Where was this photo captured?'

'I don't know,' Vishwanathan said, then clarified, 'it was given to us.'

Though unusual, Arjun had come across this sort of secrecy or ignorance before.

'What has she done?' he asked.

'She's murdered someone,' Vishwanathan said, 'and she was involved in making a large sum of money disappear, money that belongs to my partners and me. We want this handled discreetly, no police.'

'Don't worry about that. What else do you have for me?'

He had come here to turn the case down, but now he found himself unable to say no.

'That's all. The photo, the phone number and the name. It's very . . . *sensitive*.'

'Is that why you need a detective from outside Mumbai?'

'We think you're the man for the job.'

26

'Who did she kill?'

'A bar dancer called Savitri Rao.'

'Where did this happen?'

'At a guest house in Vakola.'

'How much money disappeared?'

'A sizeable amount.'

'Where did the money disappear from—the guest house?'

'Yes. She killed the dancer and took the money.'

'Were they friends, the two of them?'

Vishwanathan hesitated a moment. 'Yes, but we didn't know about it.'

'Why did she take the money? Any motives?'

'She just stole it. That was her motive.'

'Well, this will be tough,' Arjun said. 'And the police must be looking for her too.'

A hotel staff passing by smiled at Vishwanathan, who nodded in return.

'I know,' he said. 'But we believe she's somewhere close by.'

'Where was she last seen?'

Vishwanathan hesitated. 'We're not sure.'

Arjun shook his head. 'It's getting tougher.'

'Which is why you'll get twice your normal fee. If you find her.'

'So I was told. That's twenty lakhs then, with 25 per cent up front.'

'If you give me your account number, I can—'

'Sorry, I'll be taking cash for this one.'

Arjun didn't know whom he was dealing with, and didn't want to leave a trail. Vishwanathan stared at him for a moment. 'Of course.' He reached beside him and brought up a slim briefcase which he opened a crack. He took out five bundles similar to the one given to Arjun the previous night.

'Here,' Vishwanathan said. 'Your advance.'

Arjun took the money, noticing as he did that the other man's left hand was missing its small finger. He reached for a financial daily on the coffee table between them and wrapped the money in it.

'I'll get started on it,' Arjun said. 'Any other expenses, I'll bill you later.'

'Such as?'

'Travelling. Hospitalization. Paying bribes, if the need arises. Accommodation in outstation cities.'

'I see. That should be okay. Here, take down this number. You can reach me at it.'

Arjun fed the ten-digit number into his phone.

'Where will you start?' Vishwanathan asked him.

'Agnes Pereira's phone number,' Arjun said.

'Okay. We don't have much time, all right? The police are looking for her as well.'

'I get that. Is she an Indian citizen, by the way?'

'As Indian as idli–sambar,' the other man said as he stood up to leave. 'Can I give you a lift? Where are you staying?'

'Somewhere nearby. It's all right, I think I'll have a coffee here before I leave.'

They shook hands again, and soon Vishwanathan was striding away. It had been a short meeting. Arjun pretended to busy himself with his phone, glancing up at the entrance from time to time. Vishwanathan was standing at the top of the steps, his left hand with its missing digit on his hip, the other holding a cell phone to his ear. The time was 4.21 p.m. Arjun made a mental note of it. The white Mercedes he had seen entering the hotel came around and stopped, and Vishwanathan got into the back before the vehicle moved again. A rich client. In Arjun's experience, they were the most crooked ones.

He sat in the chilled lobby for a while, the newspaper-wrapped bundle of notes in his hands, and pondered on what had

28

happened. Why had he changed his mind? It was a challenging assignment. He looked at the photo again. Good posture, a bit on the skinny side, straight hair falling down to her shoulders. Agnes Pereira. What was the story? Was she someone's wife, mistress, girlfriend? He turned the photo around and studied the cell number scrawled in red in a large, untidy hand, as if in a hurry.

He tried calling the number. It was switched off. Expecting that, Arjun called Computer Baba in Delhi. He asked his on-off assistant to take down two numbers: the one behind the photo, and Vishwanathan's number.

'I'll spend my whole life tracing numbers for you,' Baba said in a tired voice.

'Not you, your telecom company contact,' Arjun reminded him.

'My old guy's gone, by the way. Now it's someone new. He's hiked the rates.'

'Is that so? I'll come and talk to you about it. Meanwhile, get me something on these two numbers by tomorrow.'

Baba sighed dramatically and said, 'Tell me what you want.'

'The first number is switched off. I want the location of its last ten calls. And the second number, I want you to check whom it was calling at 4.20 p.m. today.'

'Wait a minute,' Baba said, 'these numbers . . . where *are* you?'

'Mumbai. In a hotel on Marine Drive looking out at the Arabian Sea.'

'*Waah* . . . enjoy, bhai! Go visit a dance bar.'

When he hung up, Arjun suddenly missed Delhi. Mumbai was as crowded and polluted as Delhi, maybe even more so, and at his age, the familiar evil was the preferable one. He looked around and spotted the hotel staff who had smiled at Vishwanathan, and beckoned to him.

'Yes, sir?' the youth inquired, bending at the waist and smiling. His manner reminded Arjun of Mr Vikas from the previous night.

'There's something I want to ask you,' Arjun said, smiling back at him. 'Do you know the man I was sitting with?'

'Yes, sir, I do. I don't know his name, but he comes here from time to time with his friends.'

'I see. Thank you.'

Arjun put the photo into his shirt pocket and stood up.

'Is there anything else I can assist—?'

'No, thanks. I've got what I needed.'

6

ARJUN WALKED BACK TO HIS hotel from Marine Drive. Vishwanathan seemed to be a Mumbai man, but what about Mr Vikas? Turning on to the road where his hotel lay, he crossed to the other side and entered a pharmacy, from whose doorway he surveyed the people on the road. The meeting with Vishwanathan had given him the uneasy feeling that he was being set up. The bookie he had helped put in jail a few months ago was sure to have contacts in Mumbai. Or was he overthinking this? He had already been paid the advance. On the other hand, he didn't believe that there were no phone-tracing experts to be found here in Mumbai. An assistant came up to ask him what he wanted, and Arjun left the shop. Vishwanathan's missing finger flashed through his mind, and the vague fear of the previous evening returned.

Walking back to the Diplomat, he saw two tall, well-dressed women stepping out of a smart restaurant by the road, its glass-and-wood exterior giving it the air of a new establishment. The women hailed a taxi and got in. He recrossed the road when his hotel came into view, and when he approached the entrance, a small girl in a soiled frock came running up to him. She appeared to be living out on the footpath with her mother and brother, and Arjun had given her a five-rupee coin when he had left the hotel. Now he walked past her and entered the hotel.

The Diplomat had a shabby, relaxed charm, recalling a time before liberalization, when Mumbai had still been Bombay. Arjun took the cramped lift up to the third floor. Once in his room, he opened the door that led to the tiny balcony and lit a cigarette. In front of him was the side wall of another 'Mahal', with closed windows and pipes running down its length. To his left he could see the entrance to the hotel, and the road. On the footpath, the girl's mother was arranging the flowers in her roadside stall, while the daughter played with her brother. He recalled the smile on the girl's grimy face as she had come running up to him. Arjun stubbed out his cigarette and went back inside, closing the door behind him.

He washed his face in the damp bathroom, turned on the air conditioner and lay down on the bed. Switched on the television and checked his phone. No messages so far. On his way in from the airport, while stuck in Mumbai's notorious traffic, he had sent a message to Yamini: HI, IN MUMBAI FOR SOME WORK. LET'S MEET UP FOR A WHILE IN THE EVENING, IF YOU'RE FREE. ARJUN. He had tried hard to get the casual tone of the message right, adding the words 'for a while' to indicate that it didn't have to be a lengthy meeting, and the second comma to emphasize the words 'if you're free'. Plus his name in case she had deleted his number. But four hours had passed and she hadn't replied to the message. He pressed the call button against her name, but instantly cut it.

Tossing the cell phone aside, he took the photo out from his pocket. Agnes Pereira. Was she Anglo-Indian? Catholic? Nothing in the photo appeared to supply a clue about where she was standing. The entrance of a shop or a showroom, with the letters 'ON' at the bottom of a vertical sign outside the glass. She stood leaning forward, an expectant look on her face, as if she was looking for someone or something inside. Arjun thought she was quite pretty in a waifish way. He put the photo on the bedside table and picked up the telephone to ask for some tea but then thought better of it. The minibar under the television had four small bottles of beer; he took one out. Lying back against the pillows, he felt better with the first sip of the cold beer.

Watching the news, he went over his conversation with Vishwanathan. It was possible that his client had shared everything he knew about Agnes Pereira. The murdered girl, he would have to find out about her. By tomorrow, Baba might have something on the two numbers. He picked up his phone and called Bunty. When he said he was in Mumbai, his friend burst out, 'Sisterfucker, why didn't you tell me, we could have gone together!'

'I left in a hurry,' Arjun said. 'Regarding a case.'

'Oh. What's it about?'

'So far, a missing girl. Tell me, have you recommended me to anyone recently?'

'I keep recommending you to people all the time, boss, you know that.'

'To someone from Mumbai, or to someone with a Mumbai connection?'

'I don't think so . . . someone else could have recommended you too.'

Arjun had considered that possibility.

'Anyway,' he said, 'if you remember anything, let me know.'

'Okay. Enjoy *karo*. Go visit a dance bar.'

'Bastard, I'm here on work!' he said, laughing.

Next, Arjun called his secretary. He had called her that morning from the Delhi airport to let her know he was going on a work-related trip, and that she should put their files in order and ask Chandu to do some cleaning. Now she sounded agitated.

'I told you, sir, we should have another person in the office.'

'Why, what's happened?'

'Two people came for a pre-mat check. I told the second one to come next week. We should have one more detective in the office, sir.'

'Yes, yes, I'm thinking about it. I need you to find out something for me now.'

'What, sir?'

He had tried and failed to make her stop calling him 'sir' all the time. 'Pre-mat' was 'pre-matrimonial', which usually entailed checking whether the claims made before marriage by the boy's or girl's families were genuine. Liza went out to do such cases. Arjun reached for the ticket lying on the bedside table and told her to take down the airline name, booking time and the PNR.

'I need you to find out where the ticket was booked from, okay?'

'All right, sir, but why——?'

'Just do it, I'll explain later.'

He hung up. Another detective! Where would they sit? How much salary would they ask for? But at the same time, Arjun knew Liza was right. His reputation was spreading, slowly but surely, and having another hand in the field would be an asset. He reached over for the beer and took a swig, and the next moment gave a cry of surprise and sat upright on the bed. It was that story on the news again. The Mumbai Police had identified the girl missing from Bharat Lodge in Santacruz after her friend had been murdered; she was an air hostess from Goa by the name of Agnes Pereira, and lookout notices had been issued against her. A photo appeared, and he turned and snatched the photo from the bedside table. He looked at it, and then at the girl on the television screen. She definitely looked like the same person to him. Savitri Rao, the murdered girl, was from Pune, and the forensic report had established manual strangulation or throttling as the cause of her death.

7

THREE HOURS LATER, ARJUN WAS in a taxi heading back to his hotel from Colaba. He had made the journey down south to a bar called Gokul, to take care of the first item in his order of business. Earlier, he had made a call to the counterfeiter Gullu from his hotel room, saying he had flown to Mumbai on business, and that, following a discussion with his partner, he wanted to discuss a large order, so would it be possible to meet the boss? Gullu had sounded unenthusiastic, but a short while later, Arjun had received a call from someone called Sanjay who asked him to come down to Kala Ghoda in Colaba.

They had ended up at Gokul, a vast, packed and noisy bar across from the Bade Miya eatery. Arjun had ordered beer and surmai fry for them. Sanjay had turned out to be an unassuming man, more like a nondescript office worker, but he had let Arjun know that he could ship quantities of the duplicate spares— stamped with whatever logo was required—by trucks from workshops in Pune to Guwahati, for the north-east market. Arjun had inquired about rates, and said he would get back to him after he returned to Kolkata. They had parted outside the bar, and Arjun had trailed Sanjay, making sure he himself wasn't being followed. Arjun had seen the man get into a red Volkswagen Polo parked in a nearby street, and had noted down the vehicle's number.

The taxi dropped him off near his hotel. Arjun paid the driver, and called Arun George and gave him the details of his meeting, right down to the rates and the number plate. George thanked him and told him that an operation would be mounted soon with the police. His work done, Arjun entered Tonic, the restaurant with the wood-and-glass exterior from where he had seen two women leaving earlier in the day. He was soon seated at a table for two with two measures of blended Scotch whisky in front of him. Being in Mumbai, he had decided to treat himself to something more expensive than his usual Blenders Pride. From where he sat by the wood-and-glass wall by the street he could directly see people as they stepped into Tonic. Around him were Mumbaikars who were mostly talking in English. He took a sip of his whisky and checked his phone. It was past 9 p.m., and there was still no reply from Yamini. Should he try calling her?

He knocked the rest of his whisky back. A waiter appeared, asking if he was ready to place his order, and Arjun told him to wait a while. He rose to go to the restroom. The beers and the whisky had given him a mild buzz. Coming back to his table, he noticed a woman at an adjoining table for six who looked his way and held his gaze for a moment. Arjun Arora wasn't over the hill just yet. He sipped his second drink, chewed on some salted peanuts and ran through the *dramatis personae* of his latest case: Mr Vikas, Vishwanathan, a dead girl and Agnes Pereira. Was Pereira an innocent caught up in wrong company, or was she the crooked one? And why had he, Arjun, taken the case: for the money, for the challenge? The first thing he had to do in the morning was pay a visit to the lodge where the girl had been killed.

He went outside for a smoke, and dialled his father's number. His mother answered, and told him his father was in bed, resting. He had complained of giddiness, and a doctor who had come over to check on him had said it was high blood pressure.

'You should take him to the hospital for a proper check-up,' she said to Arjun.

'Me? Do you think he'll come with me? You convince him first.'

'I'll try and do that. Where are you?'

'In Mumbai for work. I'll let you know when I'm back.'

He had long felt that he had failed his parents in some way by not getting them out of their Rajouri Garden flat, by not giving them a happier life. The woman who had checked him out inside the restaurant had stepped out with another woman now, and she came over to ask him for a light. She lit their cigarettes and handed him back his lighter, her hand brushing his as she said thanks. Slim with wavy hair, her sleeveless top showing her fair arms. I should ask her name, he thought. Just then his phone rang—it was Rhea.

'Hello, Papa,' she said.

'Hi. What are you up to?'

She was in her room, she said, doing 'nothing much', which meant she was probably fiddling with her phone. She sounded sullen, but Arjun didn't ask her what was wrong. He had made a decision not to interfere with her new life as far as possible.

'Can you come and take me away from here, Papa?'

'What? Why, what's wrong, Rhea?'

'I don't want to stay here any more! I don't know what Mama's doing here.'

He knew it must be hard for her, adapting to a new house and a new father. But what could he offer, a solitary middle-aged man who drank too much? No, it was better she stayed under the watchful eye of her mother.

'Have they been fighting?' he asked.

'Yes,' she replied in a small voice.

'Just . . . stay out of their way for a while,' he advised his girl helplessly, watching the cars moving past. 'I'm in Mumbai, by the way.'

'Doing what?'

'Oh, just some work. Can I get you anything from here?'

'Nah. Not really. I'll see you when you get back.'

'Do you want to go for that Mehrauli walk after I'm back?'

'Yeah, sure, we can do that.'

He hesitated, then asked, 'How's your mother?'

'All right, I guess. She's gone out.'

From sullen she had gone to brusque. It was difficult coping with the mood swings of a college-going teenager. 'I see. I'll catch you when I get back to Delhi.'

Arjun hung up, and pulled on the dregs of his cigarette. They'll work it out, he thought. The rage he felt at his ex-wife's new husband had cooled over the months. He had been planning a walk with Rhea through the Qutb and Mehrauli areas for some time now, to give her a better idea of topics that she had covered in a college assignment. Up ahead, through the crowds on the pavement, he could see the flower stall on the footpath outside his hotel. The woman who had asked him for his lighter was discussing a movie with her friend, her arms folded in front of her, the cigarette held at an angle. For some reason Arjun remembered the postcards his father had once brought back from a trip to Delhi. They had been in Guwahati then, staying somewhere on the outskirts of the city. He must have been seven or eight, and the postcards showing famous landmarks—the India Gate, Rashtrapati Bhavan, Connaught Place—had given his younger self a sense of a vast and varied country.

On an impulse, he dialled Yamini's number. It rang but there was no reply.

He went back inside and asked for two more drinks, and from the menu ordered some baked potato skins. He realized some of the waiters and the other diners were throwing looks his way. This wasn't a country where people hung out alone if they could help it. He stumbled on his way to the restroom. Was the whisky hitting him already? Back at his table he ate a few of the cheese-loaded potato skins (after liberally sprinkling them with both paprika and Tabasco). The restaurant was packed now, and buzzing with voices. Arjun turned and studied the crowd. At the table for six the woman who had asked him for his lighter was now sitting on the side. He smiled at her. She looked at him and then turned away.

His whisky was over; he beckoned to his waiter and asked for two more pegs.

'Are you sure, sir?' the waiter asked.

Arjun looked up at him, and for a moment saw himself through the young man's eyes: a tired, desperate-looking drunk.

'No, forget it' he said, slowly and precisely. 'Please get me my bill.'

He paid and got out of the restaurant and walked back to the hotel. The expensive cars, the people strolling about now, Mumbai by night—he felt his mood lift. So what if he was alone? He also felt himself starting to get drunk.

8

FIRST THE POUNDING HEADACHE, FOLLOWED by nausea. Arjun groped around till he got hold of his cell phone then opened his eyes. It was nearly 8 a.m., and there were no messages or missed calls on his phone. He had gone to bed in the clothes he had been wearing the previous evening. Sitting up with a groan, he saw that the air conditioner was at full blast and the door to the balcony was open. On the table in front of him was an almost empty half-bottle of whisky; he had asked the doorman to get it for him the previous night. A hazy memory of events swam past him, and he felt uneasy—he should try and forget about her.

The gnawing in his empty stomach made him pick up the bedside telephone and call room service for breakfast. As he brushed his teeth and looked at his red eyes in the mirror, the objective part of him reasoned that the travel and the lack of food had made the alcohol hit him harder. After he had taken a cold shower and worked his way through a bowl of cornflakes, a stack of toast with butter and marmalade, a double cheese omelette, two cups of hot coffee, and popped two analgesic tablets, he felt somewhat ready to face the day. Going through the newspaper on the breakfast tray he found a new detail about the Agnes Pereira case: the murdered bar dancer had apparently worked at an establishment near Haji Ali. A police spokesperson said they were looking for Pereira so she could clear up for them the events of that morning. Arjun read the story twice, analysing the information. Before leaving the room he picked up the whisky bottle to throw it in the bin, but not before pouring out the remaining liquor for a quick hair-of-the-dog drink. He left the hotel just after 9 a.m. and caught a taxi for Santacruz East.

The taxi came out on to Marine Drive and headed north. Arjun put on his sunglasses and lit his first cigarette of the day. The driver, a melancholy-looking elderly gentleman, kept glancing out of his window, as though he would rather be elsewhere. The early-morning coolness was fast disappearing, and the anonymous press of the traffic and the buildings did nothing to ease Arjun's fragile, hung-over state. How long was he going to carry on doing this with his life? His eyelids felt hot and heavy, usually a prelude to a bout of fever. The sea, glittering in the morning sun, appeared again to their left, and then they were speeding over it along the Sea Link, the salt air rushing in through the windows. The driver's mood appeared to lift, and he switched on the radio. An old Hindi film song came on, '*Leke pehla pehla pyar*', from the black-and-white Dev Anand starrer, *C.I.D.*

Coming down from the Sea Link the taxi continued along the Western Express Highway through the morning traffic, past Bandra East and Khar East, past old, shut-down mills and government colonies, with massive new high-rises in the distance, before turning right towards Vakola. Planes came down overhead towards the airport which lay beyond Santacruz East. They crossed over the Vakola Nala, the water a dirty brown, and some distance away were the dhobi shacks with washing hung up to dry above the tiny lanes.

The Bharat Lodge was in a sleepy little lane in the Kadamwadi area of Santacruz East. A peepul tree dominated the entrance to the lane, under its spreading branches a few rickety old shops: a laundry, a newspaper and stationery shop, a grocer's.

A faded-red postbox and a grimy transformer on the other side of the road completed this picture of old-time Bombay. The lodge was a dirty, white box-like building which lay ahead of the tin-roofed shops. Arjun asked the driver to park a little ahead and walked back to the lodge. What had the air hostess and her friend been doing in a dump like this?

A rusty orange gate, a dusty little driveway, and inside the building a reception counter, a curly-haired youth sitting behind it in the semi-darkness reading a book and biting his nails. On one wall was an old poster with an image of Christ's crucifixion and an evangelical message of the Catholic Church. Next to the counter was a gloomy flight of stairs. Arjun took off his sunglasses and introduced himself as a reporter from a newspaper who wanted to ask a few questions about the murder. The receptionist got to his feet and regarded Arjun incuriously.

'I've already spoken to the reporters,' he said.

'I've come all the way from Delhi,' Arjun said, taking out two five-hundred-rupee notes from his wallet and rolling them up in his fingers, making sure the receptionist saw them. 'I'm willing to pay for your time.'

The receptionist leaned over the desk and looked down the empty corridor, then plucked the notes from Arjun's hand.

'It happened two days ago,' he began in a low, hurried voice, 'in the morning. The girl who's disappeared had come two days before that, in the morning. She had taken a room on the first floor. The one who was killed came to stay with her the next day, at night.'

'You allow guests to stay over?'

'Yes, we charge them for an extra bed. But girls going up to a gent's room is not allowed.'

'Of course,' Arjun said, and asked if he could see the room, at which the receptionist shook his head and said he would get into trouble with Mr Joshi, the manager.

42

'So what happened that morning?'

The receptionist appeared to think. 'I was here, reading a newspaper, when the first girl, the air hostess, went out to buy cigarettes.'

'How do you know what she went out to buy?'

'Because she asked me where she could buy cigarettes. The grocer's shop nearby doesn't sell them and you have to walk down to the end of the lane to find a paan shop. She came back about fifteen to twenty minutes later—'

'Would it take her fifteen to twenty minutes to go buy cigarettes from the paan shop?'

'She must have gone to the grocer's too. She was carrying a plastic bag.'

'Okay. So after she came back . . .'

'She went upstairs. About thirty minutes later, she came down with her bag and went out. I found it a bit strange, so after a while I went up to the room . . .'

'What sort of bag? Was it the same bag she was carrying when she checked in?'

'Yes, the same bag, with two straps, the type you can carry on your back.'

'A backpack. Did anyone else come in during that time, when she was gone?'

The receptionist hesitated. Above them a door banged shut and a man spoke loudly. Arjun wiped his face with his handkerchief and repeated his question.

'No, there was no one.'

'So what did you see when you went up to the room?'

'The door was half-open. It swings open when you don't lock it. The other girl was lying on the bed, her head to one side, her eyes open. I knew there was something wrong with her. So I came down and called the manager, who informed the police at the Vakola *thana*.'

'You didn't go inside the room?'

The receptionist shook his head. Something he had said wasn't sitting well with Arjun.

'How did the room look? Did it appear as if a struggle had taken place inside it?'

'No. It looked like a normal occupied room. The plastic bag the air hostess had come in carrying was on the bed as well. I think there was juice and biscuits inside.'

'When the other girl arrived, did she have a bag or anything with her?'

'Just a ladies' bag, a large one. The police found it inside the room.'

'The first girl, did she leave in a hurry or walk out calmly? Did she speak to you?'

'She just walked out. She didn't say anything to me.'

'And you didn't ask her if she was checking out?'

'I didn't think she was . . . her friend was still in the room.'

'What if her friend had climbed out of a window?'

The receptionist smiled. 'All our windows are barred.'

'I see. And you're sure no one came in when the air hostess was out?'

'Yes, no one came,' the receptionist said and drummed his fingers on the desk. 'You better hurry, my manager will be coming soon.'

'Just one last thing, have you seen either of the two girls here before?'

A shake of the head: no.

'What impression did you have of them?'

'They seemed very friendly with each other.'

'Where do you think the air hostess has gone?'

A shrug: I don't know.

'Where had she come from? Can I see your register?'

'Somewhere in Goa, I think,' the receptionist said, turning around to pick up a register which he placed on the counter. At the same time a voice echoed down the corridor: 'Excuse me, sir, you are checking in?'

It was a short, balding man wearing a pair of thick glasses, his head tilted upward to take in the taller world around him. Arjun just about had the time to spin the register around and have a look before the receptionist took it back from him. The address against the name of Agnes Pereira simply said 'Fontainhas, Panaji' and had a familiar ten-digit phone number at the end. The short man strode up to the reception and barked something in Marathi, to which the receptionist replied sullenly in the same language and turned around.

'Which paper you are coming from, sir?' the manager asked Arjun, again in English.

'The *Times of India*,' Arjun said. He knew the interview was over.

'You are having a visiting card?'

'Not really, I'm a freelancer based in Delhi. Have a good day.'

Arjun quickly exited the reception area and walked out to the road. Somewhere down the road to his left was the paan shop, while to his right was the grocer's under the peepul tree—he turned right.

9

IT WAS AN OLD TIN-ROOFED shop, the shelves in its interior hidden in a semi-darkness that was reminiscent of the lodge's reception. Like the rest of the lane, a place forgotten by time. Arjun had a sudden intimation that Agnes Pereira had been attracted by precisely that. It was a strange feeling, one that took him a moment to shake off. The wizened, white-haired owner was chatting with a customer, another elderly man in faded pyjamas and a thin sweater. Arjun asked for a half-litre bottle of cold water. As the owner shuffled towards the fridge, the other customer asked, maybe in an attempt to show the new customer how much he knew, 'So what's going on with the murder case? Anything new?'

The owner shook his head as he came back with the bottle. 'Nothing new, but I think the police are being clever.'

Arjun's ears pricked up as he paid for the water.

'Clever? What do you mean?'

'They haven't told anyone . . .' the owner started, then glanced at Arjun and promptly shut his mouth.

With a quickening pulse Arjun turned around, opened the bottle and took a drink.

'Haven't told what?' the other man asked.

'Oh, nothing. What did you say you wanted?'

Arjun took out his phone and pretended to make a call, while listening to the conversation behind him. His intuition was correct: the receptionist was hiding something.

'Two kilos of *atta* and half a kilo of *masoor* dal,' the customer said, and then asked, 'but the girl was here that morning, you said?'

'Yes, she was,' the owner said, weighing the atta, 'and she was asking me what this place was like before.'

'A bar dancer and an air hostess,' the customer said, and made a dismissive sound.

Arjun walked back to where the taxi was waiting for him. Outside the entrance to the lodge stood the manager, looking upward as if sniffing for something. The taxi driver turned the vehicle around and asked Arjun where they were going next. Arjun thought for a moment before he said, 'Take me to Haji Ali.'

They headed back south the way they had come, via the Bandra–Worli Sea Link. It was hotter now, the taxi's windows were down as its air conditioner wasn't working, and the vehicle exhausts swirled around them at the red lights. Arjun touched his forehead with the back of his hand; he definitely had a fever coming on, probably caused by spending the night under the air conditioner's direct draught. From time to time he looked back, trying to see if anyone was following him. The only thing that caught his attention though was an impressive purple Bugatti Veyron.

He tried to put in order what he had learnt. The air hostess had come from Goa and checked into a dingy lodge, had been joined by her friend, the bar dancer, the next day. She had stepped out the morning after to buy cigarettes and supplies. She came back, and after a while walked out of the lodge with her backpack. So had she strangled the bar dancer herself, or was there something else to it that the police—or the receptionist or the shopkeeper—knew, something that had made the air hostess leave the room? And where did Vishwanathan's assignment to track down the air hostess fit in with all of this?

Just before they got to Haji Ali Arjun sent a message to Baba: HAVE YOU FOUND OUT ANYTHING??, and forwarded the same message to Liza. He got down, paid the taxi driver and then stood on the road by the Worli coast and lit a cigarette. In front of him, out in the black, oily waters of the Arabian Sea, and connected by a curved walkway with litter strewn below it, was a low, white structure constructed on an islet: the mosque and dargah of Haji Ali. Arjun stood there a while in the midday sun, feeling curiously overheated with his impending fever. He watched the devotees, several women among them, buying flowers and *chadar*s from the vendors at the beginning of the walkway and slowly walking out to the tomb where the saint lay buried. He remembered snippets from an article read long ago: a Muslim merchant from Bukhara who had made Mumbai his home; a structure more than five hundred years old. What made people go and pray and hope for divine intervention? Arjun was not particularly religious. What had remained in his mind were his mother's stories of the Bhagavad Gita—Arjuna grappling with his dilemmas and Krishna's advice to him. *No one who does good work will ever come to a bad end, in this world or the next.* But what about his father then, who had got shot in the kneecap in Manipur just for performing his duties? Arjun flicked his cigarette into the sea and crossed the busy road.

The Silver Moon dance bar was down Tardeo Road and on a street cutting into Tulsiwadi. There was an unimpressive entrance with dark wood and dark glass flanked by other buildings, and just after the entrance was a heavily carpeted and curtained room where several bodybuilder types were watching a cricket match. They stared at him as he crossed the room to the second set of dark-glass doors. Once inside, Arjun halted in his tracks for a moment. The large, circular, glass-panelled room lit with coloured lights was empty and deathly quiet. Was he here too early? Suddenly, a loud Hindi film song with an insistent tabla beat came on, and one by one girls in shimmering dresses and salwar kameezes rose from a sofa in a dark corner. He was the first customer of the day.

Arjun sat at one of the tables, and a girl approached him to take his order. The girls were now on the dance floor, dancing half-heartedly and looking his way. He felt like a customer at a bazaar, trying to pick a chicken or a fish that would then be cut up for him.

The girl came back with the beer—he had asked for a lager—and Arjun asked her to join him.

'Me?' she asked, surprised. She had a slightly misshapen face and probably made most of her money fetching drinks for people.

'Yes, you,' Arjun said, flashing a five-hundred-rupee note. 'Sit here a while.'

She sat beside him, hands on her lap. He drank his beer; the cold, bitter liquid washing down his throat momentarily eased the hangover and the fever.

'Where have you come from?' she asked him in a rough, direct way.

'I'm here on business,' Arjun said. 'What's your name?'

'Chandni,' she replied, and Arjun smiled. Where would Mumbai be without its clichés?

'You don't like my name?'

'No, it's a very nice name,' Arjun said, slipping her the note. 'I once knew someone by that name.'

'Really? Then I guess it was written in your fate to meet me.'

The other girls had given up now, and were merely looking on with curiosity. Only one of them was still moving her body—a fair, young girl in a blue sari who gazed defiantly at Arjun.

'There was a girl who worked here, Savitri Rao. Did you know her?'

'The one who was murdered in Kadamwadi?'

'Yes, her.'

'She hadn't been coming to dance for some time. We thought she had played some big game, got set for life. Now look what's happened to her.'

'Any idea who might have killed her?'

'She mixed with a lot of crooked people.'

'Really? What sort of people?' Arjun asked. He had the feeling she was trying to act important, repeating gossip which she might have heard from the other girls.

'Gangster types. The police raided her flat once, looking for money. Do you know she had two flats in her name? One in Saki Naka and the other in Jogeshwari.'

'Was she married?'

'No, people in our line aren't so lucky.'

'She had a friend, Agnes Pereira, an air hostess. Did she ever come in here?'

'Air hostess?' Chandni frowned. 'What the fuck would an air hostess come in here for? And give me some more money for sitting here and answering your stupid questions.'

Arjun gave her another five hundred, paid for his beer and left the dance bar. Stepping outside, he saw one of the bouncers standing on the street smoking a cigarette. Arjun asked him for a light and tried to make small talk with him.

'What time do your customers start arriving?' he asked the muscular youth.

'Around afternoon. You finished so fast?'

'I was looking for someone, but she's not around.'

'I've been here just a week, so I couldn't tell you where she might be.'

'Oh, I found out. Savitri Rao. The girl who was murdered in Kadamwadi. Have you heard about it?'

The bouncer shook his head and ducked back inside. Arjun stood there smoking his cigarette. A bar dancer who had owned two flats, and she had been friends with Agnes Pereira. He tried to imagine the dance bar at night, crowded, raucous, money being flung at the girls by the richer patrons. Maybe someone like Vishwanathan? Might Agnes Pereira have been given the money by her friend for safekeeping? His phone buzzed with a message—from Liza. She had found out that his ticket had been booked online by a travel agent in Delhi's Paharganj.

As he was walking back on Tardeo Road towards Café Noorani where he had decided to have his lunch, his phone rang. It was Computer Baba. He told Arjun that the last ten calls from Agnes Pereira's cell phone had been made from Mumbai, Goa and Gokarna.

'Go what?' Arjun asked.

'Gokarna. It's in Karnataka. A temple town with beaches, somewhat like Goa. Nice holiday you'll be having, Arjun bhai.'

'I prefer the hills,' Arjun said. 'When was the last call made?'

'Yesterday morning.'

While he had been on his way to Mumbai. 'Let me guess, to a Goa number?'

'No, to a Mumbai number. I'll look it up for you.'

'And the other number?'

'No records, it's a virgin,' Baba said with a snort.

'No records? Hmm. I'll call you later.'

He cut the call even as Baba tried to bring up the topic of his payment. So Vishwanathan had given Arjun a number that had been procured specifically for him. Which probably meant Vishwanathan was taking precautions against Arjun trying to find out who he was in contact with. The paranoia returned, and he halted at the doorway of a building to scan the crowded, sunny road. Trouble usually showed up when you least expected it. And why had Agnes Pereira fled to Gokarna, of all places?

When he got to Café Noorani, he sat down at one of the inner tables and ordered a meal he had first had years ago:

roomali roti, tandoori chicken, seekh kebabs, dal and phirni. He also asked for some green chillies and lime. Twenty minutes later, as he bit through the last piece of the charred-yet-succulent chicken and scraped the rice pudding out of the earthen bowl, he felt a great sense of well-being. Even if someone were to shoot him on the road outside or bundle him into a van, he would have the satisfaction of this meal. He paid the bill and burped loudly as he got up from the table.

He caught a taxi back to the hotel. Along the way, he called up Vishwanathan's virgin number.

'I might know where she is,' he said when his client picked up.

'Where?'

'I still need to do some digging around. But why did you say it was a guest house? It was a lodge. And if you had said Santacruz I would have made the connection faster.'

'Guest house, lodge—same thing. And Vakola falls in Santacruz. What connection?'

'To the story on the news. The police will have the number with them as well.'

'They don't work fast, Mr Arora. *We* have more motivation to track her down.'

'Did she murder the girl?'

'Yes, I believe so.'

'The dead girl. Did you know her?'

A pause. 'She was an acquaintance.'

'I'll need some more money. Another 25 per cent.'

'That'll make it half of your fee, Mr Arora.'

'That's right. The other half after I find her. Put the money in a bag and have it delivered by this evening to the reception at Hotel Diplomat.'

He wanted half the money, his regular fee, in case he was in a position later where he couldn't reveal the girl's location. He wasn't too worried about Vishwanathan finding out where he was staying. Back in his room, he called up the reception, made a few inquiries about night buses, and informed them about a package that would be dropped off for him. He told them he would check out in the evening to catch his night flight back to Delhi. Then he called Liza, asked about the agency's affairs and told her to book him a seat on a night bus from Mumbai to Gokarna. He also asked her to run an online check on Agnes Pereira, and added that she was an air hostess. After that, he swallowed a paracetamol and got into bed.

10

IT WAS LATE EVENING WHEN he awoke. The only light in the room came in through the open balcony door, along with the sounds of traffic. Lying there, it took Arjun a moment to figure out where he was. A terrifying sense of desolation washed over him. He no longer had all the time in the world, time was surely running out for him, and his body was in a slow, irreversible process of decline. Life had narrowed down, with only death at the end of it. Several minutes passed before he could pull himself together and get up from the bed. He had work to do. The tablet had helped, but he knew his fever was far from gone. Checking his phone, he saw a message from Liza with his PNR, the bus number and his pick-up point. The spare parts case had been a factor in his coming to Mumbai, but now he wondered if he wasn't heading to Gokarna to delay meeting his daughter.

He took a shower, packed his bag, drank two cups of tea and left the room. At the reception he picked up his packet with the money, and mentioned once more that he was headed to the airport to go back to Delhi. Walking out of the entrance the flower seller's girl accosted him again, and this time he gave her a hundred-rupee note. He caught a taxi a little way down the road and asked to be taken to Dadar. The taxi driver took a different route from Arjun's morning ride, this time through Kamathipura's red-light area and then past the railway chawl colony. He sat looking out at the crowds and the evening lights, his mind feverishly swinging between the air hostess who might now be on some beach and the emptiness of his own life, when Yamini called.

'Arjun, I am sorry about yesterday,' she said.

'It's okay,' he managed to say. 'I can understand.'

'I thought I would call you later . . . and then the boss wanted to take a few of us out for dinner. I thought it would be better if I didn't call you then . . . so I'm calling you now. Where are you? Do you want to meet up?'

She has a life of her own, Arjun thought—how could he not realize that? He said, 'Some other time maybe. I'm leaving Mumbai now.'

'Oh . . . but . . . I'm so sorry, Arjun. We can still meet if you have time . . .'

'It's too late now, Yamini,' he said, suddenly tired of her, of Mumbai, of his situation. 'I have to go now.'

'Well, the next time you're here, let me know. I'll take you to—'

'Goodbye, Yamini,' he said, and hung up.

He wouldn't be calling her again. It was over, finally, and more than anything else, he felt a sense of relief.

The taxi dropped him off at a crowded street corner, and he went looking for a wine store. He bought a quarter-bottle of rum and some Coke, mixed the two standing in a dark lane, and smoked as he drank. He was doing this after many years. At a brightly lit food stall, he ate two platefuls of buttered bun with eggs and then got back to the pick-up point. The Volvo sleeper bus came crawling down the road a while later and squeezed into a parking spot. Arjun got in, leaned his seat back, took another paracetamol and lay down.

His fever and the alcohol put him in a strange, psychedelic state as the bus crawled out of Mumbai city. Passing through a slum area, he saw a row of brightly lit leather goods showrooms, with air conditioner units fixed outside the tiny rooms above the shops. When he next opened his eyes, they were moving through the dark, featureless countryside, the bus at times speeding alarmingly to overtake other vehicles. He kept drifting in and out of sleep, till they stopped at a vegetarian restaurant on the highway.

Later, stretching his legs in the parking area where the buses stood, he lit a cigarette and looked up at the stars in the night sky. He remembered a midnight halt in sub-zero temperatures on a bus from London to Edinburgh on a snowy February night, when he had gone to sign up for the Iraq assignment. Back inside the bus he took the photograph out from his shirt pocket and studied it in the light from the overhead lamp. Agnes Pereira. She didn't look like someone capable of murder—but looks could be deceiving. Was it she who he was searching for, he wondered, or something within himself, some memory of lost youth?

Gokarna, when they finally got there by mid-morning, turned out to be a laid-back, dusty little temple town, the small bus station dotted with white backpackers and Indian pilgrims, and the walls of houses made of laterite-red-stone blocks. Arjun made some inquiries, then took an auto to Kudlee beach, the first of the 'tourist' beaches, as opposed to the 'Indian' beach where the pilgrims went. The auto took him along a road and then down a rough path where it dropped him, and Arjun walked further down through the dry undergrowth and trees and into the backyard of a family's hut. Cursing the auto driver, Arjun wound his way through the small huts and fields, his backpack slung across his shoulder, till he came out to the beach, where his sneakers sank into the sand. He took them off and stood there a while looking around: the low hills on either side of the small bay, the ocean, the gentle waves lapping up, the cows and stray dogs and foreigners meditating on the beach, the string of shacks under the palm trees with their usual slate-and-coloured-chalk menus on display. After the long journey, there was something underwhelming about it all. There were apparently two more beaches ahead of this one; would he have to scour all three for her?

First he had to get himself a room. But none of the shacks were empty, the makeshift huts or rooms behind them were all full of backpackers. At the third or fourth 'Sunset Café', at the end of the stretch of beach, some rooms were available, its stocky, lungi-clad manager said. He had a livid scar on one cheek. The café itself was a mess with workers and guests just waking up, some already lighting joints, and there was a dingy, crumbling two-storey house behind. Upstairs, there were small cubicles for five hundred rupees a day, with a shared bathroom. Most had skinny, unwashed, half-dressed foreigners inside them, the doors open to let in the air. The journey and the heat had set Arjun on edge, and he finally tramped up to the only 'concrete' hotel on the beach, apparently built in violation of coastal laws, and paid Rs 1500 for a room with a double bed and sand-strewn tiles. At least the room was a storey up, he thought, and had a balcony with chairs and a view. Plus the money in the backpack would be safe. Arjun washed and lay under the fan. His fever hadn't run its course yet. He wondered how long it would take him to track her down.

11

ARJUN BEGAN HIS SEARCH AT midday. He had changed
into an old pair of shorts he had stuffed into his bag just in case,
a faded grey T-shirt and his worn bathroom slippers—the overall
effect was not just inconspicuous, he thought, but positively
down at heel. Before leaving the hotel, he handed his room key
to the sleepy-looking receptionist and asked him to get the room
cleaned. He had put a lock on the backpack zipper, and locked
it inside the cabinet.

Arjun trudged past the shacks in the glaring heat towards
one end of the beach; he wanted to start from the beginning. He
kept an eye out for anyone who looked like Agnes Pereira. There
were just a few backpackers out on the beach now, swimming or
getting a tan. Unlike the beaches in Goa, there were hardly any
tourist families here. Stray dogs and cows loitered in the sand,
and a middle-aged white woman wearing a red bikini and several
bead necklaces was feeding a skinny cow a few bananas. She
smiled at Arjun as he passed; he nodded at her and kept walking.

The first shack was a rough structure of wood-and-bamboo
matting on a rocky outcrop below a low hill, with small,
colourfully painted wooden rooms. As Arjun stepped up inside,
a pack of stray dogs tore after a cow on the beach. This caused
a stir of excitement among a group of young women and men
sitting at two tables, Australian by their accents, and Arjun
noticed three big-built Indian men looking hungrily at them.

He showed the photo to what seemed like the head waiter and asked if he had seen her recently. The man stared at it with a frown, then shook his head. He was here every day, he said, and hadn't seen her. Arjun went around repeating the procedure at the other shacks, where people were cooling off with a beer or lunching on seafood. At each place he looked at the worker's face as he asked the question. Some looked curious, some indifferent, but none of them showed a spark of recognition. They were mostly young boys, some Nepali, some from Assam, some from the south. The dreadful prospect of repeating this across two more beaches dragged Arjun's spirits down.

At one café a solitary woman sitting beside the entrance and reading a book looked like the air hostess: slim with straight, black hair. But when he went in he saw she was bony, with a prominent nose, and most probably an Israeli or European. After about eight or nine shacks, he came to one just by the hotel property. It was called 'Everest Café'. A stray dog was sleeping on the sandy floor, and in a corner a group of revellers were playing trance music on a portable speaker and smoking grass. Arjun looked around—rickety tables, bone-like structures hanging from the high roof, a sign advertising Wi-Fi. Through a door at the back he saw a long, gloomy kitchen, and beside it another open door and a pathway which led to several rough huts.

'What you want to eat, sir?' a voice asked him in English.

It was a thin, stoned-looking youth with curly hair in a dirty white shirt. Arjun took the photo out of his pocket once again and asked the same question: Have you seen her? As he looked at it, the youth's eyes widened and he breathed in sharply.

'Do you recognize her?' Arjun asked in Hindi.

He shook his head slowly. 'I haven't seen her.'

Arjun didn't say anything, just nodded and put the photo back in his pocket. He went and sat down at a plastic-covered table in a corner by the open frontage and lit a cigarette. The youth was having a word with another waiter. Was Agnes Pereira in one of the rooms behind? This was one of the places he had unsuccessfully approached in the morning for a room. Arjun waited till the youth had moved away, then raised a hand and beckoned to the other waiter.

He was young and well built, with Mongoloid features. Arjun ordered a cold beer and fried prawns, then asked the boy where he was from.

'I'm from Assam,' he said in heavily accented Hindi.

'Where in Assam?' Arjun asked.

'Sonitpur district.'

'Tezpur?'

The boy smiled, shook his head, and said, 'Near Bhalukpung.'

Arjun nodded, and asked his name.

'Manoj,' the boy said, leaving his surname out.

Arjun watched him walk away towards the kitchen. A Hindu name, so he was probably a Hindu Bodo, or a Karbi, or an Assamese, or maybe even a Nepali. He remembered Bhalukpung at the foothills of the Arunachal Himalayas from his army days. A beautiful landscape, marred by forest encroachment and government neglect, and where there had risen militant groups, a new faction morphing out of the original after every ceasefire or agreement so that extortion and kidnappings could still be carried out.

Manoj came back with the order, and Arjun made some more small talk with the boy. He discovered that the other waiter's name was Krishna, and that he was from somewhere near Siliguri. He didn't ask Manoj about Agnes Pereira though. Some of the revellers were shouting now, in British-accented English, and a girl was showing off her hula-hoop skills. Arjun drank his beer and ate the passable fried prawns and kept an eye on the goings-on.

After a while he got up to go and take a leak. The toilet was at the back among the huts, a rough tin-and-bamboo structure with two doors, whose pipes would invariably lead out into someone's fields. Arjun looked around the place but saw nothing of interest. He returned to his table and lit another cigarette. There were no waiters around at the moment, so he went up to the group of Brits, took out the photo and asked if any of them had seen her. They took the photo from him and examined it with interest, passing it from hand to hand. Someone turned down the music, and the hula-hoop girl took off the hoop to study the picture.

She said, in a thick accent that seemed further thickened by grass or beer, 'Can' be sure, but I mite ha seen summun like 'er . . . em . . . two, three days back.'

'Here? In this place?' Arjun asked.

The girl nodded, handing the photo back to Arjun. She was young, pale and wore cargo pants and a yellow bikini top.

'What about your friends, might any of them have seen her?'

'They only got here yest'day. Like I said, I seen 'er like, two or three days back.'

'And you haven't seen her since?' he asked, to which the girl shook her head.

'Wot's it 'bout, she gone missin', mate?' a skinny young man in a vest asked Arjun.

'Something like that,' he replied, and went back to his table.

Thirty minutes and a second beer later, Arjun walked out of the shack into the hot afternoon sun. He turned and saw the first waiter, Krishna, talking to Manoj while they both looked furtively in his direction. There was no sign of the girl, but Arjun had an idea as to who might be able to help him.

X

As night fell, he was back at Everest Café, sitting at the same table as before and drinking his own cocktail of cheap vodka and Sprite with a wedge of lime. The place was crowded, with foreigners and a smattering of Indian tourists, and Arjun felt his age amid the bare skin and tattoos and medley of languages. Near him sat two Russian men who seemed to be drinking only mineral water. Out in the darkness he could hear the waves gently washing up on the shore, and further down the beach some people had lit a fire.

A scruffy youth, his right hand and forearm enclosed in a dirty plaster, attended to Arjun. He kept an eye out for the first two waiters, Manoj and Krishna. They were around, but were avoiding his table, laughing and joking with the foreigners instead. He checked the time on his cell phone—in a while they would be leaving, and then hopefully he would get a call. Watching them, it struck him how they were accepted at face value, as individuals, by the foreigners. While with Indians, questions about their community and where they hailed from betrayed too much about them, as it had to Arjun.

He asked the waiter with the broken hand for a second drink (he had bought a quarter-bottle of vodka, which was with the cashier behind the counter—they weren't supposed to be selling the hard stuff in there). A woman in a faded multicoloured robe walked in, looked around and smiled at Arjun before making her way to a free table. It took him a moment to recognize her as the person who had been feeding the cow on the beach.

As he drank his vodka he kept looking at his cell phone, waiting for the call. Hanging from the high, thatched roof were those large bone-like segments, which Arjun supposed, after talking to the waiter, were from a whale which had washed up on the beach during the rainy season.

He found himself looking at the woman in the robe, who looked up periodically from her tablet with a fixed half-smile, something which suggested a forced optimism. How old could she be? Not younger than him in any case. His phone rang, and when he picked it up, a gruff voice at the other end said, 'They're here. Come now.'

Arjun stepped out after paying for his vodka. He made his way towards the far end of the beach, to the second-last place where he had inquired about a room, the third or fourth Sunset Café on the beach. The waves lapped gently in the dark and he recalled the woman's figure in the bikini, a more attractive sight than in the gown.

There was reggae playing at the café, and the two waiters, Krishna and Manoj, stood before a table where the stocky, scar-faced manager sat beside a police inspector in a tight uniform, a pair of dark glasses perched on his nose, with a bottle of Kingfisher beer and two mugs between them. The manager motioned for him to sit, and Arjun pulled up a chair in the sandy floor opposite to them. The sight of the inspector had thrown him a bit, but he took a deep breath and concentrated on the two waiters. He hoped that the inspector wouldn't ask for the photograph, *if* he had learnt about it from the waiters and the local thana hadn't been sent a photograph of Agnes Pereira.

'It took me just two minutes to open their mouths,' the manager boasted to Arjun. 'She's gone to Manali.'

Arjun had come here in the afternoon and told the manager he was looking for a girl whom two waiters at Everest Café knew about. He had hinted that he was there in an official capacity, and the manager had agreed to have a word with the waiters. Arjun had surmised, correctly it now seemed, that the manager was one of the heavies on the beach.

'Manali?' Arjun looked at the two sullen-faced waiters. 'How do you know?'

The manager said, pointing at Manoj, 'His cousin brother works there in a hotel.'

'She asked us if we knew how to get to Manali by train,' Krishna blurted.

'What's your interest in this girl?' the inspector asked, lifting his beer mug.

'I'm looking for her, she's gone missing,' Arjun said to the inspector, and then asked Manoj, 'So she's already left for Manali?'

'Yes, sir, she's left,' Krishna replied again. 'Day before. We told her to take a train to Goa, to catch another train to Delhi from there, and then to get on a bus to Manali.'

'He's not asking you!' the manager yelled at Krishna. 'He's asking your friend!'

'Are you with the police, intelligence bureau, something like that?' the inspector asked, lighting a cigarette.

Manoj now looked up and said to Arjun, 'I gave her the name of the hotel where my cousin works, that's all.'

'I'm a private detective from Delhi,' Arjun said to the inspector, then asked Manoj again, 'Which hotel is that? And what's your cousin's name?'

'Royal Residency. His name's Bhim.'

'A detective?' The inspector's eyebrows went up behind his sunglasses. 'What has this girl done?'

Arjun had to think on his feet.

'She ran away from Delhi after her marriage was fixed by her parents.'

The manager had a question of his own: 'From Delhi to Gokarna, then up to Manali?'

'There's a boyfriend. They must be planning to meet in Manali. She must have come to Gokarna to leave a false trail.'

The waiters looked spellbound by this Bollywood-style story, but the inspector was of a more cynical type. He asked Arjun, 'What's her name? What does her father do?'

'Sheetal Marwaha,' Arjun said off the top of his head. 'Her father's a minister.'

'Hmm,' the inspector said, and inclined his head and blew out a stream of smoke.

64

The manager picked up his mug, and Arjun took this chance to ask the waiters, 'Where's the train station here?'

'Gokarna Road,' Krishna answered again. 'There's a travel agent behind the next Sunset Café on the beach. I had told her about it too.'

'Why did you lie to me, that you hadn't seen her?' Arjun asked.

'I thought you might be with the police,' Krishna said, 'inquiring about drugs.'

'Did she give you her phone number, by any chance?'

The two of them shook their heads. Arjun looked at Manoj, and said, 'Don't breathe a word of this to your cousin, okay?'

'Don't worry, he won't,' the inspector said. 'I give you my guarantee. If you need any more help, let me know.'

'Thank you,' Arjun said to him and the manager. 'I better go see about my ticket.'

'Have a beer with us,' the manager offered, but Arjun was already standing up.

'Some other time maybe,' he said with a forced smile.

As he walked out of Sunset Café he could hear the manager shout at the two waiters, 'Now what are you standing here for? Go, get out!'

Arjun strode as quickly as he could towards the next Sunset Café; luckily the inspector hadn't asked him more questions. He hoped the travel agent was still open, that there was a train heading out of Gokarna Road station tomorrow, and that he could still get a berth on it. If Agnes Pereira was headed to Manali, the quickest way he could intercept her was to take a train to a nearby city with an airport and catch a flight to Delhi, and then hire a taxi for Manali. Had something spooked her in Gokarna? Or was Manali part of her plan? Drugs money, the Russian or Israeli mafia—what might she be involved in, apart from Vishwanathan and the bar dancer's murder?

Trudging through the sand in the dark, he looked inside Everest Café as he passed by. The woman in the gown appeared to be eating a solitary dinner. Ten—even five—years ago he might have approached her, with an eye on what might follow. Now, after Mumbai and Yamini, it struck him as just too much trouble.

12

TWELVE HOURS LATER ARJUN WAS sitting on a bench on the platform of the sleepy Gokarna Road station, his backpack at his feet. He was waiting for a train from Kerala headed to Pune in Maharashtra. The station was about fourteen kilometres from the beach, and he had taken an auto to get there. Waking up in the morning he had felt fresh and rejuvenated; the fever had run its course. A train headed to Madgaon in Goa had just pulled in and left, taking with it most of the tourists who had been waiting at the station. There now remained only a middle-aged French couple, and a young Russian couple in Indian attire, all going to the Osho ashram in Pune, plus some locals looking curiously at the foreigners. At one point Arjun had to get up from his wooden bench to shoo away a stray cow that had starting poking its nose into the French couple's luggage; they seemed unable to make up their mind whether to chase it away for fear of hurting someone's sentiments.

Arjun was going to Pune because Liza had booked him on a Pune–Delhi flight the previous night, after she had found that all Goa–Delhi flights out of Dabolim were fully booked for the next two days. He had called her from outside the travel agent's office, and later managed to get himself a *tatkal* ticket on the Pune train. The travel agent had recognized Agnes Pereira when Arjun showed him the photograph, and said that she had purchased two tickets: Gokarna to Madgaon, and Madgaon to Hazrat

Nizamuddin station in Delhi. She would have already reached Delhi on the Rajdhani Express, he added. Arjun had asked him if she had made any inquiries about Manali, and the agent said she hadn't. But, he said, she had looked up something on one of the two Internet-connected desktops in his office that he hired out in half-hour slots, then asked to use his phone for a call, and after she left he had noticed that she had written down a number on the newspaper on his desk: 0911. He hadn't heard what she had been talking about as he had stepped outside his office to attend to a group of tourists. The travel agent seemed okay about sharing the information with Arjun, but he claimed it would take him a long time to look for her name among the receipts, and besides he ran the place alone. When asked if he was sure it was she who had written the number down, and not anyone else, he said he was, as he had been reading the newspaper while she had been on the Internet. But when Arjun asked if he could see the newspaper, he said a customer had been reading it and had taken it with him. He said he remembered the number as it reminded him of 9/11.

After a long wait the train to Pune appeared, emerging through the heat haze shimmering in the distance, before halting at the platform for just a minute. Arjun got on with his backpack. It had been years since he had gone on a train journey. In his compartment were two stout, middle-aged Malayalees, and a younger one who made container tins for a living and travelled to the Gulf, besides a Scottish backpacking couple on their way from Sri Lanka to a place near Pune called Castle Rock. The big-boned girl offered them all slices of papaya, and the bearded boy told Arjun how some tea estates in Sri Lanka still had Scottish names. By afternoon they had climbed up into the hilly section of the Konkan railway line. Outside, in the mellow sun, were glimpses of the dark, hazy hills receding into the distance, and the rock walls and forest beside the line, along with several dark tunnels. Inside was the chill of the air conditioning, the high smell of Railways food and the boredom of the journey in his cramped upper berth. Arjun took out the photo of Agnes Pereira and studied it. Was she scared and on the run, or did she have a plan? And what did 0911 signify? A key to a combination lock? A room number? A code of some sort? Or even a reference to the 9/11 attacks? He cast his mind back to what he had seen from the auto on the way to the train station: the curving sweep of the beach from up above and the shimmering sea, then the sleepy little villages, and finally the flatland where seawater was let in through locks and evaporated to collect salt, the water reflecting the clouds and the sky. In a while he fell asleep.

The train got to Pune early next morning. Stepping out, Arjun saw several people sleeping in the station compound under bright lights. He caught a taxi. It was cold and still dark. His first stop was a wooden double-storeyed residence on Dastur Meher Road, an old Parsi locality, where he dropped off the money at a *hundi* transfer, getting in return one half of a torn currency note. He didn't want to risk checking into a flight with so much cash on him. Nearby was Dorabjee Restaurant, more than a century old, where Arjun had heard they still cooked their Parsi dishes on charcoal fires. But it was too early in the morning for it to be open. Then he proceeded to the airport, which was barely fifteen kilometres away (it hardly took him twenty minutes at this early hour). The morning flight to Delhi was on time, and by 11 a.m. they were coming in to land on a sunny and smoggy day.

From the airport he took a taxi to CR Park, where he first stopped at his office to check on business. Liza greeted him irritably, which he supposed was because of the pending matrimonial investigations. He told her to go out and start working on one case, and asked Chandu to take care of the office, putting through any customers who turned up either to him or Liza via the office landline.

'What if the call comes when I'm sitting inside the boy's house talking to his mother?' Liza asked.

'Put your phone on silent then. Chandu, if she doesn't answer, call me, got it?'

The boy nodded, his eyes wide and serious. He was being given a lot of responsibility.

'And don't worry, Liza,' Arjun continued, 'we'll get another detective soon.'

'Good to hear that,' she snapped, switching off her desktop and getting up from her seat, 'but we've already lost a couple of customers.'

'Don't worry, we'll get some more. As long as the big cases keep coming to us we'll be fine. Which reminds me, my Mumbai flight ticket was booked from Paharganj?'

'Yes. I got in touch with our contact at the airline, and he got back the next day saying it was an agent's ticket. A to Z Tours and Travels in Paharganj.'

'You have the address?'

Liza looked through her cluttered desk and picked up a Post-it which she handed to Arjun. He glanced at the note before returning it to her.

'The girl I asked you to look up, anything on her?'

'Yes, she's been working as an air hostess. I confirmed with the airlines. Seems to have done a bit of modelling before that. That's about it. Couldn't seem to find her on Facebook.'

So the news channel was right. But how had the information got to them so quickly?

'Look after the agency,' he said to them. 'I should be back in two or three days.'

'But you've just returned,' his secretary complained. 'Where are you going now?'

'I'll tell you when I get back.'

Arjun opened the tinted-glass door and stepped out, leaving the two employees of Nexus Security wondering where their boss was headed next.

13

HE WALKED THE SHORT DISTANCE from his office on the Kalkaji road to CR Park's B Block, stopping at Market No. 1 to pick up a packet of cigarettes. The midday temperature was still high, and he built up a sweat walking back to his flat with his backpack slung from one shoulder. He had worked alone all these years; why couldn't his secretary understand that it was still a process of adjustment for him?

Letting himself into his second-floor flat, he brought in the past few days' newspapers from the balcony, all coated with a patina of dust. It looked like there would be no more rains for a while. Arjun took a shower, changed into a fresh pair of jeans and a half-sleeved shirt, and rang up the taxi driver whom he had called the previous evening from the train.

'Yadavji, you'll be here at two, won't you?'

But Yadavji, who had been driving back with a family from Dehradun, had met with not one but two punctures along the way, and was going to be late. Arjun could have driven himself, or called for another taxi, but he figured a reliable driver would come in handy.

'I'll wait for you,' he said. 'Call me when you get to Delhi.'

Then he called his client. Vishwanathan seemed surprised that Arjun was in Delhi.

'Well, she's somewhere this side, in north India.'

'North India is a big place. Where exactly?'

'That's what I'm trying to find out,' he found himself saying. Somehow he didn't trust Vishwanathan enough to tell him the whole truth.

'Let me know the moment you find her, okay? And don't try to do anything, just keep her in your sight.'

With that he hung up. The uneasy feeling returned to Arjun, telling him he was somehow being set up. He had his usual fee; he could call off this search without any loss and get started on one of their pending matrimonial checks. But the photograph of Agnes Pereira on the coffee table drew him back. Who was she? What had she done? Was this about the money she had supposedly stolen? Or was it something else?

His stomach growled—he hadn't eaten since the plane—and he decided to order lunch. He picked chicken korma and roomali roti from the takeaway started recently by his butcher at the nearby Savitri complex. While he waited for the food to arrive, he turned on the television news and flipped through the newspapers. There was a bottle of beer in the fridge, and after debating with himself for a while, he went and opened it. The television news didn't have anything about Savitri Rao, and the few stories in the old newspapers told him nothing new. The police were looking for the missing suspect. But what did the police know that they weren't sharing with the public? The only person who could clarify matters for Arjun was Agnes Pereira herself.

His food arrived and he ate after finishing his beer. The korma, as usual, was excellent, tangy and creamy from the curd added to the chicken, and he polished off the remaining gravy with his last roti. He had tried to run a restaurant once, but experience had taught him that a good cook didn't necessarily make a good restaurant owner. With his lunch done, he went down to his car, wiped away some of the dust on the windshield and bonnet, and got in. The meal had improved his mood, and he started the engine and put on some Kishore Kumar.

Half an hour later he was driving up Kasturba Gandhi Marg towards Connaught Place. He found a parking lot in CP and walked to the underground metro station from where he caught a train to the nearby Chawri Bazar station. Built 125 feet below the ground, and accessed by four sets of escalators, the station was one of the engineering highlights of the Delhi Metro, and Arjun exited on to a narrow street flanked by hardware stores and juice shops. Threading his way through the people and scooters and rickshaws he entered a similar street nearby where he made his way to a shop that dealt in all manner of pipes. When he asked for a Mr Gupta, he was shown into a cramped inner office, where an accountant handed him his money upon receipt of the torn currency note he had been given in Pune. Arjun put the bundles into his backpack and returned to the metro station, where the presence of the cash didn't raise an eyebrow at the security check. Business worth crores of rupees was transacted here every day and what Arjun was carrying was small change. Exiting at Rajiv Chowk station, Arjun caught an auto to Paharganj. Not his favourite mode of transport, but it would be the quickest.

A to Z Tours and Travels occupied the ground floor of a building with a vertical green-and-purple neon sign saying 'Shiva Guest House' jutting out on one side. It was in a lane with several other hotels and lodges, the type favoured by budget travellers and grimy backpackers. Arjun asked the auto to wait some distance away and walked up to the travel agency. It was a small office, probably with living quarters behind it, and the walls were crowded with tourism calendars and posters. A portly man sat at a desk typing on a keyboard. Arjun scanned the ceiling and the walls; there appeared to be no CCTV cameras, at least none that he could see.

He sat down at the desk, his backpack with the money between his feet, and cleared his throat. The portly man looked up. Arjun said he wanted a flight ticket. He had decided against a direct line of inquiry.

'Flight ticket?' the man asked. 'International, national? Group, family, single person? Tomorrow, next week, next month? Tell me the details please.'

An emaciated white couple looked at Arjun suspiciously from the old sofa on which they sat poring over a tourist guidebook. In front of them was a low table with more guidebooks and some pamphlets advertising township developments on the outskirts of Delhi.

'I wanted to ask about discounts. On Delhi–Mumbai flights. A friend of mine told me to come here. This is where he gets his tickets done. In fact, he booked a Delhi–Mumbai flight for someone just a few days ago.'

'What's your friend's name?'

'Vikas.'

The portly man frowned. 'I don't know any Vikas.'

Arjun described his visitor: a large-built, middle-aged man, bald, with a round head. The man behind the desk shook his head.

'The ticket was done in the name of Arjun Arora.'

'How do you expect me to start looking for passenger names?'

'Is there anyone else who sits here?'

'No, it's just me. Tell me when you want to fly, I'll see what discount I can offer.'

'All right. I'll come around later. I keep flying down to Mumbai on business.'

The portly man grunted, but didn't say anything, waiting for Arjun to leave.

'Who owns this place, by the way?' Arjun asked casually. 'Are you the owner?'

The man raised his eyebrows and pointed upward, then resumed typing.

'Thank you,' Arjun said and got up. He ran his eyes over the office again.

Once outside, he looked up at the ageing white facade of the guest house. So the hotel owner or owners also had a travel agency. That was interesting. 'Vikas' appeared to be an alias, as he had suspected. Could finding out about the hotel maybe tell him something? He made a mental note to ask Bunty.

While returning to Connaught Place in the auto, Arjun's phone rang. It was his taxi driver, Yadavji, who said he would be at the flat in CR Park within the hour.

'I'll be ready,' Arjun said.

He hefted the backpack. The money he had with him; now it was time to track down the girl.

14

IT WAS PAST 8 P.M., and Arjun was in the back seat of Yadavji's taxi as it sped north on the highway heading out of Delhi towards Himachal Pradesh. It was a twelve-hour drive from the capital to Manali. While leaving the city, the chaotic traffic along the settlements on its northern fringes—a mix of trucks and buses and cars—had slowed them down. At one point they passed a massive garbage landfill with a slum-like township near it. Now with the dark countryside around them, Yadavji gladly stepped on the accelerator of his white Indigo.

Arjun smoked his Gold Flake as he watched the steady, alert profile of the taxi driver focused on the headlight beams stretching out before them. From time to time a truck or bus would come barrelling down the middle of the road from the other side; he would switch the lights on and off, and if he got no reaction, would at the last moment swerve to the left. He knew the man from two years back, when an investigation into a businessman's murder had proved that the driver, already behind bars, was innocent and a family friend guilty of the murder. After he had got out of jail, Arjun had asked him to come and work for him, but Yadavji preferred his independence.

They were in Haryana now, passing Karnal. The temperature had dropped considerably. All along the highway were identical colour hoardings for Pachranga pickles, made of a mix of five vegetables. They stopped at a dhaba serving vegetarian food in

Panipat, where Yadavji arranged for a half-bottle of Blenders Pride which the two of them shared at an outside table before having their roti and dal. Travelling on the highways at night could be risky, and Arjun was reassured by the taxi driver's watchful presence. He was a quiet fellow who could spring into action when required. Arjun would have preferred to travel during the day, but he wanted to get to Manali as soon as possible, in case Agnes Pereira had other travel plans.

They set off again, and the monotony of watching the headlights cutting through the dark soon lulled Arjun to sleep. When he woke up the taxi had stopped moving. It was the dead of night, and he figured they were somewhere in Punjab. To one side was a line of shuttered shops, and across the road was a deserted petrol pump with a Bolero parked beside it. Two police constables who had halted the taxi walked up and told Yadavji to get out. Arjun rubbed his eyes but kept his mouth shut. The taxi driver was led to the waiting vehicle, where Arjun noticed a shadowy figure.

When he returned Arjun asked him, 'How much did they take?'

'A thousand rupees,' Yadavji said, starting the car.

Arjun handed him two five-hundred-rupee notes from his wallet.

They were out of the town in a while, and presently he saw irrigation canals stretching out across darkened fields, followed by columns of eucalyptus trees beside the road. The road grew bumpy, with hillocks to one side. Yadavji drove on, seemingly impervious to fatigue or the growing chill. Arjun realized he had never asked the man about his family. If only Sonali had been with him. But she was out of his life forever. Was this what he had left her for, travelling alone through the night in search of a girl who might or might not be there? He could sense the familiar dark clouds gathering in his mind, and wished they had bought another half-bottle of whisky at the dhaba. Instead he lit another cigarette. Up ahead, he could vaguely make out the darkened silhouette of the hills of Himachal Pradesh. The girl—he wondered again if this was part of her plan, or if she had come north on the spur of the moment. And that number: 0911, 1190.

In the early hours of the morning they began climbing up into the hills. The moon broke free from the clouds. It was cold now, and Arjun put on his fleece-lined leather jacket. He remembers a night drive from Tezpur to Tawang in an army Gypsy with his father. He is six or seven then. His mother has stayed behind in Guwahati, and he feels grown-up travelling like this with his father. The driver sits hunched forward concentrating on one blind curve after another, a sheer drop to their right, and Arjun sits in the front seat with his father's arm around him. He wrapped his arms around himself at the memory. He was alone now, bereft of any protection.

The sky gradually lightened up. At the town of Mandi, vendors were helping load vegetables on to trucks. Yadavji stopped at a dhaba on a hillside and got down and stretched. His eyes were red, and Arjun told him he could take the rest of the day off after they got to Manali, which was about five hours away. As they were eating their breakfast of oily aloo parathas, double omelettes and sweet, milky tea, a Volvo bus stopped outside and its passengers trooped out, a motley group of locals and tourists.

The sun rose steadily as they moved on, and Arjun looked out at the early-morning sunshine on the green hills. They passed small towns perched on hillsides with little houses and mango and apple trees. He remembered his dream: of retiring one day and living in a small Himalayan village. The road narrowed and skirted the edges of a gorge through which the Beas flowed, the river sometimes alarmingly far below them, and meadows and isolated houses far above on the towering cliffs. He noticed palm trees sticking out of the shale above the river's edges. At the Larji hydro project they entered a long tunnel, dusty and with dim lighting, before coming out on the other side at Aut in the Kullu Valley.

There were apple orchards and stone-and-timber houses with upper balconies and slate roofs, then a narrow road through Akhara Bazar in the crowded town of Kullu, before the river appeared again running alongside the road. Past the town of Bhuntar, there was a police checkpoint where they were waved on. Yadavji said they were looking for foreigners and it could have been so; the Israelis had taken over areas in remote villages where they paid the locals to cultivate marijuana to be turned into hashish for sale in Manali, Delhi and Goa. As elsewhere in India, it wouldn't have been possible without paying off the police, who shared the proceeds with their superiors. There appeared villas and resorts, taxis and Indian tourists outside them, and river crossings and rafting camps by the churning waters of the river. Arjun looked out at the scenery of white water, boulders and conifers, and wondered how it must have been a hundred years before. A huge mound of rubbish greeted them as they entered Manali. The town itself was packed with tourists from Delhi and Punjab crowding the Mall Road area— and this wasn't even the peak summer season.

Hotel Royal Residency was above the Mall Road, and Arjun asked Yadavji to drop him there. The driver had said he would be staying at a lodge he knew on the outskirts of the town, and Arjun agreed, saying he would call him if needed.

15

LARGE RED PILLARS AT THE gate, a short gravelled driveway and a shiny neocolonial building. Arjun was surprised Manoj's cousin was working at a place like this; he had expected something rather basic. Around them were more hotels, similarly ugly buildings, and in the distance he could see the snow-capped Rohtang Pass.

Arjun walked over to the open-plan coffee shop beside the lawn. He ordered a coffee, and when the shiny-faced young waiter brought it to his table, Arjun asked him if he knew a waiter from Assam called Bhim. When the young man nodded, Arjun asked if he could fetch him as he had a message from a family member. The waiter said that Bhim was on the night shift and might be asleep. He hurried off towards the hotel. Arjun sipped his coffee and looked around. There were expensive vehicles in the car park, and overdressed tourists sitting on the lawn. He had come to Manali years ago with Sonali and Rhea, and even back then it had become one of those Himalayan hill towns overrun by tourists from the plains. The Mall Road had reminded him of Lajpat Nagar in Delhi, and the Israelis on their bikes were similar to the Punjabis—they stuck together, dressed identically and ate their own food. A rough poster on a nearby pillar caught his attention: it advertised a reward of Rs 5 lakh for help in finding a missing Israeli who had been last seen riding out of Manali on an Enfield.

The waiter reappeared from the direction of the hotel, but he was alone. He crossed the short stretch of lawn and told Arjun that he had passed on the message to Bhim who had been sleeping. Arjun nodded, imagining a cramped room somewhere at the back of the hotel, clothes hung on a rope strung above the bed. He drank the rest of his coffee and lit a cigarette. What would he do if Agnes Pereira made an appearance now? Shortly he saw someone walking towards him, a younger, slimmer version of the waiter Manoj. His uniform looked as if it had been hastily pulled on. Arjun asked him to sit but he remained standing.

'I'm Arjun,' he introduced himself, extending a hand.

'Bhim,' the boy said. His hand was hard and calloused.

'I met Manoj in Gokarna. He's your cousin, isn't he?'

Bhim nodded.

'Have you spoken to him recently, say in the last two or three days?'

Bhim shook his head. He said, 'You have a message for me?'

'Actually, I wanted to ask you something. But first, are you from Sonitpur district in Assam as well?'

Bhim nodded again.

'Nepali?'

'No, Mising.'

Arjun nodded, and said, 'I was in Sonitpur district too. When I was in the army.'

Bhim seemed to grow more attentive. Arjun took the photo out from his shirt pocket and passed it to the young boy.

'Have you seen this girl around here? She might have checked into the hotel.'

He watched closely but the boy's face displayed no sign of recognition. Handing the photo back to Arjun, he suggested inquiring at the reception.

'Okay, I'll do that,' Arjun said. Had the long trip been in vain, or would he have to check into the hotel himself and find out?

'How's my cousin?' the boy asked.

'He's fine,' Arjun said, waving to the first waiter for the bill. 'What about you? Do you go home often?'

The boy's face brightened. 'I'm going home next month. To help with the paddy harvest.'

At the reception desk Arjun introduced himself to the cautious-looking man as a detective from Delhi and showed him the photo.

'Have you seen this girl? Her parents have asked me to find her.'

The man looked at the photo closely before shaking his head and handing it back.

'Do you have a room with the number 0911?'

'No, all our rooms have three digit numbers.'

'What about 009? That would be room 9 on the ground floor?'

'Yes, it is.'

'Who's in it now?'

'It's occupied by . . .' the receptionist consulted the register before him, 'by an elderly couple from Kolkata. Just the two of them.'

'What about 119? Room 19 on the first floor?'

'We only have twelve rooms on each floor.'

So that was that. Arjun walked down the steps to the gravelled driveway and took out his cigarette packet and lighter. What to do now?

An Innova tourist taxi entered the car park through the gates, and Arjun's eyes went to the number plate, which had a Himachal Pradesh registration on it. Suddenly it struck him—a four-digit number! He almost cried out at the realization.

Lighting a cigarette, he waited till the entire family had spilled out of the vehicle, before walking across to it. The driver was a thin, dark man in a bulky sports jacket.

Arjun greeted the driver, before asking him, 'I'm looking for a vehicle with the number 0911, possibly a taxi. Do you know it?'

The taxi driver frowned and shook his head. He said Arjun should inquire at the taxi stand, and that he was going there himself. The driver gave him a lift to the stand, which was spread across a dusty plot near where Mall Road started. Arjun got down and asked one or two other drivers about 0911, but drew a blank. Would he have to get the information from the regional transport office in Kullu, if at all it was a Himachal-registered vehicle? Frustration welled up inside him. A wild goose chase, he thought, that's what I'm engaged in. He caught a glimpse of himself in a taxi's mirror. The words stencilled on it: OBJECTS IN THE REAR VIEW . . . for the second time something clicked in his mind. He walked back to the driver who had given him the lift.

'What about 1160? Is there a taxi with that number?'

'Double one . . . of course, that's the number of Kapoor's taxi.'

'Is he here?' Arjun asked, looking around at the different white-painted models.

'Ask that fellow over there, he'll know.'

Arjun hurried across to the Indica taxi the driver had pointed at. His sudden hunch had been that the travel agent might have seen the number written on the newspaper in reverse, and not realized it, especially if the 6 was written with a curve: then 1160 might have looked like 0911. If he *was* correct, he might get luckier still; in his experience, drivers were not averse to sharing information, maybe because they got both clients and new jobs that way.

Arjun asked the lean, old sardarji with the bushy beard where Kapoor's taxi was.

'You're here too late,' the man said, wiping his greasy hands with a cloth, 'he went back to Delhi yesterday.'

'Oh!' Arjun feigned disappointment. 'He's already left!'

'You want to go to Delhi? I can take you.'

'No, I had to collect something from his passenger . . . the girl. I thought she was reaching today!' He looked around, trying to act frustrated, then turned to the sardarji. 'Wait, do you know where he dropped her?'

'At the Beas View guest house, he told me.'

'Where's that?' Arjun asked with a quickening pulse.

'On the other side of the river,' the sardarji said. 'Do you know her?'

'Yes, she's an old friend of mine from Delhi.'

16

ARJUN CAUGHT AN AUTO FROM the Mall Road. It went down to the bridge above the Beas and clattered across the iron plates before going left on the Rohtang Pass road. Tourist vehicles of all shapes and sizes clogged the road coming down from the pass into town. Some distance ahead, the auto turned right and started climbing up the hillside laboriously. Just when Arjun thought it might stall, the driver stopped by the roadside at an unmarked gate flanked by a brick wall. He could see a two-storeyed wooden house some way in, with the side of a large white building that looked like a hotel above it. The auto driver told him the wooden building was the guest house. Arjun paid him and got down with his backpack. He opened the creaking gate and went in along a walkway flanked by overgrown patches of grass. To his right, beyond a few apple trees, he could see a new-looking single-storey structure. A straight-backed, silver-haired gentleman in a green pullover emerged from it. When he came closer, Arjun saw a maroon scarf around his neck, suggesting a background in the armed forces, or on a plantation.

'Do you have a room available?' he asked. 'In the guest house, not the hotel.'

'Are you alone?' the man asked, his eyes inspecting Arjun.

'Yes. I've come from Delhi. I'll spend a day or two here, and then head to Leh.'

'We do have one free room at the moment, Mr . . . ?'

'Arora. Arjun Arora. You can call me Arjun.'

A helper led him up the wooden staircase on the right side of the house to the upper floor where he opened the first door and went in. Arjun waited on the balcony, looking out at the upper end of the Kullu Valley. Down below he could hear the waters of the Beas rushing through the boulder-strewn riverbed, while the pine-clad mountain ridges rose up at the end to the Rohtang Pass, where clouds now obscured the jagged, snow-covered peaks. Beyond the pass lay the arid wastes of Lahaul and Spiti. Could she be headed there?

'Everything okay, sahib,' the helper came out and told him. He was a young boy in his teens, and the permanent half-grin on his face along with his shabby clothes hinted at something stunted. He reminded Arjun of someone.

'What's your name?' Arjun asked, taking the room key from him.

'Hari is my name, sahib. I work here. If you need anything, let me know.'

Arjun was still deciding on how to broach the subject of the girl when he heard the gate opening with a creaking noise. Looking down, he saw a tall girl walk in with a plastic bag in her hand. She was wearing a pair of dark trackpants and jacket, and her hair was tucked inside a beanie. He knew without any doubt that it was her, and when she looked up at them it was like a confirmation. The plastic bag—biscuits and juice again? He forced himself to turn to the boy and ask for a cup of tea. Below them, he could hear footsteps and a door opening and closing.

'Chai,' the boy said, then, 'do you want biscuits?'

'Yes, bring me a packet of Marie biscuits if you have them.'

'Marie biscuits? We have three packets.'

'That girl who just came in, when did she arrive?'

'Yesterday, sahib,' the boy said with his incomplete grin. 'She's staying below.'

86

'How long is she staying here for?'

The boy shrugged, then said, 'She gave some clothes to be washed today morning.'

Arjun went in to have a look at his room. It was low-ceilinged and basic: a double bed, a bathroom at the end, a table and a chair and an almirah, a television and a fireplace. Just the way he liked it. He took off his jacket and put the backpack into the almirah, then washed and went to sit on one of the cane recliners out on the balcony. The boy Hari returned a while later with a tray on which were a thermos, a cup and saucer, and a packet of biscuits. He drank his tea and ate the biscuits, dipping them into the tea first, and looked out at the mountains. The owner had told him that he only gave out rooms to people who knew about the place, or if anyone stopped by to inquire, which most people didn't as they assumed it was a private residence. He had served with the SSB in the north-east, and the adjacent hotel, the Manali Crown, was run by his two sons, one of whom had been in the Assam Rifles, while he himself looked after the guest house. Arjun hadn't mentioned his defence background. He now poured himself a second cup of tea and lit a cigarette. Later he went back into his room and called Vishwanathan.

'I've found her,' he told his client, 'and I'm keeping an eye on her.'

'Where?'

'Manali.'

'Keep her in your sights, and wait. I'll have someone there by tomorrow.'

'From Mumbai?'

'Maybe. There's an airport at Kullu. He'll contact you once he's there.'

'And the rest of my payment?'

'He'll settle that with you.'

'What'll you do with her?'

'That doesn't concern you.'

But it does concern me, Arjun thought as he hung up. He had tracked her down for his client, and felt responsible for what could happen to her. Next he called Bunty, and asked if he could find out about A to Z Tours and Travels and its parent, the Shiva Guest House.

'I'll ask around,' his friend said. 'Just give me a few days. I'm going crazy with some factory orders right now. Are you back in Delhi?'

'I was, now I'm in Manali.'

'Bhai, wah, you're having a good Bharat darshan. Have you found the girl yet?'

'I have.'

'Good, then you can treat me to some whisky and mutton when you're back.'

'What's the matter, boiled vegetables and roti for dinner again?'

Bunty's wife, Harpreet, kept trying to include her husband in her weight loss programme, saying it would work better if they could motivate one another.

'How can a bachelor like you understand my pain? Call me when you get back.'

Arjun went back outside and lit another cigarette. Bunty had a devoted wife, three children, and his parents staying along with him.

The unmistakeable sound of a couple of Bullet motorcycles came down the road, and the hammering got louder as they stopped near the gate. A mixed group in sunglasses and rough attire, lean and tanned, all of them. They looked like ex-Israeli army conscripts. Presently Agnes Pereira appeared below and walked out to meet them. Now she had a pair of Wayfarer sunglasses on, along with the beanie, and it struck Arjun that no one would connect her to the photo shown on television. She climbed behind a youth with a crew cut, her arms going around his middle. Arjun watched them ride away in single file. So Agnes Pereira had come here to meet her friends. He considered going down to her room and trying to pick its lock, but decided against it. The front was open, and a worker could show up to clean the room at any time. Instead he went into his bathroom and switched on the geyser to have a bath.

17

IN THE AFTERNOON HE WENT down to have lunch at a Tibetan restaurant on the Mall Road, in memory of the time he had been there with his family. He had a beer, fried rice and some passable sushi made with canned tuna. The place was noisy with tourists, including a group of loud American students at the adjoining tables. A miniature replica of the restaurant behind the counter had a flag on it that said 'Next time we serve you in Tibet!' and Arjun saw flyers for a lounge bar somewhere on the Left Bank, which was what the other side of the river was called, and where the Israelis usually stayed.

When he came out, it was overcast and drizzling, and the Rohtang Pass in the distance was still obscured by clouds. He bought some Delhi newspapers at a news stand, and two bottles of Himachali apple wine on an impulse, before walking back through the traffic and the crowds to the guest house. Past the bridge the sides of the road running down to the river were strewn with rubbish, and the taxis packed with tourists kept coming down from the pass. From Manali to Shillong—it was the fate of all old hill stations. Climbing up the road to the guest house, Arjun reflected that at any rate, if she had given her clothes to be washed it meant she would be staying for the day, at the least. Maybe she was planning to travel further ahead with her friends.

He opened the gate slowly so that it didn't creak and walked up to the ground-floor veranda. Both the rooms were silent, with their curtains drawn and doors locked. She was still out with her biker friends. Arjun went up to his room and sat out on the balcony reading the newspapers. Soon the drizzle stopped and the sky cleared, filling the valley with an ethereal light. Arjun put the papers aside and watched as the sun sank lower in the sky. On the other side of the river, towards the town but across a bridge over a stream, were the shacks and buildings of Old Manali. The people in the other room on his floor were out as well, as indicated by the lock on the door. He alone waited here, the private eye on the trail of the dame with the money. It came to him that this was how the rest of his years would be spent: a solitary man, waiting for someone to show up. He yawned and was soon asleep.

Sometime later, the hammering of motorcycle engines woke him. The Bullet gang had returned. The bikes halted in a line on the road. Agnes Pereira alighted and opened the gate, holding what looked like a pastry box in her hands. She walked to her room without glancing back or up, as if deep in thought. Arjun, lying back on the recliner, let his eyes run over the motorcycles. One painted a light tan had a single seat on springs and was occupied by a blonde girl. The motorcycles rode away down the road and towards the town, their rhythmic beats fading in the evening air. Arjun closed his eyes again.

When he came awake a second time, it was almost dark. He went inside his room, pulled the curtains, turned on the lights and pressed the bell. When Hari turned up, he asked for a cup of tea. He was watching the news on BBC when Hari returned with the thermos.

'What will you have for dinner, sir?' the boy asked him.

'I might be going out,' Arjun said. 'Till what time can I order dinner?'

'Till 8 p.m. Kitchen is closed after that.'

'Who does the cooking, you?'

91

'No sir, my mother,' Hari said, and gestured towards the rear of the house, where Arjun had spotted a rough shack.

'What about the girl in room number one, is she having dinner?'

'Yes, sir. Rice, dal and sabzi, sir.'

'Hmm. I'll let you know in case I want dinner.'

He handed Hari a fifty-rupee note from his wallet, and the boy bowed and backed out of the room. Maybe it was the newsreader's accent, but Arjun suddenly knew who the boy reminded him of. The orphan Smike in *Nicholas Nickleby*, a movie he had watched as a schoolboy on Doordarshan in Shillong (or was it Tura, or maybe Dimapur?), one of those sleepy towns in the north-east his father's construction supervision work had taken them to. That reminded him to call his mother, and she told him that his father had fallen down in the bathroom that morning after another spell of giddiness. Arjun was alarmed.

'Why don't you take him to the hospital?'

'He refuses to go, what can I do! You know he hates hospitals.'

'Has he hurt himself?'

'Just a few bruises. It must be his blood pressure again.'

Arjun exhaled in despair. 'I'll come and take him to the hospital when I'm back.'

'Are you still in Mumbai?'

'No, in Manali. I should be back in a day or two.'

He hung up and felt the sadness he always did when he contemplated his father's life. A Partition refugee in his childhood, he had gone to Calcutta as a young man and then to the north-east looking for work, where he had met and married Arjun's mother, a Nepali. But a militant's bullet in Manipur had crippled him, and his parents had returned to Delhi. What if his father had a stroke or a heart attack tomorrow? What would become of his mother? It seemed to him that he was groping in the darkness, ignorant about the purpose of life. He thought of the brother he had lost at birth, and it surprised him, for it was something he never thought of.

He called his daughter but she was somewhere outside with friends and told him she would call back later. Reluctantly, he hung up. Rhea seemed to be hanging around with a new set of people now, frequenting expensive places. He made a note to have a word with Sonali about how much pocket money she was getting. It wouldn't do to have her growing up being able to afford anything she wanted. Arjun switched off the television.

Downstairs, he stopped on the veranda and lit a cigarette. The lights were on in room number one, and he could hear the canned laughter from a television sitcom. What choices in her life had led Agnes Pereira to this guest house in Manali? Hopefully he would find out tomorrow. Going down towards the river, he called Yadavji. The taxi driver said he was in the dining hall of the lodge watching an Ajay Devgn action film on television with a *paua* of Bagpiper whisky for company. Arjun told him to stay put, and said he would call as soon as something came up.

18

HE WALKED ALL THE WAY in the dark to the town from where he took the road that crossed the other bridge over the Manalsu Nala to Old Manali. He went up the narrow, winding road lined with German bakeries and Israeli restaurants, their ubiquitous coloured-chalk menus on slates, and shacks selling dyed T-shirts and robes and Internet cafés offering tour packages. It was all a variation of Gokarna—spirituality and adventure combined in a convenient package for Westerners with return tickets.

The street lights and shops dropped away as he walked up, and then he spotted what he had been looking for: the tan-coloured Bullet with the single seat, with the same number plate. It stood along with a couple of other Bullets under a small, double-storeyed traditional Himachali house made of timber and stone blocks, and Arjun saw that the entrance was a ladder placed on one side. His hunch about finding them here had been correct. He clambered up the shaky ladder, emerging into a low-ceilinged and low-lit carpeted room with several short tables where people sat cross-legged holding chopsticks. Coloured menus of Korean food hung on the walls. The owner or manager, who looked Korean, was sitting with his legs tucked under the counter, his bespectacled face bathed in the blue glow of a computer monitor. Beside him was a fridge.

The blonde motorcycle rider was among a group of eight or nine; Arjun saw that the table beside hers was free, and he made his way to it. Unfamiliar smells hung in the air, and he saw some people had small burners at their tables with bubbling hotpots on them. The man sitting at the computer got up and came towards him. Arjun could hear the blonde girl and her companions talking in the French-sounding accents of modern Hebrew. There was a faint smell of hashish in the air, and soft electronic music playing out of the computer on a pair of speakers.

After consulting with the man wearing the glasses, who was the owner, Arjun ordered a hotpot and a half-bottle of Blenders Pride. The whisky came first, and he tossed back a quick peg, feeling the welcome anaesthetizing effect. A familiar handmade poster up on one wall caught his eye: it was the reward poster for the missing Israeli biker. His hotpot arrived, along with the burner, and a plate arranged with slices of chicken and pork, and diced vegetables and mushrooms. Arjun put some of this into the simmering stock and poured himself a second drink. Then he quickly turned off the gas, before making a show of trying to get it started again with the gas lighter that had been provided. He noticed the blonde glancing his way, and he gestured that his lighter wasn't working, so could he borrow theirs please? The girl handed it over with a lean, sinewy arm, and Arjun relit his stove before handing back the lighter and saying thanks.

'You're welcome,' the girl said in accented English.

'Where are you from?' Arjun asked her. 'America?'

'No, Israel.'

'Ah, okay. You all having a good time in India?'

She said yes, smiling and nodding along with her friends who clearly wanted to return to their conversation as soon as this stranger stopped talking to them.

'In Manali for long?'

95

'We leave for Ladakh tomorrow,' she said.

'Enjoy your trip. Cheers.'

They raised their beer glasses and turned away, and were soon back in the midst of their animated conversation. Was Agnes Pereira planning to leave with them? Arjun felt she might. In which case he would have to follow her, which would mean calling Yadavji. But what time would his client's representative turn up? He took out a piece of mushroom and then a slice of chicken from the broth and put them into his mouth. The smell of the hashish, though faint, clung to the back of his throat for some reason. He felt a craving for rice and the thick *pahari* dal they cooked in these places. He checked his cell phone. It was half past seven. He would have to make do with the hotpot tonight.

He depleted the rest of his whisky at a steady pace accompanied by the bits cooked on the stove, even as he listened to the hushed babble of voices around him.

'I entered India eighteen years ago,' a British accent somewhere near him said, 'from the south, and then I worked my way up north to the Himalayas. I've been in Manali the past five years running a restaurant with my wife. I met her in Goa. I go home once a year, meet my mum and dad and sis. But do you know what I really want to do?'

'What?' Arjun heard a voice ask, and found that he too was curious about the answer. Convert to Hinduism?

'I want to go on a train journey around India to see how it's changed since I first set foot in the country.'

'That . . . that sounds like a great idea,' an admiring voice said in north Indian–accented English.

Arjun turned to look. Two middle-aged men, the British one lean with close-cropped hair—almost like a white Arjun. The smell of the hashish was making him feel sick now—and he knew why. It reminded him of the psychopathic butcher in the brothel from a few months back, and the underground execution chamber in Ramadi from a few years ago, places where he had inhaled the same sickly-sweet aroma. He pushed away the plate of raw meat. The Israelis had finished their beer and dinner and were leaving, and Arjun waited ten minutes—long enough to polish off the whisky in the bottle—before paying and leaving.

Walking back along the now dark and deserted road to the guest house with the waters of the Beas rushing past below, he found himself thinking about the conversation he had overheard. Would he consider a train journey around India? He supposed he would get tired of his own company. Letting himself into the guest house, he saw the light still on in Agnes Pereira's room. The other rooms on the ground floor and the first floor had their lights on now. Stepping on to the veranda he could hear the low murmur of the television from her room. He came around to the side of the building to take the staircase when he saw the silver-haired owner, now in a green blazer, coming down the stone-lined path at the back of the hotel. Arjun greeted him, and said he would stay on a day or two more. He asked the gentleman if the other guest house rooms would be free the next day as he might have some friends who were planning to come in from Delhi.

'Sorry, they're all booked,' the old man said. 'But inquire tomorrow. Goodnight.'

'Goodnight, sir,' Arjun said, and watched the man slowly move towards his house. He reminded Arjun of a former commanding officer of his, a Garhwali who consumed butter in large quantities but had still managed to remain trim as a knife.

He went up to his room, where he turned on the news and opened a bottle of the apple wine. It was sweeter than he would have liked, but it was better than nothing. His thoughts returned to the girl in the room below him. Was she staying another day then? He remembered Vishwanathan's missing finger and suddenly felt anxious. If he managed to wrap up things by noon the next day, he could collect the rest of his payment and start back to Delhi with Yadavji. The level of wine in the bottle had dropped to half, and he yawned and felt an immense sleepiness that dragged down his eyelids. His last thought before he fell asleep in the armchair was of the woman in the red bikini on the beach in Gokarna, her lean, sunburnt body glistening with lotion.

19

AT SOME POINT IN THE night he must have switched off the television and the lights and crawled into bed because that was where he found himself when he woke up. He had been woken by the sound of a chair being dragged outside his room. His first thought was of the people in the next room, but something made him get up and peer through the curtains. Outside on the balcony stood Agnes Pereira, in the same clothes as yesterday, with her back to him and a camera in her hands. Arjun went to the bathroom and quickly washed and smoothed his ruffled T-shirt and jeans and pulled on a track jacket. He didn't look too much the worse for wear, he reflected; there had been rougher days.

He pressed the doorbell for Hari and then opened the door. She turned, startled. She had finely chiselled features and translucent, almost greenish eyes. Like a cat, he thought. Her hair was pulled back in a ponytail.

'I'm sorry,' she said in a soft voice, holding up her camera. 'I came up to take a few pictures.'

'No problems,' Arjun said, leaning on the balcony railing beside her and breathing in the cold morning air. 'It's beautiful, isn't it?'

The sun was coming up from behind them, its rays inching down into the valley, gradually lighting up the green-and-brown mountain slopes, while the rocky riverbed at the bottom was still covered in cold shadows. In the far distance were the snow-covered peaks of the Rohtang Pass.

'Yes, it is,' she said, raising her camera again. 'I wish I could live here.'

Arjun thought he detected a note of sadness in her voice. Glancing at her sideways a sudden doubt struck him. What if he was mistaken about who she was?

'Are you a photographer?' he asked.

'Oh no!' She laughed, a small girl's giggle. 'I'm just a . . . tourist.'

'Arjun,' he said, holding out his hand. She hesitated, then shifted the camera to her left hand and extended her right hand. It felt cool and delicate to his touch. 'Rosalyn'.

Was that her real name, or a cover, like with the beanie and sunglasses? Hari came trotting up the wooden staircase. Arjun asked him for tea and biscuits, and asked her if she would have a cup of tea.

'Thank you, but no. I'll get back to my room.'

She smiled, to tell him not to mind perhaps, and Arjun felt his heart miss a beat.

'How long are you here for?' he asked, surprised at how he had just felt.

'Oh, I don't know, just hanging around. What about you?'

'I'm leaving for Ladakh in a day or two.'

'Ah ha,' she said, and took a step sideways to look into his room. 'Well, I'll see you around.'

'Sure. You can come up anytime you want to take photos, okay?'

She smiled again, and put the lens cover on her DSLR camera and went down the staircase. Arjun went and got his cigarettes and sat on the cane chair on the balcony and lit one. What had happened to him? At his age, it was a dangerous feeling to have, and besides, he had tracked her down on the request of a client.

As for her name, surely she wouldn't be going around as Agnes? Hari came up with his tea after a while, and Arjun asked him for aloo parathas and two poached eggs for breakfast, with some chilli-and-mango pickle. The guest in room number one had ordered her morning tea but not her breakfast yet, he said upon being questioned, and got another fifty-rupee note in return.

Arjun stepped into the shower after Hari had brought his breakfast up to his room. He was standing with his head bent letting the hot water beat down on his neck and back when he heard a familiar sound. He wrapped a towel around himself and stepped out of the bathroom. Through the curtains he saw the gang of bikers, now in full riding gear with bags strapped to their machines. He saw her come out and talk to them, following which they rode away. She stood there a while looking down the road, then came back inside. Arjun felt relieved. She was staying put for the moment.

He had worked his way through the filling breakfast and a second cup of tea, and was considering calling Vishwanathan when his phone rang. Arjun answered it.

'Is this Arjun Arora?' a deep, low voice asked.

'Yes. Who is this?'

'The person you're waiting for. Where are you?'

'At the Beas View guest house on the other side of the river. When will you be here?' Arjun asked, but the man had already hung up.

For the next hour or so Arjun sat and tapped his feet or paced up and down the space around his bed. If they wanted to take her back to Mumbai, would she go of her own accord? Or would the police in Manali have to be involved, in which case she might be taken out of their hands. At one point he almost went down to warn her.

The gate creaked and Arjun rushed to the window, but it was only the young couple in room number two on the ground floor leaving the guest house. It was nearly eleven. About ten minutes later the gate creaked again. This time Arjun was sure it was him: a tall, lean man in grey trousers and a brown-and-white high-neck sweater. He seemed perfectly commonplace, except for his hands, which even at a distance appeared unusually large. Arjun heard footsteps coming up the staircase, and then the doorbell rang.

20

HE OPENED THE DOOR.

'Detective Arora?' the man asked.

He was taller than Arjun, and his eyes were dark and cold. Arjun nodded and the man stepped inside. Arjun closed the door and turned around.

'Where's the girl?' was his next question.

'On the ground floor. In room number one.'

'Alone?'

'I think so.'

'You're not sure?'

'Ninety-nine per cent she's alone.'

Arjun picked up his cigarette packet and lighter, but the man interrupted him.

'Take me to her.'

They stepped out to the balcony and went down the staircase. The man's hands were like a pair of wicketkeeper's gloves, Arjun thought. On the ground floor he knocked on the door of room number one, and it opened slightly to show Agnes Pereira. Or was it Rosalyn? He would soon find out. Arjun could hear the television inside. She seemed to be caught between a frown and a smile at the sight of Arjun.

Then the man stepped past Arjun and pushed the door open. Before Arjun could react, the man was inside the room holding a gun in one oversized hand. There was a look of confusion on Agnes Pereira's face.

'Get inside and close the door,' he hissed at Arjun, 'otherwise I shoot her.'

Arjun did as he was told. The delicate features of Agnes Pereira's face now twisted in horror, and she let out a terrified scream.

'Shut up!' the man shouted. 'Get inside the bathroom, go.'

He waved the gun at Arjun, who saw that it was a small automatic fitted with a stubby silencer. 'You move to the bathroom too, detective.'

The bathroom was at the far side of the room. Arjun had to pass the man to get to where Agnes Pereira was. He considered going for the gunman's arm, but the man shrank back towards the television, as if he had read Arjun's mind. Canned laughter rang out from the television sitcom. As the laughter faded, there came a loud rapping on the door, startling all three of them. The man whispered to Agnes Pereira: 'Go open the door. Whoever it is, tell them everything is okay, got it?'

She stood where she was, her lips quivering.

'Do as I say, otherwise I'll shoot you in the back of your head!'

Agnes Pereira walked past the bed and moved towards the door. The man turned the gun on Arjun and whispered, 'You don't try anything, okay? I'm watching you too.'

The door opened a crack, and Arjun heard the voice of the housemaid asking if everything was all right.

Agnes Pereira replied in a steady voice that a rat had scared her and that was all. The man had his attention on the door now, and Arjun looked around. Where he stood there was nothing within his reach. The lighter! He quietly took it out of his jeans pocket and held it between his fingers.

'Rats?' the maid said in an amused tone. 'We don't have rats here.'

'Maybe it's the first one,' Agnes Pereira said.

She has presence of mind, Arjun thought. The maid went away, and Agnes Pereira closed the door and turned around. Then she started shaking, tears running down her cheeks.

'Well done,' the man said. 'Now get inside the bathroom. Both of you. Move!'

Arjun could imagine what was to follow. He could see himself and the girl lying together on the bathroom floor, a bullet hole through each of their heads. It was a set-up, just as he had suspected!

As she went past the man, Arjun took a small step forward and sent the lighter over the bed with a flick of his wrist. It fell with a clatter on the wooden floor. The man's head swivelled at the sudden sound. Arjun pushed the girl aside and was on him in two steps, pushing the gun up with his left hand and hearing the bullet pop and thud into the ceiling even as he stiffened his right palm and drove it hard into the man's thorax. A stifled cry escaped the man's lips and he fell back towards the wall. Arjun caught hold of the gun with both hands and twisted it around to face the man. They struggled, the man's acrid breath on Arjun's face—and the gun went off. The man slid down to the floor, surprise etched across his face. Arjun stood over the still body for a moment, breathing hard, horrified at this sudden turn of events. A man had been killed, but now was not the time for reflection.

He turned to the girl. She was shaking violently, one hand pressed against her mouth as if to stop herself from screaming. He would have to handle this delicately.

'Listen to me carefully,' he said slowly. 'I'm not here to hurt you, okay?'

He saw her eyes go down to the gun he now held in his hand, so he tossed it on to the unmade bed, within reach of both of them.

'You're in shock right now, so you have to breathe deeply till your adrenaline levels normalize,' he said kindly. 'Do you smoke?'

She wiped her tears with her hand and lowered it, but continued staring at him.

'Do you smoke?'

She nodded. Arjun took out his cigarette packet, retrieved the lighter from the floor, and lit two cigarettes, one of which he passed to her.

She sat down on the bed, looked at the gun, then took a drag at her cigarette.

'How can I trust you after what just happened?' she asked in a small voice.

Arjun could see fear in her eyes, and defiance as well.

'You can pick up the gun if you want to,' he said. It was a calculated risk. 'You saw it, didn't you, he was planning to kill us both? I know you were in Bharat Lodge where your friend was killed, and I know you came here from Gokarna.'

'But . . . how? Who are you?'

'You're Agnes Pereira, aren't you?'

A slight nod from her.

'I'll be honest with you, okay, Agnes? And I want you to do the same with me.'

She swallowed, then nodded, and took another deep drag.

'My name is Arjun Arora. I'm a detective from Delhi. I was called to Mumbai where a man called Vishwanathan with one missing finger gave me your photo and your phone number and told me he wanted you found. Do you know him?'

She shook her head, and wrapped her arms around herself and shivered, as if cold.

'He said you had taken a large sum of money from him and his partners.'

'I don't know anything about that,' she said in a flat, emotionless voice.

'I thought so,' Arjun said, even as he wondered, or is that just what I want to believe?

21

ARJUN SAT DOWN ON THE chair beside the wardrobe and looked down at the body of the man.

'Have you ever seen him before?' he asked Agnes Pereira.

She shook her head, and looked away. But he thought he saw it now: the lodge in Mumbai, the dead girl, Vishwanathan's offer.

'He strangled Savitri Rao, didn't he?' Arjun asked.

'I don't know, maybe.'

'Then why did you scream when you saw him?'

'He said he was going to shoot me.'

'You have seen him before, haven't you? Where?'

She looked away again, smoking. Arjun stubbed out his cigarette in the ashtray and squatted by the body. He took out the wallet from the dead man's back pocket and his cell phone from his front pocket and placed them on the ledge below the wall-mounted television. The blood was oozing out from the entry wound in the stomach, discolouring the white-and-brown sweater. Arjun got to his feet, caught the corpse's arms, and started to drag it along.

'What are you doing with . . . the body?' she asked, alarmed.

'Taking it to the bathroom so that the blood doesn't soak into the floorboards.'

He pulled the body into the bathroom and propped it up in a corner of the shower area. Arjun looked at it for a moment before washing his hands at the sink. The tables had been turned. But could he trust the girl?

He came out and picked up the wallet and the phone and sat down in the chair.

'How are you feeling now?' he asked her.

'A bit better. But the body . . .'

'We'll have to get rid of it.'

She stared at him, then started sobbing again. Arjun had to fight an impulse to comfort her. Instead, he said, 'Don't think about it. I'll take care of it.'

'Are you going to kill me too?'

'No! I told you I was hired to find you. For some reason, they wanted both of us dead.' Not just some reason, it came to him now: so as not to leave any traces behind. 'Are you sure you don't know about the money?'

'What money? This isn't about any money.'

'Then tell me what it's about.'

She looked down at the floorboards instead, a hangdog expression on her face. Should he feel sorry for her? He opened the wallet and inspected its contents. Money, visiting cards, scraps of paper and a driving licence. Issued in Kanpur, Uttar Pradesh, in the commonplace name of Pawan Kumar. Arjun brought the card closer to look at the faded photo under the scuffed lamination. It was hard to be sure whether it was the same man. He scrolled through the call list on the mobile, a basic model which looked as though it had hardly been used. The first number was the one Vishwanathan had given him, the second his own number: it was a burner.

'Tell me what happened in Mumbai,' he said to Agnes Pereira.

'I thought you knew what had happened.'

'I want to hear your version.'

She took a deep breath, turned to look at the television and said, 'Savi had come to see me. She stayed the night. We were meeting after a long time. In the morning, I went out to buy some stuff—'

'What did you go out to buy?'

'Just . . . stuff. Cigarettes. Biscuits. Juice.'

'Okay. And then?'

'I came back and opened the door, and Savi was lying there dead. I mean, at first I thought she had gone back to sleep again—'

'She had woken up when you had gone out?'

'Yes, she was up. I thought she was sleeping, but then I noticed she wasn't breathing. I went up to her, and realized she was dead. I . . . I panicked.' She moved her hands as if trying to illustrate her agitation at that point. 'So I just picked up my bag and ran out of the place. I was terrified I would be accused of the murder.'

'How did you know it was murder? She might have died of a heart attack.'

'She was perfectly fine when I left!'

'You would be accused of murder even if you ran away.'

'I was scared! I wasn't thinking straight. When I'm faced with a difficult situation, my first instinct is to run away from it.' She added in a murmur, 'I think it's something I inherited from my mother.'

'You didn't see anyone in the room? The dead man?'

'No, no one.'

'When you got back, how long were you in the room for?'

'Maybe five minutes, at the most.'

He remembered the uneasy feeling he had got while talking to the receptionist, who had said Agnes Pereira had been upstairs for thirty minutes. So between the two of them, one was lying.

'Nobody tried to stop you?' he asked.

She shook her head.

'What were you doing in the lodge, Agnes?'

'Meeting a friend.'

'This Savitri Rao, she had a lot of money with her?'

'Maybe, I don't know.'

'What were you really there for?'

'My friend's dead, dammit! Murdered!' She got to her feet and went around the bed to the door and paced up and down.

'Calm down,' Arjun said. 'You don't want anyone knocking on the door again.'

'You were the one who knocked first. How do I even know Arjun is your real name?'

'Trust me, it is.'

She came back and sat down on the bed and asked him for another cigarette. Arjun tossed her the packet and the lighter. Lighting one, she leaned back and blew out a thin stream of smoke. 'Oh god, what a mess. What am I going to do now?'

'We'll figure something out.'

'We?'

'Your life's in danger, Agnes. I think we should stick together.'

She thought about it, then said, 'Thank you for saving my life.'

'I was saving mine as well.'

'This client of yours, what do you know about him?'

'At the moment, his name, and that he is missing a finger.'

'I thought you said you were a detective?'

'They called me to Mumbai.'

'You have lots of cases outside Delhi?'

'He offered me twice my normal fee.'

She looked at him. 'So the hunter ends up as the hunted.'

Once the shock had subsided, she seemed a different, more assertive person. It wasn't a side she had displayed that morning. He got to his feet and looked into the bathroom, as if to confirm the body hadn't moved. The room suddenly seemed unbearably claustrophobic to him. He needed something to drink, a cold beer maybe.

'Let's go out of here,' he told her. 'I feel as though that fellow's listening to us.'

111

22

THIRTY MINUTES LATER, THEY WERE sitting at a wooden table out in the sun in front of a traditional Himachali house run as a restaurant by an Italian woman. It was off the road that climbed up from Hotel Royal Residency. Arjun remembered the place from his visit with Sonali and Rhea, and the thin-crust pizzas they had been served. The house was supposed to be more than a century old. Beside his bottle of Kingfisher was his and Pawan Kumar's phones. The gun was in the inside pocket of his jacket. The dead man in the bathroom—Arjun found it hard to believe he had actually killed him.

He took a long draught of his cold beer and wiped his lips.

'You sure you don't want any?' he asked Agnes Pereira.

She shook her head. 'No thanks, I don't usually drink. Can I have a cigarette?'

Arjun was about to tell her that she was smoking too much, but thought better of it. The sight of a second dead body within a week couldn't be helping her. She had changed into jeans and a leather jacket, and put on a blue baseball cap and her sunglasses. He looked around at the families and couples at the other tables, outside and inside the restaurant, and felt envious of their normality. And, though he was reluctant to admit it to himself, he was scared. Below them was the cluttered town, and after that the mountain slopes beyond the river, with buildings and resorts scattered about. A hydroelectric plant's transmission station rose up at one point; Arjun recalled it was owned by a company that also owned a shopping centre in Delhi's Greater Kailash II. Agnes Pereira smoked, examining the patterns in the wood.

'How old are you, by the way?' he asked.

'Twenty-two,' she said, and looked up. 'Why?'

Arjun shrugged. 'Just curious. You look older. Say, mid-twenties.'

'Not a very flattering thing to say.'

'I'm not trying to flatter you. I'm trying to save your life.'

'How are you going to do that?'

'Let's eat first. I think better on a full stomach.'

The waiter brought them two thin-crust pizzas on wooden trays, a pepperoni for Arjun, and a margherita for Agnes Pereira. Her eyebrows went up as she saw Arjun sprinkle chilli flakes all over his pizza and then douse it liberally with Tabasco sauce.

'How can you have so much chilli?'

'Something I inherited from my mother,' Arjun said, and tore into a slice. The crunch of the warm crust along with the melted cheese and smoky pepperoni took him back over the years, to when the ordinary pleasures of a family were still something he could count on.

He had left Agnes Pereira to go up and lock his room, and had asked her to wait for five minutes before locking her own room and walking out of the gate. Waiting on the balcony he had been engaged in a conversation with a middle-aged man from Bangalore occupying the next room with his wife. The man had kept asking Arjun questions, especially after he had said that he was headed to Ladakh. Routes, fares, food, clothing—the questions were endless. And in the middle of it all, he had seen Agnes Pereira opening the gate and walking out. Agonizing minutes had passed before he was able to make an excuse about checking on his flight tickets and leave the guest house. He had hurried down to the highway, fearing she might have decided to

113

disappear again, and then sighed in relief as he saw her walking alone by the roadside.

Now he finished his pizza, drained his beer and lit a cigarette. She was eating hers with a knife and fork and was only halfway through. He took her photo out of his shirt pocket and showed it to her.

'This is what I was given,' he said. 'Where was this taken?'

She looked at the photo with an expression of disbelief.

'I don't know,' she finally said, handing the photo back.

He started to ask her another question but stopped himself. Better to give her some more time. Looking at the photo again, something occurred to him. The letters 'on' in lower case at the bottom of the vertical sign outside the glass pane; could it be Nikon, Canon, something like that?

'You were going to save me, you said?' she asked, chewing on a mouthful of pizza.

'First we need to dispose of the body,' he said, 'and then we need to get out of here.'

'How? And where do we go?'

'Leave it to me, I have an idea,' he said, thinking of Yadavji. 'And we should get back to Delhi. Maybe take a flight.'

'Why not go to Ladakh?'

'The more isolated the place, the easier we'll be to spot. There might be more men coming after us now. Delhi will be safer. It's . . . familiar.'

He had almost said 'home'.

'Where do we take a flight from?'

'There's an airport at Kullu, about fifty kilometres from here. We can get the tickets in town after this.' A thought struck him. 'Wait a minute.'

'What?'

'They might have your name on a watch list at the airport.'

'No problem. I have a driving licence in another name.'

114

'You do?'

'Don't look so suspicious, it's from my modelling days, when I didn't want people to know where I was staying.'

'We should be safe then. What is it, Rosalyn?'

'Yes. What's the idea you have for disposing of the . . . body?'

Arjun picked up his phone and dialled Yadavji's number. The taxi driver sounded as though he had been taking a nap.

'Come to the Beas View guest house at seven in the evening,' Arjun told him.

'Who was that?' Agnes asked him with a frown after he had given directions to the guest house.

'Relax, it's just a driver I know.'

'You know a driver? Then why don't we drive down to Delhi tonight?'

'I thought about it,' Arjun said. 'But I don't know how safe it'll be.'

He recalled the policemen who had stopped the taxi in the middle of the night in Punjab. For the right price, anything could be arranged in India. And something told him Vishwanathan was a man with a long reach.

'Another thing,' he said.

'What?'

'We'll have to stay somewhere else tonight. So settle the bill once we get back.'

'But why?'

'In case you have another visitor tonight,' Arjun said.

23

THEY WALKED DOWN TO THE crowded Mall Road where Arjun withdrew money from an ATM and used it to buy two tickets from Kullu to Delhi for the next morning. The travel agent in his cramped upstairs room glanced briefly at the driving licences in the names of Arjun Arora and Rosalyn D'Costa before entering the names into his laptop. With the tickets in an envelope, they caught an auto going to the Left Bank. Arjun stopped it at the point where the road branched off uphill and paid the driver. He asked her to go ahead, and lit a cigarette and waited. Below him the white-flecked waters of the Beas rushed by, and nearby was a line of auto-parts shops. Further up the road, above the guest house and the hotel, was a small Buddhist monastery, and then a cluster of shops and cheap lodges and a hiking trail that wound up into the mountains. Arjun waited for two minutes after she had opened the gate before walking up himself. He was booked under his own name at the guest house, and in case more of Vishwanathan's people tracked her till here, he didn't want Hari or the owner or anyone else to put two and two together.

As he came up the walkway, he could see her inside her room through the open door. She had changed into her track jacket. He climbed up the staircase to the balcony and a while later heard her door close, just as he had asked her to do. The two other doors had locks on them like the previous day. He sat on the cane chair looking out at the valley below. He had got himself into a mess, but experience had taught him to keep his wits about him.

He checked the other phone which he had kept on silent. There were several missed calls from Vishwanathan's number. Arjun thought for a moment, then took out his phone and rang his client. He had rehearsed what he was going to say.

'I'm still waiting for your man,' he said when Vishwanathan picked up.

'He hasn't contacted you yet?'

'He called me a few hours ago. But he didn't turn up.'

'Where are you?'

'At the Hotel Royal Residency.'

'My man told me he was meeting you at some guest house.'

'I had called him there to check him out first. But he never turned up. I'm back at the hotel now.'

'Where's the girl?' Vishwanathan's voice was tight, on the edge.

'She's left for Ladakh with a group of bikers.'

'Fuck! *Fuck!* All right, listen, you follow her. Find her, let me know where she is.'

'You better ask your man to do that, Mr Vishwanathan. I have to get back to Delhi.'

'Listen, you. I hired you to tra—'

'Track her down. Yes, you did, and I found her too.'

'I'll pay you more, Mr Arora.'

'It's not about the money. I've been away for more than a week and need to get back to my office in Delhi. Something urgent I need to attend to.'

'You listen to me! I said I want her tracked down!'

'I'm sorry, Mr Vishwanathan, I've done as much as I could,' Arjun said and hung up.

His phone buzzed, and then the other phone's screen lit up. A smile slowly spread across Arjun's face. Let the son of a bitch stew for a while, he thought.

117

He went into his room where he packed his things into his backpack and then rang the bell. When Hari appeared, he asked for tea and Marie biscuits, and his bill.

'You're leaving, sir?' Hari asked.

'Yes. This evening. I'm taking a taxi back to Delhi.'

'Come again, sir,' Hari said, a forlorn expression on his face.

'Certainly,' Arjun said, smiling at him. 'And listen.'

'Yes, sir?'

'If anyone comes and asks about me, keep your mouth shut, do you understand?'

The boy nodded his head vigorously. 'Yes, sir!'

Arjun drank his tea, paid his bill (with a generous tip for Hari), and then locked his room. The sun was no longer at its zenith, and the light outside had started softening. As he went down the staircase, he wondered if this was going to be his last visit to Manali.

He looked about to make sure no one was around, and knocked on the door of room number one. Agnes Pereira opened it wordlessly and went back to the bed. There was a movie on the television, an old cowboy western. Arjun pulled up a chair near the bed and sat down. The bathroom door was locked.

'Are you okay?' he asked her.

She nodded, holding on to a pillow. Indoors, she looked younger. Arjun wished now that he had lied about how old she looked.

'Have you paid your bill?'

'Yes. I told the owner I was leaving for Ladakh this evening with some friends, and that we would halt at Keylong for the night.'

'You *were* planning to go to Ladakh, weren't you?'

She turned to him. 'You *were* spying on me, weren't you?'

'Observing would be a better word. Were you?'

118

'Yes, I was.'

'Why didn't you leave with your friends?'

'I was tired of travelling. I wanted some peace and quiet for a few days. Maybe I would have joined them later.'

'Why did you decide to come here all the way from Gokarna?'

'My friends asked me to join them. I thought it was a good idea. You told me you were going to Ladakh as well?'

'I was trying to gauge your reaction. Tell me, how are you friends with an Israeli biker gang?'

'I had met them on a flight from Goa to Delhi last year, and we kept in touch.'

'You're an air hostess, aren't you?'

'Was. I don't know if I still have my job.'

'Don't your friends know about the murder?'

'I told them what had happened. That I was being framed. They said they'd help me.'

'Your phone, you've kept it switched off?'

'Yes. How did you find me, by the way? I thought I was being careful.'

'It's a long story, I'll tell you some other time. What were you looking for in Mumbai?'

'Well, that's a long story as well.'

She sank into silence, and they watched the movie. The horses galloping across the prairies, the laconic cowboy, the grimy villains, the whistled tune—they took Arjun back to Shillong, where a neighbour would hire a VCR every Sunday along with several war and cowboy film cassettes which he would invite all the neighbourhood children to watch.

'How come you like cowboy movies?' he asked her.

There was no reply, and he turned and saw that she had fallen asleep, with her mouth slightly open. Looking at her, some sixth sense told him that he was being drawn into something

119

which could prove fatal. But it was making him feel alive, and at his age, what could be wrong with that?

Arjun watched the movie till its end, and by then the light outside had started fading. He got up to pull the curtains and put on the lights. On a side table was the pastry box. He flipped back the cover and saw the remains of a slice of cheesecake. Beside it were two blister-pack strips of tablets. She stirred on the bed, then sat up and gave a long yawn.

'Sorry, I don't know how I fell asleep.'

'You'll need the rest. We'll have to leave for the airport early tomorrow morning.'

'I need to use the bathroom. Can I keep the door open?'

'Go ahead.'

She opened the bathroom door and went in. A while later he heard the flush being pulled, followed by the sound of a tap being opened. She came out and said, 'There's blood all over the floor.'

It was strange how matter-of-fact she seemed about it now. Arjun wondered if he was reading her right. He went into the bathroom; the blood had pooled around on the tiled floor. He knew that by now the flow of blood would have lessened.

'Do you have a pair of rubber gloves, by any chance?'

'I should, let me check.'

'And a room towel.'

She did have a pair of gloves she had bought in case she decided to colour her hair. Arjun put on the gloves, squatted and started mopping up the blood with the towel.

'Why don't you just wash it away?' she asked from the doorway.

'Wait and watch. Now give me a large plastic bag please.'

She brought him one, and he put the bundled-up towel inside it, taking care not to get any of the blood on the outside. He hung the bag on one end of the towel rack, then bent down and lifted the heavy, limp body and moved it around. Then he used the hose beside the toilet to wash the blood off the floor. He could make out that the outlet from the bathroom opened into a covered drain. Just then there was a knock on the door.

'Oh shit!' Agnes Pereira exclaimed. 'Who could that be?'

'Go and open the door. Act normal. Whoever it is, don't let them inside.'

As her footsteps moved across the room Arjun was struck by the thought that it could be a partner of the dead man, a backup. In which case . . .

He heard the door open, and then Agnes Pereira inquiring, 'Yes?' He braced himself for a shot, or for a scream from her. But it turned out to be a voice he knew.

'Madam, do you want some tea?' Hari asked.

'No, thank you,' Arjun heard her say. 'I'll be leaving in a while.'

She came back to the bathroom door. 'False alarm.'

Arjun washed the blood off the gloves at the sink, then took them off.

'I'm going upstairs,' he said. 'The driver will be here soon. You better get ready.'

'I hope you know what you're doing, Arjun.'

It was the first time she had used his name. He smiled and patted her arm.

24

GOING UP THE STAIRCASE, HE looked to his right. In the gathering gloom, he confirmed an earlier observation: the electricity line for the guest house, a thick, weatherproof cable, ran across from a wooden switchboard at the rear of the owner's residence, with a large fuse box on the board. He guessed these two units had their own connection, with a separate transformer for the hotel up above. In his room he turned on the lights, and then opened the bottle of wine and sat out on the balcony. Yadavji would be here soon. He listened to the sound of the river down below, and wondered where the couple in the next room could have gone.

By the time the taxi driver called to say he was on his way, Arjun was almost through with the bottle. It was dark now. He told himself he would sort out the mess surrounding the girl and then go dry for a long spell. He thought of her strangely greenish eyes. Was it some sort of coincidence, re-visiting places in Manali he had earlier been to with his wife?

The white Indigo pulled up across the road from the gate and then its lights went off. Arjun drained the last of his wine and went into his room to pick up his backpack. It was time to move. The lock and key he left dangling on the outside latch. He went down the staircase to the lower veranda, looking around, but like the previous evening there was no one to be seen. The lights were on in room number two though. He rapped thrice on Agnes Pereira's door and went out to the taxi. The front of the hotel where the road wound up to it was bathed in white light, but down below, the area around the guest house was poorly lit. Yadavji had got out, and Arjun gave him his backpack and told him to put it in the front seat.

'There's been some trouble,' he told the taxi driver. 'Someone's been shot.'

Yadavji appeared unfazed by this piece of information.

'Is he still alive?' he asked calmly.

'Unfortunately not. We have to move him.'

'To a hospital, or . . . ?' Yadavji asked, showing his quick grasp of the situation.

'Somewhere else. Somewhere deserted.'

'It'll be done. Do you want me to help?'

'No, you get behind the wheel.'

Arjun went back in. She was waiting in the doorway of her room. He went up the veranda and into her room.

'Done packing?' he asked.

'Yes,' she said, pointing to a compact red suitcase standing by the television.

He went into the bathroom, hoisted the body, turned it around so he was holding it under the arms from behind, and backed out into the room. He placed the body in a sitting position by the front door. The sweater was soaked with blood, but the flow appeared to have been staunched. The body had been drained of most of its blood. Unbidden, there arose a memory of a grimy flat, of being tied to a chair, and the butcher taking out his knives and telling Arjun he would be drained of his blood before being skinned. He caught hold of a table to steady himself.

'Are you all right?' Agnes Pereira asked.

'I'm fine, just a bit of a head rush.'

He retraced his steps to the bathroom. No drops or stains anywhere, apart from the bathroom. He took the plastic bag

123

with the blood-soaked towel off the end of the towel rack, tied the mouth, and handed it to her.

'What's this for?'

'You'll see.'

Taking the hose from beside the commode, he washed the blood off the bathroom floor. The entire episode, from the time of the shooting, had taken on an unreal air for him, like something out of a film. When he was done, he looked around the bathroom. All clear. Just one more thing. He tore off a length of toilet paper, crumpled it up, and went and stuffed it into the stomach wound of the corpse.

'I'm going to put off the lights now, okay? Keep the door ajar and wait for me.'

She nodded, her face serious now, a student paying attention.

Arjun let himself out, went along the veranda, and walked on ahead to the back of the owner's residence. Everything was quiet, and from the hotel above he could hear a man laughing. He looked around to confirm it was all clear, then opened the fuse box. Next he checked the lines, and pulled out a fuse halfway—the entire guest house area went dark. He hurried back to her room. In room number two he could hear the young woman complaining to her husband.

Agnes Pereira opened the door for him. 'Now what?'

'Help me carry him to the taxi outside. We have to laugh and talk loudly, because this fellow has had too much to drink and can't walk. Do you understand?'

She nodded. They bent down, propped him up by the arms, and took him out to the veranda. The couple in the next room had opened their door and come out by now.

Arjun let out a peal of laughter, and said, 'This is the last time you're going to drink so much, Jolly Singh!'

'Just because you're sad that I'm leaving,' Agnes Pereira carried on.

The body was heavy, and tilted to one side, so Arjun crouched slightly as they pulled the dead man along towards the gate.

'When your wife sees you . . .' he said loudly.

She let out a long, nervous burst of laughter, and Arjun joined in as well. He pushed the gate open with his foot. The final few steps were the longest. He felt as though the entire population of the hill was looking down at them. And what if a car were to come up the road now? Yadavji opened the rear door, and Arjun manoeuvred the body into the back seat. When he straightened up and turned around, however, everything was dark and peaceful. He could see the couple on the lower veranda talking to someone who looked like Hari.

'Now go and get your suitcase,' he said to her. 'And don't forget the plastic bag.'

He got in beside the body from the other side and immediately lit a cigarette. The alcohol and the tension were making him sweat, and his mouth was parched. The seconds passed agonizingly. He expected the lights to come on any moment—and people to start shouting. Instead, Agnes Pereira came out of the gate, dragging her suitcase along.

'Yadavji, help her put her suitcase into the back,' he said.

The first part was over. Now for the equally risky second part.

25

'TAKE THE CAR AHEAD, PAST the hotel,' Arjun told Yadavji.

The Indigo climbed up the bend in the road and went past the brightly lit hotel. Further ahead it was dark, with the outline of the monastery under the cliff. Arjun asked him to stop the vehicle and step out. He got out himself. A chill breeze was blowing, and in the distance he could see a few lights at the top of Old Manali.

'Don't tell me you're dropping him here, beside the road?' she asked from inside the car.

'That's not why we stopped. Yadavji, open the dicky, please.'

With the rear compartment of the car open, Arjun and the taxi driver brought the body out. They dumped the body on the newspapers that Arjun had asked Yadavji to line the trunk with, and jammed it against the suitcase so that it would remain on its back. They closed the lid and got back in the taxi.

Arjun told him to head back the way they had come. Yadavji turned the car and switched on the headlights, and they saw two figures swathed in red walking up on the side of the road. They were monks, one short, the other even shorter, and as they crossed them Arjun saw it was a wizened old man and a very young boy. He wondered if it might count as a favourable omen.

'Where are we going now?' Agnes Pereira asked, sounding worried.

'Some place deserted,' Arjun said.

She sniffed the air. 'Have you been drinking?'

'Yes. To help calm my nerves.'

At the guest house the lights had come back on. The boy must have checked the fuse box. When they came down to the highway, Yadavji turned left.

'I don't think we should enter the town,' Arjun said.

'We won't,' the taxi driver replied.

He carried on straight instead of turning right at the bridge. For a while the road ran above the river, then the two parted. They passed shops, hotels, a petrol pump where a Volvo bus was pulling out, and more hotels and resorts. Arjun found a bottle of water in the taxi and took a drink. He remembered all of this as a barren area, with just the road and trees and fields. At the rough-and-ready settlement of Jagatsukh, he saw a sign advertising the lounge bar whose flyer he had seen at the Tibetan restaurant on Mall Road. They went over a concrete bridge, passed one or two more resorts, then were out in the dark countryside, with what looked like apple orchards on the slopes above the road. When Arjun asked him, Yadavji said the road went on to Naggar Castle before joining the main Kullu–Manali highway.

All of a sudden, the car's headlights picked out a police barricade on the road, with a group of khaki-and-leather-jacket-clad policemen standing beside it. It was too late to turn back. One of the men raised a hand, and Yadavji slowed down.

'Keep calm and act normal,' Arjun said. 'Let me talk, unless they talk to you.'

The taxi came to a halt. Two men came around to the driver's side. Arjun looked out of his window at a wire fence and fields in the darkness.

'Where are you going at this time?' one of the two men asked Yadavji.

'Naggar Castle,' he replied.

Arjun remembered there was some accommodation in that area. The castle had been the residence of the old rulers of the Kullu Valley.

The other man switched on a torch and played it over the front and back seats of the taxi. Arjun rolled down his window.

'Where are you coming from?' the man asked.

'Delhi,' Arjun said. 'There was a traffic jam on the way. We were stuck for more than two hours.'

'What's in the dicky?' the first one asked.

'Their suitcases and my bag,' Yadavji said.

'Open it,' the second one said calmly, his torch still on.

Arjun felt his heart hammering but forced himself to act normal. He said, in a relaxed tone, 'Let us go, sahib, it's been a long journey and my wife's not feeling well. She's three months pregnant and the doctor asked her to get as much rest as possible.'

'And you brought her all the way from Delhi in a taxi?' the first one said.

'We've come for a holiday. If you let us go . . .'

Arjun was considering the last option of a bribe, but their colleagues were nearby. Just then the attention of the two men shifted to something behind the car. Arjun heard the growl of a large engine, and turned to look. It was the Volvo bus from the petrol pump.

'All right, you can go,' the second policeman said, not even looking at the car as they moved towards the bus.

'Thank you,' Arjun said, and rolled up his window.

Yadavji started the vehicle and they pulled away from the roadblock. In the rear-view mirror Arjun could see the two cops motioning for the bus driver to get down.

No one spoke for a while. It was Agnes Pereira who finally broke the silence.

'Three months pregnant?'

'Better than telling them we have a dead body in the trunk,' Arjun said.

They crossed small villages with old-fashioned, double-storeyed stone-and-timber houses, then fields with the valley sloping up on the far side. It somehow reminded Arjun of the road from Shillong to Cherrapunjee. They reached a forest with tall fir and pine trees and huge boulders scattered about them. The road wound its way down through this stretch. Yadavji drove a little distance, then stopped by the side of the road and killed the headlights. There were insects calling, but otherwise it was quiet.

'Okay, let's get this over with,' Arjun said, getting out of the car.

The trunk was opened, and then he and Yadavji carried the body up to the boulders, where they propped it between two large stones. Arjun looked around, and was satisfied the dead man couldn't be seen from the road. He went back to the car where Agnes Pereira sat smoking a cigarette. When he asked her for the plastic bag, she took it out from under the front seat. He also asked her for the rubber gloves and the bottle of water.

'What are you going to do?'

'Spread some blood around so that it'll look like he shot himself here.'

'How long will you take?'

'Not too long. If anyone stops to ask, say your husband's gone to take a leak.'

Arjun climbed back to where the body was and put on the gloves.

He said to the taxi driver, 'Go back to the car and gather up the newspapers in the trunk. And see if there are any bloodstains.'

He took out the pistol and put it in the dead man's right hand, then pulled out the wad of toilet paper. After that he took out the towel and wrung it over and around the body, dripping the blood on to it. He washed his hands with the water from the bottle. Then he put the towel, the toilet paper, the empty bottle and the gloves into the plastic bag. He stood for a moment in the darkness looking down at his handiwork. In his career as a detective he had strayed over the fine line into criminality several times, but this was something new. Just like how the girl was making him feel.

As he was walking back to the car, a pair of headlights coming from down below swept over the tree trunks. Arjun shrank against one of them till the vehicle had passed.

Yadavji had in the meantime gathered the newspapers into a bundle. Arjun asked him to stuff them into the plastic bag and tie it up.

'No blood anywhere, except for a stain on the suitcase,' he told Arjun.

'We'll clean it at the lodge. Let's go.'

On their way back, Arjun stopped the taxi near a rubbish dump with a few stray dogs and tossed the plastic bag in it. Some way ahead they saw that the police barricade had been pulled to the roadside and the men in uniform had disappeared.

'Must have collected enough for the night,' Yadavji said.

'What if they had stopped us again?' Agnes Pereira asked him.

'I would have said that you wanted to stay in Manali. And opened the dicky.'

The taxi driver was cool and collected, and hadn't even asked for an explanation. Arjun made a note to ask him again if he wanted to join the agency. He looked at Agnes Pereira. She was staring out of the window, a pensive look on her face.

'The worst is over,' he said to her. 'When they find the body, there'll be nothing to connect it to us. We'll be in Delhi tomorrow morning, and then I'll figure out the next step.'

She replied without turning to look at him: 'Whatever you do, I can never go back to my old life now.'

26

THE LODGE YADAVJI HAD BEEN holed up in was on the outskirts of Manali. It was a misshapen white-and-red structure that gave the impression of having been built and then extended haphazardly.

'*This* is where we're staying?' Agnes Pereira had said in disbelief when she saw it.

Arjun pointed out to her that the adjacent parking area was screened off with tin sheets, hiding the car from the road, and that the lodge would be the last place anyone would think of looking for them.

'You can say that again,' she muttered as she followed him in with her suitcase.

The owner, an old acquaintance of Yadavji's, was a former sweet-shop owner from Meerut who had landed up here via Delhi some years back. The taxi driver introduced Arjun and gave a story about this sahib he knew whose request for an additional night at their hotel hadn't been granted and they had been out on the streets literally when he had run into them and decided to bring them back here. The owner gave them a double room at a discount, and there were no formalities such as signing the register.

Arjun asked Yadavji to arrange for a half-bottle of Blenders Pride and agreed to meet him in the dining hall in a while. The room given to him and Agnes Pereira on the second floor smelt damp and dusty, with a thick brown carpet and matching curtains. The first thing he did was to pull apart the single beds and put a side table between them, then take out an extra bed sheet and blanket for himself from the flimsy almirah.

'Just to make things clear,' he said, opening the bathroom door.

'I'm glad,' she said.

She was sitting on the foot of her bed and going through the shakily transmitted channels on the television.

He said, 'Oh, and you better scrub that bloodstain off your suitcase.'

A while later, they went down to the dining hall at the rear of the ground floor. There were eight tables with curry-stained tablecloths, some of them occupied, and the windows at the front and back were tinted, giving the place a kitschy air heightened by the dim lighting and the shiny, synthetic curtains. Yadavji was in a corner with the bottle watching a B-grade Hindi film on the wall-mounted television. Arjun knocked back a drink, and ordered a Fanta for Agnes Pereira.

'What do you want to eat?' he asked her as she flicked through the menu.

'Don't know. Maybe some soup.'

'That might not be a good idea here. Yadavji, what's good to eat here?'

'Chicken curry and roti,' was the answer, and she agreed to go for that.

Arjun ordered for them, and poured another peg.

'You drink quite fast,' she commented.

'I don't like to waste time,' he replied.

There was a break in the movie, and a waiter switched to the Hindi news. After a story on high pollution levels in Indian cities, there was one on a murder case and the missing suspect, an air hostess by the name of Agnes Pereira. Yadavji leaned forward to get a better look at the photo, then dropped his gaze to look at her. She had bent her head and was looking past Arjun at the wall.

'Is anyone looking at me?' she asked him when the story had ended.

'No, no one's noticed,' Arjun said. 'But I think you better finish your dinner and go back to the room.'

'All right.'

'Where did they get that photo of yours from?'

'It must be from the airline.'

She drank her Fanta. After she had eaten and left, Arjun said to the taxi driver, 'You've been of great help.'

'My pleasure, sahib. It's always interesting working with you.'

'Why don't you start working for me? I'll pay well, and you can carry on with your taxi work as well.'

'Let me think about it.'

They finished the half-bottle, and asked for another one. Disposing of the dead body together had given them a sense of companionship, however temporary. Arjun briefly gave the other man an inkling of what had happened, adding that he believed the girl had been framed in the murder.

'Are you sure about it?' the taxi driver asked him.

'That's what it seems like,' Arjun said, not mentioning the doubts he had felt.

'And the man who hired you now wants you dead as well?'

'I think that was his plan. So that there wouldn't be any loose ends left.'

By the time they had finished their whisky, they were the only people left in the dining hall, along with a sleepy waiter. Arjun asked him to heat up their food, and went through eight rotis and two helpings of chicken curry. After saying goodnight to Yadavji and reminding him about the flight timing the next morning, he managed to stumble up to their room where he let himself in with the spare key he had asked the waiter to get him.

The television was on but she wasn't in the room. Nor was she in the bathroom. The panic that struck almost turned him sober, before he noticed the curtains were slightly apart. She was standing on the small balcony, looking out into the night and smoking. He could hear the waters of the river rushing by somewhere down below.

'Was it your first time, killing someone?' she asked.

'No. Not my first time. It doesn't get easier, if that's what you want to know.' Attempting to lighten the mood, he added, 'But you can get used to it.'

She thought about this, before asking, 'Is it okay if I watch TV for a while before turning in?'

'Suit yourself,' he said, drawing back the curtains. 'Just keep the volume down.'

Then he turned back, having spotted something in her other hand.

'You told me you had switched off your phone.'

'Just checking my messages. I'll switch it off now.'

'Were you calling someone?'

'That's none of your business.'

He started to reply, but then held his tongue. Once inside, he collapsed on his bed and pulled the blanket over himself. Before he fell asleep he tried to think of the first man he had ever killed—where had that been? When he had been in the army, in Assam. The memory made him feel old and tired. His last thought was that he hadn't wished her a goodnight. Maybe it was for the better.

27

THEY BOTH WOKE UP LATE the next morning, and only had time to wash and have a cup of tea brought up by a waiter before setting out for the airport. Agnes Pereira plugged in the earphones of her MP3 player and looked out of the car window. She appeared to be in a sullen mood. Arjun didn't bother trying to find out why. He wasn't feeling too cheerful himself. There was a telltale pulsing in the big toe joint of his right foot which indicated that an attack of gout was on its way. At least she was wearing her sunglasses and cap, as he had asked her to, and had her hair gathered at the back with a band. Yadavji dropped them off at the airport at Kullu, at Bhuntar actually, and Arjun paid him and told him to head down to Delhi and call him at night. The arrival and departure building was a compact structure, and some distance away from the short runway on the valley floor, separated by a fence, was the Beas again. As the plane took off and climbed out of the bowl of the mountains, Arjun drank a half-litre bottle of water and swallowed an anti-inflammatory tablet.

He spent a part of the short flight back to Delhi looking at the mountainous landscape of Himachal Pradesh sloping down to the plains of north India, which were covered, as usual, by the winter haze of vehicle exhaust and smoke from fires. Then he opened a financial newspaper he had found in the rear pocket of the seat in front of him. Agnes appeared to be taking a nap;

he could, however, still hear the beat of the music from her earphones.

They landed in Delhi around mid-morning, and came out of the terminal to get a prepaid taxi. There had been a brief moment of anxiety—on the way to the exit, a sniffer dog had seemed interested in her suitcase, where the spot of blood had been, but the commando holding its leash pulled it away. Arjun felt relieved when they got into the vehicle outside; in spite of her precautions, it would have taken just one sharp-eyed security personnel to look at her and make a connection to the photograph that could have been passed around by now. It was a pleasantly cool day, and as the taxi sped along the long, straight roads leading out of the airport, she finally took off her earphones. Arjun wound down his window and lit a cigarette.

'Listened to enough music for the day?' he asked.

'The battery's over,' she said, looking out at the low buildings passing by.

'Is anything the matter?'

'Oh, nothing. Just that there might be someone else coming to kill me.'

He decided to leave her alone. He could understand the stress she was under, on the run with two dead bodies on her trail.

When they reached the office of the agency, she went in ahead of Arjun and looked around with interest.

'There's a bathroom in there,' Arjun told her. 'You can wash up if you want to.'

'I will, thanks.'

Liza was out on pre-mat work, Chandu informed Arjun, looking up from some rough notes of the secretary he had been typing out on the computer. The two of them seemed to have worked out an efficient working relationship, Arjun thought. Now if he just had one more detective . . .

When Agnes Pereira was done, he told her she could watch television in the outer room while he finished some work in his office. He stepped inside and called his secretary from his desk phone to let her know he was back. Liza was somewhere in west Delhi, and said she would be back some time in the afternoon.

'As soon as you can,' Arjun said. 'There's someone here I want you to meet.'

With that done, he looked inside his desk drawer for a new writing pad. He started jotting down the points of the case, beginning from the rainy night Mr Vikas had turned up at his flat. It was hard to believe that it had been just a week ago. Now here he was, his life mixed up with the girl sitting in the outer room switching channels on the television. Who exactly was Vishwanathan? Maybe Poppy Barua could help him with that. And he needed to get Agnes Pereira talking. What had she been doing in Bharat Lodge? Who had killed Savitri Rao and for what? There was also the matter of putting her up someplace safe for the time being. He returned to his notes, which he would type on his laptop later on. Ever since he had opened the office, he had given up his usual black notebook in favour of a more rigorous approach. Though the notebook still came in handy for jotting down the odd impression or scrap of information. When he was done, he picked up the landline and dialled Liza's extension and asked Chandu to tell the girl to come in.

She came in and sat down across from him, looked around, and said, 'So, this is it?'

'What do you mean?'

'I thought a detective's office would be . . . I don't know, different. But it looks . . .'

'Just like any other office?' Arjun said.

'Yes. I imagined photos on the wall, maps, cigarette smoke, a whisky bottle maybe.'

'I don't smoke in here, and the bottle is in my flat.'

'Where do you stay?'

'Nearby. Are you hungry? Do you want to have lunch?'

'I guess so,' she said, and it struck Arjun that she would look better with a couple of kilos more on that frame of hers.

Kolkata Hot Pot, in the basement of the adjoining building, would not in other circumstances have been Arjun's first choice, but now he didn't want to move around in the open with her. Plus he wanted to be near the office in case his secretary got back early.

'Not the best of places,' Arjun said, leading her down the steps and into the darkened interior, 'but the noodles are decent enough.'

'Don't worry,' she said, 'I've eaten in worse places.'

They sat at one of the small marble-topped tables, and Arjun waved to a waiter. The place was more than half-full, with students and working professionals, mostly Bengali from the conversation floating around. Arjun ordered two plates of chicken chow, and she asked for two Cokes along with that. After the waiter had left, she asked him, 'What happens now?'

'We need to find a place for you to hide, somewhere you can lie low for a while till I figure out what's going on. As you said, there might be someone else looking for you now.'

'And if you can't figure out what's going on?' she asked, fear in her eyes.

'I will. That's my job.' Arjun hoped he sounded reassuring. 'But for that to happen, you need to tell me the whole story, and we need to go over what happened in Mumbai one more time.'

She pursed her lips, looked down at the table and nodded. Over their lunch of greasy noodles with lukewarm Coke, she went over the events that had occurred in the lodge. He sought the occasional clarification or explanation as she spoke, her voice low, but there was nothing that differed from her earlier account. In the end she said, 'But you were right, I have seen him before.'

'Seen whom before?'

'The man you killed. After Mumbai, I fled to Goa—that's where I'm from.'

'Let me guess. From Fontainhas in Panaji?'

'Yes, the old Portuguese quarter. My grandmother had a house there. Though nobody lives in it now.'

Arjun wanted to ask her why but he didn't want to break the flow of her account.

'I was looking at the street outside through the windows on the first floor. I was still scared. This was the day after the . . . incident. And I saw this man, tall, with abnormally large hands, pass by a couple of times, looking up at the house. After a while, I got the feeling that when it was dark he would try to get into the house. I knew then that I had to get away.'

'Was there no one you could have gone to?' Arjun asked. She shook her head.

'I packed my things into a bag and locked the house and left through a back door. I didn't know what I was doing, I just went and got on to a bus going to Gokarna.'

'Why Gokarna, of all places?'

'I thought some place remote would be safe.'

'And from Gokarna you just decided to go up all the way to Manali?'

'My friends asked me to come over.' She gave a snort of laughter. 'I don't think they actually expected me to turn up. I thought I would be safe with them, and disappear with them to Ladakh for a while.' She shook her head at the thought.

'At the travel agent's in Gokarna, did you write down something on a newspaper?'

She stared at him, seemingly mystified, then said, 'Yes, maybe I did.'

139

'Why would you write down a four-digit number? You wouldn't remember it?'

'I don't know, I was under . . . pressure. Maybe out of nervousness. So that's how you managed to find me?'

'That's part of the story, yes. Why didn't you ask for the driver's number instead?'

She exhaled in irritation, and said, 'I really didn't want to call up someone from my cell, which was switched off. The guys at the hotel gave me his taxi number, and I told them to ask him to wait in the parking lot in the railway station.'

'But you didn't stay at the hotel, did you?'

'No, my friends recommended the guest house. I thought it would be safer than the hotel. Then, you showed up.'

'Wait, how were you in touch with your friends, through your phone?'

'I turned it on from time to time to check my messages.' She looked around at the thinning lunch crowd. 'Can we get out of here, please?'

As they were walking up the steps, an auto came to a halt before the agency's office. Liza stepped out of it. She raised her eyebrows. 'Hot Pot?'

'We have a guest,' Arjun said, looking at her meaningfully as Agnes walked behind him. 'Come inside, I'll explain.'

As they walked up to the agency he asked her how the pre-mat check had gone.

'Girl's side were correct in their suspicions,' she said. 'I found out from a neighbour that the boy had been married before. The first wife died mysteriously in a kitchen fire.'

'Well done,' Arjun said, opening the door to let the two women in. 'So,' he began, taking a deep breath, 'this is Agnes Pereira. Agnes, this is Liza Thomas, my secretary. Agnes is having a bit of a problem, Liza.'

Was it his imagination, or was his secretary inspecting the girl with a look of disapproval? He quickly proceeded to give Liza a condensed version of the case so far, with Chandu listening avidly, before telling her, 'So this client planned to have both of us killed, do you see?'

'So what do we do?' Liza asked, concerned.

'We need to find a safe place for her for a few days. I was thinking of your place,' he said, trying to gauge her reaction. Hopefully she won't object, he thought. 'It's not too far from here and you have a separate entrance.'

Liza had rented a flat in National Park near the Lajpat Nagar metro station.

She paused for a few seconds, and then said in a tone Arjun recognized well, 'Can we have a word in *private*, sir?'

He asked Agnes Pereira to wait a while, and stepped into his room with his secretary.

'Isn't she the one accused of murder?' she hissed. 'How can I have her in my house?'

'That's what the police are saying, but I think she's being framed for the murder.'

'And what about our client?'

'Didn't you hear what I just said? He tried to have both of us killed!'

'Exactly! What if he sends someone to my flat to look for her?'

Arjun had considered the possibility, but hadn't thought about it seriously until Liza had put it into words.

'I won't let it happen. You have my word,' he said solemnly.

'All right,' she said after a while. 'But just for a few days.'

'Thanks, Liza.'

'But not tonight.'

'Not tonight?' Was there a lover, someone who came to see her late at night?

'Actually, one of my aunts—my father's cousin—and her husband and their son and his wife and *their* children are all at my place now. But they'll be leaving tomorrow for Uttarakhand. To see some holy places. She can stay till they come back.'

Arjun nodded, and turned to look through the dark glass at Agnes Pereira. Where was he going to put her up tonight though?

28

AGNES PEREIRA SAID, 'YOU KNOW, if it's too much of a problem for you, I can stay in a hotel.'

It was half past seven in the evening, and she had just opened the door for him at his flat after he had returned from CR Park's Market No. 1 with some groceries.

'You'll be safer here,' Arjun said, depositing the plastic bags on the dining table. 'This is the prepaid SIM card you wanted. I suggest you keep your phone usage to a minimum, though.'

'Thanks, I will. I'll pay you back, okay?'

He waved his hand at her suggestion. She had asked him to withdraw some money with her debit card, but Arjun had advised her against it, in order to avoid leaving a trail.

'We can settle that later,' he said, and took the grocery bags to the kitchen.

'Hey, why are you limping?' she asked. 'Are you hurt or something?'

'Gout.'

He waited for her to say something about alcohol and meat, as people usually did when they heard that. From what his doctor had recently told him though, they were looking at it more as a metabolic imbalance nowadays, with a new drug to lower uric acid levels. He would soon have to start a course again. But going easy on the meat and alcohol would help.

Instead, she said, 'My grandmother used to have it. Gout. She . . .'

Arjun turned to look when she paused, and saw her looking down at the floor, grimacing. Had she been reminded of something?

'You were saying?' he asked, arranging the groceries on the kitchen shelves.

'Oh, yes. She would use baking soda when she got an attack. A teaspoon of baking soda in a glass of water twice a day.'

'Really? Maybe because baking soda is alkaline. In that case, *khar* would work too.'

'What's that?'

'Water filtered through the ashes of burnt banana-tree stem. They do it in Assam. The water is then used to cook vegetables and dal in. An alkaline solution.'

'How do you know that? Are you from Assam? Where are you from, by the way?'

'Where am I from?—that's a good question.' Arjun held up a tin of paneer. 'Will this do for dinner?'

'You'll cook?'

'Yes. Why?'

There was an amused look on her face now. 'Nothing. Sure, paneer would be fine.'

'I'll cook you a good dinner. You could do with a bit of weight on your bones.'

'What's that supposed to mean?'

'Nothing. Just that you look thin. And tired.'

He opened the tin and emptied the paneer in a bowl. Next he took a bunch of spinach from the fridge and washed the leaves in the kitchen sink. He could hear her walking around the sitting room, going out to the balcony, then coming in and entering the second bedroom, where he had told her she could sleep, before coming out again.

'So, tell me,' she said, standing by the kitchen door.

'Tell you what?' Arjun asked without looking up.

He was going to blanch the leaves lightly, puree them in the food processor, and then use that as a base for his palak paneer.

'Where you're from.'

'For that, you'll have to tell me where you're from too. All right?'

'You already know that.'

'I want details. Do you want a cigarette?'

They went out to the balcony where he lit up for both of them. She had showered and changed while he was out, and she smelt fresh and clean, her hair still slightly damp. The night was cool, and he had put on the fan instead of the air conditioner in the sitting room.

'I was born in Shillong,' he said. 'My father was a Partition refugee, he was just a child then. He moved from Delhi to Calcutta looking for a job, and then to the north-east as a construction company supervisor. He's Punjabi. My mother's a Nepali. He met her in Shillong in the late 1960s. I'm the only child.' And a brother who didn't survive, he thought.

'Have you always been a detective?'

'No, I was in the army. I was a major.' Then I nearly got court-martialled, he thought, and then I was a mercenary in Iraq. 'What about you, Agnes?'

She was looking out across the park dimly lit by the yellow lights.

'I grew up in Goa,' she said. 'I was raised by my grandmother and my mother. I don't have too many memories of my father. Nobody spoke about him after he disappeared, and after a while I stopped asking about him. My mother passed away two years ago, and my grandmother followed her a couple of weeks back.'

'Sorry to hear that,' Arjun said. 'And where do you stay?'

'Pune. But most of the time I'm flying around the place.'

He tried to picture her in a flight attendant's uniform: someone who would turn heads.

'Do you like the job?' Arjun asked her, stubbing out his cigarette in a flowerpot.

'It's okay, I suppose. Doesn't anyone look after these flowers?'

'My wife used to,' Arjun said, going back into the kitchen.

She followed him in, watching as he drained the water from the spinach, pureed the leaves, and added the paste to the oil he had heated in a kadai and tempered with garlic. As the mixture sizzled and smoked, she said, 'It looks like you know what you're doing.'

'I do. So go sit down, watch some TV, and let me get dinner ready.'

'It's funny, but I don't know any men who can cook. I can barely make Maggi and tea myself. My grandmother and my mother were okay cooks. I guess I just didn't want to learn. I had all these dreams of going to different countries, doing different things.' She paused and said, 'Can I have a drink? You said you had a bottle in the house.'

He stopped stirring the palak in the kadai and looked at her.

'I thought you said you didn't drink?'

'I do, once in a blue moon.'

'Let me finish cooking and then I'll open the bottle. In the meantime, why don't you put on the news and check if there's anything about you.'

Arjun drained the brine from the paneer and slid the pieces into the bubbling gravy—in this recipe he didn't fry the paneer—and put the gas on simmer. He checked the fridge and saw that he had some cream left, to add to the gravy at the end. Then he washed some rice and put it in the rice cooker; hot, fluffy rotis would have been nice with the palak paneer, but he wasn't in the mood to spend time making them now. Asking the girl to make them was out of the question, by her own admission.

He went to the cabinet near the dining table and took out the bottle of whisky.

'I only have Blenders Pride,' he said. 'Will that do?'

29

ARJUN POURED OUT TWO PEGS in the kitchen and added water to both the glasses. Just one drink, he told himself, I'll go dry from tomorrow. He came out and placed both glasses on the table in the sitting room. She was sitting on the sofa, so he took one of the chairs beside it.

'Nothing about me or the dead man,' she said, switching between news channels. 'Can I put it off?'

'Sure. Put on some music instead.'

She said cheers and sipped her whisky—he could see she had to steel herself—then went over to the CD player on one of the shelves. She was half his age and she was in his flat drinking with him. Arjun wondered if he had done the right thing by bringing her home.

'This is like, really ancient,' she said, going through his CD collection. She put on a Dire Straits disc, and the mellow sound of Knopfler's guitar filled the room.

'Do you like them?' he asked as she came back and sat down.

She nodded. 'The room I'm in,' she said, 'did it belong to your daughter?'

'Yes, it did.'

'How old is she?'

'She's in college.'

'And your wife?'

'We're separated.'

'How is she taking it?'

'My wife?'

'Your daughter.'

'She seems okay.'

Arjun leaned back in the chair and closed his eyes. His daughter. And his parents. He had to see them soon. He heard Agnes Pereira say, 'There's something I want to show you.'

Arjun opened his eyes and said, warily, 'What?'

'You wanted to know what I was looking for in Mumbai, didn't you?'

She put down her glass, got up and went to the second bedroom. He could hear the zipper of her bag opening and closing, and then she was back.

'Have a look at this,' she said, and handed him a small red cloth bag.

The material was old and faded, and there was a drawstring around the mouth. Arjun remembered bags like these from his childhood; women would use them as a purse. He opened the bag and turned it over. What fell out were a pair of earrings, a folded piece of paper, and a black-and-white photograph of a European-looking couple.

'What are these?' he asked, puzzled. 'Who do they belong to?'

'I found the bag among my grandmother's things after she passed away. It's the reason I'm sitting here right now.'

'I don't understand. And what's that piece of paper you're holding?'

She showed it to him. 'Regent's Clinic', it said at the top in an antique-looking font in blue. Below it was a typewritten doctor's report dated September 1960. The uneven words on the yellowing paper said that the patient Agnes Carvalho had a case of severe adenomyosis, and that a hysterectomy was recommended immediately. The doctor's name was Phiroze Mistry, and the clinic's address was in Bandra, Bombay.

Agnes Pereira said, 'Agnes Carvalho was my grandmother. At least that's what I believed till a couple of weeks ago. She passed away in her sleep one night. The maid found her in the morning. When I got there the next day, there were two or three neighbours at her place and her brother's son, my uncle, whom I had never got along with. We buried her at the nearby cemetery, and the next day I cleaned up the place with the maid. At the bottom of the almirah in her bedroom, I found an old biscuit tin, those flat, round foreign ones. I hadn't seen this tin before, I was sure of that. When I opened it, I found these things inside.'

Arjun asked her, 'Wait, what do you mean, you believed she was your grandmother?'

'Read the medical report.'

'I have, but I'm not a doctor.'

'Adenomyosis is an abnormal condition of the uterus that causes bleeding and pain. Also infertility. A hysterectomy is when a woman's uterus is removed. If she underwent the procedure in 1960, then how could she have given birth to my mother in 1962?'

'You're sure she had this procedure?'

'She must have. Otherwise she could have died. And even if she somehow didn't, she would still be unable to have children.'

Arjun looked at the photograph. The man wore a white shirt, his thick hair side-parted and combed back, while the woman wore a plain dress, with her hair in a bob. There was something stolid and heavy about the unsmiling couple, something at odds with the light, delicate features of the girl before him, assuming they were in some way related.

'Did you find anything else inside the tin?'

'No, I didn't. Just the medical report, and the three items inside the bag.'

'Do you have photos of your grandmother and of your mother?'

'Yes, I do.'

While she went to get them, Arjun took a large gulp of his whisky and then turned the photo around. There was a faint impression of a rubber stamp on one corner, but the three words had faded away. Angling the photo towards the light, he could make out the second and third word though: 'Studio', followed by 'Bombay'. Unfolding the piece of paper, he saw, spelt out in capital letters in faded black ink, a name: 'BOBBY'. It was followed by an address in the city's business district of Fort. The earrings were in yellow metal, possibly gold, inlaid with beads of a black stone-like material, and were shaped like teardrops. Agnes Pereira came back and handed him two photos.

One was in black-and-white, taken inside a studio, and showed a tall, well-built woman in a knee-length skirt and polka-dotted blouse or top. She was dark-complexioned, and her curly hair was cut short. Something about the photo seemed familiar, then he spotted it: the flower-and-bird pattern on the cloth behind her was the same as the one behind the couple in the other black-and-white photo. He turned it around, and saw a similar rubber-stamp impression, but too faint except for the last word 'Bombay' to be made out. So both photos were likely to have been taken at the same studio.

The other photo was in colour, and had an oversaturated look. There could be no doubt that the woman in it was related to Agnes Pereira. It was taken in an overgrown garden, and the woman wore what had been called baggy pants in the mid-eighties, and a cream-coloured jacket with the sleeves pushed up. Her hair reached her jawline, and there was a rebellious look about her. Arjun thought the woman to be in her mid-twenties, so that would tie in with when Agnes Pereira said her mother had been born.

'That's my mother,' she said. 'It was taken by a friend of hers in Bangalore.'

Arjun looked up at her. He could see now where she got her looks from.

'What was her name?'

'Susan Carvalho. My grandmother gave my mother her own title.'

'You are your mother's daughter,' he said, 'no doubt about it. And about your grandmother, you could be right.'

'Could be? I know I am.'

'Do you think she meant for you to find the biscuit tin?'

'I don't think so. Maybe she couldn't bring herself to throw those things away.'

'What about her husband? Your grandfather. What did he look like?'

'Nobody knew. She was working in Bombay, and came back with a baby one day. Which was my mother. She never went back.'

'She didn't have any photographs of him?'

Agnes Pereira shook her head.

'So you think she might have adopted your mother?'

'Yes. But there are no records of that.'

'This couple in the photo, they bear no resemblance to your grandmother, or even to your mother for that matter.'

'That's what I thought as well.'

'What about the doctor's address?'

'I went to have a look. The clinic still stands in the same place, but the doctor died a long time ago. And they don't have any records going back further than thirty years.'

'What about the address on the piece of paper, did you go there?'

'I did. I went there from the clinic. It's a furniture showroom, looked like a pretty high-end store. I went there the first time and asked for Mr Bobby, but they said there was nobody by that name there. I asked if I could see the manager or the owner, and

151

they asked me to come back the next day. When I returned the next day, the owner met me, and took me into his office. He was an old man, in his sixties or seventies. I told him my story, and asked if he knew a Mr Bobby. He said he would ask his father, who had started the showroom, and get back to me.'

'You told him where you were staying?'

'Yes, after he asked me.'

'What was his name, this old man?'

'He introduced himself as Anil Mehta.'

'And he said *his* father had started this furniture showroom?'

'No, I mean, his father was the owner of the building. I got the feeling that the old man's son ran the place. He got a phone call while I was there and he told the person that his son Nikhil was the one they needed to contact about the order.'

'Did you see this Nikhil?'

'No, I didn't.'

'What happened after that?'

'That evening Savi came to stay with me. And the next morning . . .'

Arjun finished the rest of the whisky in his glass, and wondered if he should have a small second. What he had been told seemed improbable enough to be true. The stories of Indian families could at times be stranger than fiction.

'What was the name of this furniture showroom?' he asked.

'It was called Expression.'

He recalled the letters 'ON' in the CCTV photo Vishwanathan had given him.

'So you knew where that photo of you would have been taken, right? Expression?'

'Yes, but I didn't know whether I could trust you.'

'Fair enough,' he conceded. 'Did Savitri Rao know anyone by the name of Vishwanathan?'

'I don't know.'

152

'Did she have someone else's money with her for safekeeping?'

'I don't know, okay? Can't you see, the man you killed must have mistaken her for me? Now can you give me another drink, please?'

Arjun picked up the empty glasses and stood up. It was time to give her a break from the questioning. As he poured them two more pegs, he went over her story. Was the murder of her friend Savitri Rao a result of her decision to go looking into the story behind the items in the biscuit tin? In which case the bar dancer's death would appear to be a case of mistaken identity. Or was it really about the money, as Vishwanathan had claimed? Money which Savitri Rao might have been entrusted with, and which had then disappeared? But the killer in Manali hadn't been interested in finding out anything from Agnes Pereira.

30

HE SPREAD OUT ALL THE items before him on the glass-topped coffee table: the cloth bag, the note with the address, the medical report, the pair of earrings and the photographs, including the one Vishwanathan had given him. Agnes Pereira went out to the balcony with his packet of cigarettes. He considered the items one at a time. Were the items from the biscuit tin the reason she was supposed to have been killed? In that case, someone at the clinic or at the furniture showroom could have passed on word about her. But what could have been the motive? Which was why he wasn't ready to let go of the Savitri Rao angle just yet. He picked up the earrings. They were well made, and looked valuable. Turning them around in his fingers, he spotted a marking on the reverse side of both: a double M. Someone's initials?

She came back inside and looked at him studying the items.

'Have you figured out anything?' she asked.

'What do you think? These earrings, did you ever see your grandmother or your mother wearing them?'

'No, I'd never seen them before.'

'Do you have any idea where your father is now?'

'The last I heard, he was in Mangalore with his second family. He left us when I was three or four years old.'

'What was his name?'

'Simon Pereira. He was a businessman of some sort. My grandmother couldn't stand him. I think she was secretly happy he left. So I grew up with those two ladies.'

'They seem to have done okay,' Arjun said. He stretched and let out a long yawn. It had been a long day and he needed to hit the sack. He could go over all of this tomorrow. He drained his glass and stood up. 'Let's have dinner.'

They ate at the dining table. Rice, palak paneer and salad. She watched with interest as he broke off a sliver of a raja mircha with a spoon from a pickle bottle, and poured some of the oil over his rice.

'You're a chilli addict, aren't you?'

'I suppose so,' Arjun said. 'How do you like the food?'

'It's great. Who taught you how to cook?'

'I must have picked it up from my parents.'

'Are they still around?'

'Yes. They're here in Delhi.'

'You're lucky. I have no one now. I can't stand the handful of relatives I have, and I don't want to see my father ever. I'm not surprised about us not being descended from my grandmother, you know. I remember my mother always had this sort of fantasy about us living in a large house with plenty of servants. I think she wanted me to marry someone rich.'

'How did your mother die?'

'She had a problem with her drinking. That's why I hardly touch the stuff.'

'What did she do for a living?'

'Oh, secretarial jobs. She just seemed so miserable all the time.'

'Wouldn't she have had a birth certificate?'

'No, I looked. I suppose in those days you could make do without one.'

Something else occurred to him. He asked, 'Did your mother suffer from gout?'

155

'No. Why?'

'Just asking. What about you?'

'I don't have it either. Only my grandmother did.'

His phone rang—it was the taxi driver.

'Yadavji, have you reached Delhi?'

'Yes, a while ago. Is everything okay?'

'All fine. Once again, thanks for your help.'

'Don't mention it, sahib.'

'I might call you again sometime.'

'Whenever you want.'

Agnes Pereira asked him who it was. When he told her, she asked, 'Is he, like, a source of yours?'

'No, more of an occasional assistant.'

'Do you have to be very clever to be a detective?'

He laughed at that 'Not really. Though it helps. Most of all, you have to be observant and capable of analysing information. Some more rice?'

'No, thanks, I'm stuffed.'

After dinner she sat down to watch a television show. He served them both some sweet curd in bowls. Soon she was engrossed in the soap, smiling at the punchlines. Arjun allowed himself a proper look at her, something he had avoided so far. The lean legs tucked up on the sofa, the small breasts under the T-shirt and the slim arms. He remembered how he had felt when she had smiled at him on the balcony of the guest house that morning. He finished off his curd and told her he was going to bed.

'Do you mind if I—?'

'Go ahead. Just keep the volume down. Goodnight.'

'Goodnight.'

In his bedroom he changed into a pair of shorts and a vest, washed and brushed his teeth. He checked his arms in the mirror; he still had muscle definition. He turned off the bedroom lights and opened a window at the rear to smoke a last cigarette. The back lane behind the house was quiet and dark. From the sitting room he heard faint laughter from the serial. Gout was usually a hereditary condition. His father had it. If Agnes Pereira and her mother didn't have it while the grandmother did, then it was another detail confirming Agnes's theory. As he lay down on his bed he wondered if she might knock on his door sometime in the night.

X

There was someone knocking at the door, and when he went to answer it, he saw it was the police. They took him down to the patrol car and in the back he saw the man he thought he had killed in Manali. There was blood and dirt all over his clothes, and as Arjun was pushed into the vehicle he saw maggots crawling out of the man's stomach. The inspector said they would take both of them to the court and then to the jail, to be lodged in the same cell. Arjun woke up with a start in the darkness. Reaching for his cell phone, he saw it was 4 a.m. It was a Saturday. He decided he would go for the football game on Sunday.

Arjun lay in bed till 5 a.m. watching as a faint light crept in from behind the curtains. She hadn't come to him in the night, but then what had he been expecting? He was a middle-aged man with greying hair. Putting on an old pair of sneakers, he went down to the park below for a run. The pain in his big toe had eased up, and he knew he had got off lightly this time. There was no one around this early in the morning, and he could feel a slight nip in the air. After four rounds he sat down panting on one of the benches. It had been a while since he had last run, and the cigarettes weren't helping. He watched as the sky lightened in colour. How many more sunrises were left for him to see? Looking at his flat on the other side of the park, where the large neem tree was, it struck him how lifeless his balcony looked. He had given up on it. Would there come a time when he would do the same with his detective work? The thought scared him, and he got up from the bench. On his way out of the park, he passed two old ladies talking about a wedding.

Back in the flat he took a shower, changed into a clean pair of Wranglers, and put on a Spanish league game rerun on one of the sports channels, with the volume turned down. She hadn't woken up yet. He made himself a cup of tea, sat down on the sofa and considered the items which were still on the table. On the television there was a rough tackle near the box followed by a free kick, which went wide. He felt something taking shape at the edge of his thoughts, some idea about the situation he now found himself in. I need to get more information, he thought. He picked up the two black-and-white photographs and studied them again. Then he went to the bedroom and got his magnifying glass. He turned on the light in the sitting room and studied the reverse of both photos. Comparing the old rubber-stamp impressions he thought the first word might be 'Royal'.

His laptop was on the dining table, and he switched it on and inserted the dongle. He first searched for Expression, adding 'furniture store Mumbai' after it, just to confirm it existed. He went through the search results. It seemed to be, as Agnes Pereira said, a high-end store for the well-heeled of Mumbai. Adding the name 'Bobby' didn't bring forth anything useful. Next he searched for 'Royal Photo Studio Bombay'. A handful of results turned up, but how would he know if any of them had been in existence way back in 1960? He shut his laptop and jotted down a few more points in the writing pad. A furniture store and a photo studio, how could the two be connected? Or was the connection Agnes Carvalho, a woman who had passed away a few weeks ago? Nothing seemed to make any sense.

His maid turned up after a while—of late she had started coming thirty minutes earlier than her usual time. Arjun put the items on the coffee table into an envelope and collected the newspapers from the balcony, hoping that Agnes Pereira wouldn't get up just then. He asked the maid not to make breakfast and not to sweep the second bedroom as he had a guest there. She threw him a questioning look before tucking in the loose end of her sari and tackling the dishes. Ever since his wife and daughter had left the house, she seemed to regard him with a mix of suspicion and anger.

He went to the bedroom to go through the newspapers, moving to the sitting room when the maid came in to wash the clothes in the bathroom. There seemed to be no mention of a suspicious death on the outskirts of Manali. He became aware of a tinge of fear lodged somewhere at the back of his brain, troubling him now and again like an itch he couldn't scratch. He made a note to check the Internet later on. After the maid left, he carried the garbage bag to the nearby *dhalao* on the main road where the *kabariwallah*s were bringing in the morning's collections. He had to wait a while to cross the road to Market No. 3 as the cars rushed past on their way to schools and offices. He bought bread, eggs and milk from a kirana shop and a packet of cigarettes from the paanwallah beside it. At Punjabi Chik-Inn, the workers were sitting outside listening to film songs on their cell phones and chopping onions. When he got back to the flat, she was awake, dressed in a pair of pyjamas and a T-shirt that made her look, he thought with a twinge of guilt, like a college girl. He was glad she would be leaving that day.

'Time for breakfast,' he said to her.

31

HE DROVE TO HIS OFFICE by way of Market No. 2, where he stopped at a pharmacy for a couple of strips of tablets to keep his uric acid level low. He took one with a glass of water when he got to the office. Chandu was already there cleaning up the place. On Saturdays, they opened a bit early and tried to close early as well. He had asked Agnes Pereira to wait in the flat till he came back to pick her up.

'Don't open the door for anyone,' he had told her. 'I'll call you before I head back. And if you see anyone suspicious, call me.'

'What if I want to order something for lunch?'

'Give them the building number and go downstairs to collect it. But don't step out into the street.'

Arjun now went into his room and took out the laptop and the writing pad from his backpack, and started updating his notes on the case. As he typed, he could feel a strong impulse pushing him forward to resolve this matter at the earliest. It was not just his and the girl's lives being in danger, but also the mystery of her background, which a part of him felt he could relate to.

When he was done he googled 'Doctor Phiroze Mistry', but only a thirty-four-year-old doctor by that name in the UK's NHS showed up, and then he searched for 'Murder dead man Manali forest', but that didn't yield anything relevant either. Could it be that no one had come upon the body as yet? If there were dogs in the area, they might have started feeding on the corpse. He recalled his dream, and tried to remember if they had left anything incriminating at the site. Liza had arrived by then, and came in to use the bathroom.

'You're here early today, sir,' she said when she saw him.

Was it an innocent comment, or did he hear something else in it? He spent the next hour going through the correspondence and files of the agency's cases. The secretary of the automobile association had sent him a mail of thanks, informing him that they had, with the help of the Delhi Police, managed to nab all the members of the gang of counterfeiters, along with the advance money. They were also on the trail of the ringleader in Mumbai. He went through the report his secretary had prepared the previous day about the suspicious groom. The first wife had died in a kitchen fire in a suspected dowry case, but the family members had all given alibis to the police. Liza's report might save the life of their client's daughter, but who could guarantee it wouldn't happen to another girl? And some other organization like the Automobile Parts Manufacturers Association might soon ask him to track down another counterfeiter's gang. Sometimes, it seemed to Arjun that Delhi was one vast criminal enterprise, varying only in degrees of seriousness. He thought about the men he knew in the police force, and understood how they developed a fatalistic, case-by-case approach to morality. He made a few changes to the report before mailing it back to Liza. At 10.30 a.m. he sent Chandu to get the thermos flask filled with tea from the stall in Market No. 1. Sipping on the tea, he sent a text message to Bunty suggesting they meet for lunch, and set out in his car. There were a couple of things he had to take care of. He also had to call Poppy Barua for a favour, but right now was too early in the day for the newswoman.

Mid-morning on a Saturday wasn't exactly the best time to turn up at Nehru Place. It had taken Arjun as much time to

161

find a vacant spot in the vast, dusty parking areas below the tall buildings as it had taken him to get there from CR Park. People milled about under the shadows of the buildings looking for cheap deals on laptops and desktops, software and even clothes and books. Budget restaurants on the ground floors of the buildings served oily, filling food, while a couple of policemen on the beat kept an eye on the proceedings. It appealed to Arjun's sense of irony that one of the world's largest software companies had their offices nearby, even as young boys roamed the corridors around Nehru Place clutching stacks of pirated software that included the company's products. You bought a copied DVD, took it home and put it into your computer, then called the boy for the product activation key which would be given over the phone. All for less than a hundredth of the actual price.

Arjun jostled people on his way up the steps and along the corridors of the building where Computer Baba's shop was tucked away in a corner. Today it was full of customers standing amid cartons and boxes of hardware parts. Baba was on the phone, and he raised a hand when he saw Arjun, asking him to hold on. When he put the receiver down, a young man told him he had come to collect the Dell laptop which had crashed.

'Oh, *haan*, that one,' Computer Baba said distractedly as he looked around his desk. 'Come on Monday and collect it.'

From above the false ceiling came the voice of Baba's assistant who repaired laptops up there: 'Monday? How can I give it on Monday? I have other laptops to fix—and you haven't got me the hard drive for the Dell.'

'So I'll get it today,' Baba snapped. 'And you better fix it first thing Monday!'

'One day I won't turn up,' the disembodied voice continued, 'and then you'll learn.'

'This place is full of computer technicians, do you hear? I can get an ITI-pass for what I'm paying you.'

Arjun came out of the shop and leaned against one of the outer pillars and lit a cigarette. There was a cool breeze up here. Looking at the crowds down below, he wondered what the daily turnover of the entire market would be. A few hundred crores at least. By the time he finished the cigarette Baba had called him in and drawn out a stool for him.

'How did you happen to remember this humble servant of yours?' Baba said, his left hand on the computer mouse while his right kept sweeping back his greasy, wavy locks.

On any other day Arjun would have told him to cut the bullshit, but today he decided to humour his go-to techie.

'I was passing by, thought I'd see how my dear friend is doing.'

'Very nice of you, Arjun bhai, what can I say, with business the way it is, I'm just managing to keep myself alive.'

'Yes, I can see that. By the way, did you manage to get what I asked for?'

Baba opened a drawer, rummaged around, and brought out a printout.

'List of last ten calls from Agnes Pereira's phone. You thought I forgot?'

'I knew you would have it ready, Baba.'

'But the rates have gone up now, Arjun bhai. There's a new fellow . . .'

Arjun tossed on the table a sheaf of five-hundred-rupee notes held together by a rubber band.

'That takes care of all the old assignments,' Arjun said. 'We'll discuss this one later.'

'As you say,' Baba chirped, handing over the printout and taking the money.

Arjun went through the list with its ten entries while Baba counted his money. The calls had been made from Mumbai, Goa and finally Gokarna. The last column showed the receiver's number and name; in Mumbai she had called Savitri Rao and a city landline listed in the name of a Robert Chacko, in Goa she had called her airline office and Robert Chacko again, and in Gokarna she had called a Navin Sood who had a Delhi address, and finally Robert Chacko again.

'Chalo, all accounts settled,' Baba said, pocketing the money. 'My old telecom guy has left, transferred out of Delhi. He introduced me to someone in his office, but this *chutiya* wants a higher rate now. Anyway, let me see if I can bargain a bit. Arjun bhai?'

'Yes?' Arjun looked up from the list, wondering what he could be looking for.

'You look lost. Working too hard? Let's go and have some fresh juice, my treat.'

The unseen repairman reminded Baba not to forget about his zarda and paan masala.

'You don't do any work, just chew bloody zarda and paan masala all day, *haramzada*!' Baba yelled.

As they made their way down the building, Arjun asked Baba who the repairman was.

'An old employee of mine. A good worker, but he talks too much.'

They made their way to a juice stand on the ground floor where incense wafted out from between mounds of carrots and mosambis, bananas and pomegranates. Baba asked for two large glasses of mosambi juice, and Arjun asked the man not to add masala to one.

'You should have a bit of that masala,' Baba said. 'Helps with digestion.'

'My digestion is fine.'

'Well, your health is certainly tip-top. Arjun bhai, I was thinking, you know.'

'What?'

'We have to keep working our whole life, isn't it?'

'That's true. Unless you go on KBC and become a crorepati.'

'I was never good at general knowledge. But computers, I don't know why, I understand everything about them.'

Arjun knew that Baba had grown up working in various computer shops in Nehru Place, teaching himself along the way about the innards of the machines and the code language that ran them. The man behind the stand had peeled the fruits, put them through a juicer, and was now pouring the juice from one mug to another to build up the froth.

'So you want to stop working now?' Arjun asked, as he took his masala-free juice.

'When did I say that? What I meant was, we work all the time, so we need some time to relax and enjoy ourselves too, right?'

'Right,' Arjun agreed between sips, wondering where Baba was going with this.

'A friend of mine in Bangkok has called me over there. I was thinking of going for a week or two. Only thing is, I've never been abroad. How is it? Do you need to keep anything in mind over there?'

'How long has your friend been there?'

'Nearly three years. He works in a clothes shop owned by an Indian.'

'Stick to your friend and you'll be fine. It's a big city, so be careful of your money.'

'Thanks for the advice, Arjun bhai. How much for our juice, Tiwariji?'

Walking back through the crowds towards the parking lot Arjun thought about Baba's query. He hoped Baba's friend didn't try to convince him to stay back in Bangkok. It would be a bother trying to find himself a new techie. Or was Baba just trying to put himself in a better bargaining position? He got into his car, and as he waited for the parking attendant to push out the car parked in front of him, he glanced at the list of phone numbers and names once again. He was about to put it back into the envelope with the other items when it suddenly occurred to him: Bobby and Robert Chacko—could there be a connection?

32

THE DRIVE TO WEST DELHI where his parents lived was a long one. By the time he crossed the old Hyatt on the Ring Road it was noon. Bunty had replied to his message, suggesting they meet at Select Citywalk around two, but Arjun didn't want to go there and had suggested the Swagath branch in Malviya Nagar instead. I should check out some of these new places, he thought, maybe with Rhea. There seemed to be all sorts of small, new restaurants coming up in the city—Russian, Moroccan, French—but he and Bunty always seemed to end up in their old haunts. Looking at the dashboard clock he decided it was safe to call Poppy Barua, and clipped on his hands-free Bluetooth device. She turned out to be on her way to Jaipur in a taxi.

'What for?' Arjun said.

'Don't ask. The newspaper's sponsoring an event and I've been asked to attend.'

'Good for you.'

'Yeah, listening to boring speeches during the day and fending off drunken men in the evening. Why don't you come over? I can get you a pass.'

'I would love to but I'm in the middle of a case.'

'Pity. Anyway, I have the new J.K. Rowling book with me.'

'I didn't know you were into Harry Potter.'

'I'm not. She's written a novel for adults.'

'When do you get back?'

'Tomorrow. I don't intend to stay a minute longer than necessary. I've seen enough of Jaipur for a lifetime, thank you.'

'Would you mind finding out something for me?' Arjun asked. 'There might be a story in it for you.'

'I'll have to see. But tell me about it.'

'You must have heard about the murdered bar girl in Mumbai? Savitri Rao? Yes? Okay. I want to know more about her and the friend who was with her in the lodge. Also about a well-built businessman of some sort called Vishwanathan who has a missing finger. And the Expression furniture store in Mumbai, when it was opened, something about the owner. Possible?'

'Could be done, but it would have been nice to have a little more on the man,' Poppy Barua said cautiously as she noted it down in her pad. 'The bureau chief in Mumbai is an old friend. So you're saying the man with the missing finger and the Expression store are linked to the murder?'

'Could be, yes.'

'I could ask him to send out a reporter again, but he'll want something in return.'

'There will be something in it for you guys,' Arjun said.

He was now coming down the Moti Bagh flyover, with the gleaming white gurdwara to his left. Up ahead, the pillars of the under-construction overhead metro line rose up from the middle of the road.

'Why don't you go down to Mumbai and find out, Arjun?'

'I was in Mumbai, but I don't intend to go back soon. Someone there wants me dead.'

'Oh my!' she said, and giggled. 'Sorry, that wasn't an appropriate response.'

'No problem, I'm still alive.'

'Let me ask him and get back to you.'

'The reporter should talk to the receptionist in the lodge. And to the owner of a grocery shop near the lodge, I believe he knows something.'

'Mm-hm.' Arjun could hear the faint scratch of a pencil on a pad. 'So when do I get to see you?'

'Soon. I'll be waiting for your call. Bye.'

The conversation left him feeling down for some reason. He called his secretary, as much to ask her for something as to listen to her always chirpy voice.

'I want you to look up two things for me.'

He told her about the various Royal Photo Studios, and the dead girl Savitri Rao.

Liza said, 'So the studio should have been . . .'

'Operating in the late fifties and early sixties. Get their numbers from the Internet and call them. And anything interesting you might find online about Savitri Rao, all right?'

'Okay. Sir, you think this Agnes Pereira could have committed the murder?'

'It was most likely someone else,' Arjun said, 'but we'll have to make sure of that.'

He wasn't ready to let go of the bar girl angle to the case just yet. The call over, he took off his Bluetooth device. He didn't like using it, but you couldn't risk talking on your phone in the car nowadays, just like driving after a few pegs too many. Delhi was slowly losing all the charm of its old ways.

33

ARJUN GOT TO RAJOURI GARDEN and found a free spot down the road that ran past the cluster of buildings where his parents had a flat. Before he got down he took out the earrings from the envelope inside the dashboard and put them into his pocket. As he walked back to the entrance gate, he saw on the other side of the road the press-wallah ironing clothes in his brick shack with his coal-fed iron, his frail wife beside him dutifully folding the shirts and pants into stacks. They had been here even before Arjun's father had bought the flat, which was more than twenty years ago. Someday I'll come here and find them gone, he thought, just like all the other things in my life.

He shook the thought off as he walked up the staircase to the second-floor flat. As always he first looked out from the balcony at the sprawl of buildings under a blanket of haze and the small park down below with its patches of grass. When he rang the bell, his mother came to open the screen door in her dressing gown. She looked tired, her hooded eyes drooping.

'You've finally come,' she said, putting her arms around him. 'What were you doing in Mumbai?'

'I had to meet a client,' he said, returning her hug.

In the sitting room the old sofa set with its yellowing wood frame and faded green cushions seemed to be waiting to remind him that, in the end, all effort was wasted.

'How is he now?' he asked, following his mother inside.

'Better. He's resting in bed most of the time.'

'Will he go to the hospital?'

'Ask him, he's in there. Let me make some tea.'

She veered into the kitchen before he could stop her, so he carried on down the corridor to the second bedroom at the end. His father was sitting up in bed, looking out the window at the faded blue sky outside. The ceiling fan was turning slowly, and there were a couple of newspapers on the bed. Arjun cleared his throat, and his father turned. The normally fierce eyes seemed unfocused, as if he were far away somewhere. Then he returned to the moment.

'How are you feeling?' Arjun asked.

'I'm okay now,' Arora senior replied brusquely.

Arjun pulled up a chair to the foot of the bed. He was determined not to let the old man make him angry today. His father was wearing a dhoti, which he sometimes did at home, a habit from his Calcutta days, and Arjun could see the twisted flesh and ligaments of the damaged kneecap. Mr Arora smoothened the dhoti to cover his knee when he noticed his son looking at it.

'Where's your mother gone?'

'She's making tea.'

'It'll be time for lunch soon and the woman is making tea,' Mr Arora grumbled.

'I asked for it, I wanted to have a cup,' Arjun said, and his father grunted.

Mr Arora put on his glasses and picked up one of the newspapers. For a while, Arjun looked at the short silver-grey hair and the shoulders that were still broad, then took the plunge.

'At your age, this high blood pressure thing could be dangerous. You fell down in the bathroom the other day. I want to take you to a hospital and get a full check-up done.'

His mother came with three cups of tea on a tray, and Mr Arora looked up at her then at his son. His reply surprised Arjun, who had been expecting another bad-tempered outburst.

'I'm feeling better now, so let's see. The doctor gave me new medicines. Give me a couple of days, maybe we can go after that.'

Arjun couldn't think of anything more to say. His mother came and sat near him on the bed and they drank their tea.

'How's Rhea?' she asked him.

'She's okay,' Arjun said. 'Busy with her friends. You know how it is at this age.'

'Yes, like how you would disappear for the entire day when you were in college.'

Mr Arora snorted. 'If he had only studied then, instead of going and joining the army.'

'How many times will you keep saying the same old thing?' his mother muttered, and Arjun held up his hand to tell her it was okay, he wasn't going to lose his cool today.

'Bring her here sometimes,' Mr Arora said. 'We need to see her, we're her grandparents.'

'I'll tell her,' Arjun said. 'I hardly get to see her myself nowadays.'

They sat in silence for a while drinking their tea. Arjun thought about the girl back at his flat, and that reminded him of the earrings. He took them out from his pocket and showed them to his mother.

'These are lovely!' she exclaimed. 'Are you going to give them to someone?'

'Of course not. I need to find out about them.'

She held them up to the light and looked closely. 'Beautiful, and this inlay work of black stone . . .' She looked at Arjun, her eyes suddenly lighting up. 'Where did you get these?'

'Something to do with one of my cases. Why, have you seen them before?'

'Maybe in a film magazine . . . I used to buy a lot of *Filmfare* in those days . . . before you were born. I think this style was popular for a while.'

She turned to Mr Arora.

'Do you remember we used to go to the Anwar cinema hall in Tezpur?'

'We went to many halls,' he said testily. 'Kelvin in Shillong, Anwar in Tezpur.'

'Nice movies in those days,' she continued. 'Good stories, good actresses. Madhubala, Munni, Meena Kumari, all those people.'

His father grunted. 'Meena Kumari died from drinking too much. And Munni was murdered or something like that.'

'Munni was in that movie, remember?' she appealed to her husband again. 'She played the sister of the hero . . . and she dies in a train accident while trying to save the life of the girl her brother loves. What was the name of the movie? Everybody was crying in the hall. I remember that.'

'So many tragedies in those movies,' Mr Arora said, and allowed himself a smile.

Mrs Arora handed him the earrings, collected the cups and put them on the tray, and stood up.

'I'm getting old,' she said to her husband, 'that's why I can't remember.'

'We're both getting old,' Mr Arora told her as he examined the earrings.

She had reached the kitchen when Mr Arora called out to her, 'Train accident . . . do you mean that movie *Toote Hue Dil?*'

Mrs Arora came back to the bedroom. 'Yes, I think that was the one!'

She smiled at her husband; looking at them, Arjun was reminded of how long they had spent with each other. In the end, what was life but having someone by your side?

'Munni,' Mr Arora said, 'kidnapped or murdered. Imagine that.'

'When would that have happened?' Arjun asked, amused by this banter between his parents. The name of the actress sounded vaguely familiar.

'When?' Mr Arora turned to look at his wife. 'A long time ago, wasn't it?'

'Yes,' she said, 'it must have been sometime after we got to Delhi.'

Mr Arora handed the earrings back to his son.

'That's pure gold,' his mother said, 'and the black stone must be onyx. Who gave them to you, Arjun?'

'A client,' he said vaguely. 'So they're worth a lot of money?'

'Yes,' Mrs Arora said. 'They would have been very expensive to make. Will you have some rice? There's chicken curry from last night.'

'No, I have to meet someone for lunch,' Arjun said. 'I'll be off now.'

'Come and have dinner one of these days,' his mother said. 'Bring Rhea along too.'

'I'll do that. Maybe tomorrow. I'll let you know.'

34

HEADING BACK TOWARDS SOUTH DELHI, Arjun
reflected on how normally the visit had gone. Maybe his
father was finally mellowing. Arjun would have to take him
for a check-up one of these days. Who knew how much time
he had left? And what would become of his mother after that?
Her life now revolved entirely around taking care of his father.
Time was slipping away—Arjun felt it was already too late. He
remembered the earrings, and slipped them into the envelope in
the dashboard. He tried to think where he could get the earrings
tested.

About forty-five minutes later, Arjun reached the Malviya
Nagar market. Looking at the weekend rush he parked some
distance ahead of the block. Walking towards the hotel, he called
Sonali to ask about something that had been on his mind for
some time.

'How much pocket money does Rhea get nowadays? I just
wanted to know.'

'Why do you want to know that?' his ex-wife asked.

'She seems to be hanging out at expensive places, five-star
restaurants, nightclubs.'

'Well, she's got a new set of friends, she's popular. What's
wrong with that?'

'How much do you give her a week, Sonali?'

'I don't keep track, okay? Her friends come from rich families, and I don't want her to feel out of place among them.'

Arjun gritted his teeth. He knew very well what was to follow.

'I hope it's nothing more than one or two thousand a week?'

She snorted with contempt. 'Which world are you living in, Arjun? Besides, I have my own business, and I don't ask you for money. Rhea has started earning, and that money goes into a savings account.'

Arjun took a deep breath and exhaled. He could have brought up the argument Rhea had told him about, just to hurt her, but he felt no desire to do so.

'It's just that at this age, she shouldn't be able to afford whatever she wants.'

'Oh, don't you worry about that, I've made sure she knows what's important in life.'

'I'm sure you have, Sonali. Bye.'

He made his way past the crowd and the cars and scooters to the entrance of Swagath, where he lit a cigarette and took a few hurried puffs. He wanted everything clear-cut and well defined in life, he realized, that was his problem. It must have been something he had inherited from his father.

In the dining area on the first floor, Bunty Chawla sat alone at a table for six with a glass of water before him and a phone in each hand with which he was carrying on two simultaneous conversations. One was a large, folding model with a keypad, the other a smartphone with a six-inch touchscreen, and as Arjun took a seat on the other side Bunty lowered the large phone face down from his left ear and lifted the other phone to his right ear. He was dressed in his usual combination of jeans, a white T-shirt and a black waistcoat.

'Yes, I'm here. What? Okay, tell Srivastava to check the invoices against the orders one more time to make sure. Then you call up that *sala chutiya bania* in Kanpur and tell him we've sent him exactly what he asked for. He called whom? Achha, wait, just hold.'

Bunty switched to the phone in his left hand now, and his voice turned smoother.

'Ha, tell me, Khan sahib. No, no, just some routine factory work. Yes, yes. I think you should talk to the SHO at the Safdarjung police station first and get some information. Then I'll see what I can do. If needed we can try and meet Madam herself. Ha, yes. Khan sahib, just hold for a while.'

Arjun looked on as his friend juggled the two calls, one to do with his factory that manufactured bathroom fittings, and the other with his position as a general secretary in a political party. A waiter sidled up to their table and waited for the calls to end. Bunty Chawla carried on talking, and Arjun marvelled at the amount of information his friend could process simultaneously. When he had hung up on both men, (claiming he was stepping into a conference at the Habitat Centre), Bunty looked up at the waiter.

'Haan, ji. Get us two large pegs of whisky. Arjun, what'll you take?'

But Arjun shook his head, so Bunty reconsidered and asked for a bottle of beer.

The waiter nodded, then asked, 'Sir, when are the other people coming?'

'Arré, they're on their way. There are traffic jams all over the city. My friend took two hours to get here from Rajouri Garden, isn't that so, Arjun? Now get us the beer and the menu.'

Confronted with this the waiter slunk away. Arjun asked him to get just one beer mug.

'What'll you have then?' Bunty demanded. 'Rum and Coke? It's too early for that.'

'I'm not drinking,' Arjun said.

This news so astounded Bunty that he stared at Arjun with an open mouth for a while. He finally said, 'But why? Have you fallen in love?'

Arjun laughed. 'Nothing like that, *paaji*. I'm just taking a break.'

'I guess your liver needs it by now. *Aur bata*, how was your Bharat darshan?'

As he told his friend the details of the Agnes Pereira case till date, Arjun realized he had missed his usual sounding board. The waiter returned with a bottle of beer, and Arjun asked him for a cold Coke. They ordered appams, chicken stew and vegetables stir-fried with coconut, with Bunty insisting they not order dosa or vada or sambar. When Arjun finished his story, Bunty drank some beer and closed his eyes. Then he opened them.

'So where is this girl now?'

'At my secretary's place,' Arjun said, sipping on his Coke.

'The south Indian girl I recommended to you? How is she doing?'

'She's a smart one. Very helpful.'

'Hmm. But this girl, Agnes whatever her name is, she's not your client, is she?'

'No. Vishwanathan's my client. But he tried to have me killed as well.'

'What do you think? *Why* would he try to have you killed?'

'So that I wouldn't open my mouth about Agnes Pereira, perhaps?'

'Well, you survived. And you're in Delhi now. No son of a bitch from Mumbai can touch you here. I think you should tell her to move, and tell your client where she is.'

'I did that once—and I almost died.'

'Arjun, would you do the same thing if you had been asked to find a grown man?'

'What's that supposed to mean?'

'How old is this girl?'

'Mid-twenties. Listen, Bunty, it's not that, okay? She's a nice girl and she's in trouble.'

Bunty shrugged and mopped up some chicken stew with a piece of appam.

'I'm just giving you an objective view of the situation,' he said.

'I know. But those things that the girl showed me, the photograph and the note and the pair of earrings, I think there's something more to the whole story.'

'Could be, but why do you want to get into it?'

Arjun started to explain but then thought better of it. His mind was made up, and he knew better than anyone that no one could change it for him now. Instead he asked, 'Have you heard of an actress called Munni?'

'I only know *Munni badnam hui*,' Bunty said with a grin, referring to the popular Hindi film song.

'I learnt a long time ago,' his friend continued, then let out a small belch, 'sorry, I was saying that I learnt a long time ago that in business you need to leave your sentiments aside and concentrate on the main objective, which is making money.'

'Well, I have my usual fee with me,' Arjun said, 'so I'm not running at a loss. What about that guest house in Paharganj, did you manage to find out who it belongs to?'

'Shiva Guest House? Something odd there. I asked my accountant to have a look, and he says it's in the name of a firm registered in Mauritius. Blue Wave Capital.'

'That's strange. Any names? Owner? Board of directors?'

'It's a bit secretive. I've asked him to find out though. So your ticket was booked . . .'

'At the travel agency below the guest house. The agency is supposed to be owned by the guest house. I know it might not be anything but I just wanted to check.'

'As you wish, *kancha*, I'm always here to help you. Bhai, wah, that was a good meal!'

Bunty was the only person who was allowed to address him by that term.

'Next time we should try the dosa and sambar.'

'Sisterfucker, I had enough of that for a lifetime when I was in college!'

Bunty snapped his fingers, and their waiter came hurrying over.

'Don't tell me you've given up on sweets as well?' he asked Arjun.

They ended up having warm gulab jamuns soaked in sugar syrup. As they ate their dessert, Arjun asked, 'What's a good hospital to take an elderly person for a full check-up?'

'Your mother or your father?'

'My father.'

'You can take him to Apollo. I took my father there some time back. How's he?'

'Okay, but he's getting old.'

'A time will come when they won't be there,' Bunty said, suddenly sombre. 'It really scares me.'

It was such an uncharacteristic comment from his friend that this time it was Arjun who was at a loss for words. Then Bunty waved to their waiter again.

'Bring us our bill. I don't think our friends will be joining us.'

35

ARJUN DROVE TO HIS OFFICE, where he leaned back in the chair in his room and closed his eyes. His friend had asked him why his client had tried to have him killed. What if it wasn't to silence him about the girl, as he had thought? What if *he* was a target as well, along with the girl? The fatigue from the last few days of travelling hadn't fully left him. Just five years ago I wouldn't have been this worn out, he thought. After ten minutes, he opened his eyes and got up to wash his face. He returned to his desk and picked up the telephone to call the landline in his flat. Agnes Pereira picked up after a couple of rings but didn't answer straightaway. Arjun could hear the canned laughter from one of her television shows.

'Trying to make sure it's not anyone else?' he asked.

'I wouldn't want to answer if a girlfriend had called you, would I?'

Her answer made him pause for a moment. He asked her if she had eaten.

'I ordered a burger and fries from McDonald's,' she said.

'I hope you—'

'Don't worry, I only gave them the building number, and I went downstairs to collect it.'

'Did you see anything suspicious outside?'

'I did see two policemen going around the park on a motorcycle.'

'Really? Listen, I'll be there in a while to pick you up, so get ready, okay?'

She sighed. 'All right.'

'Agnes.'

'What?'

'Your grandmother, was she fond of Hindi films? From during her day?'

'Hah! No way. She was into jazz and Hollywood movies.'

'A Goanese in 1950s' Bombay, right?'

'Yes. She must have seen two or three Hindi movies in her whole life. Why do you ask?'

'Oh, it's nothing. See you in a while.'

He hung up and went to the outer room, where Liza was typing on her computer and Chandu was sorting the files in the cabinet.

'Aren't you all done for the day?' he asked.

'Nearly,' his secretary said. 'Just give us half an hour.'

'*Theek hai*. You managed to check those two things?'

'Yes, I did.' She looked up and flexed her fingers. 'There are *several* Royal Photo Studios in Mumbai, as you said. I spoke to a few of them. They have been around for ten, maybe fifteen, years at the most. One person said he had heard of an old studio by that name but had forgotten the location. I'll try calling up a couple more studios.'

'Hmm. And the other thing, the murdered girl?'

'Savitri Rao? *Very* shady female she was, sir. From whatever I read, she was involved with gang members and police, keeping their money for them and things like that.'

'I see. Call me when you get home, okay? I'll come by and drop her.'

'Why don't you bring her here, then drop both of us at my place?'

'I don't want her to be seen with you in public. Just to be on the safe side.'

'As you wish, sir.'

He started to say something to her, but instead turned around to ask Chandu how it was going. Ten minutes later, Arjun was driving back to his flat. Agnes opened the door and asked him if they were leaving.

'In a while. My secretary will call me when she gets home.'

'I don't think she likes me.'

'Oh, come on. You'll get along fine with her.'

He went out to the balcony to light a cigarette, and she switched off the television and followed him. The weather was pleasant, with a faint breeze. A couple of children were playing football in the park, running after the worn ball on spindly legs.

'Did you find out anything?' she asked him, helping herself to a cigarette.

'I'm working on it.'

'Was that why you asked about the Hindi movies?'

'I was just checking something. Your grandmother, your *step*-grandmother, where was she working in Bombay?'

'It was a British firm, I don't recall the name. She worked there, and one day she came back to Goa, with my mother. That's all I know.'

'Could you find out the name of the firm? From some relatives maybe, friends?'

'I'll see what I can do. We lived a very, how do I say, isolated life.'

He turned to look at her. Why did he feel that her life struck a chord with him?

'What makes you want to find out? After all these years, why not just let it go?'

'Suppose you came to know that the person you had thought of as your grandmother all along hadn't given birth to your mother, but had brought her home from somewhere, wouldn't you want to know?'

183

'I guess so.'

'Of course you would.'

They smoked in silence for a while. Arjun stubbed out his cigarette in a flowerpot.

'There's something I haven't asked you. How were you friends with Savitri Rao?'

'You want to know how I could be friends with a bar dancer who slept around with men, right? I'll tell you, I have nothing to hide. I moved to Pune when I started modelling. I told my mother I was in a college there but that wasn't true. I just wanted to get away from Goa, and I didn't want to stay in Mumbai. So I went to Pune. Savi tried getting into modelling as well, but she was heavily built. A model can be dark in this country but not plus-sized. We met and we became friends. She was a lovely, lively person. Her boyfriend took her to Mumbai telling her he would get her into the movies, but instead she ended up in a dance bar. So that's the story of Savi and me.'

'I see,' Arjun said. 'The couple in the photograph, any idea who they might be?'

She shook her head.

'Your grandmother's colleagues, perhaps?'

'I don't know. Like I said, my grandmother hardly discussed her life in Bombay.'

'Well, think about it. Anything she might have said at any point. See if you can remember.'

'Okay, detective.' She sighed loudly. 'Listen, I'm sorry if I'm being difficult. It's just . . . a strange situation. But I appreciate your help.'

'It's all right.'

'Do you want to have some tea?'

'Yes, please. Black, with some ginger.'

While she went to the kitchen he lingered on the balcony, trying to recreate in his mind the features of the stolid couple in the black-and-white photograph. How could they be connected to the woman Agnes Pereira had grown up believing was her grandmother? And what secrets had been hidden by her friend, the bar dancer? Down in the park, a maid watched on as a small boy chased a couple of pigeons.

'Tea's ready,' Agnes Pereira called from inside.

'I'm coming,' he said, unwilling to move away from the sight of the boy playing.

An image came to him: an infant, a girl, being stolen from her parents, and then being handed over to someone else in return for money. A chill went through him. He had seen evil in the course of his work, and he knew how it could corrode one's soul. Was he doing the right thing by trying to help this girl? Was he wrong to ignore Bunty's advice?

'Drink your tea,' Agnes Pereira said at his elbow, 'it'll get cold.'

'Thanks,' he said, taking the cup from her.

She took a sip from her cup, and said, 'It's a nice place you have here.'

'I suppose it's okay,' he said, and looked at her out of the corner of his eye.

He was glad she was leaving, but knew a part of him would miss her company.

36

HALF AN HOUR LATER, LIZA sent him a message saying she had got home. Arjun carried Agnes's bag down to his car and drove with her to the nearby GK-II market. He drove slowly, looking in his rear-view mirror to see if they were being followed. Greater Kailash II was now prime real estate in the capital, but nearly half of the plots had been bought by well-off Hindus fleeing the civil war in 1970s' Afghanistan, in what had then been a new development beyond the refugee colony of CR Park. The market was where a few months ago he had asked Bunty to hand over money to a cricket betting ring in the case involving the missing accountant and the butcher.

Arjun drove up towards the end of the market, noting as he did that the last remaining budget pub in the market had disappeared. His ex-wife certainly knew what she was talking about. He parked his car, looked around, and asked Agnes Pereira to get down before taking her bag out from the car. He knew that a couple of autos hung around where the lane cut away from the back of the market, and he went to one that had a square of transparent plastic in the back and said they wanted to go to the Nehru Place metro station. As the auto retraced the route they had come by, Arjun kept looking back through the transparent square.

'Aren't you being a bit too careful?' she asked.

'You think so? I saw a grey van behind us in CR Park.'

That silenced her, till the auto came out on to the Outer Ring Road and moved towards the side of the Savitri flyover to take a U-turn. They saw the van speeding away over the flyover. She muttered, 'All right, I take that back.'

From the Nehru Place metro station they went two stops ahead on the overland line and got off at the Lajpat Nagar metro station, from under which Arjun caught another auto to take them the short distance to his secretary's rented flat in National Park. He got down and helped her take out her bag. Looking up, he saw Liza's face appear over her balcony; she must have heard the racket made by the auto.

'Aren't you coming up?' Agnes Pereira asked.

'No,' he said, looking around again, 'I think it's better I don't.'

'I'll see you later then?'

'Yes. Be careful, and stay out of sight.'

He watched her go up the narrow steps at the side of the building, then waved at his secretary and got into the auto. Arjun asked the driver to drop him at the GK-II market. As the auto went swerving through the road towards Amar Colony, he replied to the message his secretary had sent him a while ago: 'Look after her. It's just for a few days. And keep an eye on what she does. See you on Monday.'

When he got back home he sprawled on the sofa and tuned into an EPL game on the television. It felt good to have the house back to himself. It occurred to him he was turning into a misanthrope. There were just a few fingers of whisky left in the bottle, and he considered going out for some more, then decided against it. It wouldn't do to give in so easily. He would stay dry today and go for the football game tomorrow. A while later, he got up to make himself a cup of tea.

Thirty minutes into the first half, he was engrossed in the game in faraway Manchester where the spectators were already bundled up in mufflers and thick jackets. The score was 1–0, and when his phone buzzed, his first reaction was to ignore it. I'll just look at who it is and call back later, he thought, and reached for the phone. It was Vishwanathan's number, so he muted the television and answered the call.

'Good evening, Mr Arora,' the familiar voice said. 'How are you?'

'Busy,' Arjun answered.

'I hope you're not giving your other clients the same service that you're giving me?'

'What do you mean? I found the girl for you.'

'I sent another of my men. Someone very resourceful, good at *jugaad*, as you north Indians might say. He found out that you were staying in the same guest house where the girl was. And that a body was recovered some distance away from Manali town. The face and hands chewed up, possibly by stray dogs. You don't have to be a genius to put things together.'

Hari? Arjun thought. No, it couldn't be him. Maybe the silver-haired ex-forces man?

'I have no idea what you're talking about,' he said.

'Where's the girl, Mr Arora?'

'In Ladakh, for all I know. Where I told you she was.'

'You're helping her, aren't you? Are you fucking her as well? That ripe, young body?'

Arjun closed his eyes and took a deep breath.

'I don't know what the hell you're referring to, Mr Vishwanathan. Now listen, I did what you asked me to do, for half the agreed price. Now stop calling me!'

'You're threatening me, Mr Arora? Do you know what I can do to you?'

'I don't know and I don't care. I don't want to hear from you again, do you understand? This case is closed!'

He banged the phone on the table and went out to the balcony and lit a cigarette, then kicked the plastic chair with the wobbly leg, sending it crashing against the iron grilles. He peered at the margins of the park, looking for anyone lurking in the dark and keeping an eye on his flat. Watching the rest of the match, he calmed down and focused on what steps he should take. On the face of it nothing was making sense, so he had to approach it from another angle. Something told him the items in the biscuit tin might hold the key.

When the game was over—a 2–2 draw—he sat down at the dining table and switched on his laptop. The first thing he looked up was adenomyosis, the condition Agnes Carvalho was said to be suffering from. It was, as Agnes Pereira had said, an abnormal condition of the uterus that caused much bleeding and pain, leading to infertility, and was frequently treated, at least in the olden days, by removing the woman's uterus. One of the main causes of adenomyosis was a botched abortion. Arjun opened the envelope which was on the table and took out the two black-and-white photographs. What could be the link between the couple and the single woman in the Bombay of over half a century ago?

And what of the earrings? It occurred to him that a jeweller friend of Sonali's might be able to get it checked. His parents' conversation came to mind, and he typed in 'Munni Hindi film actress' on Google. His father had said she had been kidnapped or murdered. There was an entry in Wikipedia, along with a sepia-tinted photograph from the early 1960s of a thin, oval-faced young woman in a sleeveless blouse and a sari, her hair piled up in the fashion of the day. He read the opening paragraph with interest. 'The actress turned into a recluse in the mid-1960s, and then in 1993 disappeared from the house in Delhi where she had been staying. The noted film director of yesteryears Babul Biswas, who owned the house, was a suspect in her disappearance, but nothing was ever proved against him.'

Arjun clicked on the director's name, and was taken to the entry on him. He was, as Arjun now remembered, a successful director from the 1950s and 1960s, a period regarded as Bollywood's golden era, when social concerns had been wedded to artistry and commercial appeal. Biswas had worked on a string of such movies, and *Toote Hue Dil* with Munni had been one of his biggest hits. The director was still alive, Arjun noted, which meant he would be in his eighties now. He returned to the page on Munni. 'She was one of the lesser-known actresses,' a famous actor had said. 'Not as well known as Meena Kumari and Madhubala and the others.' After *Toote Hue Dil* she was on her way to becoming a big star, but then stopped acting for some reason. Like a lot of early Hindi film heroines, she came from a family of dancers and musicians, people who took part in *mujra*s. As they were mostly Muslims, they had to take Hindu names to appeal to a wider audience.

Arjun read through the colourful and ultimately depressing account of her life: a family background in music and dance in which she had been trained from an early age, the family's move to Bombay after Independence, the mother—who was said to wield an iron fist over her daughter—finally succeeding in getting her a foothold in the film industry in the mid-1950s, a steady flow of films for her, culminating in the success of *Toote Hue Dil*, which dealt with the issue of women's emancipation. After that movie, however, Munni became a recluse, spending the last decades of her life alone in a house in Delhi that had been given to her by Babul Biswas, a director she had worked with. Various theories were put forward by her fans—a broken heart, a loss of interest in acting, a quarrel with her domineering mother—but Munni declined to provide an explanation, or even to talk to the press. Her disappearance after years in isolation brought forth new explanations—murder, suicide, a move to an ashram in the Himalayas, a move to a foreign country under a new identity—but when no trace of her was found, she was gradually forgotten. The entry ended with her filmography, and Arjun realized she had acted in a few films where the music had been scored by Kishore Kumar, one of his favourite singers. It surprised him that he didn't recall anything about her life.

Going through this historical life story, a sense of familiarity struck him. What could it be? When he scrolled back to the top of the page, he saw it. He took the third photograph out of the envelope, the one of Agnes Pereira's mother. Though separated by over two decades, and by colour film, there was an unmistakeable resemblance between the two women. The features of the woman in the colour photograph weren't as fine, and were slightly more prominent, but it wouldn't be far-fetched to say that they were sisters. Or even a mother and daughter. Arjun sat there for a long time looking at the two photos, then shut down his laptop.

He hardly noticed what he ate for dinner that evening. He was still thinking about Agnes Pereira's story. He finished the last of the sweet curd and then called Poppy Barua. Maybe she could tell him something about Munni. She told him she was in her room at the resort with a bottle of champagne and the new Rowling book.

'Cheers,' he said. 'Aren't you at the event?'

'I said I had a headache and got away. I *would* have got one in a while with the wretched music they were playing.'

'You sound like an old lady, Poppy.'

'I *feel* like one. How come you called? Changed your mind?'

'Unfortunately not. You'll have someone look into the Mumbai thing, won't you?'

'Haan, baba, I will. I have it noted down.'

'I just wanted to ask you about something. What do you know about Munni?'

'About who?'

'Munni. The old Hindi film actress.'

'She had disappeared from that director's house, na? It was big news back then. Nobody knew what happened to her. Why are you interested in *her*, all of a sudden?'

'I just am. So you don't know anything about her?'

'Not really, no. But you know who would? Prakash Saxena.'

'Who's he?'

'A retired professor working on a history of Bollywood. I know this because I met him a couple of days ago at the Habitat Centre. You should go see him.'

'Where does he stay?'

'Defence Colony. If you're interested, I can ask him for an appointment.'

'Tomorrow morning, if he's free.'

'I'll try and persuade him.'

'Thanks.'

'Don't thank me. Just get me something I can use, okay?'

'I will. Goodnight.'

He put on a movie and watched it for a while. Ten minutes later, his phone buzzed with a message from Poppy Barua. Prakash Saxena had agreed to meet him at eleven the next morning. Arjun then called his daughter to check that she hadn't changed her mind about their Sunday excursion.

'Of course I haven't, Papa,' she said.

'Late afternoon, all right? I have a game and then I need to meet someone.'

'Who?' she asked, and he could discern his wife's interrogatory manner in that word.

'A retired professor. Something to do with a case. I'll see you tomorrow then.'

It wasn't 10 p.m. yet, so he watched the action movie to its end before going to bed. Smoking a last cigarette at his bedroom's rear window, looking out at the dark and deserted service lane, it suddenly came to him that he had forgotten about the single Delhi number which had been on Agnes's call list which Computer Baba had given him.

37

'RUN, ARJUN, RUN! STOP HIM!'

The shouts of his teammates egged him on, but as he sprinted, Arjun could feel the tightness in his chest constricting him from drawing a full breath. He slowed down to a trot and watched the other team's striker pull ahead and, thankfully, shoot over the goalkeeper and the crossbar. Arjun's team was down 1–0, and with barely five minutes to go had pushed all its men forward, when a striker from the opposite side had broken free. Arjun being nearest to him had given chase, but had been brought up short by his smoke-choked lungs.

The remaining few minutes in the empty stadium ringed by concrete seats played out uneventfully. Arjun tried to remember how long he had been smoking. The first cigarette—or a beedi most likely—would have been in one of those schools in the north-east he had attended, government schools with rebellious students where he had learnt to depend on his strength to protect him as an outsider. Maybe when he was around ten. So that was more than three decades of smoking. It was high time he quit, or be diagnosed with cancer soon.

When the game ended, the score unchanged, they gathered in the players' shelter for the post-game routine: water bottles from the icebox, some glucose, bananas and light banter. An outsider almost everywhere on account of his Punjabi–Nepali heritage, it was here among these weekend footballers that Arjun sometimes felt most at home.

'What happened, boss, you seemed to be struggling a bit at the end.'

It was their goalkeeper, Debu, a Bengali journalist.

'I couldn't breathe properly for a second there,' Arjun said.

'I've been telling you for years, stop smoking.'

'This time I think I will.'

A voice piped up behind them, 'Smoking-woking *kuch nahi*, Arjunji is getting old.'

It was a short Assamese doctor called Gogoi with a smooth, round face and an ever-present smile. He would be around Arjun's age.

'I can still repeat my squats with you,' Arjun taunted him.

'Try *karo*,' Gogoi said, beaming at everyone.

'Yes, yes,' the others shouted, 'we want squats!'

Arjun put himself in a squatting position with his thighs parallel to the floor and his back to one of the fixed plastic chairs, where Gogoi clambered up. It was something they had tried out years ago, just after their football matches had started. Back then, Arjun had squatted with Gogoi on his back for fifteen repetitions. Now the doctor hoisted one and then another stout, sweaty leg around Arjun's neck and placed his hands on top of his head. Debu held Arjun's hands to steady him, then let go. With his hands placed lightly on his knees, Arjun raised himself up, feeling Gogoi's load falling on his thigh muscles.

He cranked out six repetitions with ease, the rest of the players keeping count. The next three he slowed down, feeling the weight on his knees, and by the tenth he could feel his thigh muscles giving up. He lowered himself and motioned for the doctor to jump off.

'Ha ha, *maine kya bola*?' Gogoi asked. 'From fifteen down to ten!'

'That's because you're ten kilos heavier! Too much pork and rice.'

'What to do, yaar, it is our national dish!' Gogoi explained with a smile.

Arjun took off his sweat-soaked T-shirt, poured some water over himself and towelled himself dry. Then he pulled on a fresh T-shirt.

'You see,' he said to Debu, 'my muscles are still okay.'

'It's stamina that counts boss,' the goalkeeper replied.

'Where it counts I still have it,' Arjun said with a wink, and then, to change the subject, asked, 'how's your family?'

'They're fine.' Debu made a wry face. 'I have to go and help my son with his maths for the final exams.'

'What class is Tarun in now?'

'Seven, getting to eight next year.'

Arjun nodded and zipped up his kitbag. He noticed that ever since his divorce had become common knowledge, his teammates avoided asking him about his family. Which suited him fine. The goalkeeper was moving away when Arjun called out, 'Hey, Debu.'

'What?'

'Do you know Prakash Saxena, by any chance?'

'Prakash Saxena . . . you mean the history professor?'

'Yes, him. What sort of a person is he?'

'A gentleman. Old-school guy. Why?'

'Oh, I have to meet him for something.'

'He'll serve you lots of wine, just see.'

'Wine?'

'Yes, his wife makes it herself.'

'How do you know that?'

'I went to his house for dinner one time with some friends.'

'Sounds promising.'

On his way out to the parking lot with Lalrinzuala, the Mizo bureaucrat, and Elias, the Khasi architect, they discussed the day's matches coming up in the EPL.

'Bring some beer in the afternoon and join me,' Lalrinzuala invited them.

'Sorry, man, have to go visit some relatives who're in town,' Elias said.

'I'm tied up too,' Arjun said.

'I've given up on you, Arjun,' Lalrinzuala said, 'you're busy even on Sundays.'

Waiting inside his car with the windows down after he put on the air conditioner he reflected on what his old friends had told him. He was losing stamina. And he didn't seem to have free time. Not that there was anyone waiting for him at home if he did. But his muscles were still strong, as was his will. He pulled up the windows and started back towards Delhi.

38

ARJUN WAS BACK IN CR Park about forty-five minutes later. It occurred to him on the way back that it was only on Sunday mornings that you could truly detect the character of an Indian city's road—minus the traffic, minus the lights and police vehicles. He took a shower and changed into a pair of jeans and worn leather moccasins, retaining the black T-shirt. It was only 10 a.m., and he didn't want to get to the professor's house early, so he made himself a cup of tea and switched on his laptop. He had already eaten a large breakfast of toast, fried eggs and baked beans before the game. Arjun searched the websites of the English newspapers he had seen in Manali, the *Tribune* and the *Times of India*, and went through their Himachal news.

Twenty minutes later, he shut the laptop, a grim look on his face. The cup of tea with the two Marie biscuits on the plate beside it stayed untouched. Instead he lit a cigarette. An unidentified male body had been found in a patch of forest on the outskirts of Manali. Its face and hands had been chewed off by semi-wild stray dogs. And another dead body had been found in the residence on the grounds of Hotel Manali Crown, a kukri driven through it. He was the father of the hotel owners, and a retired widower. Arjun remembered the silver-haired man in a green pullover, his maroon scarf always tucked into his white shirt. He had cautioned the boy Hari, but he hadn't thought about the old man. Vishwanathan had someone capable and cruel on the job. Someone who would be on his way to Delhi, if he wasn't already here.

He took the cigarette out to the balcony and looked around the park again. Nothing untoward so far. But he would have to be careful. He went to the bedroom, opened the locker inside the almirah and took out his Smith & Wesson 30-1 model .32 revolver. He loaded the gun with his Sellier & Bellot .32 long bullets and put it back. Then he called his secretary and asked about Agnes.

'Sir, she was watching TV till what time I don't know,' Liza said, sounding annoyed. 'And she's still sleeping.'

'Let her be,' Arjun said. 'She's had a rough couple of days. I'll call again later. Bye.'

As he hung up, it occurred to him that he should have given some money to his secretary to help out with the food expenses while her guest was there.

Driving to his appointment with the professor, his thoughts returned to the two dead bodies he had just read about. The first he had killed himself, in self-defence. He was glad he had been spared the sight of the chewed-up face and hands. The second was harder to contemplate. Someone his father's age, leaving behind grieving children and grandchildren. Yet another piece of collateral damage caused by him.

He came down the Moolchand flyover, took a left into Defence Colony, and drove around for a while among the two- and three-storey houses looking for the address. He finally located it down a lane near the Defence Colony market. It was a squarish, whitewashed two-storey dwelling, the veranda on the upper floor shaded by bamboo blinds and its edges lined with earthen pots holding flowers and shrubs. The simplicity of the structure was like a reminder of an older Delhi—another link to the past.

The nameplate beside the gate simply said SAXENA'S, and when Arjun opened the gate, a thin, middle-aged white man came to the front door on the ground floor.

'Professor Saxena?' Arjun inquired.

'He is upstairs,' the man said in what seemed like a Spanish accent, smiled, and closed the door.

In the driveway beside the house was a grey Wagon R, and ahead of it a dust-covered Fiat, a Premier Padmini. Arjun stood there a while looking at the old car before going up the steps at the side of the house and ringing the doorbell. Around this old house a few high-rise apartments were coming up, all anonymous glass and steel and wood.

The door was opened by a sprightly looking man with a white beard. He wore striped pyjamas and a faded blue T-shirt with the words 'Stanford University'. A pair of glasses hung from his neck by a cord, and a ball pen was placed behind one ear.

'Professor Saxena? Arjun Arora.'

'Oh, Poppy's friend. Come in, please.'

The sitting room was cool and airy, its shadows filled with all manner of handicrafts and antiques: masks, paintings, carvings, hangings. Two framed posters on a wall caught his eye: one appeared to be of a left-wing documentary on tribals, and the other of the Manipuri activist Irom Sharmila. As Arjun took it all in, an elderly woman in a starched cotton sari entered the room.

'Is this Poppy's friend?' she asked.

'Yes, his name is Arjun Arora,' the professor said.

'Sorry to disturb you on a Sunday,' Arjun said.

'Oh, rubbish,' the professor said, rubbing his hands. 'Sit down. Mala, how about a glass of wine for our guest? You do drink, don't you? I know it's early, but it's a Sunday.'

'A glass perhaps,' Arjun ventured, sitting down on a varnished wood chair.

'Excellent! Never trust a man who doesn't drink, I always say. And a glass for me as well, Mala.'

He beamed at his wife and, after she left the room, came and sat next to Arjun.

'Poppy told me you wanted some information on an old actress?'

'Yes. Munni. I believe you're writing a book on Bollywood?'

'A history of Bollywood. I always wanted to combine my subject, history, with one of my passions, which is Hindi cinema, and now that I'm retired I finally have the time to work on it. Munni, unfortunately, is just a small part of a chapter.'

'Why unfortunately?'

'Because she was so interesting! She never became as popular as she should have though. Which is why she's in a chapter on lesser-known actresses. I have to listen to my publishers too.'

'What I'm looking into is her private life. Whatever you might happen to know.'

Mala Saxena came in with a tray on which were two glasses filled with a pinkish liquid.

'Ah, here it is! Which one is this, Mala?'

'The apple one. I had bottled it in the winter.'

Something in her voice triggered old memories in Arjun.

'Here, Mr Arora,' the professor said, and handed him a glass. 'Good health!'

Arjun raised his glass and took a sip. It was surprisingly good, fruity, astringent and with a decent percentage of alcohol.

'Where did you learn to make wine?' he asked.

She replied, 'One of our neighbours in Calcutta was an Anglo-Indian lady. She taught my mother, and I learnt by helping my mother.'

Now he realized what was familiar in her voice. An old-Calcutta English. During their infrequent visits to Calcutta, he remembered one of his father's friends who worked in the railways and whose sons spoke in a similar tone.

'And then she refined her skills when we were in the US,' her husband said.

'I don't usually drink wine,' Arjun said. 'But this is very good.'

'Thank you,' Mala Saxena said with a shy smile.

'But *why* don't you drink wine?' the professor wanted to know. 'In a hot country like India, it's preferable to spirits. And the health benefits!'

Mala Saxena saved him from having to answer. 'He's here on some other work, Prakash.'

'Oh yes, sorry, I get carried away talking about my wife's wine, you know! So, the actress Munni. But before that, what do you do, Mr Arora?'

The framed posters had told Arjun that they might not be comfortable with the armed forces and detectives. And he knew Poppy Barua didn't tell people what he did for a living. He said, 'I assist in the work of a law firm. This is for a client of ours.'

'I see. Just for my own curiosity. If Poppy has referred you, I don't need to worry. By the way, do you know that as a young man I nearly studied law instead of history?'

Arjun murmured that he didn't. Mala Saxena left, saying she had some work in the kitchen. She came and placed the tray on a side table near them, and then quickly removed the pen from above her husband's ear. Thankfully for Arjun, the professor put aside memories of his student days and started on the story of the actress.

39

'WHERE DO WE START?' PROFESSOR Saxena wondered aloud. 'To begin with, how much do you know about Munni?'

'Just what I've read on the Internet.'

'Ah, but not everything is on the Internet, is it?'

'No. Which is why I'm here.'

'She was born Rukhsana Syed to a famous, or infamous rather, dancer of Lucknow, Sultana Begum, in the year 1930. Sultana Begum was what you would call a courtesan or a *tawaif*. You must have heard of the term? This was part of the culture of Lucknow when it was the centre of the court of Awadh. The nobility and the rich and important of the city would go to see these women recite ghazals, sing and dance. It was high culture though, and not just mere prostitution. They were something like the geishas of Japan, skilled in the arts. This milieu reached its peak as the Mughal Empire declined and its princes and nobles whiled away their time in the pursuit of pleasure. With the arrival of the British, Victorian mores of conduct slowly took root, and after the horrors of the 1857 mutiny, the rulers ensured that the courtesans were hidden from view. That was the beginning of their decline.'

Professor Saxena paused to take a sip of his wife's apple wine, and smacked his lips.

'Coming back to Sultana Begum. She had her kotha in the Chowk area of the city, and by all accounts she was a very talented woman. She was also supposed to be an accomplished painter. Sultana Begum herself was born in 1912. Think about that. A hundred years ago.'

'Was she from Lucknow?'

'Yes, and her mother was reportedly a dancer as well. The profession ran in the family in those days. As you can imagine, Sultana Begum had many admirers. Local traders and nawabs and small-time royalty, as well as certain English officers.'

'Do you have any photographs of this lady?'

'I have one, which I'll show you in a while. But it was taken when she was much older. Photography wasn't a common practice before Independence, or even after it. I sometimes wonder what it would have been like if people had cell phones or digital cameras in those days. The wealth of archival material we would have had!'

'But there would have been less mystery that way.'

'True. One's imagination and a thorough investigation can reveal hidden truths.'

It seemed to Arjun as though the professor was referring to the case he was on.

'Sultana Begum, did she have any brothers or sisters?'

'She had an elder brother. He lived in Lucknow all along. Later in his life he became a cloth merchant.'

'Was Sultana Begum married?'

'Yes. Twice. And both times to musicians. The first was a Hindu, and the second was a Muslim. I think she had a son with her first husband, and he died at an early age due to some sickness. That marriage fell apart, and then she married the other chap. He was a tabla player from Allahabad called Firdaus Syed, nearly fifteen years older than her. It is believed Sultana Begum's mother fixed the match. This was in, let's see, yes, in the year 1929.'

'She would have been just seventeen then?' Arjun observed.

'Exactly. A good listener, I like that. You must remember that in those days a girl by the age of sixteen was considered a woman—ready to be married off and bear children. I could tell you so many stories about the fate of women in those days. But coming back to the story, Sultana Begum married a second time in 1929, and gave birth to a daughter a year later. She was called Rukhsana Syed, as the musician's title was Syed. He claimed to be of Arab lineage, but there is no way of verifying that. After the death of her son, Sultana Begum's devotion to her daughter was absolute. It was something the musician didn't like. Apart from that, he had a problem of his own, which was that he was overly fond of the bottle.'

Professor Saxena paused again, this time to check a message that had arrived on his cell phone.

'One second, let me answer this,' he said.

Arjun swallowed the last of his wine, and wondered if he would be offered a second glass. He looked around the sitting room: among the decorative items he could spot a brass *xorai* from Assam, wooden dragon masks from Bhutan and bamboo mugs from Nagaland.

'Sorry, where were we?' the professor asked.

'The second husband had a drinking problem,' Arjun said, impatient now to get to the daughter's story.

'Ah yes. The drunken musician. And besides that, with the independence movement spreading across the country, things were getting even tougher for courtesans and their patrons. The family's fortunes dwindled, and at one point, somewhere in the mid-1930s, Syed went back to Allahabad. But Sultana Begum was not some weak, helpless woman. She soon found herself a new protector, a British army major by the name of Montgomery Edwards. So even though her public appearances had dwindled, she was helped financially by Major Edwards, who was then posted in Lucknow. This allowed her to spend time with her daughter, whom she began to teach singing and dancing, as a sort of future insurance. From what I gathered during the course of my research, Major Edwards, even though he had a wife and children back in England, was very fond of Sultana Begum. There was talk that he even planned to leave his wife and settle down in Lucknow. But who knows if that was a story spread by Sultana Begum herself? Fast-forward to the Second World War. Around 1942 or '43, Major Edwards was sent to Burma, from where he never returned. Sultana Begum's finances were in bad shape again. By now Syed had died in Allahabad due to his drinking. Rukhsana Syed was growing into a beautiful young woman, learning the arts of singing and dancing and poetry from her mother. And wouldn't the mother, with her hard commercial streak, have seen the potential in her daughter?'

'I'm sure she would have,' Arjun said, fascinated. 'So she had already started performing by then, the daughter?'

'Oh no. Sultana Begum was far smarter than that. She was grooming her daughter for something bigger. After the end of the Second World War, when her daughter was sixteen, and when she must have realized Major Edwards wasn't going to come back, she decided to move to Bombay, to look for work in the film industry. By then the Hindi film industry had grown in size, and producers were on the lookout for new actors, technicians, make-up artists and musicians. Lucknow was one of the places that supplied artistes, and someone Sultana Begum knew wrote to her from Bombay suggesting she come over.'

'So mother and daughter moved to Bombay just before India's independence?'

'Not straightaway. Sultana Begum's mother was ailing, and by 1946, people knew the British were going to leave soon. The old lady passed away a couple of months before Independence.

Then came Partition and all the massacres. Many families from Lucknow moved to Pakistan. In December of that year mother and daughter caught a train to Bombay. So you can say that 1947 was as momentous a year for Rukhsana Syed as it was for our country.'

40

THE PROFESSOR PAUSED FOR ANOTHER sip of wine. Arjun's hopes of being offered a second glass were ebbing by now. The story moved forward.

'In Bombay, they stayed for a while with a family friend of Sultana Begum's, before renting a room in the city's Byculla area. The early years were tough for mother and daughter. Sultana Begum, though still striking, was now in her mid-thirties. It was too late for her to start as an actress and she knew it. Somehow, she got the odd role here and there, taught actresses and extras dance steps, and even did backing vocals on a few songs. The daughter had grown taller and was even more stunning now. But she had to wait a long time to get what Sultana Begum was after ever since they had arrived in Bombay.'

'An acting assignment.'

'Not just an assignment, Mr Arora, a starring role.'

'But she was good-looking, and knew how to sing and dance.'

'True, but even at that time, when in people's minds the film industry wasn't a place for respectable girls, there was still competition. For the money, for the glamour. And there were always people willing to go the extra mile. Finally, in the year 1952, four years after they had set foot in Bombay, a north Indian producer called Jivan Nath showed an interest in Rukhsana

Syed. Sultana Begum, who was forty by then, was asked to come and attend meetings regarding a big-budget movie Jivan Nath was planning. Gradually these turned into visits in the evening, from which Sultana Begum would return late at night. A few weeks later, when the roles were announced, Rukhsana Syed's name was missing.'

Professor Saxena shifted in his chair, and gave Arjun a sad smile, waiting for the implication of his words to sink in. After a while he resumed.

'I've often wondered about that period in their lives. Imagine the daughter cooking the evening meal and waiting for her mother to come home. When she got home, after being used by the producer, she would have to put on a smile and describe all the great things that were going to happen to her daughter after the movie came out. Maybe they even rehearsed parts of what they imagined Rukhsana Syed's role would be. And then the news from the producer, and the bitterness.'

The professor lapsed into silence. Outside, a car drove past with loud Punjabi rap playing. Arjun asked, to rouse the professor from his reverie, 'But she did eventually manage to get a foothold in the industry?'

'Yes, she did, eventually. But that experience would have scarred both mother and daughter, made them trust no one. They carried on as before, but now Sultana Begum was colder than ever. She made her daughter start working in small parts, no longer content to wait for that one big role. That was when her name was changed to Munni, to make it more acceptable— after Partition—to the largely Hindu audiences. As she started to get more work, their finances improved. And this was when the mother began running her daughter's life with an iron fist. It could have been to ensure her daughter didn't get hurt, and also for assuring her own financial security as she grew older. Three years later, in 1955, Rukhsana Syed got her first starring role, in the film *Qayamat* directed by S.K. Gulati. It was one of those early Hindi thrillers.'

'What sort of a reception did it get?'

'Nothing great. It was your average run-of-the-mill movie. But it allowed Rukhsana and her mother to get a foot into the Bombay studios—and there was no looking back from that point on. Soon she had a secretary, a house in Bandra, and a car as well. And controlling everything was Sultana Begum.'

'What car did she buy?' Arjun asked. 'And did she drive it herself?'

'I'm not sure, it was some American model. She must have had a driver.'

'Okay. And what was the secretary's name?'

'The secretary? Let me see, I think it was someone called . . . Mr Palekar.'

'I was just curious,' Arjun said.

Professor Saxena nodded. 'In 1960, she got a part in *Toote Hue Dil*, directed by Babul Biswas, with whom she had already done a few films. It was released around Diwali the next year and was a big hit. Even though she was the co-star, it was Rukhsana's performance that everyone talked about. She had reached the top rung of Hindi film actresses, and Sultana Begum, who was close to fifty now, finally seemed to have reached a comfortable place in life. But, as you know, that wasn't to be.'

'Something to do with Rukhsana's private life?'

'Definitely. You know, I believe that people with talent who have to struggle much longer than is normally required to get their dues end up with some sort of inner damage that makes their lives very difficult—even after achieving success. It's almost as if they could only be content while still struggling to make it. A couple of months after the release of *Toote Hue Dil*, and with offers for starring roles in hand, Rukhsana Syed and her mother disappeared.'

Arjun leaned forward towards the professor. 'For how long?'

'Oh, a couple of months. When they showed up again in Bombay, the press went crazy. I was in school here in Delhi then, and I read about it in the papers. I remember because that was when the India–China war was on as well. I don't think you were born then. We were routed up in the passes of what was called NEFA. Arunachal Pradesh. It was a blow to India, and it's hard to imagine now the mood of despair that settled over the country.'

'A couple of months? Did Munni, I mean Rukhsana, have anything to say about it?'

Professor Saxena shook his head, and sat back in his chair. Looking at him, Arjun realized the man would be around his father's age, maybe a few years younger, but from a more privileged background. The professor continued, 'Neither mother nor daughter had anything to say about it. The same went for her secretary, who had been seen a couple of times around Bombay. There were many rumours, of course. I think it was one of the first celebrity scandals in independent India.'

'Why a scandal?'

'There were several rumours, but it was generally accepted that she must have gotten pregnant, and then terminated the pregnancy, or her mother, who ruled her life, made her do so. Or she lost the child at birth. Keep in mind though that there was no news of a pregnancy, and how could there be? She wasn't married.'

'Or the child was born and given away,' Arjun said. 'Since she was missing for a couple of months.'

'That was one of the rumours too. But I doubt it, looking at what happened to her next. After a few half-hearted shoots for her films, she stopped showing up. It was soon revealed by one of the newspapers that she had moved to a house in Delhi owned by the director Babul Biswas, and had quit both the

Hindi film industry and Bombay. I think Biswas must have used his contacts to stop the newspaper from reporting where his house was. It became known much later, by which time people had lost interest in her. If she had been upset about giving away her child, she could have brought it back.'

'And what happened to the mother?'

'She went back to Lucknow. Her daughter must have forced her to.'

'So the director Babul Biswas might have been involved with her?'

Professor Saxena shrugged. 'He had a reputation in Bombay and Calcutta as a ladies' man, and by all accounts he was interested in Rukhsana. But I doubt he had anything to do with her. He was a professional, and he didn't romance his actresses. Besides, Sultana Begum wouldn't have allowed it.'

'So who were the other men?'

'The person she was supposed to have been involved with before that first disappearance was a friend of Babul Biswas's. A fellow called Riyaz Sheikh, a businessman from Delhi who had invested in Biswas's films. He was rich, and Muslim, but he had a wife and children back in Delhi. It might not have been such a problem, what with polygamy still around back then, but I think Sultana Begum didn't like him and tried to keep him away from her daughter.'

'Was there anyone the mother *did* approve of?'

'There were a few: Raj Bedi the actor, a politician named Dinesh Chadha, and even an English businessman called Jones. The mother had a soft corner for the English.'

'For her to get pregnant, she must have had to get away with the person, regularly maybe. But you said her mother kept her in a tight grip.'

'True, but as she grew more successful and more money came in, she started getting more assertive. She bought another flat and another car, and her mother was living a life of luxury. Sultana Begum had to loosen her grip a little. But look how it turned out in the end.'

It was a grand tragedy, Arjun thought, reaching for something and then achieving it, only to have that destroy your life. It was a story that somehow appealed to him.

'So in 1963 she came to Delhi,' Arjun said, 'and turned into a recluse?'

'That's right. For more than a decade there was no news about her. Then sometime in the mid-seventies, just before the Emergency, a newspaper reported that she was staying in a house in Sundar Nagar. Babul Biswas's house. There was a bit of interest for a while but then it died down. One reason for that could have been that she had never been a true pan-Indian star; another was that she hardly did anything. The newspaper found out that a couple from Lucknow living in the house did all the housework and shopping, and that Rukhsana only left the house thrice a week to attend a meditation class.'

'And then the next time she's in the news is when she disappears?'

'Correct. In 1993. The husband of the maid came forward to write a complaint that Rukhsana had disappeared from the house one night. The police investigated but nothing ever came of it. After three decades in that house, she had vanished.'

'The couple from Lucknow?'

'They were interrogated, but in the end they were let off. As for the rumours this time, well, I'm sure Wikipedia must have given you all the theories.'

'What do *you* think happened?'

'I don't know. Maybe she walked out of the house and left for someplace else. Maybe she was murdered by someone for her money. I really don't know. But that was almost twenty years ago, and if you're here now on behalf of a law firm, then you might have some information about her, am I correct?'

The professor looked into his eyes, and Arjun cleared his throat and moved in his chair.

'It's just that there's a case which seems to have an indirect link to Rukhsana Syed. And since the matter hasn't come up in court yet, I'm sure you'll understand that we have to maintain a certain degree of confidentiality.'

'Oh yes, of course. But, as I said, her life holds an interest for me, so I might be able to help out.'

'That's why I came to you. By the way, you mentioned you had a photo of the mother?'

'Yes, I do. Let me get it for you.'

Professor Saxena left the room. Arjun took out his phone and checked the time. It had been a long conversation. And that single glass of wine had left him badly needing a drink. In his mind he went through the main characters in Rukhsana Syed's story. He would have to take down the notes later in the day, so as not to lose anything. The professor returned a while later and handed Arjun a black-and-white photo.

'Here she is, one of the few photographs of Sultana Begum.'

It looked like it had been taken inside a studio, with lights and props visible in the background. A group of five people, two men and three women, all smiling, as if they had successfully wrapped up a shoot. One of the women was Rukhsana Syed, aka Munni, her hair done up in a bouffant, and one of the men Arjun recognized as Babul Biswas, dressed in dark trousers and a white shirt with rolled up sleeves. Sultana Begum was at one end, a tall, imperious woman with a haughty stare. Arjun looked closely at her face. The bone structure no doubt was somewhat similar to Agnes Pereira's. He realized she would have been a stunning-looking woman in real life; the camera made the planes of her long face look too harsh.

'This man and woman,' he asked, pointing, 'who are they?'

'Riyaz Sheikh and his wife. It must have been the first or second time he met Munni.'

'I see. Quite a striking woman, the mother. When did she pass away?'

'It seems she's still alive somewhere in Lucknow. A fellow film aficionado had told me. No one knows where she stays though, and I don't know if it's just a rumour. I would have liked to go and dig around, but as I said, Munni is just part of a chapter in my book.'

'Lucknow?' Arjun said, remembering the city he had visited years ago while still in the army. 'But that would mean she's, what, a century old?'

'Yes, a hundred years old. Can you imagine? Living history. If she's alive, that is.'

From inside the flat, Mira Saxena called out to her husband, 'Are you going to get me my chicken from the market?'

'Yes, I am!' he shouted back, then said to Arjun, 'Sorry, some guests coming over for lunch.'

'I'll make a move as well.'

'You should go and have a look. Lucknow.'

'Well, let's see,' Arjun said. He had come here out of curiosity really; who knew if there was anything to it? He glanced at the photo again before handing it over, and something caught his attention. The earrings Sultana Begum was wearing—could they be . . . ?

He said, 'Can I . . . keep this photo for a while?'

'Why not? On one condition though.'

'What's that?'

'You let me know if you find out anything. All right?'

'Sure, that should be okay.'

He stood and shook the professor's hand. 'Thank you. You've been very helpful.'

'Anytime, Mr Arora.'

'One last question.'

'Go ahead.'

'The address of the house in Sundar Nagar?'

Saxena told him, and then opened the front door for him. Arjun walked down to the street and got into his car. As he drove away, he saw the professor standing on the landing and looking down at the street. For some reason he reminded Arjun of the manager outside Bharat Lodge in Mumbai.

The story might not be connected to the Agnes Pereira case, but Arjun found himself wondering where Munni might have disappeared.

41

HE DROVE TO THE DEFENCE Colony market and went up the stairs of the building beside the cramped parking lot. At the bottom was an open kebab restaurant, above it another restaurant, followed by a two-level restro bar or lounge bar or whatever its new avatar was supposed to be. Arjun went to the top storey and out to the little terrace where he sat at a table for two, lit a cigarette, and asked for a gin and tonic. It was a Sunday, after all.

Most of the tables around him were taken by young people, some smoking, some sitting outside with the weather just about allowing it. He watched them talk and laugh as they swiped their touchscreen phones; it was like watching another species of humans. Rhea would fit in here with them, but she was different, his own flesh and blood, and as complicated as him. His drink came, and he downed half of it at one go. Now that he was here, he didn't feel like hanging around for too long. He went through the professor's story again in his head. Putting it together with Agnes Pereira's account, Arjun wondered if there wasn't a slight chance that Munni had given birth to a daughter who had ended up being adopted by Agnes Carvalho. But how exactly could it have happened? Caught up as he had been in the professor's strange, old narrative, there were things that he had forgotten to ask. In any case, he could call up Prakash Saxena at night, when he was typing out his notes of the meeting. On the face of it, he had not got any real leads—apart from the fact that the missing actress's mother might still be alive in Lucknow. Should he go and have a look? It was his intuition prodding him on, and he knew better than to ignore it. Still, he couldn't discount the fact that Agnes Pereira, or someone known to her, might have taken Savitri Rao's life over the money Vishwanathan claimed to have lost.

He finished his G and T and asked for a repeat. As he drank, he thought of Munni's life. Something traumatic had happened to her just as she had reached the top rung of her profession, something so wounding that she had gone into a self-imposed exile for thirty years. And yet, after the harshness of the performing life, and being under her mother's control, those years she had spent on her own with the visits to the meditation centre might have been the happiest of her life. So had she walked out and disappeared, in which case she might still be alive somewhere, or had someone killed her? He took out the photo he had taken from the professor and studied it. Sultana Begum's earrings: Arjun couldn't really make out from the photo. He finished his drink and went down a floor to the cash counter to pay the bill. The prices made him wince—this was a city for the rich.

Driving back to CR Park, he put on Led Zeppelin and stepped on the accelerator. It had been a while since he had listened to his favourite band. Back at his flat he dug out his magnifying glass and studied the photograph. His initial impression was correct: Sultana Begum was wearing a pair of earrings similar to the ones he had with him. There were too many connections to be ignored. It looked like he would have to travel to Lucknow, after all.

For lunch he made himself three ham-and-cheese sandwiches. He put on a repeat game from the German football league and ate the sandwiches, washing them down with a glass of juice. He felt like having some ice cream or sweet curd after that, but didn't have any in the fridge, so he had to settle for a half-eaten bar of chocolate he found behind his bottles of chilli pickles on the dining table. It was a quarter to three now, and he watched a part of the second half of the game before leaving the flat at 3 p.m.

It took him half an hour to get to Canning Road via the India Gate roundabout. As he waited at a red light, a brand-new hoarding for a residential project in Greater Noida called the Platinum Court Towers caught his eye. Driving away as the light turned green, he tried to recall where he had seen that name recently. He parked a little way down the street from the apartment building where Rohit Khanna had his duplex. Rhea picked up the second time he called and said she was on her way down. Waiting for her, Arjun looked around. This was only the second time he had come here to pick her up. With its blocks of government flats and its proximity to India Gate and the Supreme Court, there was something grim and lifeless about this part of town. Not that Rohit and Sonali would notice it, Arjun thought.

He saw her in the rear-view mirror walking down the pavement towards his car, engrossed in her phone as usual. She was dressed in a light-green and light-blue salwar kameez, something he had rarely seen her in, and she seemed to have grown even taller.

'Hi, Papa,' she said as she got into the car. 'How are you?'

'Alive and kicking,' he said as he turned the key in the ignition. 'What have you done to your hair?'

Her free-flowing mane was now flat and glossy, cut to a bang at the front and in an angle at the sides, coming down from her ears.

'Do you like it? I'd got it cut for a fashion shoot.'

'It looks . . . interesting. What sort of fashion shoot?'

'A *proper* one. Mama knows the owner of the design label.'

'So you're thinking about this seriously? I mean, after college?'

'I don't think so. It all seems so . . . I don't know, shallow.'

Arjun smiled to himself. He wondered what Sonali would say if she heard that.

'What are you smiling at?' Rhea asked.

'Me? I wasn't smiling.'

'Come on, I saw you. What, you think I can't guess? Have I told Mama about it? No, I haven't. She still thinks I'm going to become the next Indian supermodel.'

He allowed himself a grin this time. It felt good that his little girl still confided in him.

'Become a supermodel, marry a rich industrialist, travel to Paris and London, you don't want any of that?' he asked.

'Nah. I have other plans.'

'Really? Like what?'

'I want to go to America to study. Sociology, history, something like that. I haven't decided yet.'

Why had he assumed that she would want to hang around in Delhi forever, as he had done? Life was one long process of letting go; he of all people should know that well. I need to find a place somewhere up in the hills, he thought. One day it would be time to retire, to bid farewell to this city and this life.

'So you'll be out of my life then,' he said, trying to sound flippant.

'Don't be so dramatic. There's the Internet. And I want to return to India later on.'

'Good. Then you can look after me when I'm old.'

'But before that, I want to spend a year doing some travelling and writing.'

'As long as your mother allows you to,' he muttered, but Rhea pretended not to hear.

He was coming down Aurobindo Marg, and carried on straight instead of taking the left that headed towards Andheria Modh. The top of the Qutb Minar was visible ahead of them. He was curious as to what had happened between Sonali and Rohit Khanna, but since Rhea seemed to have forgotten about the matter, he decided not to rake it up. Leaving the car in the parking area outside the Qutb complex, he bought two tickets from the counter and they went in. It being a Sunday, there were quite a few people around. It had been a while since he had been here, but that initial sight of the massive lower storey of the minar tapering upward had lost none of its power to impress.

'Magnificent, isn't it?' Arjun said. 'The highest minaret in India, seventy to seventy-five metres high. Too bad you can't go up any more.'

Rhea pointed to the closed doorway. 'So they used to let people climb up to the top?'

'Yes. Your mother and I did it once. I remember there were 379 steps in all.'

'Wow, that's a lot of steps,' Rhea said, angling her phone upward to take a photo. She asked a woman to take one of her with Arjun, then looked up at the minar again.

'What are those?' she asked, pointing upward.

'Balconies. Where each storey ends.'

'No, below them. The carvings.'

'Calligraphy. Look, it goes around in a band. On the top two storeys they're done in marble, see that white up there?'

'What do they say?'

'As far as I know, they're verses from the Quran and historical details.'

Walking towards the open-plan masjid beside the minaret, Rhea asked him, 'Our professor in college told us that the minar was built as a symbol of victory and power by the kings of the Delhi Sultanate. Do you think that's true?'

'Yes. But it had a practical aspect too. It would have served as a lookout tower and as a place to announce the prayers.'

Once they were inside the masjid, Rhea wandered off on her own, taking photos of the iron pillar and the remaining portion of the prayer screen with its arches, which had a similar sort of calligraphy inscribed on them along with intricate floral designs. Watching his daughter, Arjun was reminded of Professor Saxena's remark about photography with cell phones and digital cameras. He had visited the Qutb complex twice before, first with his parents and then with Sonali, and as on those occasions, he tried to picture the people who had first swept down on their horses from the mountains of Afghanistan nearly a thousand years ago to build these stark new structures. What sort of people would they have been? A hard, driven people, with a sense of righteousness and destiny about them—a sinewy race of conquerors on horseback. He imagined a camp at dusk, the newcomers cooking their meals of meat and rice on fires, while the defeated populace watched from their tattered tents some distance away. It was strength that gave rise to power. He saw Rhea beckoning to him from within the farthest pillared cloister, and went over to join her.

'Look at the motifs on these,' she said, running a hand over a pot carved into a pillar.

'Recognizably Hindu,' Arjun said. 'What did they tell you about them in college?'

'Umm . . . that it was part of a new architectural style that combined elements.'

'They would say that, wouldn't they? These pillars were taken from several temples that stood in this area. Muhammad of Ghur and his men sacked the city that stood here.'

'I didn't know that. Really?'

'Of course, look here.' He stepped to the edge of the cloister and pointed up at a figure on a pillar. 'Some sort of goddess or devi, the face has been chipped away.'

'Oh yeah!' She looked up with interest at this new twist to an old story. 'My god, if people knew about this there would be trouble, wouldn't there?'

'I don't think so. People in our country aren't bothered with history—they're only interested in comfortable myths. Come on, let's go and have a look at the other stuff.'

The shadows were lengthening as they walked around the other structures in the complex, tombs mainly, austere and stark constructions made of the same materials used in the minar: sandstone and marble. Finally they stood before the Alai Minar, the large, rough, uncompleted first storey of a minaret on a platform.

'Delusions of grandeur,' commented Arjun.

'This was built by the Khilji sultan Alauddin, wasn't it?' said Rhea.

'Yes. He was going to build something twice as big as the Qutb Minar. Unfortunately, he died just a year or two after work began on the project, so it was abandoned.'

'We should get going, Papa.'

He could make out she was getting bored. The sun was sinking towards the horizon, colouring the smoggy air a vivid orange-pink hue.

'We could come again some other day. In the winter. Maybe have a look at the Mehrauli Archaeological Park.'

'Sure! Now I want to have some coffee and cake.'

'There's a coffee outlet right over there.'

'Not *that* one. There's a new café in Mehrauli village, let's go check that out.'

X

They came out and got into the car. Arjun drove around the Qutb complex and past the Qutb colonnade, most of whose celebrity-run establishments had been shut down, before entering the dusty makeshift parking area opposite the subdivisional magistrate's office. They walked down the narrow, crowded road towards the village.

'I hope you found it useful.' Arjun said.

'Yes, it'll be helpful for the end-of-term essay we have to do.'

'Write down your notes when you get home.'

'*Yes*, Papa, I'll do that. Look, that's another structure.'

To their right was a weathered octagonal structure with a dome: Adham Khan's tomb. Stray dogs, beggars and idlers lounged on the crumbling steps leading up to it. He watched as she positioned herself to get the structure lengthwise on her camera screen, minus the street life below it. The men looked at her with vacant eyes, their brains dulled by grass or tablets or smack.

The café was somewhere within the damp lanes of this urban village. Like Shahpur Jat and Hauz Khas, Mehrauli offered an Indian version of hipster cool. Arjun followed his daughter, content to allow her to ask for directions. They found the café and went in. It was on the ground floor, small and dark, and decorated with wood and red wallpaper in the manner of a Japanese teahouse. Arjun saw two or three couples in the gloom, and a bearded youth working on his laptop. Rhea ordered her coffee and cake, while he asked for a cup of Darjeeling tea. She busied herself with her phone as they waited.

'What are you checking?' he asked.

'Updates. Twitter, Instagram, Tumblr. And Pinterest.'

'No more Facebook, ha?'

She wrinkled her nose. Something about the phone caught his attention.

'Is that a new phone?'

'Umm. Sort of. Talking about that invasion stuff, you can't deny that a lot of good things came out of it too. Music, architecture, food.'

He saw how quickly she had changed the subject, but he decided to let it go. In fact, it pleased him in a way.

'I'm not denying it. Of course those things came about. But the people who came down on their horses from the mountains had one thing first and foremost on their minds.'

The waitress appeared then, with their order on a lacquered bamboo tray. Rhea kept her phone aside and took a spoonful of her red velvet cake.

'Want some?' she asked, but Arjun shook his head.

Rhea continued, 'It's yum. Okay, coming back to the invasion, but there were invaders all the time from the west. And Hindus from the south ventured into South East Asia as well.'

Arjun let out an exasperated sigh. 'Yes, but that still doesn't change what I said. These people came down to conquer. They didn't have an eye on the history books—they were just doing what they wanted to, what they felt they had to do.'

Rhea didn't reply, and instead lowered her head and concentrated on her cake. He saw that he had upset her. A sudden feeling of shame came over him. Since when had proving a point become more important to him than his daughter's feelings?

'Let's forget about all that, okay? Do you want some more cake?'

She shook her head, unwilling to talk just yet. Then he remembered what he had been meaning to ask her all along.

'Your grandmother wanted you to come over for dinner. What about today? We could go straight from here.'

She looked up at him. 'Today? I'm supposed to meet some friends for dinner, Papa.'

'Oh. Some other time then.'

'I want to come and see them. It's been so long. Sometime soon, okay?'

His disappointment faded. At least she thought about them. The day had gone well; there was no need to try and pack more into it. He sipped his tea, and, as a peace offering, Rhea showed him the photos she had taken. The last one of the tomb made him think of the wasted men on its steps. History as tragedy—it reminded him of the story of Rukhsana Syed.

'Have you heard of an old actress called Munni? No? There's no reason you should have. Anyway, she was an actress in the 1960s; your grandparents remember seeing her on screen. Then she turned into a recluse, and sometime in the 1990s, disappeared from a house in Delhi.'

'Disappeared? How?' Rhea asked.

'That's what I'm trying to find out.'

'Someone's asked you to?'

'Sort of. Might be connected to a case of mine.'

Arjun handed the phone back to her and waved at the waitress for their bill.

'Why did she turn into a recluse?' she asked.

Arjun shrugged. 'Nobody seems to know.'

It was early evening as he drove back with Rhea towards central Delhi. They were near Lodi Garden when her phone rang. She looked at it and cut the call. As they were going past India Gate the phone rang again. This time she answered, telling the caller in a curt voice that she was going out with friends that night. Arjun asked who it was.

'Some guy who's been asking me out on a date,' she said in an irritated tone.

'One of your old friends?'

'No, just some random guy.'

'I hope you haven't lost touch with your old friends?'

'I haven't, but at this age things keep changing, Papa.'

He had forgotten how it had been in college. Now I just have a single friend, he thought, and he's someone from my college days.

They had turned on to Canning Road when he finally brought up what had been weighing on his mind.

226

'Listen, Rhea, I know you're a big girl now and you're earning for yourself, but don't go overboard with the spending, okay?'

'I won't, Papa,' she said with a firm politeness.

He had wanted to ask her how much she got every week from her mother but decided against it. Enough lectures for one day. He dropped her near her house and said bye and watched her walk away. He wasn't a religious person, but he said a prayer for his daughter anyway.

As he drove home, Arjun played back the scene in the café. Unlike his investigative work, when it came to his opinions, he was too rigid, too stubborn. It made him a burden as a human being—a sobering thought.

Back at the flat, he turned on the lights and took out the bottle of Blenders Pride. But something made him stop. Let's see how many days I can keep going, he thought, and put it away. He switched his laptop on, made himself a cup of tea and began typing out the professor's narrative. Occasionally he wrote down a question on a notepad.

About forty-five minutes later he called up Prakash Saxena.

'This is Arjun Arora here. I'm sorry but I have to trouble you again.'

'I was expecting your call. Tell me how I can help you.'

Arjun drew the notebook closer.

'A few questions occurred to me later. The first one is about the house in Sundar Nagar. Who lives there now?'

'Well, a year or two after Munni disappeared, Babul Biswas's wife and son moved in. They were staying in a flat near Gole Market till then. Babul Biswas now lives with them, but he's close to ninety and doesn't receive any visitors. I know because I tried to meet him.'

'What about the son, what does he do?'

'Siddharth Biswas, he's an executive in a management consultancy firm. McLoyd & Company, I think it was.'

227

'Mm-hm,' Arjun said, writing it down. 'You mentioned Sultana Begum had an elder brother. Do you know anything about his family?'

'No, I don't. He died in Lucknow, so they might be there.'

'What was his name?'

'I don't know that either.'

'Munni's secretary, Mr Palekar, any idea where he might be now?'

'Sorry, no. He disappeared from the public eye along with Munni.'

'Okay. Um, Munni's admirer, Riyaz Sheikh, what happened to him?'

'I think he died a couple of years after she disappeared. His family still runs the cosmetics company he founded.'

'And the Englishman Jones?'

'Jones was jailed for running a fraudulent insurance business. I believe he left for England after being released.'

'The meditation centre you said Munni visited regularly, where was this?'

'The Natural Life Studio. You must have heard of it.'

'You mean the one in the Qutab Institutional Area?'

'Exactly. But back then it was just an ordinary meditation centre.'

'Started by the eccentric businessman Kailash Swami, wasn't it?'

'Yes. The man famous for drinking his own urine in his private jet.'

'I've heard that story. The couple who stayed with Munni, what happened to them?'

'I can't say. They disappeared, the way servants do in India.'

'What about her money? Her assets? Who controls those?'

'The two flats in Mumbai were in her mother's name. Sultana Begum—or one of her relatives—sold them after Munni

228

disappeared. The bulk of her money was in a trust which Babul Biswas had made her open. Sultana Begum tried to gain control of it, but from what I know, Babul Biswas filed an appeal and the Bombay High Court kept her away from the money.'

'It would be a considerable amount, I guess?'

'Oh yes. With the interest it's earned, there must be several crores by now.'

'I see,' Arjun said, noting down the information. 'One last question. Do you know anything about a pair of gold earrings which Munni might have worn in her films?'

'I couldn't tell you about that. See, my interest in her as an actress is historical. I think you'll have to ask someone else for what you're looking for.'

'I understand. Thank you for your time, professor.'

Arjun hung up, and started to update his file on Munni. When he was done, he let out a loud yawn, and then another. It had been a long day and he needed to get to bed. He thought of calling his secretary to ask about Agnes Pereira, but decided it could wait till the morning. Once again, he looked at the points he had jotted down on the notepad. He realized there was one more thing he had to find out: the police officer who had investigated Munni's disappearance. There were too many questions piling up. But he knew where he had to go first thing in the morning.

42

JUST PAST TEN THE NEXT morning, Arjun was walking through the M Block market in GK-I. Most shops in this cramped south Delhi market had just opened and the only people around appeared to be college girls who had skipped their classes. He looked into the outlets as he walked past: expensive branded clothes, flashy shoes and bags, a department store, a luggage store, a coffee shop. The staff, many of whom were girls from the north-east, stood around chatting or checking their phones, taking things easy before the day got busy. Arjun stopped at the black-marble-and-glass frontage of Amritsar Jewellers. Behind the reinforced glass were heavy, elaborately designed pieces of jewellery, meant for well-fed women trying to show everyone who they—or rather, their husbands—were. Sure enough, as he entered the cool, well-lit store after being frisked by a moustachioed guard carrying a pump-action shotgun, he saw two young, plump, overly made-up ladies idly browsing pieces. He asked one of the staff if Harvinder was in, and a while later, a lanky, turban-wearing sardar in glasses and a black shirt stepped out from behind a curtain at the back.

'Arjun. After a long time. Come into my office.'

Harvinder 'Harry' Bains ran the family-owned jewellery store which his grandfather had started in Connaught Place and his father had shifted to GK-I. Harry was a friend of Sonali's from school, and he had helped Arjun out in the past. When

230

in college, he had had dreams of becoming a sculptor and an artist, but in the end the demands of making a living had taken precedence.

Arjun stepped into the room past the curtain. Harry Bains sat at his desk. Behind him was a large safe, to his right a bank of six CCTV monitors showing the inside and the outside of the shop, and in front of him several forms. As Arjun sat down he felt he could understand the sorrowful expression which Harry always seemed to wear.

'Busy?' he asked.

Harry nodded. 'Sales tax matters. What brings you here?'

Arjun took the pair of earrings out from a pocket of his jeans and laid them on the forms. 'What can you tell me about these, Harry?'

The jeweller picked up the pair and examined them with interest.

'Where did you get these?' he asked.

'A client,' Arjun said.

'Are they for sale?'

'No. But I want to know more about them.'

He didn't mention the Munni connection—let Harry figure it out on his own if he could.

'I would say they're more than a century old. Or at least seventy to eighty years old. This is gold, 20–22 carat. And this black material here is most likely onyx, or it could be jet too.'

'Jet?'

'Yes, a fossilized form of coal. It was used in some types of Victorian jewellery.' Harry looked up with a gleam in his eyes. 'What you have here is most probably mourning jewellery.'

'What's that?'

'Jewellery worn when mourning for a deceased person. It could go on for years. Hence the black stone. You would have rings, brooches, necklaces, all kinds of ornaments. But always

231

with black. And if the family could afford it, gold. You've heard of Queen Victoria?'

'I have. Victoria Memorial. Empress of India.'

'She lost her husband while in her early forties. And for the rest of her life, she dressed in black, and wore only mourning jewellery. That's how it became popular in England.'

'So you think this pair came from abroad?'

'I'll have to check, but yes, it looks like it.'

'The initials at the back. Do you think they could be the owner's?'

'The double M? Might be, or they could be the initials of the jeweller who made them. Is your client selling these? I would love to add them to my collection.'

'Not at the moment, no. But how do you know so much about mourning jewellery?'

'Oh, it's just something I picked up in the trade,' Harry said. 'Much more interesting than your usual wedding sets. If you leave them here with me, I can run a test and tell you the exact age and where they're from.'

'How long will it take?'

'Say a day or two. I'll give you a call.'

'Okay, Harry.'

'What'll you have? Tea, coffee, a cold drink? I can't offer you the other drink.'

'It's all right, Harry, I have to get back to the office.'

'How are Sonali and Rhea? Give them my regards.'

'They're fine. I'll tell them. Call me when you find out.'

Arjun got to his feet and came out of the office. The two women were still trying on necklaces. Walking to the parking lot, Arjun thought about what Harry had told him. *If* the earrings were an original pair from England, what were the possible English connections to the case? There were two: Major Edwards, Sultana Begum's one-time lover, and the conman

Jones, one of Munni's admirers. Might Jones have stolen the earrings from somewhere and presented them to Munni? And how had they then landed up with Agnes Carvalho, the younger Agnes's grandmother?

The parking lot was dusty and unkempt, and near where he had left his car was a mobile restaurant on wheels offering the usual fare of chow and chilli chicken and momos. There were two young Nepali boys by the back door, one washing utensils with water from a drum and the other kneading dough in a pan. He was about to get into his car, then went back to the restaurant and asked them to pack two plates of chicken momos for him.

From GK-I he drove the short distance back to his office. His secretary and his helper had already turned up and were starting off with the week's work. He had called Liza earlier that morning, to inquire about Agnes. His secretary had sniffed and said that the girl was following her usual routine and was still asleep in the sitting room after having watched television late into the night.

'Let her be,' Arjun had said, to which his secretary had immediately retorted, 'Yes, I know, she's had a hard time.'

He was still annoyed with her response so he walked straight into his room with a curt 'good morning', and he could have sworn he heard a snort before she responded. He switched on the ceiling fan—the heat was subsiding and they could do with lower electricity bills—and turned on his laptop and checked his email. When he was done he searched the Internet for mourning jewellery. Looking at the gold-and-black-stone ornaments he realized that Harry had pointed him in the right direction. But what was the link between the earrings and the attempt to take the air hostess's life?

Pulling out his notepad, he jotted down names and possible links. Bobby and Robert Chacko. The Mehtas at the furniture store. A Delhi number: Navin Sood. A pair of earrings from England and a baby. Savitri Rao and the missing money. The answer to the question that had occurred to him between Harry's showroom and the parking lot now came to him: someone, maybe the couple in the photograph, had given a baby girl, maybe Munni's child, to Agnes Carvalho along with the pair of earrings as a reminder or proof. Who could tell him more about that? Only one name came to him: Sultana Begum.

Arjun was about to go to his secretary's desk, but something else nagged at him. What was it? Something from the previous day? Between meeting the professor and meeting his daughter. He spun the notepad around on his desk. When he closed his eyes it came to him. The hoarding for the Platinum Court Towers project in Greater Noida. It had seemed significant to him, but why? He looked it up on the Internet. It was a new project coming up near the Greater Noida Expressway, but a recent ruling by a central environmental agency had halted its construction, saying the towers had exceeded their height ceiling and were too close to a protected waterbody. With the Yamuna having been turned into an open sewer, and groundwater depleted across the area, it would appear the agency's ruling was arbitrary, but to Arjun it seemed that the money which had changed hands in the past for bending the rules was no longer helping.

The website of the project's promoters had nothing on the ruling, but Arjun suddenly realized why he had given the hoarding a second glance. It was the *name* of the project. Clicking to enlarge a photo of the promoters' brochure, he recalled seeing copies of the same on a table at the A to Z Tours and Travels office in Paharganj. Was it just a coincidence, or could there be a deeper link between the promoters and the Mauritius-registered capital firm? Before looking into that, however, he had to go to Lucknow, and before Lucknow he had to check out the meditation centre Munni used to visit.

He stepped out of his cabin and gave Chandu some money to get a thermos of tea from their usual shop in Market No. 1. Liza, whose fingers were flying over her keyboard, ignored him. Arjun placed the packet of momos on her desk.

'Something to have along with the tea,' he said.

She looked, but didn't ask him what it was.

'So had she got up by the time you left your place?' Arjun asked.

His secretary nodded, but didn't look away from her computer.

'Like I said, it's just for a few days.'

Liza stopped typing and looked sideways at Arjun.

'TV and late nights, I can understand. But she's calling someone on her cell phone and taking these tablets . . . I'm a single woman staying alone, sir. What if something happens?'

'What sort of tablets?'

'White tablets, I saw her having them last night, almost one every hour.'

Arjun recalled the strips he had seen in her room in Manali.

'Was she acting strange after having them?' he asked.

'I don't know, she hardly talks to me,' Liza said grumpily.

'Well, they could be some medicine she's supposed to have.'

'And whoever she's calling, it's so secretive. I'm telling you, sir, it's worrying me.'

'I'll give her a call and find out, okay? Meanwhile I need you to book me a ticket.'

'Sure, sir. Which film?'

'I haven't been to a cinema hall in years, Liza. A train ticket. The Shatabdi Express to Lucknow.'

'Oh. For when?'

'Tomorrow morning.'

She noted it down on a Post-it. 'What about the photo studios and Savitri Rao?'

'Keep digging.'

He went back into his cabin, and in a while Chandu came in to give him a cup of tea along with a few momos. As usual, the tea bordered on the oversweet. No matter how many times he had asked Chandu to tell the tea seller, it made no difference. He was attending to some paperwork when Liza called him on his landline.

'No tickets for tomorrow, sir. But if you want you can go day after.'

'All right. Get me a ticket.'

'And what about your return ticket?'

'I'll do that once I get there.'

He put down the receiver and looked at the incomplete forms on his table. All of a sudden, he felt restless, unable to concentrate. The moment he had shot the man in the guest house in Manali returned to him. Who knew if Vishwanathan had sent someone after him? He locked his laptop away in a desk drawer and told his secretary he was stepping out for a while.

43

ARJUN DROVE AROUND AIMLESSLY FOR a while, even as he kept an eye on his rear-view mirror. He went through Kalkaji, past Narendra Dev College into Govindpuri, and on to Alaknanda, middle-class residential neighbourhoods with the usual scattering of roadside shops. I know the roads and the names of the places, he thought, but nothing beyond that. He felt a sudden pang of sadness for something he had never been a part of: a community. Not in those small towns in north-east India, nor in the schools there. The circumstances of his background and his upbringing meant that he was always an outsider. Was that why he had become a detective? He came to Tara Apartments: if he kept going straight, he would reach the Mehrauli–Badarpur road, with the ruins of Tughlaqabad Fort nearby. He turned right and headed towards GK-II. He remembers wood-plank houses with rusty tin roofs, rain, mud, overgrown vegetation, men wearing gumboots and smoking beedis—a forgotten corner of the world. Deep in his heart was a nostalgia permanently nursed by loss. The turning for CR Park was up ahead. He had nowhere to go but his flat.

Once he was home, he took out his cell phone and called Agnes Pereira on her new number.

She answered hesitantly. 'Yes?'

'It's me, Arjun.'

'Oh, hi. I thought you were never going to call me.'

'How are you doing?'

'Fine. Dying of boredom.'

'Just a few more days, trust me. I'm working on it.'

'I think your secretary hates me.'

'Give her some time to get used to you.'

'Used to me? It's not like I'm a six-foot-two guy farting all around her place.'

'She's a bit worried about those tablets you're popping. What are they for?'

'I *need* them. They're not drugs, okay?'

'And you're in touch with someone on your phone? I told you to lie low.'

'Some personal business of mine,' she said. 'Can I come see you today?'

'Why?' Arjun asked, knowing he couldn't say no to her.

'This whole business. The dead people. I feel like I'm losing my mind. I need to talk to someone. To figure out what's going on. Do you understand?'

'Mm-hm.'

'So can I come over?'

'Not now, I've got a couple of things to do. Maybe later. Call me before you come.'

'As you say. Bye.'

For a moment he wondered if he should call her back. Instead he got up from the sofa and went back outside. Let her come over, he decided; he needed to sort out the matter of the tablets and the phone calls with her. He got into his car and turned on the ignition. Where would he go? To the starting point of the story he found himself entangled in. How ironic it was, he thought—he had been hired to track her down, and now here he was trying to help her.

As he crossed the Inner Ring Road and headed north, he thought about the information that Poppy, Bunty, Liza and

Harry were supposed to gather for him. It struck him that he was lucky to have a network to fall back upon. Maybe he wasn't as isolated as he liked to think. While he waited for them to get back to him, he had some scouting of his own to do.

Arjun went under the flyover beside the Oberoi. On Mathura Road now, he turned right into Sundar Nagar. Up ahead were the ruins of Purana Qila, supposed to be the sixth city of Delhi, and built on the ruins of the historical Indraprastha. Sundar Nagar was now one of the old-money residential areas of the capital, but Arjun had met people who remembered it as a marshland beside the Yamuna that had served as a camp for Hindus fleeing the fighting in Kashmir in 1948. There were large mansions built around small, neat parks, and the market consisted of sober handicrafts stores and coffee shops and several bank branches. Arjun drove past a guest house where he had once been called to investigate the murder of a visiting businessman from south India. He found a free parking spot near the market and walked over to the address Prakash Saxena had given him.

It was in the middle of a row of houses facing a park, and had a plain, whitewashed outer wall and a guardhouse beside a simple iron gate. The modest three-storeyed white-and-blue structure seemed somewhat out of place next to the houses with ornate balconies and high gates. Arjun soon learnt that Prakash Saxena had been correct about the former director's social schedule. As he was studying the place where the actress had lived out the last decades of her life, a wizened face with wispy white hair peered out of the guardhouse and angrily asked Arjun what he was looking at.

'This is Babul Biswas's house, isn't it? I have an appointment with him.'

'Is that so?' was the bad-tempered reply. 'There are no appointments for today.'

'My name is Arjun Arora. Check with your sahib, he might have forgotten.'

'No appointments for today!' the man repeated fiercely. 'Or for tomorrow.'

The face disappeared inside the guardhouse. Arjun took a last look at the director's house before retracing his steps. The car in the driveway had been an ordinary Maruti, unlike the sedans and SUVs he saw inside the other compounds. What did that tell him? That the director was a man of simple tastes? Did his wife and his son share that quality with him?

At the far corner of the park, on the outer side of the brick wall and railing, was a press-wallah's modest establishment: bamboo posts, a faded tarpaulin cover, a makeshift ironing board made of a plank on bricks, and a man filling glowing coals into a cast-iron press. Next to it, an old cycle leaned against the park's brick wall. Arjun had earlier walked past him without a second glance, but now the old man caught his attention. The neighbourhood press-wallah usually had a fair idea of the locality's gossip.

He stopped and asked the old man if he had a matchbox. The man nodded, propped up his iron, put a hand into his pyjamas and drew out a matchbox. Arjun took it from him, lit a Gold Flake and handed the box back. The man had a smooth brown scalp, and was lean and straight-backed.

Arjun thanked him, then asked in Hindi, 'That house over there behind the white wall belongs to a director, doesn't it?'

'Yes,' the old man said, getting back to ironing a shirt. 'A famous director from the olden days.' *Purana zamana* was the term he used.

'I went to meet him, but the guard chased me away. Wouldn't let me talk to him.'

The old man chuckled as he turned the shirt over.

'He's a peculiar fellow. But I've heard the director doesn't meet people nowadays, he's too old.'

'I wanted to find out if we could interview him for a television programme. About the actress Munni. You must have heard about her?'

The old man chuckled again as he folded the shirt and laid it on top of a stack of ironed shirts. He picked up a packet of beedis from a corner of his ironing board and lit one.

'She used to stay in that house,' he said to Arjun. 'That was a long time ago. I was still here then.'

'Really? So you must have seen her around?'

'She didn't come out of the house. People said it was because of a broken heart. But I did see her a few times. And also on the day she disappeared.'

'You saw her?' Arjun asked in disbelief.

The old man nodded, a smile on his lips as he exhaled.

'She used to go to an ashram thrice a week. A taxi would pick her up and drop her home later in the afternoon. That day I saw her coming back late. It was almost dark.'

'You're sure it was her?'

'She always wore a white sari.'

'Did you know the taxi driver?'

The old man shook his head. 'He was a new driver, from some taxi stand outside.'

'So that was the last time you saw her?'

'No, that was a while later. I finished my work late that day, and was just about to leave for home, when I saw a woman in a white sari coming from the other side of the park. She came out of that gate and went towards the market. I thought it was strange, her coming out of the house like that. I went home, and it was only the next day that I learnt from the couple who looked after her that she had disappeared.'

'Are you definitely sure it was her?'

241

'Yes, I'm certain.'

'You knew the couple?'

'Yes, they would come by to give me things for ironing. Only sometimes. Bedsheets and tablecloths, never any clothes.'

'Where are they now?' Arjun asked, sensing a breakthrough.

But the old man shrugged. 'Who knows, they must be dead by now. The police kept coming to question them. One day they just left the house and caught a train back to Lucknow.'

'Do you remember their names?'

'The man was called Bholu. The woman's name, I've forgotten.' He flicked away the end of his beedi. 'It happened a long time ago.'

Arjun could sense the man starting to close up again. One last thing to find out.

'That house, did it ever have a back gate?'

'No, there was always a wall at the back.' The old man shook a pair of trousers and laid it on his ironing table. 'He's a Bangali, the director. He doesn't meet people any more.'

'I'll have to try again,' Arjun said. 'Thank you for the matches.'

Arjun walked back to his car and drove out on to Mathura Road. He cut south diagonally across the city, and stopped at the INA market to have some fish curry and rice for lunch at a small Malayalee restaurant. One door had closed on him, but another had opened. You just have to keep trying. So the actress had come back late from her meditation class and then walked out of her house. Had she met someone, and then gone out a second time to meet that person again? An old lover, perhaps? From INA he carried on down Aurobindo Marg, and then turned right on the Jawaharlal Nehru University road. His next stop was the meditation centre the actress had frequented.

44

THE QUTAB INSTITUTIONAL AREA LAY to the north-west of the Qutb Minar and the area known as Lal Kot—the first city of Delhi. Beside it was the hilly, scrub-covered campus of the university. The institutional area, as its name suggested, had the offices of several foundations and centres and institutes amid its greenery. The Natural Life Studio, as it was now called, had been one of the first to move into the area, and now occupied a large plot that bordered the fringes of Lal Kot. As he drove towards it Arjun tried to recollect what he knew about the studio. Starting out as a meditation centre run by one of India's early business tycoons, a man by the name of Kailash Swami, the place had expanded and turned into a professional wellness centre. Kailash Swami himself had earned a reputation for eccentricity over the years, drinking his own urine and growing his own vegetables even as he flew around in a Gulfstream jet. Part of his studio's appeal was its reputation as an exclusive networking environment, where the movers and shakers of Delhi could work on their deals even while detoxifying. For those who couldn't afford the expensive residential fees, there were lifestyle books and products and CDs. What had been a modest retreat in the actress Munni's time was now a high-end lifestyle brand.

Arjun turned on to a narrow road that ran for a short distance between tall hedges, with trees beyond them. The road turned to the left, then to the right, and a high gate came into view. He spotted CCTV cameras atop both columns of the gate. A brick wall topped with barbed wire stretched away on either side. There was a portacabin by the gate, and a uniformed guard holding a walkie-talkie stepped out to ask Arjun what he wanted.

'I've come from a television production company,' Arjun said. 'We want to do an interview with Kailashji.'

'Do you have an appointment?' the guard asked.

'They told me to come and inquire at the reception.'

He opened the glove compartment and took out a laminated photo ID card and a visiting card. Both were in the name of Ankit Ahuja, producer, Global Asia Productions. He handed them to the guard, who studied Arjun, the cards and the silver-grey Swift, before raising his walkie-talkie and moving back towards his cabin.

The name was one of Arjun's aliases. He had his phone number in that name against an address at the German Embassy, New Delhi; he had stopped his paper bills and paid online each month. Global Asia Productions had been a stillborn business venture of Bunty's, but it still had an address and a phone number (of what was now Bunty's bathroom fittings factory), and even a basic website, still functional but without any names. Arjun could see the guard still studying the cards as he spoke. Then he came back to the car and returned the cards to Arjun.

'Okay, you can go in,' he said.

A moment later, the gates swung open and Arjun drove in, only to be stopped at another portacabin with several guards standing outside. Here they checked the car (and him) using under-vehicle mirrors and handheld metal detectors, before waving him on. The level of security came as a surprise to him. But then they did have high-profile guests inside.

Arjun turned the Swift left into a paved parking area where among the other vehicles were three white Toyota Fortuners with tinted windows. As he got out of his car, he spotted at least three more CCTV cameras up on the lamp posts. The main building was directly in front, a long, low structure with an overhanging roof that reminded him of a tea garden clubhouse. Nowhere were the words Natural Life Studio to be seen. The brand consultants must have impressed upon Kailash Swami the need for understatement. Inside, it was airy and well lit, and a girl in a light-blue sari behind a desk asked him what he was looking for. Arjun repeated what he had told the guard.

'From which channel have you come, sir?'

'Not a channel. A production company. We package shows for foreign and Indian channels.'

That seemed to impress her, but she wasn't going to let him have a walkover.

'What do you want to interview Kailashji about?'

'We're producing a documentary on the old Hindi film actress Munni.'

'The one who disappeared?'

'Yes, her. She used to come here for meditation classes. So we'd like to talk to Kailashji about his memories of her.'

The girl frowned, and turned to look at the office behind her. This was obviously not something she had dealt with before.

'He usually doesn't do interviews,' she said, 'but if—'

Her sentence remained unfinished as the telephone on her desk beeped. She picked it up, and Arjun could see her body immediately stiffen.

'Yes, sir,' she said, 'yes, sir . . . no, sir . . . yes, sir.'

Who could it be? Arjun looked up, and saw two CCTV cameras pointing at him. The girl put the receiver down gingerly, then said, much to Arjun's surprise, 'Kailashji wants to see you.'

She hadn't even asked him his name. Someone seemed to have noticed him.

'Did you mention the interview?'

'He wants to meet you first,' she said, and pressed a buzzer on her desk that summoned from the office behind her a young man in a light-blue uniform.

'Was that Kailashji, the person who called you?' Arjun asked, but the receptionist was already giving instructions to the muscular, earnest-looking young man.

A class of some sort appeared to have finished, for a group of people in white saris and white kurta pyjamas came down the corridor from the left, smiling and talking.

'This is Harmeet,' the girl said to Arjun. 'I've told him to take you to Kailashji's residence. Please follow him.'

'I will. Kailashji stays here in the compound?'

'Sometimes, yes. He has a house here. It's right at the back.'

'I see. Just one thing . . . when were all these new buildings made? Earlier this was just a meditation centre, right?'

'Yes. This was the first building, in fact. The other buildings were begun after the mid-eighties. The plot was expanded and Kailashji built his residence in the early nineties.'

'Thank you for the information,' Arjun said, and flashed her a smile.

The mid-eighties were when Delhi had begun expanding with new money, after the Asian Games, and the early nineties were when the Indian economy had been opened up. Kailash Swami's studio had been well placed to take advantage of the favours provided by its influential clients, no doubt in return for other services.

Arjun followed Harmeet along the corridor to their right, passing the studio's lifestyle store. A tall woman in slacks and heels with blonde streaks in her hair was examining what appeared to be a bar of natural soap. They came out into the sun. In front of them was another similar structure.

'What's that for?' Arjun asked Harmeet.

246

'They have classes there,' the guide said curtly, turning left along a pathway that wound around the building they had just exited before straightening out and leading to a gate set in a low brick wall topped by more barbed wire. A uniformed guard stepped out of a cabin beside the gate to frisk them. The same uniform as the guards at the main gate, but this one wore a holstered pistol. A second guard opened the gate, and then they were in the inner sanctum of the Natural Life Studio.

What surprised Arjun was the space: an immense lawn stretching all the way to the back, with a line of small cottages on the left, each with its own manicured hedge in front. It seemed like something from an American movie: an exclusive retreat for the well-to-do. Maybe that was where Kailash Swami had got the idea from. He counted eight cottages, and at the far end, three low buildings like the ones outside, one after the other. To the right of the lawn was a tree-shaded walk at the end of which was another walled enclosure, from behind which rose an elaborate white mansion—probably the Swami's residence.

The guide led him down a path that skirted the trees. Attached to each tree was a small board with the tree's common and scientific name, as in a government park. Arjun noted the higher walls in this inner compound, a large transformer hoisted up on poles between the trees and the mansion's walls, and the discreet security booths with faces looking out. Curiously, they seemed to be the only people about. He thought of asking the guide a question, but held his tongue. He was lucky to have got straight inside; no sense in spoiling things now.

They reached the small, iron-barred gate set into the walled enclosure. It gave a view of the marble-clad mansion and had a CCTV camera above it. Another pair of security guards— how many of them were around?—let them in, and Arjun saw a gravelled driveway to the right of the house that ran to the corner of the outer enclosure where there was a broad metal-

and-wood gate, which was probably where the Swami's vehicles came in from. As they entered, he could see the edges of another lawn at the back of the house. To the left was a large cemented circle with red and black markings that Arjun recognized as a helipad. Beyond it was what appeared to be a garage and an office of sorts.

A bald man of Arjun's height, barefoot and dressed in white linen trousers and a white cotton shirt, stepped out of the front of the house.

'So you want to do an interview with me?' he asked Arjun.

45

'YES, OUR PRODUCTION COMPANY IS interested,' Arjun said.

He hadn't expected to get to the heart of Natural Life Studio so quickly. Had someone been waiting for him? Kailash Swami regarded Arjun with a steady, unblinking gaze. He grinned to reveal a row of brilliant white teeth.

'Nice to know I'm considered newsworthy,' he said.

His voice was deep and smooth, while there was something predatory about his smile. It reminded Arjun of a shark. The impression was strengthened by his eyes, which seemed hypnotic in the intensity of their stare.

'Not news really,' Arjun said. 'We're working on a documentary on the actress Munni. That's what we wanted to talk to you about.'

The smile faltered for a beat, then returned.

'Why not? Come inside.'

Arjun turned to look but his guide had slipped away unnoticed.

'Quite a lot of security you have here,' he commented as they went in.

'For our guests,' the Swami said. 'We guarantee them 100 per cent security.'

They entered a vast, high-ceilinged room decorated with a mix of furniture, both antique and modern. A flat-screen television on a wall was soundlessly showing a train on a railway line on the Discovery Science channel. At a large wooden desk, a short-haired, feline-looking man in a white kurta pyjama was working on some papers, the computer before him showing rows of figures. There were polished wooden doors leading off to other rooms in the house.

'I didn't see too many guests,' Arjun said, following the other man across the room.

'In their classes. They have a busy schedule.'

Kailash Swami led Arjun out to a patio that ran across the back of the house. There were a couple of cane chairs around a glass table where the Swami indicated they should sit down. Flowerpots with blooms of varied colours lined the patio, from where wide steps led down to a branch of the gravel driveway, after which was the lawn, this one with rectangular beds of flowers at the far side. After that the high brick-and-barbed-wire wall with the wood-and-metal gate to the right, and beyond it the tops of *keekar* or acacia trees.

A barefoot helper appeared and the Swami asked him to get them coconut water.

'A very impressive place, I must say,' Arjun said as he looked around.

To their left, beside the lawn, the structure with the garage and the office continued, where there were carpenters working on wood, the faint sounds of sawing and hammering reaching them.

'Just something that I made,' the Swami said. 'I have no attachment to it though. Tomorrow I could leave all this and go and live in a hut by the Ganga, like I did as a child.'

He flashed that insincere smile again at Arjun, who found it hard to look away from those penetrating eyes. There was a rugged healthiness about him, a remnant maybe of his rural upbringing. Arjun recalled reading somewhere that he was in his late seventies, but in person he could pass for someone at least two decades younger.

'Where were you born?' Arjun asked.

'A village,' the Swami said, 'that no longer exists. Here's our coconut water. I believe in the natural life, Mr . . . sorry, I forgot to ask you your name.'

'Ankit Ahuja.'

'Mr Ahuja, as I was saying, I believe in the natural life. No religion, no philosophy, just exercise and meditation and fresh food.'

That smile again, and Arjun wondered if his definition of the natural life included predators and prey. He took a sip of the cool coconut water. It had been a while since he had drunk it, and the taste took him back to the hot summers in Assam, when in the absence of a fridge his mother would give him a glass of *daab* water on especially humid days.

'And other things as well,' the Swami continued. 'You must have heard about my urine therapy?' Arjun nodded, drank some more coconut water. 'One reason why I've remained so healthy. I'm eighty, but people tell me I could pass for a sixty-year-old. And I haven't fallen sick in more than ten years. You should try it sometime, Mr Ahuja.'

'It might not suit me,' Arjun said. 'I usually drink whisky.'

The Swami shook his head. 'Foreign poisons. You might consider it when your liver and kidneys start giving up. Were you ever in the army, Mr Ahuja?'

'No, I wasn't.'

'Really? There's something about your appearance. My father was in the army. He was a sepoy in the British Army.'

The smile faded, and something darker fell across his face. The moment passed.

'But why am I boring you with all this? You said you were here for an interview.'

251

'Yes. As I said, our production company is working on a documentary about the actress Munni. We wanted to talk to you about her. Would you consider it?'

'Why not? You're interested in her disappearance, I suppose?'

'Yes. Plus what sort of a person she was. You must have met her?'

'I was the one who suggested that she attend our meditation classes,' the Swami said, reminding Arjun of just how far back the roots of this case seemed to go. 'When do you want to do the interview? Do you want me to come to your studio?'

'We could come here, if that's okay. Show a bit of *your* studio as well. Next week?'

'Next week? Hmm, I should be here, but I'll have to check. I keep travelling.'

'I noticed the helipad.'

'That's just to get to the airport quickly. Call the reception in a day or two, I'll let them know when we can meet.'

'Thank you,' Arjun said. 'So what sort of a person was she, Munni?'

'Munni?' The Swami exhaled and leaned back, stretching his long, sturdy arms behind his head. 'There was a purity in her, a purity of the old days. I've looked, but people don't have that nowadays. As our country has advanced, Mr Ahuja, we've lost something, and most people don't know anything about it. Everyone's looking ahead, not behind.'

The Swami's words made Arjun wonder about the vanished hamlet by the river. But was his image of Munni based on fantasy or reality?

'She had withdrawn from the world by then, hadn't she?'

'Yes, she had. People had hurt her. She needed peace.'

'Sir . . .' someone called out to the Swami.

Turning, Arjun saw it was the feline-looking man at the doorway.

252

'Excuse me for a second,' the Swami said, and hurried back inside.

Arjun ran his eyes over the property again. The lawn looked pristine, even more so than the one outside, and he thought he knew why—the waist-high fence around it continued without a break except for where the wall was at the far end. There seemed to be some exotic flowers growing in the broad flower beds at the end of the lawn. In the silence he could hear the hammering and sawing coming from the rooms at the far left. The Swami returned.

'Sorry, I had to check on something with my secretary.'

Arjun waved his hand to show it didn't matter. Kailash Swami took a seat.

'That road,' Arjun said, pointing towards the gate at the corner of the high wall. 'Where does it come in from?'

'It comes in from a road connecting Qutb to the JNU campus. In the old days, it was all open. But then I had to think of my guests.'

'How do you water your flowers?'

'Excuse me?'

'Those flower beds, how do you water them? The fence runs all around the lawn.'

'Micro-drip technology. A few ml of water for each flower morning and evening.' The Swami added, 'A friend who was in the Israeli military got it for me from his country.'

'I see.'

'Checking out your location?'

'Something like that. Kailashji, the day Munni disappeared, she left late from here, didn't she?'

A frown creased the broad forehead. 'Who told you that?'

'We've been doing our research.'

'She was helping me prepare a brochure for the institute that day—we used to call it an institute then—that's why she was late.'

'She took another taxi home after that, didn't she?'

A faint smile appeared on the Swami's lips. 'Am I a suspect in her disappearance?'

'Not at all. But you were one of the last people to see her alive.'

'Well, come next week and I'll tell you everything.'

'All right. Just one last thing, do you know if she met someone that day? Someone important in her life, someone who might have been connected to her past.'

Kailash Swami slowly shook his large head. 'She was her usual self that day, as far as I can remember. Quiet.' He stared fixedly at the faraway flower beds, and his eyes glazed over.

After almost a minute, Arjun said, 'I'll get going then, Kailashji. Looking forward to seeing you next week.'

The Swami rose and shook Arjun's hand. It was, to Arjun's surprise, a rough, calloused hand, almost like a labourer's. He seemed older all of a sudden.

Arjun walked back through the long room where the secretary was still at the accounts. His guide was waiting for him outside the gate to the mansion, and walked back with him to the reception, where there was a new girl behind the desk. He walked out to the car park.

Driving out of the studio's premises, Arjun thought about the Swami, and the disappearance of the actress. He remembered a poster for a missing biker in a Manali restaurant, an Israeli biker. As he turned on to the main road, he realized the Swami had asked him for neither the name of his supposed television production firm nor his card. And then his question to Arjun about the army—were there things the old man knew but was hiding?

46

IT WAS EARLY EVENING WHEN he got back to his flat. There were boys still playing cricket and football on the field outside; Arjun made himself a cup of tea and stood on his balcony watching them. The case—if it could still be called that—seemed to be slowly grinding to a halt. Should he just follow Bunty's advice and drop everything? But then where would that leave Agnes Pereira? Then there was the matter of Vishwanathan's man who might already be in Delhi. Arjun yawned; he felt tired. It seemed to him that by going dry he had forced his body to try and balance itself. Maybe he ought to try out the Swami's urine therapy as well. He settled down on the sofa for a short nap and was soon fast asleep. At one point he was dimly aware of his cell phone buzzing on the coffee table, but he ignored it and turned around on the sofa. A while later it buzzed again—this time he picked up.

'Are you at home? Can I come over?' It was Agnes Pereira.

'Yes. Give me half an hour.'

'Is anybody there?'

'I'm taking a nap.'

'Oh. Sure. See you in a while.'

He was awake now, but didn't get up from the sofa. Dusk had fallen, and even with just the fan on, it was slightly chilly in the room. The lights had come on in the buildings across the field. Arjun lay in the growing darkness and thought about the approaching winter: fog, and the luxury of sleeping under a blanket. The small cast-iron grill he had in the kitchen needed to be cleaned. Then he could call Rhea over for a barbeque some day. Maybe some of her friends as well.

A while later, the doorbell rang. He went and opened the front door. The stairwell light was on, and he could see she had used a bit of make-up: lipstick and eyeliner. She was dressed in a cotton salwar kameez which gave her a different look. He was looking at her, not saying anything, and she slipped in past him. Arjun knew what was coming next. He was only human, after all, a lonely man.

He locked the door and followed her into the dark flat.

She pressed a switch on the wall by the dining table and the tube light above the sofa flickered to life. There was a sombre and watchful air about her.

'Is anything the matter?' Arjun asked, but she shook her head.

'Okay. Watch some TV, make a cup of tea, if you want. I'll take a quick shower.'

As he was soaping himself in the shower cubicle, he realized she hadn't uttered a single word. He hoped she hadn't had a row with Liza. Standing under the shower, letting the water run over his body, he tried not to think of her, just a few feet away.

There was a soft knock on the door. He turned off the shower and stood still, not trusting his ears. Then another knock. He remembered he had left the bedroom door unlocked. Wrapping a towel around his waist he went to the bathroom door. 'Yes?'

'Arjun?' Something in her voice made him open the door without asking any questions.

What he saw made him involuntarily pull in his breath. She stood before him with her head slightly bowed, her lean brown body clad only in a black lace bra and panties.

'Agnes,' he whispered.

She looked up, put a finger to his lips and pushed him back with her other hand, stepping into the bathroom with him. It was all very unreal for Arjun, like something in a dream. Their lips met, teeth knocking, and he found himself responding to the hunger in her. The towel dropped to the floor and he felt her slim fingers close around him, already hard and pulsing, and start stroking him. Arjun thought he could taste cigarettes and chocolate in her mouth. She broke off to look at him, and he caught her by her shoulders and backed her against the wet wall, where he peeled off her panties and took off her bra, then taking her firm nipples in his mouth and sliding his fingers into her wetness, he made her moan. He had almost forgotten what it was like, to take, and give back, pleasure.

She wrapped her arms around him and he bent to grab her by the back of her thighs and lift her up, even as she spread her legs and freed one hand to guide him in, gasping as he buried himself deep in her. He built up a steady rhythm, the girl clinging on to his wet body, and to his surprise he found himself thinking of Sonali. Let this be an exorcism, he thought.

He drew himself out of her, not wanting it to end too soon, and guided her towards the bathroom mirror, where he made her turn around and place her hands on the marble slab with the sink before entering her from behind. Her eyes were clouded now, with lust and pleasure, and as Arjun thrust in and out of her, feeling himself inching closer to the brink, something made him grab her hair and pull it back, raising up her face for him to see. Then he turned her around, made her sit on the marble slab and part her legs for him again. When they were done, he washed himself at the sink while she picked up her wet undergarments.

She handed him the towel to dry himself.

'What was that?' he asked her, unsure of what exactly had happened.

257

'I was thinking of you,' she said, taking the towel from him. 'I needed someone.'

'Anyone?'

'No, just you.' She lifted herself on her toes and gave him a kiss on the lips.

Arjun put on a pair of boxer shorts and a T-shirt and went to the kitchen to make some tea. She put on her salwar kameez and came and sat on the sofa.

'I hope no one followed you here?' he asked.

'I don't think so. I went to South Extension first and then caught another auto.'

'Well, be careful. I think the man who hired me has sent someone to Delhi.'

'I trust you'll protect me. How's the investigation coming along?'

Something in her tone made him pause. What was she *really* here for? Or was he just imagining things?

He carried two cups of tea out of the kitchen and placed them on the dining table.

'Come here, I want to show you something.'

He switched on his laptop and opened the entry on Munni on Wikipedia.

'Have a look at this,' he said, drawing out a chair for her.

She sat down and went through the article. He watched as she got to the end and scrolled up to look at the photo of Munni, just as he had done. Then she sat back in the chair.

'Oh my god! You don't mean . . .'

'Possibly. That's what I'm trying to find out.'

She stood up, walked slowly up and down the room with her arms folded. Arjun sat down at the table to check his email. Agnes Pereira came back to the dining table.

'But it could be, you know,' she said, 'there was always something . . . lost . . . about my mother, I felt.'

She stood near him and picked up her cup of tea. He could make out her pert, little breasts under the cotton garment, and he pulled her to him and buried his face in her, feeling her hands come down to fondle his hair. He breathed in her smell of soap and talcum powder deeply. He had gone for so long without this softness in his life.

Arjun took her to the bedroom where they made love again, at a more leisurely pace. Later, as she lay in his arms in the darkened room, he found himself thinking of his ex-wife again. Agnes was the first woman to have come into his flat after Sonali had left.

'They do look similar, don't they?' she asked. 'My mother and that actress.'

'That's what struck me as well. It's a lead I'll have to follow.'

'She was someone always out of place, that's what I felt about my mother.'

'It's something I can relate to.'

'You said you were in the army. Why did you leave?'

'I punched a senior officer at our mess bar in Jorhat. They would have court-martialled me if I hadn't left. I was too independent for them, I guess.'

'Maybe being a detective suits you better. You make me feel safe.'

He grunted, not willing to tell her what he thought, that life was a random affair, and it was beyond anyone to protect someone forever. Somewhere, somehow, the inevitable would occur. A thought struck him.

'I hope you're . . . safe.'

'Don't worry, I use protection,' she said coolly. Then, 'I wish I could stay here.'

'That would be a bad idea.'

She let out a small laugh. 'Your maid would object?'

'That's one of the factors, yes. I hope you haven't quarrelled with Liza?'

'No. She's a sweet person. But too inquisitive. Maybe because she works for you.'

'Maybe,' he said. 'What are those tablets you're taking?'

'Anti-anxiety pills. I know I should quit them, but I can't right now, in this situation.'

'Navin Sood. Who's he?'

Arjun could feel her stiffen; he could guess her surprise: how does he know the name?

'So you *are* a detective. A friend from the airline. He gets me the tablets.'

'You should quit, those things aren't good for you,' Arjun said.

She said in a small voice, 'I know.'

There were other questions he wanted to ask her, about Savitri Rao, Vishwanathan's money and her friend Navin Sood, but for the moment he was content lying with her warm body in his arms. A while later her breath was short and shallow; she was asleep. Arjun lay still, not wishing to wake her. From the Civil Hospital in Shillong to this flat in CR Park—he had come a long way. He relaxes, his mind wanders, and he sees an image: his parents and him, just a child then, on a ferry crossing a vast river, the Brahmaputra most probably, the clouds reflecting off its grey-blue waters, the dark silhouette of a mountain range in the distance. Where had they been headed to? But he could recall just that image, hazy and unclear, his younger self looking across the water at the hills. He gently freed himself from her arms, and went to make himself another cup of tea.

He was in the sitting room going through the day's newspapers and drinking his tea when he got a call from Liza. Arjun hesitated a moment—did his secretary know where Agnes Pereira was?—before picking up.

'Sir, she's gone missing,' his secretary said with real worry in her voice. 'I tried calling her but her number's switched off. What to do now?'

'She called me a while ago. She's at a friend's place for the night.'

'Oh . . . so it's okay then?'

'Yes. She said she'll get back to your place in the morning. If she's not back by the time you leave for the office, keep your house key with your neighbours downstairs.'

He felt bad lying to his own secretary—but it couldn't be helped.

Soon after, Agnes Pereira came out of the bedroom rubbing her eyes.

'I was wondering where you were,' she said, almost like a little girl.

'Too early for me to sleep,' Arjun said, and patted the sofa. 'Come and sit here.'

She sank into the sofa beside him, yawned and picked up the remote to switch on the television. 'What's for dinner tonight?'

'Not sure. Don't really feel like cooking.'

'We could order in.'

'Okay.'

Part of the reason was that Arjun wanted her company, wanted to be close to her, as he knew this was a one-off encounter—their situation was untenable. He folded the newspaper and took his cup to the kitchen to wash it. When he came back, she asked, 'Not drinking tonight?'

'No. Going dry for a couple of days. You can have a drink if you want. Or another cup of tea.'

She shook her head. 'Just come and sit here.'

He sat beside her and she wrapped her arms around one of his and laid her head on his shoulder. She had put on one of her American soaps again, mindless entertainment, but somehow oddly comforting to him now. He felt like sharing something with her, so he told her about his visit to the Natural Life Studio, and the naturopathy that had been suggested to him, and his reply.

'You told him what?' she said, and burst out laughing with a fetching spontaneity.

When she had recovered, she asked him why he had gone there. He told her about the studio's link with Munni's disappearance, and what he had learnt in Sundar Nagar.

'So you think she might have met someone that day?'

'Maybe. Do you remember anything? Anything your grandmother or mother might have said?'

She shook her head. 'It's as much of a mystery to me as it is to you.'

'Well, let's forget about it for now. I'll get back on the trail tomorrow morning.'

Something had made him keep his upcoming trip to Lucknow to himself. He leaned back on the sofa and pulled her towards him.

47

IN THE EARLY HOURS OF the morning, he woke up to hear her mumbling in her sleep. He tried to decipher what she was saying, but she turned over and went silent. Arjun lay awake for a while. They had come back to the bed past midnight, after a dinner of pizza and Coke while watching a movie. Now he thought of the dhobi's little shop and Natural Life Studio from the previous day. There was something he had seen at the latter place which nagged at him—what was it? He fell asleep, waking up again to hear the maid bustling around the house. Agnes was still fast asleep, so he took out his clothes that needed to be washed and locked the bedroom door from the outside. He put the clothes into a bucket in the bathroom in Rhea's old room, and told the maid she could skip cleaning his room. She looked at him wordlessly before returning to mopping the floor. He got the newspapers from the balcony and read them—nothing about the Savitri Rao murder or a missing air hostess. Thankfully Agnes didn't knock on the bedroom door, from the inside, as the maid went about her morning routine. She left after making a few chappatis and some sabzi for him, along with a cup of tea. Arjun opened the door to check. She was still sleeping, and he decided to let her get up at her own time. Then he wandered about the rest of the flat aimlessly—it was a strange situation for a man of his age to find himself in. What would he say if she told him that she wanted to stay for a few days?

The doorbell rang, startling Arjun. He looked up at the wall clock. It was just 8.30 a.m. Who could it be? He went to the front door thinking it might be the newspaper man who had come to collect the bill, but when he put his eye to the peephole, he straightened up with a jerk.

'Oh no,' he muttered. 'This can't be happening.'

But he had to open the door. On the landing, looking fit and fresh in trackpants and a white T-shirt was Rhea.

'Hi, Dad!' she said.

He forced himself to smile. 'What are you doing here so early?'

'I had come to play tennis with a friend at the Panchsheel Club. The driver's downstairs.' She made her way past him, and he closed the door and followed her. She opened the fridge, took out a bottle of cold water and had a drink. 'I looked up the actress Munni yesterday evening. I found her story very interesting.'

'I noticed that.'

'Want to know something I found out?'

Arjun nodded, his eyes straying to the now unlocked bedroom door. 'Tell me.'

Rhea pulled up a chair at the dining table and sat down.

'Like you said, the actress becomes a recluse and disappears several years later. It was big news back then. Do you know the name of the police officer who was investigating it?' She smiled, enjoying this display of her knowledge.

'I don't know,' Arjun murmured, wondering what her reaction might be if Agnes Pereira happened to come out now.

'Surinder Jha. Then an ACP in the Delhi Police.'

'Surinder Jha?' He racked his brains but couldn't recall having met him anywhere.

'Yes, he's a joint commissioner now.'

Arjun was impressed with her initiative—it was something he had been meaning to look up as well. 'How did you find out?'

264

'A *lot* of reading on the Net. Your case is connected to Munni, isn't it? Do you think they might have murdered her and buried the body in the compound?'

'Well, I spoke to a witness just yesterday who says he saw Munni walking out of the house on the evening she disappeared,' Arjun said.

But something about his daughter's theory rang a bell in his mind.

'Well, thanks a lot for finding this out,' he said. 'I'm off to the office, so . . .'

She frowned. 'You haven't even had a bath.'

'I was just going to.'

He saw that she wanted to stay a while, maybe have breakfast with him, and it broke his heart to have to lie to her. 'I need to get to the office. Something to do with the case.'

She shrugged and stood up. 'All right. Bye.'

'Bye.'

Walking to the door, she glanced at the extra-large pizza box on the coffee table but didn't say anything. He heard her open and close the front door. He felt ashamed of his duplicity. Why couldn't life be simpler? The bedroom door opened and Agnes Pereira came out in an old T-shirt of his. At least she had the sense to wait, he thought.

'Has your maid left?' she asked sleepily, rubbing her eyes.

'Yes. That was my daughter.'

'Oh. What did she want?'

'Nothing. Just came to see me.'

He took two steps towards her, but froze as he heard the front door open again. A moment later, Rhea appeared, and she halted at the sight of the other woman.

'Oh . . . sorry. I left my phone on top of the fridge.'

She took a hesitant step forward, while Arjun turned and went to the fridge. When he picked up the phone, he turned back to see his daughter eyeing Agnes Pereira warily.

'This is my daughter, Rhea,' he said as he moved forward with the phone. 'Rhea, this is Agnes.'

The briefest of nods passed between the two women. Agnes Pereira made for the balcony, while Rhea took the phone from him. 'Bye, Dad.'

He could see anger in her eyes, as well as embarrassment. What could he say? Following her to the front door, he said, as she went down the steps, 'Rhea, wait.'

She paused without looking up at him. 'What? I don't want to disturb you.'

'It's not what you think. I've known her for a few days now—'

'Mom and I leave the house and you start screwing around with young girls?'

He lost his cool. 'Rhea! Watch your mouth.'

She went running down the steps. He followed her, and by the time he got to the gate, he saw her getting into the back of one of her stepfather's cars, this one a dark-blue Mercedes sedan. Arjun watched her being driven off, and felt furious. How dare she lecture him after she and her mother had deserted him? Coming back up to the flat, he came upon Agnes Pereira in his bathroom, dressed in her salwar kameez and brushing her teeth.

'Now where are *you* going?'

'I think it's better that I leave, Arjun.'

'Have breakfast at least?' he pleaded, but she shook her head.

He came out, looking for something to take his frustration out on. But what could he throw, what could he break? She came out of his room, gave him a peck on the cheek and backed away.

'Bye. I'll call you later.'

He just nodded and sat down at the dining table. No need to tell her about the keys, his secretary would still be at home. In the end, he heated up the cup of tea in the microwave and lit a cigarette, alone as ever.

48

THE OFFICES OF MCLOYD & Co. were in a gleaming high-rise called Anand Parbat Tower, a stone's throw away from Connaught Place on one of the radial roads branching off from the outer circle. The building was a towering structure of steel and glass which complimented the newly restored CP with its larger and glitzier showrooms, but all around it were the reminders of another urban India, for those who could see them: a crowded bus stop, a choley kulche vendor on a cycle serving customers, a woman and her child begging on the footpath. Arjun made his way past two guard points—at the outer gate and at the entrance to the building—before rising up in a sleek elevator to the tenth floor. Inside, young men with ties and gelled hair talked about percentage points and interest rates—a sort of double abstraction within the air-conditioned building.

The reception area was done up in an anonymous international style with glass and stark white furniture and bright lighting, and the tall receptionist with a fixed smile on her unnaturally smooth face asked him if he had a prior appointment with Mr Biswas.

'No, but tell him I'm here regarding his house in Sundar Nagar.'

'Your name, sir?'

'Arjun Arora.'

'Please have a seat while I pass on the message.'

She waited till he moved out of earshot to one of the low sofas away from her desk before she made the call. Out of the windows, he could see the concentric white buildings of CP with the park in the centre, and buildings spreading out into the haze beyond. McLoyd & Co., as far as he recalled, was an American consultancy firm that had entered India a few years back. They had three floors of Anand Parbat Tower, with banks, airlines and real estate firms in the floors below. Looking at the sprawl of Delhi from up there, he had the notion that a view like this could distort a person's perception of the city.

'He'll see you now,' the receptionist said with a bright smile. 'This way please.'

Arjun followed her as she swiped past a series of doors; he had an impression of hushed tension, people staring into their monitors. As she paused at the final door to knock, he studied her figure and decided she went to a gym. Opening the door, she stepped sideways to let him enter first. A large, grey-carpeted room with a desk in the middle, from which rose a short man with thinning hair, gold-rimmed glasses and an expensive suit. There were surprisingly few papers on the desk. At the far end of the room, it was all glass, with the blinds half drawn.

They shook hands, but Siddharth Biswas didn't introduce himself. He smiled at the receptionist, a fraction too long, letting her know she could leave.

'Sit, please. What can I do for you, Mr . . . Arjun Arora. Is that correct?'

His voice was brisk, commanding.

'That's right. First of all, I'm a detective, a private investigator.'

'Oh.' His eyebrows curved upward. 'We have those here now?'

It struck a false note, like something Biswas might have heard a senior colleague use in a different context. Arjun looked at him a while, then said, 'The first detective agency in Delhi opened in 1961.' He didn't add that it had been a one-man operation, initially.

'Oh well, I don't know much about these matters. But why are you here? Priya—she's the secretary—said you mentioned our house in Sundar Nagar. What about it?' He added with a smirk, 'It's not for sale.'

'I'm here regarding a case of mine. It seems to be linked to the disappearance of the actress Munni. You must remember that, of course?'

A look of caution appeared on Siddharth Biswas's face.

'Yes, I do. What's this case of yours about?'

'It's confidential. All I can say is that it concerns a missing girl as well.'

The director's son was quiet for a moment, then got up and walked over to the half-drawn blinds. Looking down at Parliament Street he said, 'It was a terrible time for us, by which I mean me and my mother. There were all sorts of nasty things being said and written.'

'How old were you then?'

Siddharth Biswas came back to his desk and sat down. '1993, wasn't it? Nineteen years ago. So I would have been, let's see, twenty-three years old. I was just finishing my master's.'

Arjun thought he looked older than his age. 'What do you think happened to her?'

'The actress?' he inquired, and Arjun nodded. The director's son shrugged. 'Who knows? They're not very bright, you know, these women. Fall for all sorts of sweet talk. Maybe someone lured her away and murdered her. Just a theory, mind you.'

'I see. Do you think your father ever had an affair with her?'

'What?' He let out a high-pitched laugh. 'You expect me to answer that?'

'So he did have an affair with her?'

'No, he didn't! She was just some illiterate tawaif with a grubby mother whom he felt sorry for. Are you really a detective, by the way, or some cheap film magazine reporter?'

Arjun ignored the jibe. 'So he felt sorry enough for her to give her the house?'

The junior Biswas took a deep breath, removed his glasses and put them on the desk.

'Munni was one of the reasons my father rose to where he was. So he was thankful to her too. She was supposed to live there for a short period, but then she turned into a recluse.'

'Why hadn't you and your mother moved into that house?'

'Family matters, Mr Arora. My mother was attached to the flat we stayed in, which she had inherited from her father. Whenever Baba, my father, came to Delhi, he stayed with us. The Sundar Nagar house was bought as a sort of investment.'

'And you and your mother didn't resent the house being given to someone else?'

'She was just staying there. The house was in my father's name. My mother taught at a college in Delhi University. We were far removed from the Bombay scene.'

'Was there ever any interaction between Munni and you and your mother?'

Siddharth Biswas shook his head. 'None at all.'

'And after Munni disappeared, you and your mother moved into the house?'

'Yes. Wouldn't you have done the same? My mother had retired by then, and Gole Market wasn't what it had been in the old days.'

'What did you do your master's in, Mr Biswas?'

'My master's? Economics. I was at D School.' With the hint of a smile, he added, 'Top of my class, and then I left for New York.'

'The day Munni went missing, where were you?'

270

'Where was I?' He laughed, incredulous. 'I was at the university and then I went down to CP, okay?' His face hardened suddenly. 'That's all I have to tell you.'

He put on his glasses and turned towards his computer.

'Just one last question. Did you or your mother ever visit the ashram that Munni used to go to?'

'No, we had nothing to do with that.' He picked up the phone and asked Priya to get him a file.

Arjun stood up to leave. He had reached the door when Siddharth Biswas spoke.

'Look, I'm sorry if I seemed rude, just that there are a lot of bad memories for me and my mother from that period. And to be reminded of them like this, all of a sudden . . . I'll tell you what, if you want to discuss this some more, come by the house one evening this weekend.'

'Certainly. Thank you, Mr Biswas.'

On his way out he passed the secretary who was carrying a file. He smiled at her but she pretended not to notice and walked past him.

'Bitch,' he muttered.

Once outside, he lit a cigarette, and then walked towards CP. The morning heat was starting to lose some of its intensity; another month, and the weather would be pleasant. The traffic, however, was as bad as ever. His thoughts were muddled, he couldn't concentrate. After his daughter and Agnes Pereira had left his flat, he had showered and driven to CP, more out of a desire to avoid home and office for a while than to question Siddharth Biswas. He had happened to remember that McLoyd & Co. had their offices in CP, and decided to pay the director's son a visit. He now felt that he had probably been too pushy and direct—but then why had he been invited for another meeting?

Arjun took a left and walked past Regal Cinema, now renovated, which he had visited a few times while in college

271

to watch B-grade Hindi films with friends. The old CP was now gone, though the street vendors with baskets selling belts, goggles, handkerchiefs and cucumbers still loitered about. He crossed the road and made his way down to the inner circle. A growl in his stomach reminded him he hadn't eaten breakfast, and so he walked around the curved colonnade, past women in ethnic wear selling paintings and handicrafts to tourists. He gave McDonald's and KFC a miss and instead bought two chicken patties from Wenger's and a chocolate shake from Keventers— walking around CP had awoken old college memories. He sat on a railing and ate, watching the crowds pass by, and hung around for some more time, smoking another cigarette, before calling Liza and telling her that he had come out on some work but was heading back to the office now.

49

AT HALF PAST THREE THAT afternoon, Arjun was at the gates of the Delhi Police headquarters in ITO, filling up the columns in a visitor's register after letting the policeman on duty know that he had an appointment with Joint Commissioner Jha: under the column 'Occupation' he wrote 'Self-employed'. The building was a hulking behemoth in the anonymous government-building wilderness of ITO; across the road and up ahead was the MCD headquarters, while behind it was Bahadur Shah Zafar Marg, where the newspapers in the old days had their headquarters, and where the *Times of India* still operated from. He made his way up to the eighth floor, where one of the joint commissioner's staff told him to wait his turn on one of the faded government-issue sofas in the waiting area.

Delhi Police HQ was where the capital's 80,000-strong force was controlled from. While it had its fair share of complaints about corruption and high-handedness, Arjun saw that as a natural fall-out of the environment they operated in: a money-and-power culture that fed on the politics of the capital and the region's overwhelmingly north Indian machismo, not to mention the daily floating population in the tens of thousands from the neighbouring states of Haryana and Uttar Pradesh. Surinder Jha, Arjun had found out from Bunty, was a Maithili Bihari who had been at his current post for a couple of years, joint commissioner of one of the Delhi ranges. That was after Arjun had called Jha's office around midday and managed to get an appointment by dropping a few names and mentioning the 'old film star case'—Bollywood glamour opened doors everywhere.

He waited under the glare of the tube lights, fiddling with his phone. Near him a worried-looking sardar and an overweight bania were whispering about someone's passport and a plot of land on sale. A well-built, crew-cut man in civilian clothes appeared, spoke to the staff member, and walked into the office. Some minutes later he emerged, his watchful eyes sweeping over the people who were waiting and stopping for a moment at Arjun. 4 p.m., the time of his appointment, came and went. The sardar and the bania were called in; they emerged fifteen minutes later, both of them now smiling. Arjun walked along the corridor to one of the windows and looked down at the busy afternoon traffic passing by. Come evening, this area would be one of the most polluted in all of Delhi, as a continuous stream of buses, cars and two-wheelers headed out towards Noida slowed down at the red lights.

The question of perspective, which had occurred to him that morning while looking down from the offices of McLoyd & Co., now returned to him: did the change in view as you went higher up in life alter one's perception of society? Was that what had led to Munni shutting out the outside world during the last decades of her life? It was a fuzzy sort of realization, and he made a mental note of it.

At ten minutes past five, the staff member let Arjun know that Sahib would see him now, but only for a short while as he was supposed to leave at 5.30 p.m. sharp to attend a programme at Siri Fort. Arjun entered the joint commissioner's office, aware that this would possibly be his only chance to get something useful out of the police officer.

'So why are you interested in Munni's case?' asked the person at the desk without looking up from the papers he was shuffling through, a pen in his left hand.

274

'I'm curious as to what happened to her,' Arjun answered truthfully.

The joint commissioner paused, looked up. 'I spent years looking for her. So I might understand how you feel.'

Surinder Jha had a razor-sharp side parting, wore rimless glasses and had a smooth, fair complexion that made him look considerably younger than his fifty-odd years. Arjun had a sudden image of him in an ironed tracksuit, taking a morning walk with a small dog on a leash. The domesticated appearance was completed by a large, red tiffin carrier on a table behind him, the type that could be plugged in to keep the interior warm.

'What do you think happened to her?' Arjun asked, for the second time that day.

Jha leaned back in his leather swivel chair. 'But what's your interest in her, Mr Arora? This was almost twenty years ago.'

'I'm a detective. It's come up in an indirect way in an investigation of mine.' He hesitated, then went on. 'I managed to find out that she was seen leaving the Sundar Nagar house that evening.'

The thin eyebrows went up behind the stylish glasses. 'Then you know quite a lot.'

Arjun pressed ahead. 'I also know that she was delayed that afternoon at Kailash Swami's institute. He claims that she had been helping him design—'

'A brochure, I know. He had showed it to me.' Jha looked up at the ceiling and smiled, maybe at the memory of his younger self. 'But whether *she* had been working on it, who knew? His staff, of course, all vouched for him.'

'Did she meet someone from her past that day?'

'If she did, I never managed to find out. And we never found the taxi driver who dropped her home, do you know? Someone had asked her regular taxi to leave, and by the time she left there was a new taxi waiting outside the gates. Very strange.'

'Did you talk to the director's son, Siddharth Biswas?'

'I did, yes. He wasn't too far from Sundar Nagar that afternoon, in CP. But then again I couldn't connect him to the disappearance. Were you ever in the police, Mr Arora?'

'No. Army.'

Jha nodded, looking into the middle distance now, seemingly lost in thought.

'A few years after this case, I had to go once again and see the person who calls himself Kailash Swami. A secretary of his had disappeared. He was from Swami's home state, mine too, Bihar, and I even went there with the police team. We went looking for the secretary's village, which was near Swami's old village. That had been swallowed up by the Ganga. Anyway, we found no trace of the secretary, but an old man told me an interesting story. In the village that had disappeared, there had been a boy called Lalit Prasad. He was a moody child, always in trouble with his father, and one day, while in his teens, he had disappeared. Strangely, his mother and his father went missing at the same time. Years later, when the Ganga finally eroded the village away, two skeletons came floating downstream. The old man said they knew the skeletons came from bodies that had been buried in the village upstream. And the male skeleton had one leg shorter than the other by three inches, just like Lalit Prasad's father. The old man then told me where Lalit Prasad was. Of course, he didn't use that name any more.'

'Kailash Swami?'

'Exactly. Do you know how the investigation into Munni's disappearance stopped? I had summoned Kailash Swami to the thana for questioning but he didn't turn up. The next day, a Union minister called me and told me to forget about the case if I was serious about my career. I weighed my choices, and did as he asked. I don't regret it.'

Arjun looked at him, an officer secure in his job, his marriage, his own community lobby. He must have studied at Delhi University, tried for the civil services, but got into the Delhi Police instead of the IAS. 'But sometimes you still wonder what happened to her?'

Jha nodded, a faint smile on his face. 'You cannot imagine the sort of connections Kailash Swami has. It cuts across party lines and communities. But if you come across something, let me know. I retire in a couple of years, and I would like to go out with a clean conscience.'

Arjun found that he didn't dislike the man. Like him, Jha was doing the best he could.

'What happened to Munni's servants, did you find out?'

'They disappeared as well.' He looked up at the clock on the wall, beside the framed portrait of Mahatma Gandhi. 'Well, I have an appointment. I've been invited for a documentary film festival.'

'Anything else you could tell me about Kailash Swami?'

'He claims he made a pilgrimage to Mount Kailash, and then changed his name, but that's all false. The farthest north he's gone is Haridwar. He wandered all over the country as a young man. Oh . . . and he even learnt carpentry somewhere along the way.'

Arjun remembered those rough, calloused hands.

'Where did he learn it, would you know?'

The joint commissioner stood and picked up his cap and stick. 'I'm sorry, no. All this is ancient history, Mr Arora. People in our country don't have time for it.' He gave him a smile. 'I really have to go now. I'll tell my secretary to give you my mobile number.'

Arjun rose to leave. Driving back from ITO to his office, he went over what Surinder Jha had just told him. It seemed he would have to pay Kailash Swami another visit.

50

BY THE TIME HE GOT back home after closing the office it was past 7 p.m. Liza had given him a printout of his early-morning train ticket to Lucknow for the next day, and let him know that Agnes Pereira had shown up just as she was leaving for work in the morning. His secretary's expression had been neutral, so Arjun didn't probe any further, just told her to let Agnes know that it was dangerous for her to step out often.

As he switched on the sitting room light, he saw that the pizza box from the previous night was now teeming with ants. The depressing and shameful episode from the morning returned to him. He folded the box and stuffed it into the kitchen dustbin, then tried calling Rhea, but she didn't pick up. He hoped she hadn't told her mother about what she had seen in the morning—he could do without more of Sonali's sermonizing. Next he tried Agnes Pereira's new number. No answer there as well. What a ridiculous position for a grown man to find himself in!

He took a shower, changed, and then took out the bottle of Blenders Pride and put it on the dining table. He sorely felt the need for a drink, but then there was the buffer of the last few dry days, and he put the bottle aside. But what was there to celebrate, really? At the most he had just added a few more days to his life. In the end there was only one thing he could fall back on: his work. He sat down at the dining table, switched on his laptop, and started typing in his notes right from the previous day's visit to Sundar Nagar.

Time passed, and he found himself entering into the narrative of the missing woman. As with Agnes Pereira, there was something there which appealed to Arjun: history, loss, intimations of an older India. He wondered at the same time if he wasn't straying too far from the original situation with Vishwanathan. The notes from the previous day completed, he was now on to his visit to Biswas junior's office. What did the executive think of his father's work? He had seemed to show a rather low opinion of actresses in general.

His phone rang. He reached for it thinking it was Rhea or Agnes Pereira returning his calls, but it turned out to be Poppy.

'Arjun. Can we talk?' Her voice told him she had something. In the background he could hear the hubbub of voices in the newsroom; it served to remind him how solitary his own profession was.

'Go ahead, I'm all ears.'

'I managed to get the bureau chief to send out a reporter. So you owe me a good story, okay?'

'You'll get it, I guarantee that. So what have you got?'

'You better write this down.'

He reached for a ball pen and his notepad lying on the table. 'Go ahead.'

'The dead girl, first of all. She worked at the Silver Moon dance bar on Tardeo Road—that was reported. If we go back, we see that she had an on-off relationship with a south Indian gangster named Shetty, for whom she stashed extortion money in return for a cut. That's how she managed to buy two flats in the city. Then she gets arrested six years ago, and is in jail for six. After she gets out, she returns to her old job, but there's reportedly no contact between her and Shetty any more, mainly because he's somewhere in South East Asia now—Bangkok or Hong Kong, the cops say.'

'All right,' Arjun said as he wrote. Nothing new there, except for another name.

'Next, Vishwanathan. There's nobody by that name, but we do know that there's a crooked real estate developer by the name of Kumar Sampath who has a missing finger. Apparently lost it to someone from Dubai over a missed payment.'

'Crooked in what way?'

'Land grabbing for constructing flats, at least two cases. Later, no one was willing to testify against him. And before you ask, yes, he did have links to Shetty.'

'I see.' Arjun scribbled away.

'Then the Expression store—'

'Wait, what about the lodge? Did the reporter go there?'

'I'm coming to that. The Expression furniture store is owned by an old Bombay family, the Mehtas. The interesting thing is that it used to be a photo studio before.'

'The Royal Photo Studio?' Arjun asked sharply.

'Yes, that's the name! How did you know? Anyway, the manager of the photo studio was a one-time Bollywood cameraman called Robert Chacko. There was some sort of scandal in the early 1960s over pornographic photographs being shot there, following which it was closed down for a long time. Apparently, the Mehtas retained the services of Mr Chacko, even though he was supposed to have been involved in the affair. He was popularly known as Camera Bobby. So that's the Expression store. Now moving on to the lodge . . . are you getting all of this, by the way?'

'Yes, go on,' Arjun said, writing quickly. Bobby—that was one name sorted out.

'The receptionist at the lodge wasn't too keen to talk to our reporter—she does the crime beat, by the way—but one of the things he said was the other girl had gone out that morning, had returned and then come down half an hour later with her bag, and left. After which he went up to check and found Savitri Rao dead.'

'But she had said five minutes, so one of them is lying.'

'Five minutes? Who's "she"?'

'It's her case I'm working on, Poppy. You remember I asked you about Munni?'

'Yes. And?'

'Well, it looks as though this other girl is Munni's granddaughter.'

'Munni's grand . . . wait a minute . . . she didn't marry or have children, did she?'

'That's what people have believed so far.'

'But if she's . . . oh my god! This could be a big story, Arjun. I want you to give me everything you've got.'

'I will, after I find out why some people want her—and me—dead.'

'Are you in trouble, Arjun?'

'Nothing that I can't handle. What else did the reporter find out?'

'Well, she went to the grocery shop, as you had suggested. And she managed to find out something interesting from the old owner. He told her that one of the hotel staff who had come to his shop on the day after the murder had told him that a tall man had been seen moving around suspiciously near Savitri Rao's room that morning.'

'Don't the police know about this?'

'Well, that's what she tried to find out next. But apparently the police are only interested in the girl Agnes Pereira. Who you say you're in contact with. Be careful, Arjun.'

'I will. Thanks for this. Once everything's settled, you'll have your story. But as always—'

'I leave you out of it, I know.'

Arjun smiled. 'Poppy, another thing I want looked up.'

'What is it?'

'Kailash Swami. Do you know him?'

Poppy snorted with annoyance. 'Who doesn't? The sleazeball tried to interest me in a private meditation class once. Ages ago when I used to be a reporter.'

'Any dirt you can get on him. Especially missing persons.'

'Will do. And he's someone you should be careful of as well.'

'I'm aware of that. I'll call you soon.'

'Take care, Arjun.'

There was a pause, as if she was going to say something else, but she hung up. Arjun looked at what he had jotted down—he would have to transcribe those details as well. He decided to take a break and fix his dinner. Once again, he wasn't in a mood to cook anything. Opening the fridge, he looked inside, but there was hardly anything by way of leftovers. In the end, he took half of an old loaf and made himself three toasted tomato-and-cheese sandwiches and a glass of cold coffee to go along with them.

What surprised him most was that the 'Bobby' and the address in the note, and the photo studio and the furniture store, were all linked. But only if he was looking for unrelated events, he realized. A rough idea of what could have happened was building up in his mind. The sleaze angle—he would have to ask Prakash Saxena if Munni or her mother might have done anything of that sort for money. And another thing he should have asked Poppy Barua to get checked: Regent's Clinic in Bandra. Anyway, those things could wait till he got back from Lucknow.

He worked late into the night typing out his notes.

51

AT SIX THE NEXT MORNING, he was striding along the overbridge of the New Delhi Railway Station with his backpack, making his way down to the platform where the Shatabdi Express to Lucknow stood waiting. The sight of the blue-grey carriages and the upholstered seats inside where passengers sat reading newspapers or browsing through their phones momentarily disoriented him. As he took his seat by the window he almost missed the crowds and the iron-barred windows of his early days, to be followed later by hawkers threading their way through, shouting out their wares. At exactly 6.10 a.m., the train pulled out of the platform.

Arjun watched as central Delhi slipped away; they were crossing a bridge over the sluggish, black waters of the Yamuna, after which came the endless raw-brick dwellings, factories and residential areas which stretched from east Delhi into western Uttar Pradesh. Half an hour later, the train pulled into the Ghaziabad Junction station for a two-minute halt. He checked his phone. No calls or messages from Rhea or Agnes Pereira. What was he hoping to find in Lucknow? Still, he had to keep moving. He remembered his mother's commentary on the Bhagavad Gita: didn't it say that the fruits of one's work should not be one's motive, and that one should never be inactive?

The train had picked up speed now, and the high-rises and warehouses finally gave way to wheat fields and villages, cloaked by a thin mist in the early morning. The man beside Arjun, a businessman from the capital, informed him that the train had reached Ghaziabad a couple of minutes late and that they were now travelling at around 120 kilometres per hour, which was impressive but still nowhere near the Japanese and Chinese bullet trains. Arjun was spared having to make further conversation by the appearance of the breakfast trolley. He ordered an oversized samosa and a cup of oversweet coffee, and washed it down with a uric acid tablet and half a bottle of water. It had been four days since he had touched any alcohol, and he felt better for it.

About an hour from Ghaziabad, they pulled into Aligarh Junction, again for a two-minute halt, and after that Arjun dozed off, coming awake some fifteen minutes before they got to Etawah. Arjun's co-passenger now told him that they had lost some more time after crossing Tundla Junction, and that Kanpur Central was yet to come before they got to Lucknow Junction. Arjun didn't share the businessman's anxiety; he felt a contentment of sorts, brought about by the movement of the train and the flat north Indian countryside with its fields and towns, the heartland of India—a landscape familiar from his years in the army.

The train pulled into Lucknow at 1 p.m., late by twenty minutes or so, as the co-passenger once again pointed out. Arjun bade him farewell and quickly got out on to the platform. He caught an auto from the crowded Station Road to the nearby Hussainganj intersection, where he checked into a three-star hotel he had looked up the night before on the Internet. Once he had washed, he came down looking for the receptionist. Now that he had actually reached Lucknow, the task of locating the hundred-year-old Sultana Begum seemed harder than it had in Delhi. All he knew was that she had once lived in the old Chowk area, and that her elder brother had been in the cloth business.

The receptionist turned out to have a faint idea of who Sultana Begum was—but that was it. He didn't even know if she was alive or dead. In the end Arjun took an auto past the Vidhan Sabha to MG Road, where they turned left and continued past Hazratganj and Qaiserbagh, the Gomti River flowing nearby to the right. They crossed an Imambara, and the roads grew crowded and narrow, the buildings older and shabbier. He got down in the Chowk area and walked around looking for an old restaurant. When he found one, he sat near the counter, and while his order of kebabs and roomali rotis was being readied, he asked the owner about Sultana Begum. The silver-haired owner didn't know of her whereabouts, though he said she was still alive, but informed Arjun that the elder brother's chikan-work showroom had been somewhere nearby in the cloth market.

While he ate, the owner made a few calls to find out where the shop was. Arjun had a sense, amid the crowded lanes, of an old courtesy which had lingered on from the days of Awadh, a very different sensibility from the crassness of Delhi, though both cities had a similar culture of political violence, even more so here in Lucknow. He thanked the owner, paid him, and made his way on foot to the nearby cloth market, where, after making further inquiries, he finally managed to find the shop.

It looked decades old, with a small frontage, but stretched a long way in, where women both young and old were looking at ready-made salwar kameezes in various colours and styles, all of them embellished with that delicate embroidery work that Lucknow was famous for. Arjun made his way into the interior where he spotted a middle-aged man with henna-red hair and kohl-rimmed eyes keeping watch on the proceedings and collecting the money. He moved closer to the man, and asked a helper to show him salwar suits. Arjun described an approximate size—he had an idea as to whom he wanted to present it to— then went through the pieces he was shown, letting it be known that he was a visitor from Delhi interested in the city's old culture and history. As he talked to the helper and went through the salwar kameezes, he noticed the owner looking his way a few times. He finally chose a light, cream-coloured suit and a pastel-pink one, and went to pay. Over the transaction, he struck up a conversation with the owner.

'Charming shop,' he commented. 'Must be very old?'

'My grandfather started it,' the middle-aged man replied with pride. 'You've come from Delhi?'

'Yes. Looking around Lucknow. I'm looking for someone's house actually, I wonder if you could help me.'

'Whose house are you looking for?'

'An old woman, well known once upon a time, the mother of the actress Munni.'

'The one who disappeared?' the man asked, a half-curious, half-amused look on his face, and when Arjun nodded, asked him why.

'We're interested in doing a television programme on Munni. Do you know where the house is?'

'The One Above has guided you to the right place. Of course I know where Sultana Begum lives. She's my grandfather's younger sister, my grand-aunt.'

Arjun feigned astonishment. 'Really? What a coincidence! So she lives with you?'

'Nearby. You want to interview her?'

'Yes. But I'd like to talk to her first. How old must she be now? Almost a hundred?'

The man nodded. 'Which channel have you come from?'

'It's a production house. We do documentary films for Indian and foreign buyers.' Arjun could sense a degree of scepticism in the other man, so he added, 'We pay well, of course. We'll need to show bits of Lucknow too, and your shop would be a good location.'

'All right. You want to go now?'

'Sure.'

'Let me call my son,' he said, and took out his cell phone.

They waited for the son. A stool was procured for Arjun, and a cup of tea. He learnt that the man's name was Ashraf, and that his grandfather had passed away a couple of years ago at the age of ninety-eight. They had a workshop in another area of the city where their embroidery work was done. A while later, the son appeared, a younger version of the father minus the henna and kohl, and with a different hairstyle. Ashraf asked him to handle the cash counter while he stepped out for a while with the *mehman* from Dilli.

As he followed Sultana Begum's grand-nephew, who expertly threaded his way through the crowds and traffic of the choked lanes lined with restaurants and clothes shops, Arjun asked what he thought might have happened to Munni.

'Someone must have killed her. But one thing is certain, we never took any of her money, and after she disappeared, we were the ones who had to take care of her mother.'

They cut into an even narrower lane in a residential area of sorts, and then climbed up a flight of wooden stairs to an apartment with a lengthy balcony where clothes were hung out to dry.

'This way,' Ashraf said, leading him up another flight of rickety stairs to a landing from where they went in, turning left and right past small doors, some closed, some open, furnished rooms and offices.

Arjun had the feeling of having wandered on to the set of a Hindi film from the black-and-white era. Would one of the doors open and a young Munni walk out? A few more stairs, and then Arjun's guide stopped in front of a larger wooden door, worn with age and darkened with grime.

'Here we are,' he said, and knocked thrice.

52

A WIZENED OLD MAN OPENED the door and studied them with large, mournful eyes.

'There's someone to see Begum sahiba,' Ashraf said.

'You know she doesn't like meeting people,' the man said in a low, rasping voice.

'They want to interview her, on camera,' Ashraf said, and pushed past the old man into the darkened interior. 'Where is she?'

The old man stood looking at Arjun, then turned. 'Let me go and see.'

Ashraf asked him to come in, and as Arjun entered the room he picked up a smell of dust and abandonment mixed with the aroma of spices and some sort of incense or perfume.

'I pay for all of this,' Ashraf said. 'You should put that into your film. But we never saw a rupee of Munni's money.'

Ashraf found the switch he was looking for, and a tube light flickered to life. On one side of the wooden room, there was a sofa and a divan, and on the other side, piles of cardboard boxes stuffed with salwar kameezes in plastic wrappers. That was where the perfume-like smell was coming from, Arjun realized. The old man reappeared.

'You're lucky, she's awake,' he said.

'You go in and talk to her,' Ashraf said to Arjun. 'I'll wait here.'

The shop owner sprawled out on the divan and took out a smartphone. Arjun followed the old man past the faded curtain in the doorway. Inside it was dark, and he felt for the wood-and-plaster walls of the corridor in case he lost his balance.

'In here,' the old man said to Arjun, then, 'Amma, there's someone to see you.'

He entered the small room. The only light came in from a tiny window that had a view of the bare concrete wall of a building across a narrow alley; from down below came voices and the tinkling of a cycle bell. Gradually, within the gloom, he could make out a frail, bent figure sitting on a bed.

'You can sit there,' the old man said, pointing to two stools by the window, and again to the old woman, loudly, 'Amma, you have a visitor from Delhi.'

Arjun sat on a stool. There was an aroma of fried food, again from down below.

'Who wants to see me?' a surprisingly sharp voice demanded.

The old man urged Arjun to speak, so he cleared his throat and said, 'We're shooting a documentary film. On the actress Munni. We would like to show you in it too.'

'Munni?' the old woman queried. 'Munni is dead. And what sort of a film are you going to shoot here, inside this cell where I'm locked up? I've seen how films are shot, in a studio, on a set, with actors and directors and cameramen. Are you a director?'

'I'm a producer,' Arjun said. 'And it's a documentary film.'

'I know what a documentary film is! Black-and-white movies you shoot out on the streets. What's your name?'

'Ankit Ahuja.'

'Never heard of you. My daughter Munni, *she* was a star. She could sing and dance and act. Who do you think taught her? It was me.'

Arjun reminded himself that he was talking to Sultana Begum, a hundred-year-old woman who had been born at the pinnacle of the British Raj. He said, 'Yes, she was a star, known all over India. Which is why we want to give today's generation a chance to know about her.'

The figure on the bed waved a hand in dismissal. 'She's gone. Forever. Why waste your time?'

'But how do you know she's dead? Maybe she's still alive?'

'How do I know? Because otherwise she would have come looking for her mother, this mother who made her a big star.'

'We look after you, don't we, Amma?' the old man said to her.

Her head turned towards the doorway. 'Why are you standing there and listening to us talk? So that you can go and report it to Ashraf? Move from there! Don't you see I have a guest with me?'

The old man looked at Arjun with a wan smile, then withdrew with his head bowed.

'Keeping me locked up inside here like an animal. Once the whole of Lucknow knew about me. If it was in the old days, I would have served you sherbet, paan, sweets. But this is my fate now.' Her head turned towards where Arjun sat. 'Are you still there?'

'Yes, I'm here,' Arjun said. 'Could you tell me about the old days? About Munni?'

'Those days are gone. So is Munni. She could have been bigger than Madhubala, Nargis, Sharmila Tagore, everyone. Instead she . . .' and her voice trailed off.

His eyes were adjusting to the dark; he could see that she was draped in black from head to feet. Her mental faculties seemed to be intact, but her isolation would have made her neurotic, prone to fantasies based on earlier events. Arjun had been in some strange places as a detective, but this was by far the strangest of them all. He decided to take the plunge.

'Who do you think was responsible for her death?'

'All those men, hanging around her like flies. They killed her.' Then she added, 'I can't remember any of their names. All of them must be dead too, by now.'

The last part of her reply reminded him of Prakash Saxena's description of her, a canny woman, and a survivor. He appeared to have reached a dead end, with little time left. Then he recalled something.

'Do you remember a pair of earrings? Gold borders, with black stone in them. The letters "MM" inscribed on the back.'

He thought she hadn't heard him and was about to repeat his question, when he saw her slowly get to her feet and then shuffle across to him. A whiff of damp, unwashed clothing hit him as she felt for a stool and sat down opposite him. The light from the small window fell on her face, and Arjun felt the hair rise on his arms and neck. Below the black head cover, two opaque, milky-white eyes looked out at him from a long, bony face criss-crossed with fine wrinkles.

'Do you see what's happened to me? It's a blessing in a way. I don't have to see my surroundings.' A claw-like hand reached out and clutched Arjun's wrist. 'How do you know about these earrings?'

'I came across them while researching Munni's life,' Arjun said, then added on a hunch, 'they went missing when Munni had a baby, didn't they?'

The decrepit woman opposite him sucked in her breath, and he knew he had struck close to the truth.

'Who told you this?' she asked. 'And where are those earrings now?'

'They're with someone in Delhi. Were they yours?'

She was quivering with emotion now. 'You must get me those earrings. They mean a lot to me. I want to hold them in my hands before I die.'

'I'll try and get them to you. But you have to tell me something about Munni in return.'

'I can give you something now,' she said, raising herself up and moving towards a corner of the room. 'Something which belonged to Munni. But I want those earrings. It was that *haramzadi* Stella Brown who made them disappear.'

Sultana Begum rummaged for something in the dark. Arjun made a mental note of the name she had just mentioned.

'You can have this if you want,' she said, coming back towards Arjun and handing him what looked like an old diary. 'It belonged to my daughter.'

He took it from her. An old, green Rexine cover, and inside it, yellowing pages, some of them loose, filled in a cramped hand in Hindi. Arjun looked up into those unseeing eyes. 'So Stella Brown made the earrings disappear? Who was she?'

'She was a nurse. The bitch was present when Munni had a baby. I know she stole the earrings!'

She stopped then, aware of what she had just revealed. Arjun leaned forward.

'What happened to the baby?'

'Oh, but it died. The poor thing! I didn't want to tell my daughter the truth, so I told her we had given the baby away, but then later when she insisted that the baby be returned to her, I had to tell her the truth. Oh, my poor child!'

Tears ran down from the vacant eyes. Arjun waited a while before asking her, 'Where was the baby born?'

'In Shimla, that's all I remember. Go through the diary, it'll all be written there. But you have to pay me for it. I don't have any money. All of Munni's money was stolen by that Bengali director.'

'How much do you want for it?'

'Five thousand rupees. Give it to me quickly before anyone comes in.'

Arjun hesitated a moment, then took out his wallet and gave her the amount in thousand-rupee notes. He would have preferred to simply photocopy the diary, but at least he was getting somewhere now. Sultana Begum rubbed each note between her fingers as she counted them.

'What was it?' Arjun asked. 'A girl or a boy?'

'It was a boy. I've given you her diary, now you have to get me the earrings. If you do, I'll give you more of her things: letters, photos. I have them hidden elsewhere.'

'Why are you so interested in those earrings?'

'Because they were mine! The major had given them to me. He would have made me his wife, but he never returned from Burma.' Her voice was shaking now, and she stood up and called out, 'Moin!'

The old man appeared silently in the doorway.

'Show him out, Moin,' she said. 'I need to sleep now.'

Arjun rose and bid farewell to her. As he walked down the corridor he heard the old woman call out, 'Get me those earrings. I want to hold those earrings again.'

Ashraf got up from the divan when he saw Arjun enter the room.

'I got this from her,' he said, holding up the diary.

He appeared unsurprised. 'It'll be helpful for you. Shall we leave now? I have to get back to my shop.'

On their way back, Arjun asked him about the old man and Sultana Begum's blindness.

'Moin is a relative of ours,' Ashraf said. 'He looks after her like his own mother. As for her eyes, something went wrong with them about ten years ago. Glaucoma, cataract, something like that. She's too old for an operation now. She's had a long, long life. So did she agree to appear in your documentary?'

'I think I'll have to come again to persuade her.'

Arjun parted with Ashraf outside the latter's shop, after exchanging numbers and telling him he would be in touch regarding his next visit. Then he caught an auto back to his hotel.

53

ARJUN TOOK A SHOWER TO wipe away the fatigue of the day, then called room service and asked for coffee. He stretched out on the modest-sized double bed, switched on the bedside lamp, and picked up the diary he had just procured.

Ten minutes later he put the diary aside and went over to the window, where he stood looking out at the late afternoon haze over the city and the press of vehicles on the road below. The entries in that cramped hand in the diary seemed curiously bland, brief and, more importantly, spread apart. *8 August 1958: Went and bought new sari with Amma. 12 October 1958: Film shooting is so tiring. I wish I could take a break.* Did the entries reflect the actress's lack of a formal education? A diary as a sort of prop, to prove to herself that she was doing something noteworthy? Or—and he hated to think so—could it be a fake? Then again, there did seem to be some authenticity in it. For 1962, the year Munni went missing, there were just a handful of entries, mostly for the beginning of the year, starting with what seemed like an account of a holiday. *2 February 1962: Confusing times, there's so much happening. This is a beautiful place though, and so near to Bombay.*

His coffee arrived, and he finished the pot and decided to go out for a walk. At the train station he booked his return ticket and walked around aimlessly until dusk fell. Everything felt strange, yet familiar. He didn't know whether to believe Sultana Begum's claim that her grandson had died in the hospital. Arjun recalled the horror of looking into the crone's blank eyes, but by Prakash Saxena's account she had once been a woman of charm, beauty and intrigue. Now only something of the last quality remained. Age—his father would one day pass away, and then the countdown would begin for him.

He suddenly noticed that he was across the road from a gaudily lit beer bar, with youngsters on bikes in front of it. The familiar old pull beckoned him, but he turned around and headed back. At the hotel, a waiter discreetly asked him in the lift if he wanted company, of either sex, or something to drink. Arjun excused himself by saying he would be having dinner early. But it was still too early to order, so he lay back on the bed changing channels on the television. He realized he was missing Agnes Pereira, missing the warmth of having another person near him. Was he really interested in solving her case, or was it only her? And his growing fascination with the missing actress, wanting to know what had happened to her—was he trying to solve the mysteries of his own background in a way? On the other hand, Vishwanathan's man would be in Delhi by now. Arjun was in too deep. He wondered again whether he was making a mistake by focusing on the missing actress instead of the dead girl Savitri Rao.

He called Computer Baba and asked him to find out, from the records of Agnes Pereira's old number, first, her bank account details and transactions over the past three months, and second, Savitri Rao's number and bank account and details and transactions over the same period. After that, he tried calling Prakash Saxena, but the retired professor didn't answer. Focusing on the diary, Arjun had forgotten to consider the name of the nurse the old woman had mentioned. He sent a message to Rhea: I'M IN LUCKNOW. NEED YOU TO FIND OUT SOMETHING FOR ME. IT'S URGENT. CAN YOU CALL ME? He had messaged her instead of calling, to let her know that he wanted to discuss something other than the previous morning's incident, and hopefully that would lessen her anger.

At half past seven, he rang room service and ordered dinner. When Rhea called him, she still sounded sullen. Arjun came straight to the point: 'I want you to look up a person for me. You've got a pen and paper with you?'

'Yes. Go on.'

'The person's name is Stella Brown, could be Estella Brown too, and her surname might have changed if she had got married. She was a nurse, late 1950s to early 1960s.'

'A place? A hospital?'

'Shimla. 1962. No hospital name, sorry.'

'Mm-hm. Anything else?'

'Try searching for her along with a Dr Phiroze Mistry, Regent's Clinic, Bandra, Bombay.'

'Brown would be . . .'

'An Anglo-Indian. Mistry, a Parsi.'

'Seems tough, but I'll have a look. When do you want this by?'

'The sooner the better.'

'I'll get on to it today.'

'Thanks, Rhea.'

'When do you get back?'

'Midday tomorrow.'

'I'll call you tomorrow.'

She hung up before he had a chance to even mention Agnes Pereira. The reversal of roles here appealed to his sense of irony though. A while later his 'heritage Lucknow thali' appeared, along with a scoop each of vanilla and strawberry ice cream for dessert in a steel bowl.

X

Arjun caught the express train coming from West Bengal at 5.30 a.m. It was supposed to reach Delhi at 2 p.m. (the Shatabdi from Lucknow departed for Delhi only in the afternoon). This time he was in an AC 3-tier coach, where he managed to get himself a single seat beside the aisle and by the window. The other passengers in the compartment appeared to be Bengalis from Kolkata, en route to Rajasthan for a holiday. He watched the countryside and the towns go past him in reverse now, even as he grappled with all the pieces of the puzzle in his head. It occurred to him that Stella Brown might be the woman in the black-and-white photo.

They reached Tundla Junction a little after 10 a.m., and as Arjun was looking out at the activity on the platform, his phone rang. It was Harry Bains.

'What did you find out?' Arjun asked.

'My hunch was correct. They're more than a century old, 22-carat gold. The black stone is jet, a type of coal that was mined in a place called Whitby in England.'

'That's very helpful, Harry. Any idea about the initials?'

'Well, if they were made in England during the Victorian era as mourning jewellery, then there's a good chance that the "MM" stands for "Memento Mori".'

'What does that mean?'

'Latin for "Remember Death". Basically, remember that one day you will die.'

'That would make sense, wouldn't it? Thanks, Harry.'

'When are you going to pick them up?'

'As soon as I get back to Delhi. I'm in a train, heading back from Lucknow.'

'Who do they belong to, Arjun?'

'That, my friend, I'll tell you someday over a drink.'

The train started moving. Remember Death, Arjun thought. It reminded him of the title of a poem they had studied in college: 'Death Be Not Proud'. Major Edwards had gifted Sultana Begum those earrings—but why mourning jewellery? He must have thought she would never find out the significance of the black stone. Or was it because he knew he would never return? He took the diary out of his backpack and flipped through its pages.

By 1 p.m., they had crossed Ghaziabad and were on the final stretch to Delhi. For lunch Arjun had bought himself puri and choley on a leaf plate at Aligarh, and now he waited impatiently for the journey to end. Before they reached Delhi, Arjun received two more calls in quick succession. The first was from Prakash Saxena, who apologized for having missed Arjun's call the previous evening, saying he had been out with his wife for a movie. Arjun gave him a brief update of his Lucknow trip, including his discovery of Sultana Begum herself.

'Oh, that's marvellous! What was she like?'

'Crafty. Tell me, have you ever heard about a diary belonging to Munni?'

'Oh, and you bought it from her, I suppose?'

'Yes, but how do you . . . ?'

'I forgot to tell you about that. There were a couple of similar handwritten diaries she had got prepared, maybe from an actual copy of Munni's diary. But all entries reduced to a single line or two—her life washed clean.'

'Wait a minute, so you're saying it's worthless?'

'Not entirely. It's almost certainly based on a real diary, but edited and then copied out several times. So you do have the bare bones of her life.'

'Five thousand down the drain,' Arjun said ruefully.

The retired professor chuckled. 'That's Sultana Begum for you.'

His disappointment at the piece of news was, however, balanced out a while later when Rhea called him to say that she had tracked down a Stella Smith, a former head nurse, aged eighty-three, who lived somewhere in west Delhi's Patel Nagar. She had worked at a hospital in Shimla and, more importantly, had been at Regent's Clinic in Bandra prior to that.

'You're sure about that?'

'Absolutely.'

He was genuinely impressed. 'How did you manage to find out?'

'I was totally lost at first. Then I decided to look up Anglo-Indian and Parsi associations. These people have all sorts of data, especially on the older people. That's where I found it. And by the way, this doctor, he was a consultant surgeon at the same hospital in Shimla, the Oldfield Sanatorium.'

'Oldfield Sanatorium,' Arjun repeated, looking out at the raw-brick dwellings and rubbish dumps speeding past. 'Can you message me the nurse's address?'

'I've mailed it to you.'

'Thanks, Rhea.'

'Don't thank me. I expect you to pay me.'

'Of course. When do I see you?'

He could hear Sonali's voice calling out in the background. Rhea said, 'Talk to you later,' and hung up.

There was no data signal on his phone so he had to wait till they were nearer Delhi in order to open his email and check the address.

54

THE TRAIN PULLED INTO NEW Delhi Railway Station at 2.30 p.m., late by half an hour. Arjun was waiting at the open door of his coach, backpack slung across his shoulder, and got down even before the train came to a halt. The game was afoot, as that famous fictional detective from another century would have remarked. He collected his car, covered now in a film of dust, from the parking lot behind the station, and made his way out through the congested traffic of Paharganj and Jhandewalan to Karol Bagh, from where he took the Pusa Road going down towards Siddharth Hotel. East Patel Nagar was nearby, low blocks of flats spread out amid spacious surroundings. He found the address without difficulty, but had to drive around for a while looking for a place to park, and then walked back. In his hand was an envelope with the three black-and-white photos and one colour photo; he had taken then with him to Lucknow.

It was the first-floor flat in a three-storey building with the simpler aesthetics of an older time. A group of children were playing tennis-ball cricket on the street outside. The door was opened by a fair, middle-aged man of medium height.

'I'm looking for Stella Smith,' Arjun said to him. 'Is she at home?'

The man nodded. 'And you are?'

'Sorry. Arora. Arjun Arora. Something to do with an old patient of hers.'

300

The man looked at him a while, before asking him to come in.

'My name's Stephen,' he said, leading Arjun into a cool, shaded sitting room. 'I'm her son. Let me see if Mummy's up from her nap.'

He disappeared through an open door, leaving Arjun to look at the cross on the wall, the poster of Jesus with a quote from the Bible, and framed black-and-white photos above an old-fashioned, box-like television set. Arjun went closer and bent to look at the photos of men in suits and women in dresses: weddings, parties, dances. Like the photos he held, they were glimpses of a vanished past.

'Yes?' a sharp female voice inquired, and Arjun turned.

He saw a matronly woman in a faded blue dress. Her eyes were alert behind her glasses, and her grey-white hair was pulled back in a strict bun. Stephen stood beside her. She wasn't the woman in the photo of the couple he had with him though; there had been her likeness in some of the framed photos atop the television.

'My name's Arjun Arora. I work for a firm of lawyers.' Something told him that the stern-looking woman before him might appreciate the law connection.

'Something to do with an old patient of mine, you told my son?'

'The actress Munni. You attended to her in Shimla, didn't you? She had a baby.'

'Where did you learn this?' There was something else on the woman's face now: a trace of fear.

'I've just returned from Lucknow. I spoke to Munni's mother there, Sultana Begum.'

'How did you find me, Mr Arora?'

'Through the Internet. From the records of an Anglo-Indian association.'

'And what is it that you want?'

'I want to know about the baby. What happened to it?'

She moved forward towards him, her son behind her. 'I don't want to talk about these things, you know. They happened a long time ago.'

'That's why I need to know. You might help someone looking for her real mother.'

That made her pause, and he thought he saw her lips quiver. 'I'm sorry but I'll have to ask you to leave, Mr Arora.'

'Okay. As you wish. But I'll leave my number. Call me if you change your mind.'

He came out of the flat and lit a cigarette. The tennis-ball game of cricket was still on in the street. He had been overconfident in there, rushing in blindly; he should have spoken to the son first. Arjun walked back to his car.

He had got in and was about to turn the key in the ignition when his phone rang. He was tempted to ignore it, but something made him answer. A landline number—his first thought was of Agnes Pereira. But it turned out to be Stella Smith.

'All right, I'll talk to you,' she said curtly.

Arjun returned to the flat, where Stephen now offered him a glass of lime cordial. Stella Smith settled herself into a chair by the window.

'It is about the baby, isn't it? Otherwise I wouldn't bother talking to you.'

'Yes. There's someone who believes she might be Munni's granddaughter. That's why I came to you. Can you tell me what happened in Shimla?'

She looked at the lace curtains of the window, then turned back to Arjun and started talking.

'I had moved to Shimla in the middle of '62. There was a better paying position at the Oldfield Sanatorium, and they were looking for someone experienced. I was at a clinic in Bombay before that.'

'The Regent's Clinic in Bandra?' Arjun asked.

Stella Smith's eyes widened in surprise, then she nodded. 'A doctor in the clinic told me about the job in Shimla. Phiroze Mistry. He was a consultant at the Oldfield Sanatorium.'

Arjun interrupted her. 'Why would a doctor from Bombay go all the way to Shimla?'

'Dr Mistry liked trekking, you see, and that way he could have a holiday and do a bit of work at the same time. He arrived there one night and told me that a patient was coming in, and that she was to be kept isolated for reasons of secrecy, with only me and a junior nurse attending to her. When she was brought in around midnight, I was surprised to see that it was the actress Munni. She was pregnant then, nearly full term. I remember the year because the India–China war had just started.'

'Dr Mistry was sure that you and the other nurse wouldn't talk about the patient?'

'He made us both sign an agreement which said we would lose our jobs if we did.'

'Who else accompanied Munni?'

'Her mother, whom you said you've met. A real witch she was. Then a man called Palekar and his wife, I got the feeling that he was a sort of secretary.'

'And she travelled from Bombay in that condition?'

She shook her head. 'It seemed they had been in Shimla for a couple of weeks, and Dr Mistry had kept coming up to check on her.'

'Was there no one else with them?'

'I'm coming to that. Three nights after she was admitted, Munni went into labour. Dr Mistry delivered the baby with just the two of us nurses present. It was a baby girl, caesarean section, I remember, just over two kilograms. A strange, pitiful cry she had, like a kitten. After the delivery, Dr Mistry told me that the baby would be taken away the coming night, and that Munni would be discharged the night after that. He asked me to keep her sedated.'

'So Munni didn't know if it was a boy or a girl?'

'No, she didn't.'

'But her mother would have known?'

'Yes, Dr Mistry told her.'

'I see,' Arjun said. Even there the old crone had lied to him!

'The next evening, I heard screams coming from her room. We were in the common room for nurses, listening to the news on the radio. Chinese troops advancing in NEFA and in Ladakh, and our troops in retreat, Nehru appealing for courage and sacrifice.' She paused to collect her thoughts before going on. 'I remember it like it was yesterday. I walked down the corridor, it was a cold and wet night, the old wooden floorboards sinking beneath my feet, and I was hoping that the war wouldn't spoil my plans of Christmas with my cousins in Calcutta. When I entered the room, Munni was thrashing about on the bed, demanding that her child be brought to her.'

'She didn't even get to see her baby?'

The old nurse's voice trembled. 'Dr Mistry had told us that the mother had given him instructions. I saw that the sedative had worn off and sent the junior nurse to get an injection. In the meantime, Munni grabbed hold of me and asked me whether it was a boy or a girl. I told her it was a girl. She wanted to see it. I said in a while, she could see the baby in a while, and then the junior nurse returned and I injected Munni and put her to sleep.' She bowed her head and was quiet for a few moments. Then she resumed in her normal voice: 'There was another person by then in the room. But I came to know who he was only later.'

'Are you talking about Riyaz Sheikh, a businessman from Delhi?'

'No, it was Dinesh Chadha, a politician. Not yet a cabinet minister then.'

'You mean . . . do you think he was the father?'

'I don't think so, he seemed closer to her mother, Sultana Begum. Besides, even in her half-drugged state, Munni kept calling out for a Riyaz . . . the one you mentioned, I guess.'

'So the baby survived?'

'Yes. It was taken away by the secretary's wife and Mr Chadha. There was a car waiting outside for them. I followed them out and watched the car drive away. Who knows where that poor child was taken.'

'So you have no idea where . . .'

Stella Smith shook her head. 'But I think Munni had an inkling of what might happen. Two nights after she was admitted, and the night before she delivered, I was alone with her for a while in her room. She gave me a pair of earrings then. Old earrings, gold with black stone, very valuable. In a small, red cloth bag. She had worn them in her last film. She had said that in case anything happened to her, I was to put the earrings inside the baby's clothes. So after I put her to sleep the next night, I went to the incubator room to wrap up the baby, and inside its clothes I put the bag with the earrings. I hoped they would one day somehow lead the baby back to her mother.'

Arjun nodded. 'I know which earrings you mean.'

'You've seen them?' Stella Smith asked him. 'Where?'

In response, he took out from the envelope in his hands the black-and-white photo of the couple and handed it to her. 'Do you know who they are?'

She held the photo up to the light and brought her face close to it. 'Why, these are the, what was their name, the Italian couple. The Fanuccis, yes! Where did you get this photo?'

305

'It was found along with the earrings and an address among the belongings of a woman who passed away recently in Panaji. One Agnes Carvalho.'

'The name sounds familiar.'

Arjun took out the photo in question from the envelope and handed it over to her.

'Oh, but I used to know her! She would come to the clinic in Bandra, she was one of Dr Mistry's patients. He used to treat fertility problems as well, you know.' She studied the photo again. 'Agnes wasn't married, but she had . . . problems.'

Arjun could guess what she was referring to. 'Why would she have a photo of the Fanuccis with her? How could they be connected?'

'How could they . . . I don't know . . . it was so long ago.'

Stella Smith suddenly seemed tired and frail, as if dragging those memories out had exhausted her. She looked at Arjun. 'Do you know what happened to the little girl?'

This time he took out the colour photo from the envelope, the one of Susan Carvalho.

'We believe the girl was adopted by Agnes Carvalho. This is a photo of her from Bangalore. Both of them are now dead though.'

The old nurse studied the photo carefully. 'Yes, she does look like Munni. All these years I wondered what might have happened to her, and I prayed for forgiveness.'

She started weeping, silently, with her head bowed. Memento mori, Arjun thought as he watched: Remember death. She took off her glasses and wiped her eyes.

'Don't blame yourself,' he said. 'There are other people responsible for this.'

'I suppose so. And Munni? What happened to her? She disappeared, didn't she?'

'That's something else I'm looking into. What do you think happened to her?'

'She must have committed suicide, after losing her child.'

But why after so many years, Arjun wondered. He said, 'The Royal Photo Studio in the Fort area of Bombay, do you remember that place?'

'Photo studio?' Once again she seemed lost.

From somewhere inside the flat the son called out, 'Mummy, time for your evening walk now,' before entering the room.

'Yes, Stephen, just discussing something with this gentleman.' Arjun noticed that her hearing was excellent for her age. She said to him, 'I hope I was of help to you. Must go for my walk now. I've seen many things in my life, Mr Arora, but nowadays my greatest pleasure is watching my grandchildren play. They'll be home from school soon.'

'You were most helpful,' Arjun said. 'If you remember anything more, anything at all, please give me a call. '

They both stood, and she handed him back the photos.

'You said there's a granddaughter?' she asked him.

'Yes, a young girl.'

'I would like to meet her, if possible.'

'I'll let her know,' Arjun said.

55

FROM EAST PATEL NAGAR, ARJUN drove across the city to Greater Kailash II. The retired professor had mentioned Dinesh Chadha's name as well, and Arjun tried to remember what he knew about the man. An old-time politician, one who had been jailed as a teenager by the British for taking part in the freedom movement. Won his first election from Madhya Pradesh in the 1950s. It was by the late '60s and early '70s that he had emerged, on account of his seniority, as a national-level leader. He would have been very interesting to someone like Sultana Begum, regardless of the fact that he was closer in age to her daughter. Arjun seemed to recall that he had written an autobiography a couple of years ago. But was he alive still? And what about the businessman Riyaz Sheikh?

He stopped at the M Block market to pick up the earrings from Harry Bains. Arjun then set out on the short distance to his office. It was dark by now, and the rush hour traffic had turned the underside of the Nehru Place flyover into a gridlock. Surrounded by honking vehicles, Arjun escaped once again in his mind to that cold, quiet place up in the Himalayas, his footsteps echoing along a misty street. One day he would be there. Thirty minutes later, he pulled up in front of Nexus Security. Liza was wrapping up the day's work, and Chandu was on the sofa sorting out the papers in a file on the table in front of him.

'Didn't I tell you to do that inside my office?' Arjun asked him.

'Sorry, sir, nearly over,' Chandu said.

Liza looked up but didn't say anything.

'Everything okay?' he asked her, to which she nodded.

'Any new cases?' This time she shook her head.

'Is Agnes Pereira all right?'

His secretary took a deep breath and looked up at him.

'She's on the phone all the time with her boyfriend or whoever. Last night, a car came and parked below around midnight, and she went down for nearly half an hour. And those pills, she's taking them one after another.'

'I'll speak to her,' Arjun said.

'Nearly one week she's been with me, sir. My relatives are back on Monday.'

'Just give me till this weekend,' Arjun said, going into his room.

He sat down at his desk to gather his thoughts. Taking out his phone, he considered giving Agnes Pereira a call, but saw his secretary outside and hesitated. Instead he went to his Internet browser and looked up Dinesh Chadha. The ex-freedom fighter had breathed his last at a Delhi hospital the previous year. He was survived by two children and three grandchildren. His autobiography titled *Freedom and Beyond* had been published a couple of years ago. Arjun had remembered that correctly. He picked up the phone and called Liza.

'I want you to look up someone for me. First thing tomorrow. A person by the name of Riyaz Sheikh. He was a Delhi-based businessman, passed away in the late 1990s. He was a friend of the Hindi film director Babul Biswas and had invested in a few of his movies.'

'Does this have anything to do with Miss Pereira's case?'

'It could, yes,' Arjun said, and put down the receiver.

After helping his two staff members close the office, he watched them walk off to catch their transport back home: an auto for Liza Thomas and a bus for Chandu. The Kolkata Hot Pot owner, who stayed near the Kali Mandir, and who had arrived for the night shift at his restaurant, stopped to say hi to him. Arjun lit a cigarette and called Agnes Pereira, twice, but she didn't pick up. Who could have visited her at night? Navin Sood? Or maybe even Vishwanathan's second man? You're getting paranoid, he told himself. His stomach growled, and he realized he hadn't eaten for hours.

He went to his flat, taking his backpack from the car, along with the photos and the earrings. As always, as he entered the flat he sniffed the air and checked the placement of the objects on the table by the door, to see if anyone might have been there. The lifelessness of the flat made him decide to get out for dinner. He stepped out on to the balcony to retrieve the morning's papers, and stopped to gaze up and down the lane and around the park, where a few solitary walkers were doing their rounds under the orange-yellow lights. He was about to go back inside when something caught his eye: a motorcycle, one of the new orange-and-white sports bikes, parked in the shadows to the left of his building, where the lane turned right around the park. He had never seen it there before—maybe it was a visitor's. He went back inside, locked the door, then washed and went down to his car. It was almost 8 p.m.

56

FROM CR PARK HE DROVE out aimlessly to the Outer Ring Road, then turned left under the Chirag Delhi flyover. Twenty minutes later he was driving into the vast parking lot under the Select Citywalk Mall in Saket. He usually avoided malls, but he had decided to make an exception as it wasn't a weekend and there was something else he had to pick up as well.

Most of the outlets inside the mall had customers, or at least window shoppers, but the bookshop at one of the outer lanes far from any of the entrances seemed dead with only an old man and a young woman browsing the titles. They had a few copies of *Freedom and Beyond* with them; Arjun picked up one. He walked back towards the main shopping area and took an escalator up to the first floor where the restaurants were located. Fast food, Indian-style Chinese, an 'ice bar' where patrons were being handed fur coats outside, American burgers—Arjun walked past all of them and entered an Irish pub, though the only thing Irish about it was the green on the walls and on the staff T-shirts. He had gone five days without a drink; today, of all days, he deserved one. He hoped the high prices here would discourage him from imbibing his usual higher-than-average quota.

He found a table for two in a dimly lit corner and claimed it. Not that the place was crowded: just a group of office workers being showily boisterous at the other end, two middle-aged couples and two young women. A smiling waiter appeared—he seemed mildly puzzled that Arjun was alone and didn't want any Guinness.

'It's Irish beer, sir,' he said.

'I know. Just get me a cold Foster's, please. The 650 ml bottle, not the 330 ml one.'

He looked around at the memorabilia on the walls as he waited for his beer. Did anyone else notice the absurdity of foreign working-class relics hanging in what was a place for people with money in this country? Maybe a few decades down the line Rhea would go abroad and encounter Hero cycles and stainless-steel tiffin carriers stuck up on the walls of an Indian diner. The beer arrived and he said cheers to himself. The first cold, bitter draught instantly made him feel better.

It struck him that it had been exactly two weeks since Mr Vikas had shown up at his flat. If only he had said no and not allowed his curiosity to get the better of him. Now he was stuck in a situation he couldn't seem to extricate himself from. Anyway, he had learnt some interesting things along the way. He took another sip of beer and opened the book. It didn't take him long to locate the part he was interested in: 1962, the year of the India–China war, when Munni had given birth to her daughter. The one-time cabinet minister wrote in a clean, precise style which hinted at a logical and methodical personality. The 1962 war though was covered in a slightly odd manner: for the month of October (the hostilities had started on 20 October), there was a general recounting of events and personalities connected with the conflict, with no reference to where Dinesh Chadha himself was. He reappeared in his own narrative only in the first week of November, in Delhi. So maybe the minister hadn't been in Delhi when the war had broken out, maybe he had been in Shimla with Sultana Begum. But why would he miss being in Delhi at the outbreak of a war, unless it was for something very pressing? Arjun flipped back through the pages. The year 1962 was covered sparsely, beginning with an account of a trip to Matheran a few weeks after New Year's Day, followed by a government-sponsored trip to the US during the summer. Flipping through the next chapter, Arjun came to learn that Chadha had tied the knot in the winter of 1963, at the age of thirty-five, to a twenty-two-year-old from Amritsar, in what seemed to be an arranged match.

His beer was already over, and he signalled the waiter for a repeat. Then he called Bunty. He asked him to come over for a drink if he was free, but his friend was with a group of business associates at a hotel. Arjun could hear loud voices and a television channel in the background. Once again, he was reminded of the solitariness of his profession.

'I just got back from Lucknow today,' Arjun mentioned.

'Lucknow? For what? And I thought you had stopped drinking?'

'Just took a break, Bunty. I had gone there because of that case I told you about.'

'The young girl? You're still involved in that?'

'I need to get it sorted out. For my own satisfaction.'

'I suppose you know what you're doing. Just don't sleep with her or anything.'

Too late, Bunty, Arjun thought. He asked, 'Did your accountant get anything?'

'Accountant?'

'The guest house and travel agency in Paharganj, Bunty.'

'Oh, sorry, I forgot to ask! I'll tell him to mail it to you tomorrow.'

'No problem. One more thing, you've heard of Dinesh Chadha haven't you?'

'The late minister?'

'Yes. Do you know any family members or relatives of his?'

'Let's see . . . haan, yaar, there's a guy called Sunil Chadha, builds flats and things like that, Dinesh Chadha's grandson. I met him once at a party.'

'Could you get me in touch with him? Tell him I want to talk to him about his grandfather.'

'Who do I say you are?'

'Give him the producer story. Tell him I'm doing a documentary on 1960s' India.'

'I can do that. And let's meet this weekend, okay?'

'Sure. Call me.'

He hung up and looked around the semi-occupied bar. If only there was someone with whom he could share the details of his day. He took out his phone and sent a text message to Agnes Pereira: GOT BACK FROM LUCKNOW TODAY. MET MUNNI'S MOTHER. HOPE YOU'RE STAYING SAFE. CALL ME, WE NEED TO DISCUSS YOUR CASE. Then he called his daughter. She was out with friends for a movie.

'At Select Citywalk, by any chance?' he asked.

'No, Anupam. Saket. Papa, we're entering in a while.'

'I just wanted to let you know that I managed to meet the nurse.'

'Oh, great. I hope she was of some help.'

'Very helpful. You're becoming quite the investigator.'

'Thanks, Papa. No, yaar, we're going there for dinner . . . Sorry, that wasn't for you.'

'Rhea, about yesterday morning. I can tell that you are upset, but please try and understand. It just . . . happened. She's involved in this case and wanted some help.'

'It was a shock for me, Papa. Just be careful, okay? I have to go now.'

He looked at his phone. First Bunty, now his daughter. There had to be some truth in what they were saying. He resolved to fix this case and then make a clean break with Agnes

Pereira. Drinking some more beer, he opened the book again and skimmed through its pages. A childhood in the undivided Punjab, the family's rural estates, a far-sighted grandfather who sold off all their land in the early 1940s and moved to Delhi, then Dinesh Chadha's entry into politics as a teenager in the independence movement. By the late 1950s, he was a member of Parliament, an influential and popular figure. He moved around the social circuit in Delhi and Bombay, and seemed to know quite a few actresses and socialites.

Arjun drained his glass and asked for a third beer. He reflected on how different a life Sultana Begum and her daughter had had compared to Dinesh Chadha. It was not just about privilege, but also about ancestors who had played their cards right many years ago. He skipped forward. Then the events of the '70s and '80s, starting with the Emergency, followed by the genesis of the problems in Kashmir and Punjab and Assam, all overseen by an excessively federal Centre with its hidebound bureaucrats. Dinesh Chadha had by then reached a sort of symbolic elderly statesman position. He and his wife had two daughters, one of whom in turn had a son and a daughter, and the other an only son, Sunil Chadha, whom Bunty had just mentioned. In the middle of the book was a selection of photographs from Dinesh Chadha's life, mostly early black-and-white photographs. One of them made Arjun pause: it showed the politician in trousers and shirtsleeves along with a bespectacled man outside a shopfront filled with photo frames, above which was the hoarding 'Royal Photo Studio'. The caption read: 'With the director Babul Biswas in Bombay in 1960'. So Dinesh Chadha could be connected to the photo studio as well.

Putting the book aside, Arjun called the waiter over and placed an order for dinner: sausages and mash. He drank his beer and thought of the old woman in the musty, crumbling house he had met the previous day, and the elderly nurse from a few hours before. They were players in a dark drama that stretched over the years, leading to Arjun now trying to understand the life of a politician who had kicked the bucket. The past and how it affected the present—Arjun found it fascinating. Most Indians had no concern for history, or even the present—they were people for whom their own country remained a mystery. He reviewed the case he was on: he had more or less established that Agnes Pereira's mother was the baby girl Munni had given birth to in Shimla. Now the question was: who had the father been? Though he hadn't discounted the Savitri Rao angle yet, instinct told him that Agnes Pereira had somehow put her own life in danger by digging into her past.

Arjun rose from his table to go to the restroom. He had to pass close to the entrance, and that gave him a view of the corridor outside. A man sitting alone at one of the American burger joint's outer tables caught his eye. He looked fit, had short hair and was wearing a sports jacket, and he was busy with his phone, a soft-drink glass at his elbow. Arjun entered the restroom. He was sure that none of the outer tables had been occupied when he had entered the pub. It could be a coincidence, but a lone man with a soft drink at that time of night seemed a bit strange. On his way back, he looked out again, and at the same moment the short-haired man looked up towards the entrance to the pub as well. Arjun made his decision on the spot.

Walking back to his table, he drained his last glass of beer in one go, picked up the book and went to ask for the bill. His dinner wasn't ready yet, they informed him, it would take another ten to fifteen minutes, would he like it packed? Arjun gave them his debit card and told them to forget about the food and simply add it to his bill. He walked out of the pub and then down to the ground floor, from where he glanced up at the burger place. The outside tables were now deserted again. He looked around, but couldn't spot anyone in a sports jacket.

Maybe it was the jacket that had alerted him—it was still too warm for one. He went down to the parking area, started his car and drove out into the Delhi night.

He was headed back towards the BRT corridor, when along the darkened stretch near the district court complex, a single headlight bearing down on him caught his eye. Slowing at a traffic signal, he saw that it belonged to an orange-and-white sports bike. It approached smoothly and glided to a halt beside his car, and a person wearing a familiar jacket swivelled his helmet to look at him. Arjun looked on as if in a dream as the person's right hand went inside the jacket and came out holding a revolver. For a moment he was back in that summer, watching as a police motorcycle had similarly approached his car. But suddenly, his instinct kicked in, and he sped off from the red light with a rapid 1–2 gear change. He knew there were no CCTV cameras at that spot, and his mind raced to figure out another such spot. The motorcyclist lost a few seconds putting the gun away, but was soon speeding after him.

Arjun had to slow down at the left turn on to the BRT corridor, and the motorcycle had to do the same. Arjun threaded his way through the cars, leaving angry drivers honking in his wake, till about a kilometre and a half away he had to stop at the red light below the Chirag Delhi flyover. Around him, headlights and traffic fumes and families selling balloons and flowers, while in his side-view mirror a single headlight weaved in and out of view, coming closer. Would he be crazy enough to shoot at Arjun here, among the crowds? But who would be able to track down a single motorcyclist going fast? He wished he had brought his .32 along. There was a traffic police picket just ahead but the last thing he wanted was to involve the police. The pixelated digits in red counted down while the headlight came closer. Arjun knew he needed just a few more seconds.

An auto jerked ahead by a few feet in anticipation of the light changing, and Arjun quickly moved through the gap. He could see the motorcycle's headlight and the rider's jacket behind him now in the rear-view mirror, but the light changed to green just then and Arjun floored the accelerator, shooting out of the massed traffic and leaving it behind under the flyover. The accelerator needle climbed steadily and his mouth felt dry. Till the next traffic light, it was a relatively dark and deserted stretch, with a patch of Siri Fort park land on either side. There! In the darkness that solitary headlight once again. They were now both a long way ahead of the rest of the traffic. Arjun's heart was pounding but he forced himself to stay calm. He would get just one chance to pull this off. Up ahead, he saw the lights of the next traffic signal at the crossroads. He eased back slightly on the accelerator and watched as the motorcycle gained on him.

'Come on, come on,' he said, his eyes flicking between the lights up ahead and the headlight approaching in his rear-view mirror.

Now! He lifted his foot off the accelerator even as he stamped on the clutch, pressed the brake and shifted from fifth to third gear. The car tyres squealed—and the motorcycle was beside him before he knew it. He jerked the steering wheel briefly to the right, making the side of his car bump into the motorcycle's rear wheel. Then he released the clutch and accelerated, even as he saw in his side-view mirror the bike smashing into the metal divider and then bouncing off the road, screeching and sending sparks into the air. He looked ahead. Miraculously, the light was green. No time to look back now. Going at a steady clip he took the right that sloped down to Greater Kailash I. He held his breath till he was through GK-I and on the straight stretch towards Nehru Place.

Ten minutes later, he was back in CR Park. He ran his hand over the part of the car that had hit the bike. A minor bump, no scratches or scrapes. Coupled with the lack of CCTV cameras at that spot, Arjun felt he would get away with it. Still . . . He went upstairs and poured himself a stiff whisky, sat down at the dining table and lit a cigarette. No matter whether his would-be assassin lived or died, Vishwanathan—or Kumar Sampath—might send more people after him. He thought of calling his gangster client in Mumbai and letting him know he was still alive, but decided against it. His time was running out. His hand shook as he took a drag on his cigarette. He had to bring the matter to a close one way or another. He switched on his laptop, and began typing out his notes from his meetings with Sultana Begum and Stella Brown.

57

ARJUN WOKE UP LATE THE next morning, and the first thing he did was to open the newspapers. The city news page of the first paper had a small column with the headline 'Biker Killed'. It said that an 'unidentified middle-aged man on a motorcycle' had met with an accident at night near the Siri Fort red light on Josip Broz Tito Marg and later died of serious head injuries at the nearby Moolchand hospital. It mentioned there were 'some reports of an accident' but that the police hadn't let out anything in this regard. He sat back on the sofa and considered this bit of information. Did the police really have no idea of who the man was and how he had died? Or was it something they were keeping to themselves, like the news of the revolver? Or could someone have picked up the revolver from the scene?

He checked his phone. There was a message from Agnes Pereira, sent in the early hours of the morning, after he had gone to bed. I'M SO SORRY ABOUT WHT HAPPENED. YR DAUGHTER MUST THINK I'M A REAL SLUT. I'M JST A SCREWED UP GIRL WHO DSNT KNOW WHO SHE IS. He couldn't be sure if this was a genuine message sent in the late hours after her pills, or if it was something more calculated. Hadn't she been the one who had wanted to come see him? He replied: DON'T BE SO HARSH ON YOURSELF. I'M GETTING CLOSER TO THE TRUTH NOW. SO JUST STAY SAFE, AND PICK UP THE PHONE THE NEXT

TIME I CALL YOU. That would give her some food for thought, he considered, realizing at the same time that his paranoia had heightened since the previous night's incident. More than anything though, he now felt anger. He had found himself with his back up against the wall before—now, he would show them that he knew how to fight.

A while later she messaged him again: HOW WAS SHE, MUNNI'S MOTHER?

VERY OLD, VERY FRAIL, was his reply.

The maid had left his breakfast for him—chappatis, eggs, tea—and he ate it hungrily. Dinner had just been rice, dal, two old sausages from the freezer and chilli pickle. Then he washed down one of his tablets with a glass of water. After washing his plate, cup and glass, he looked around the kitchen and then checked the fridge—he would have to go to the market for supplies. It was 10 a.m. He decided to wait till 10.30 a.m. to call his secretary on the office landline, and then chalk out his course of action for the day. As he was waiting, going through the newspapers, his phone rang. It was Bunty.

Does he know something, was the first thought that crossed Arjun's mind.

'You might have forgotten, but not me,' his friend said and chuckled.

'What are you talking about?' Arjun asked.

'Sunil Chadha. I've fixed you a meeting with him.'

'Thanks, yaar.'

'No thanks, you buy the drinks this time! First thing I did this morning even though I had a hangover. I think I need to join a gym, body is getting soft. You want to join one together? We can look at all those college girls doing aerobics in their tights, ha ha!'

'You know me, I play football. So where and when do I meet him?'

'You kick a football once a month, bhai. Anyway, it's at 4 p.m. at his residence on Aurangzeb Road. Be there, VIP *banda hai*.'

'I will, Bunty. Just message me the address.'

After he hung up, Arjun called Liza.

'Still looking, sir,' she said.

For a moment he was confused. 'Looking for what?'

'You had told me yourself, sir. Riyaz Sheikh. He had started Red Rose Cosmetics, his family still runs it.'

'Oh okay. Yes, look him up and let me know. I had also asked you to look up—'

'Yes, sir, Royal Photo Studio and Savitri Rao. I'll look them up too.'

'You can drop the photo studio. Just look up the girl after you're done with Sheikh.'

'Okay, sir.'

'How's the load for today otherwise? Is Chandu in?'

'Nothing much, sir, manageable. He's here too, sir.'

'I won't be coming in today, maybe tomorrow also. I want to finish off this case once and for all.'

'Good, sir. And the girl, I told you my relatives . . .'

'I remember. Monday. Don't worry, she'll be gone by then. And tell Chandu to do the filing work in my room.'

He hung up, took a shower, and then walked over to Market No. 1, where he bought some groceries, including sweet curd. Mr Sen was missing from behind his desk. When Arjun inquired, the head salesman said that Dada wasn't well. He looked at the empty desk once again before leaving the shop. Unthinkable, this absence of the slim gentleman in his pressed trousers and half-sleeved shirt, a plastic disposable cup of tea always at his elbow. He reflected guiltily that he hadn't scheduled his father's appointment for a check-up as yet.

When he got back to the flat he checked his phone—he had left it plugged into the charger—and found that there was a message and a missed call. The message was from Bunty, and contained Sunil Chadha's address. He memorized it and deleted the message. The missed call was from Poppy. Arjun called her back.

'Hi. Arjun. Making any progress with your case?'

Her voice sounded husky and sleepy; she would be at home, having just got up after one of her usual late nights.

'I am, yes. Just a few more things to clarify. You managed to find out about Kailash Swami?'

'Yes. In fact, I was wondering if we could meet this afternoon at the India International Centre. You, me and Professor Saxena.'

'Why the professor?'

'You'll see.'

'He thinks I'm from a lawyer's firm, by the way.'

'We'll let him keep thinking that.'

'What time?'

'Would two this afternoon be okay?'

'That should be fine.'

'So I'll see you there then.'

Afterwards Arjun went to the bedroom and emptied the backpack he had taken to Lucknow, including the shopping he had done there. For lunch he made himself a light chicken stew with carrots and cabbage, akin to the boiled food of the north-east, to go along with his rice. Before he ate he quickly went through the notes on his laptop once again. There were questions he had for both Poppy Barua and Professor Saxena.

58

THE EARLY-AFTERNOON SUNLIGHT SLANTED
INTO the carpeted lounge at IIC where silver-haired retirees
from the bureaucratic and academic fields sat in armchairs
reading or having quiet conversations. Arjun spotted the senior
editor and the retired professor in one corner and made his
way towards them. It was his second or third time here, and
the place reminded him of something: an illustrated story in
an old children's book or an advertisement in an old magazine,
something he couldn't quite place. Poppy Barua raised a hand as
he came closer. He saw there was a pot of tea or coffee on the
table between them along with a remaining sandwich on a plate.
They seemed to have been there a while. Prakash Saxena half
stood to shake his hand, and when he was seated, Poppy said to
him with a glint in her eye, 'I've managed to convince Professor
Saxena here to do an article for us.'

'I must say she's very persuasive,' Prakash Saxena said with
a quiet smile.

So that's why he was here. She looked fresh and charged,
unlike the voice on the phone.

'About what?' Arjun queried.

'Munni, and the child no one knew about. The secret
histories of Bollywood.'

'She's pointed out quite rightly that it'll be good publicity
for my book,' Prakash Saxena said, somewhat apologetically.

Surprised, Arjun said, 'I haven't quite got to the bottom of things yet.'

'That's why we're having this meeting,' Poppy Barua said. 'Coffee? Tea? Sandwiches or cutlets?'

Arjun raised a hand. 'Thanks, but I've just had my lunch.'

Prakash Saxena leaned forward in his chair. 'There was a child? How did you know?'

'Our client really, she had a suspicion,' Arjun said, looking at Poppy.

'Relax, Arjun, Professor Saxena won't start until we both give him the go-ahead.'

'Then there's the issue of confidentiality too,' he said.

'Don't worry, I've explained that to him,' she said, and the retired professor nodded. She went on, 'But let me share what I managed to find out about our friend Kailash Swami. Apart from Munni, there have been several disappearances over the years that are somehow or other linked to him.'

'A former secretary of his, for instance?' Arjun asked.

'Correct. Then a businessman who had accused Kailash Swami of backtracking on a bribes-for-contracts deal with a Central minister. Also a political rival of a state minister from Uttar Pradesh who was a regular client of the Natural Life Studio. Then people like the wife of a senior bureaucrat, which left him free to marry a lawyer he had been having an affair with. The list goes on.'

'How many such cases are we talking about here?' Arjun asked.

The editor shrugged. 'About eight to ten. Could be as high as twelve.'

'And you're sure they're all linked to Kailash Swami?'

'I can't be sure . . . they could all be your usual Delhi crimes. But once you look at them with Kailash Swami in the picture, he seems linked to everything. So that's strange.'

'I know what you mean,' Arjun said, remembering his own reaction when she had given him the details of the photo studio and Camera Bobby. Everything was linked . . . he also recalled the strange details of the story told to him by Joint Commissioner Surinder Jha.

'My god, in that case he's a . . . a psychopath!' Prakash Saxena whispered.

'We can't say that yet,' Arjun murmured. 'But there is definitely something fishy. Do you know Kailash Swami's supposed to be a carpenter as well?'

Poppy Barua shook her head as she checked her phone. He turned to Prakash Saxena.

'The Royal Photo Studio in Mumbai. There was some scandal about pornographic photographs being taken there in the early 1960s. Did you ever hear about that?'

The retired professor nodded his head slowly. 'There were rumours about that, yes.'

'Do you think either Sultana Begum or her daughter could have been involved in it?'

'I don't think so. They were certainly hard-pressed for money at one point, but it's difficult to see either of them getting so desperate. And even if that were the case, it would have happened much before the early 1960s, maybe in the mid-1950s.'

'What sort of pornography are we talking about here?' Poppy Barua asked as she put her phone back on the table. 'Hard-core images or more like soft porn?'

'My guess would be the latter,' Prakash Saxena said.

'You haven't seen those images, have you?' Arjun asked.

Poppy Barua shook her head. 'Just some gossip I got from our Mumbai bureau chief.'

'What do you intend to do now?' the professor asked him. 'Talk to Kailash Swami?'

'I've already done that, but I guess I'll have to pay him another visit soon.'

Someone called out the retired professor's name; they turned to see a tall, slightly stooped man in a white shirt approaching them.

'How are you, Prakash? Long time no see.'

Prakash Saxena stood to shake the other man's hand. 'Balbir, how have you been?'

The two men traded news of their families and other retired friends. Poppy gave Arjun a thin smile. He looked around the room as he half-listened to the two men talking. What he was reminded of, in these peaceable surroundings, were the two men he had killed: one in Manali, the other here in Delhi. He knew they would come back to haunt him once all of this was over. Balbir left, and Prakash Saxena sat down.

'I suggest you start making your notes,' Poppy Barua told the professor before turning to speak to Arjun, 'A week from now? You should be in a position to brief Professor Saxena by then?'

'Certainly,' he said. He wasn't looking forward to it, but then she had helped him.

Her phone beeped with a message; she picked it up to check, and said, 'Sorry, I have to get going. A press conference that I'm supposed to cover.'

Arjun took the chance to get up too. The retired professor said he would hang around for a while at IIC. He spoke with a wry smile, 'What will I do back at home?'

They walked out together to the car park. She commented on how pleasant the weather was and asked him where he was headed. When he told her she said, 'You're really involved in this case, aren't you?'

'I just want to get it over with, to tell you the truth. Hey, hang on a minute.'

He went over to his car and brought back the packet he had taken out of his backpack that morning.

'I got something for you from Lucknow,' he said. 'I hope it's your size.'

She took out the cream chikan-work salwar kameez and squealed in delight.

'So sweet of you, Arjun! It'll fit me perfectly.'

He looked at her face in the sun. It had fine lines and the beginnings of pouches, unlike Agnes Pereira's flawless skin. A face that bore witness to the life it had lived. There was something in her though that was too similar to him, he realized, too close to his own temperament.

'I got one for my daughter as well. I hope she likes it.'

'I'm sure she will. It's something classic.'

He lit a cigarette and watched as she drove off. A press conference, or someone she had to meet, he wondered. He walked over to his car and got in.

59

AURANGZEB ROAD WAS JUST A five-minute drive from
IIC, around the top of Lodi Gardens and up South End Road.
The proximity to Parliament made this one of the most sought-
after stretches of real estate in the capital, with ultra-modern
apartments and bungalows that went for tens of millions of US
dollars. At the roundabout, Arjun turned left from Claridges
Hotel and drove the short distance to the address. Up ahead
was Nagaland House, where the chief minister of that state had
survived an audacious assassination attempt by Naga rebels back
in 1993.

Black granite walls topped with CCTVs, a high wood-and-
metal gate, and beside it a guardhouse that seemed more like a
small office. As he turned off the road, he saw, some distance
behind the gate, a large apartment block with sleek metal balconies
and wide glass windows. All of this could be traced back to that
far-sighted grandfather of Dinesh Chadha's, Arjun thought.
An unsmiling guard in uniform came up to ask him where he
wanted to go, following which he called him into the guardhouse
to make an entry in a register while he called up Sunil Chadha to
confirm. Arjun took in the interior of the air-conditioned cabin
which included a bank of eight CCTV monitors and a pile of
newspapers on the floor, a copy of the *Loksatta* on the top.

He left the guardhouse, the gate slid open smoothly, and he
drove in and slotted his car in the 'Guests' section of the parking

lot at the ground level, from which four storeys rose up, two flats to a floor. There were Range Rovers and Porsches in the parking area, apart from the more common BMWs and Mercedeses. A mali in shorts and a full-sleeved shirt was using a hosepipe to water the patches of grass around the parking area. Sunil Chadha occupied a top-floor flat, and Arjun had been asked to go straight up. He took the lift. The place was deathly quiet, with none of the usual chatter and noise that pervaded Indian apartment blocks. Insulated walls, he guessed. On the top-floor landing, he rang the doorbell of number 42—the second flat on the fourth floor—and was reminded of the 0911–1160 that had led him to the Beas View guest house in Manali.

The door was flung open by a tall, middle-aged man dressed in scruffy shorts and a T-shirt. He was pale, unshaven and thin—a far cry from the solid and stylish Dinesh Chadha whom Arjun had seen in the photographs in *Freedom and Beyond*.

'Ankit Ahuja, the producer! It's great to meet you! Sunny Chadha!' He pumped Arjun's hand enthusiastically and ushered him in. 'Forgive the clutter, but it's how I live.'

A large sitting room that ended in a balcony with expansive views of central Delhi, but inside there were things strewn all over the place, magazines and a laptop and books on the sofa and immense glass table, food and cartons of juice and plates with leftovers on the dining table, sneakers and dumb-bells on the carpeted floor, and two empty pints of a Belgian beer in the corner.

'No problem,' Arjun said.

He pushed aside a paperback thriller on the sofa and sat down.

Sunny Chadha gave him a sheepish grin. 'No wife and no maid, so I've gone back to being a college boy.'

'Where have they gone?'

'My wife's left me.' Chadha waved a lanky hand. 'Forget about all that. Bunty told me you're doing a film. Tell me about it.'

'Well, it's about an old film actress, Munni, I don't know if you've heard of her.'

Chadha nodded thoughtfully. 'I've heard of her, sure.'

'She was a recluse during the later part of her life, and then she disappeared. We want to look at her life and times as an actress. Which means talking to people who knew her, such as your grandfather, for instance.'

Chadha let out a whinnying laugh. 'I don't know if you know, but the old man's been dead for some time now.'

'We're aware of that. Which is why we wondered if *you* would consider talking about him . . .'

'But what would I say?'

'Oh, you know, your grandfather's friendship with people like the director Babul Biswas, Munni and her mother Sultana Begum. His zest for life and larger-than-life personality. I'm sure you have plenty of stories about him.'

'He was a personality all right. It was always believed in the family—being frank with you here, okay—it was always believed that he was more interested in her mother, though she was about fifteen years older than him and her daughter was closer to him in age.'

'I've heard about that. Would you be . . . uncomfortable . . . talking about it?'

'Uncomfortable? Of course not! All that happened a long time ago.'

He went towards the dining table where he started moving things around. There was a sense of unease and restlessness in him. His privileged background seemed to have left him lacking drive and determination, as if his successful ancestors had used up all of that.

'You drink, don't you?' Chadha suddenly asked. 'I can always tell a man who drinks.' Without waiting for an answer, he went into the kitchen and returned with a bottle. 'A thirty-year-old single malt. I have an excuse to have a drink, now that you're here.'

He opened a wall cabinet and took out two glasses, into which he poured out two measures at the dining table before bringing Arjun his drink.

'If you insist,' Arjun said. It had been a while since he'd drunk whisky during the day.

'Oh, I absolutely insist! And I shall persist!' He laughed again. 'Let's toast to that grandfather of mine.'

They clinked their glasses and Arjun took a sip. It was a smooth, honeyed liquor.

'So where do you want to interview me?' Chadha asked. 'And do I have to wear a suit and all that?'

'Here, if that's okay. A suit would be good, but you can wear anything.'

'I'll have to get a shave as well,' Chadha said, stroking his cheeks.

Was he being facetious, Arjun wondered, or was that just his normal flippant personality?

'We're still a few weeks away from shooting,' Arjun said. 'In fact, the script's still being written. I was wondering if you could tell me more about your grandfather.'

'What can I say? He was a public person, so his life is well known. You should pick up his autobiography, *Freedom*—'

'—*and Beyond*,' Arjun completed. 'I was reading that just yesterday. He had an arranged marriage, didn't he?'

'Most people did in those days. Maybe it was for the better. Look at me, I married for love.' He let out a whinnying laugh again and took a sip of whisky.

'Do you think he was faithful to his wife? Given the fact that he knew so many women.' An awkward question, but Arjun had the feeling Sunny Chadha could handle it.

'Once he was married, he was a one-woman guy. He was straight that way. What had happened in the past had happened. It's a feeling I share, Mr Ahuja. All of our history, all that fighting over religion, our superstitions and beliefs, I think all of that should be swept aside.' He made a sweeping motion with his free hand. 'Look to the future, that's what I say.'

'Going back to the past again, your grandfather was pretty friendly with Babul Biswas, wasn't he?'

'Mm-hm. Very good friends. The two of them and Riyaz Sheikh, the guy who started Red Rose Cosmetics, they were quite a group at one time. Before he got married. They would meet up at the New India Lodge whenever my grandfather was in Bombay.'

'What do you think happened to Munni?'

'Who knows? Maybe someone murdered her.'

'An old lover?'

'Could be. They were quite colourful in those days, mind you. And a lot more privacy than today, what with your cell phones and Facebook.'

'True. What do *you* do, Mr Chadha? Excellent whisky, by the way.'

'Glad you like it. I dabble in real estate and construction. Nothing serious, just keeps me occupied.' He drained his glass. 'Would you like another drink, Mr Ahuja?'

'Some other time, perhaps. The rest of your family members?'

'Abroad. I look after all of our family's properties here. Well, if you're not going to have another drink . . . I need to get to one of my construction sites.'

'Sure, I guess I'll make a move too.'

Sunny Chadha collected their glasses and went to the kitchen. Arjun looked around the vast sitting room. There was an emptiness about the place that he was familiar with. Under

333

the glass table before him, on the magazine rack, was a stack of brochures along with scattered magazines and newspapers. He craned his neck to have a better look, and saw that the brochures were for the presently stalled Platinum Court Towers project in Greater Noida. It was the same brochure he had seen at the travel agency below Shiva Guest House in Paharganj. When Chadha came out, Arjun asked him where his projects were located.

'I just have one now in south Delhi. So let me know when you want to do the filming. And we should meet before that. Maybe I'll remember something more about my grandfather.' He grinned at Arjun, showing a row of uneven, yellowing teeth.

'Sure, that would be nice.'

Why had he lied? Arjun wondered as he went down by the lift. Or was Platinum Court Towers someone else's project?

The gate slid open as his car approached. He stopped and nodded to the security guard, who came over. He could see the mali sitting on a chair outside the guardhouse, reading the newspaper Arjun had seen earlier. The man lowered the paper to look at the car, and Arjun saw a crucifix showing through his half-open shirt. Something about the gardener niggled at him.

'What car does Chadha sahib drive?' he asked.

'He doesn't have a car, he sold his last one,' the guard said.

'Is he buying a new one?'

'I don't know.'

Arjun took a last look at the mali and then turned left and drove down to Khan Market, where he went into the McDonald's to order a Maharaja Mac for himself. He was hungry after that light lunch of his, and the fine whisky had acted as a sort of appetizer. He saw that he had a missed call from the office. He called back and Liza picked up.

'I've got some material on Riyaz Sheikh,' she said. 'Should I take a printout for you?'

'Just tell me what you have, briefly,' Arjun said, biting on a French fry.

'Okay. Born in Old Delhi in 1926. Came from a family that dealt in *attar* and other traditional perfumes. Went to college while working in the family shop. Started a small cosmetics unit after Independence in 1949. Within a decade, it was a recognized cosmetics company. He had married by then, and later had a son and two daughters. Reportedly had an affair with an actress hired for the company's advertisements. Also rumoured to have had an affair with the actress Munni. Health problems in later age, blood pressure, diabetes, etc. Was confined to a wheelchair after a stroke in 1997, and passed away in 2005. After his death, the family sold the company to a group of investors. Survived by his wife, who must be in her mid-seventies now, three children and several grandchildren.'

'How many grandchildren exactly?'

'Not sure, sir.'

'I want you to find out how many grandchildren there are, how old they are, how much the company was sold for and who received how much, if possible, plus where the wife and daughters are now. Got it?'

'Mm-hm, yes, sir, wife and daughters, okay,' she said, writing it down. 'Will you be coming into the office tomorrow?'

'No. Keep it closed, if necessary. You can ask Chandu to help you.'

'Sure, sir. See, that's why I keep saying we need another detective in the office.'

Arjun grunted, and was about to hang up when she said, 'Sir, one more thing.'

'What?'

'That Savitri Rao girl. After much searching on the Net, I came across one article in a Mumbai tabloid on bar dancers where they had interviewed her. She said she was planning to leave India and migrate to Australia.'

'When was this article from?'

'From April of this year, sir.'

'Did she mention why she wanted to leave?'

'She said she wanted to start a new life.'

'I see. Thanks, Liza. See you on Monday.'

He hung up and dug into his burger and fries and shake. When stuck in a complicated situation he liked this sort of meal. He felt it somehow cleared his head. Right now he had a rough idea of how Munni's unfortunate daughter—Agnes Pereira's mother—had ended up in Goa. But he still didn't know who the father had been. Riyaz Sheikh, or someone else? And how could his identity be tied up with the threat to Agnes Pereira's life? Then there was the information Poppy had given him regarding the disappearances surrounding Kailash Swami. Did Munni's disappearance hold the key to this case? And of course, there was still Savitri Rao to consider. He would have to call Agnes Pereira and Computer Baba.

Arjun finished his shake and the last few fries. Across from him were a group of teenagers, boys and girls joking and laughing. He saw himself, Bunty and Sonali there, but in a tea shop under a peepul tree in Delhi University. There were no second chances in life, but like most lessons, it was one that was learnt too late. He cleared his tray at the bin and walked out into the Khan Market evening and lit a cigarette.

60

DRIVING BACK TO CR PARK, Arjun put on some Led Zeppelin. Waiting at the South Extension flyover for the lights to turn green, he looked at the vehicles around him in the smog, even as Robert Plant sang:

In the days of my youth, I was told what it means to be a man . . .

Could there be any more motorcycle-borne assassins out there looking for him, he wondered. His phone buzzed. It was Bunty. Arjun paused the song and answered the call.

'Kancha, where are you?'

'South Ex. Headed home.'

'Chalo, I'm coming over with a bottle.'

'I thought we were meeting on the weekend?'

'Then what is it today? Thank god it's Friday!'

'Any occasion, Bunty?'

'We haven't said cheers for a while, so I thought I would come over to your place.'

'Theek hai. I should be there by seven.'

'Okay, ji.'

Arjun pressed play and stepped on the clutch as the traffic started to move.

Good times, bad times, you know I had my share . . .

The doorbell rang just a few minutes after Arjun got home, and he asked Bunty to wait while he took a shower. He came out of the bedroom ten minutes later in his boxers and T-shirt to find his friend sitting on the sofa watching a Hindi comedy film and chuckling to himself. The bottle of Blenders Pride he had brought with him had been opened, and there was half of a peg before him.

'You couldn't wait for me?' Arjun asked, lighting a cigarette.

'Wife called, I need to get back after a while. An uncle of mine from Punjab has turned up.'

Arjun went into the kitchen to get himself a glass. He felt a stab of irritation upon hearing his friend's explanation, followed by a familiar, old feeling of anger tinged with self-pity. Why couldn't the world just leave him alone? He made himself a stiff drink before sitting down in one of the single-seaters.

'You shouldn't have come if you have guests,' he said without looking at his friend.

Bunty, who had been leaning forward to pick up his glass from the table, froze.

'Arré, yaar, what are you saying? He's that uncle of mine who lost the MLA elections. I have to go and see him, even if I don't want to. He had to land up at my place today, of all days. You aren't angry, are you, Arjun? If you want, you can come to my place, we'll continue there.'

Arjun waved away his friend's suggestion with a grin. You couldn't stay angry with Bunty for long.

'It's okay, have your peg and run back home.'

'Let me finish three pegs then you chase me out. Aur bata, how's the young chick?'

Arjun ground out his cigarette in the ashtray and blew out the last of the smoke. 'She's fine. It's just me who's gotten entangled in this whole business.'

'I had given you some advice at the beginning, if you remember. So what have you found out?'

'She could be the granddaughter of a Hindi film actress from the '60s who had disappeared.'

338

'Munni?'

Arjun nodded and knocked back his drink. 'The guy from Mumbai wants this girl dead, but I still can't figure out why. I was nearly killed myself.' He briefly told Bunty about his encounter with the motorcyclist the previous night.

'They tried to kill you here, in Delhi? Sisterfucker, if I could get my hands on that fellow! Do you want me to arrange a guard for you from a security agency?'

'I can take care of myself, Bunty. What I need to find out is who the girl's father was. I have a feeling that's where the answer lies.'

He told his friend about his trip to Lucknow and his meetings with the director's son and with Sunny Chadha. Bunty shook his head as he heard the details.

'It's too complicated for me, yaar. Maybe your Mumbai guy wants her dead for the reason he told you: she stole his money.'

'But then why try to have *me* killed as well?'

'To tie up all the loose ends. So you can't tell anyone when you realize that you found her only for him to get rid of.'

'No, that seems too . . . simple. Her problems seem to have begun from when she started digging into the items she found in that biscuit tin.'

'Biscuit tin! Listen to yourself. Why do you want everything in life to be complicated?'

There was some truth in what his friend was saying, Arjun reflected. He wondered how Bunty would react if he told him that he had slept with Agnes Pereira. Which reminded him that he needed to call her. They sat for a while in silence watching the film. One of Bunty's two phones on the glass-top table buzzed. He picked it up and read the message.

'Achha, my accountant has sent you that mail about Blue Wave Capital.'

'Let me have a look,' Arjun said, and got up.

'Can't you wait?' Bunty complained. 'Enjoy your drink?'

'After I get to the bottom of this.'

He brought the laptop and opened the email. Blue Wave Capital was, as Bunty had said, registered in Mauritius. The company had interests in South Asia in stocks, real estate, commodity-trading firms, hospitals and hotels, among which was listed, curiously, Shiva Guest House in Delhi's Paharganj. The company's board of directors had a few Anglo-sounding names followed by some Indian or South Asian names, one of which stood out for Arjun: Kumar Sampath, who, going by the information Poppy had collected, could be Vishwanathan's real name. Another name caught his attention: A.K. Mehta. Could he be the Anil Mehta from the family which owned the furniture store?

'Anything useful?' Bunty asked, pouring himself another peg. 'This is my last one.'

'Mm-hm,' Arjun grunted, reading the mail a third time. Links within links, it was all getting too complicated. And yet, there was something at the margins of his mind, nagging at him. Something he hadn't been able to connect. What was it?

'By the way, I almost forgot. I heard something interesting today about that Chadha's grandson.'

'Really?' Arjun put down the laptop and picked up his glass again. 'What is it?'

'I heard it from a property dealer I know who operates from Connaught Place. It seems the grandson is fighting a court case with his cousins over their grandfather's property on Aurangzeb Road.'

'There's an apartment block there now. They must be fighting over who gets how much rent.'

'This dealer said the grandson is fighting for a fifty-fifty share, while his cousins want it equally distributed among the three of them.'

'How reliable is this guy?'

'Quite reliable. He's been in the business for over thirty years now. Knows all the old families in the city.'

Arjun nodded. 'Have you heard of the Platinum Court apartment project, Bunty?'

'Sounds familiar. Where is it?'

'The other side of the Yamuna. But I read something about it being stalled. Could you find out who's behind the project from your property dealer friend?'

The brochure he had seen in the travel agency in Paharganj and then in Sunny Chadha's place—was there a connection there as well?

'I'll find out tomorrow, all right?'

Bunty checked his phone again, gulped down the rest of his drink and got to his feet.

'Time for me to leave. Don't finish the whole bottle.'

'I'll leave a peg for you. Find out about that project, okay?'

Arjun went out to the balcony, lit a cigarette and watched Bunty walk to where he had parked his car on the other side of the road, across from the park. It was a cool night. Winter was slowly approaching—soon another year would have gone by. A feeling of having wasted his life crept upon him, and he tried to shake it off. He stubbed out the cigarette in a flowerpot with a dead plant and was about to go back in, when he noticed a silver-grey SUV near where Bunty had parked come to life and drive off. Another car he had never seen around here.

He went back inside and called a number from his cell phone. When the other person picked up, he said, 'Commissioner Jha? This is Arjun Arora here, the detective.'

'Mr Arora. Managed to find out anything new?'

'I'm working on it. I went to Lucknow and traced Munni's mother, and she led me to an Anglo-Indian nurse here in Delhi who was present when Munni gave birth to a girl.'

341

There was a silence, then the Commissioner spoke, 'I'm impressed. You seem to be a very persistent man.'

'I never learnt when to give up.'

'But what happened to Munni?'

'I feel I'm getting closer to finding out. Could I ask you for a favour?'

'Go ahead.'

'There's a crooked builder in Mumbai by the name of Kumar Sampath. Might also use the name Vishwanathan sometimes. A big-built man with the little finger of his left hand missing, apparently over a missed payment to a Dubai don. Could you ask your contacts in Mumbai to look into this fellow, especially any Delhi connections he might have?'

A pause. 'How long have you known this character, Mr Arora?'

'I met him for the first time two weeks ago.'

'I see. And you think he's connected to Munni's disappearance?'

'Possibly, yes.'

'I won't promise you anything, but I'll see what I can do.'

'Thank you.'

'All the best, Mr Arora.'

He fixed himself another peg, and then did something he had last done ages ago: he put the slightly less than half-full bottle away in the cabinet near the dining table, surprising himself in the process. Could he be turning over a new leaf? For dinner, he made some *arhar* dal along with a mixed vegetable sabzi and a salad. The only indulgence he permitted himself was a spoonful of ghee over his hot rice and dal. It was with a feeling of satisfaction that he washed his plate and then settled down on the sofa to watch some news before going to bed.

61

ARJUN HAD ONCE READ SOMEWHERE that alcohol interfered with the body's REM sleep cycle, and that had seemed to explain why he had fewer dreams in his sleep as he grew older. But it was an exceptionally vivid and surreal dream that brought him awake in the early hours of the morning. He had somehow landed up in the Bombay of the 1960s, and was being driven around by a taxi driver who pointed out the sights to him and then brought him to a photo studio where Arjun had been instructed to ask for 'Bobby'. This character, a slim, taciturn, elderly gentleman, had taken him into an inner room where Agnes Pereira, her hair in a short bob, and draped in a sheer, see-through sari with nothing underneath, was posing for a photographer who was using an old-fashioned box camera. A group of men stood by in one corner, smoking and looking at her silently, among them Dinesh Chadha. A moment came when she dropped the only garment she wore, and strode up to Arjun in only her heels and asked if he had a cigarette with him.

He came awake with his heart pounding and, in the dark, became aware of an unfamiliar sound. Going to the window, he pulled the curtain aside to see a steady stream of rain falling in the orange glow of the street light in the back lane. Strange, a shower at this time of the year. He went back to bed but couldn't fall asleep. Thoughts of Agnes Pereira mixed with memories of monsoon rains drumming on the tin roof of their small house in Shillong. A sense of incompleteness gripped him. Life was the biggest mystery of them all. He checked his phone: 4.30 a.m. In the end he got up and made himself a cup of tea and sat down at the dining table with his laptop and notepad, going through and adding to his notes on the case.

His secretary would start looking into Riyaz Sheikh that day. He would give Agnes Pereira a call after a while. Of his would-be assassin there was no further news. Even if someone had noticed a silver-grey Swift, he thought, there were thousands of these cars in the city. And if the police had the number, then they would have already paid him a visit. His dream came back to him—the look on Dinesh Chadha's face. Only a dream, but was his subconscious trying to suggest something to him? He lit a cigarette and jotted down a few points on the notepad. Something that had been bothering him since the previous day was now clearer: could there be a connection between Kailash Swami, with his training as a carpenter, and the furniture store in Mumbai? And if A.K. Mehta on Blue Wave Capital's board of directors was the same man who was associated with the furniture store, then maybe, looking at where his Mumbai ticket had been booked from, someone had been keeping an eye on Arjun for a while now?

The maid came in at 6.30 a.m., and Arjun collected the newspapers from the balcony and sat down on the sofa to go through them. It was now drizzling outside. As far as appointments went, he had to call Siddharth Biswas to confirm their meeting for the evening. And he needed to talk to Kailash Swami once more, see if he could ferret out something about the suspicious disappearances. Maybe he would go to the office for a bit, later in the morning. All the while the maid sullenly went about her duties, banging the dishes in the kitchen sink. He tried talking to her as she made his usual breakfast—parathas, an omelette and a cup of tea—but all he got out of her were monosyllabic replies. Eventually he grew annoyed and gave up. If only she asked him how Rhea and Sonali were, so that he could give her some news of them, instead of putting on that stern face of hers. On one or two occasions, he had contemplated asking her to leave and finding a replacement, but that would have been even more of a bother, so he settled for the lesser evil. It occurred to him that once this whole Agnes Pereira business was over, he should ask Rhea to spend a night in her old room, and give the maid a surprise in the morning. That might help thaw the ice. He went into her room to have a look, and unpacked the Black Eagle device and put its batteries into the charger pack. In case he had to use it any time soon.

He had his breakfast after the maid left. Then he took out his revolver and pulled it apart, and was cleaning it over a newspaper spread on the dining table when his phone rang. The landline number seemed familiar, and when he answered it he was surprised to hear Stella Smith's voice.

'Good morning, Mr Arora.'

'Good morning, Mrs Smith. You've remembered something, I hope?'

'I was thinking about it after you left. So many memories. Then I remembered. But I had to wait till my son left for work, he was a bit upset yesterday after you had left.'

'I'm sorry if I—'

'No, it's all right. It's just that he found out I had been crying.'

'Thank you for calling me.'

'As long as it helps that poor little granddaughter in some way. All right, the Italian couple, the Fanuccis, were living in Bombay. The husband was working in a shipping firm. I remembered that they had come to see Dr Mistry too at the clinic in Bandra. I guess it might have been about the wife. They didn't have any children, you see. And Dinesh Chadha, he must have been a friend of theirs.'

'Must have been? What do you mean?'

'Many years after Shimla, I happened to read this article in a magazine about Dinesh Chadha. I was working in Delhi then. Anyway, it mentioned one of his daughters who went to Italy to study designing and stayed for a while with a family friend, the Fanuccis. That's what I recalled last night.'

'As far as I know, Dinesh Chadha had two daughters, which one do you think it was?'

'I wouldn't know about that, sorry. And the other thing, that photo studio that you had mentioned,' she paused, and Arjun could hear her taking a deep breath, 'I remember that at one point there was a scandal about indecent photographs of actresses being taken there.'

'When was this, do you remember?'

'Early '60s, before I moved to Shimla. There were rumours that Munni had appeared in a few of those photos before she had become famous. That her mother had forced her to do it. The photos were supposed to be sold to wealthy people in India and abroad.'

'Really?' Arjun opened his notepad and scribbled down a few details. 'But was it ever proved?'

'No, just a rumour as I said, but a lot of people were talking about it back then.'

'Where were Munni and her mother staying in Shimla before they came to the hospital, would you know?'

'Yes, I made inquiries after they had left. They had stayed in a house owned by someone from Delhi. I even went to have a look at the place once. A charming little cottage up in the Summer Hill area. But after that incident, no one seemed to have stayed there.'

'Did you ever get the feeling, Mrs Smith, that Munni might have wanted to get rid of the baby? Or did it seem like she wanted to keep the baby?'

'I've thought about that too, Mr Arora, and I can't say. I've seen women who didn't want to keep their child turn out to be lovely mothers, and I've seen intelligent women from good families who made terrible mothers. But one thing I do know is that Munni's mother had her mind made up: that child was going to be given away.'

'And the father, who do you think he might have been?'

'That I can't say, Mr Arora, and it wouldn't be wise for me to speculate.'

'But if you had to guess?'

'It wouldn't be proper for me to do that. I prayed for that girl, you know. Let me know if you manage to find out what happened to poor Munni. I have to go now.'

'Yes, but . . . Mrs Smith?'

She had already hung up. Arjun put down his phone, and resumed cleaning his gun. The Fanucci family, Munni's possible porn photos and a house in Shimla owned by someone from Delhi. This case was getting more complicated than even the tandoor murder case he had been involved in a few months ago. He used a small brush to spread a few drops of oil inside the barrel and the bullet chambers, then put the gun back together and loaded it. There was no time to lose now.

He called Agnes Pereira's new number, and for once she picked up.

'Morning. Are you alone over there?'

'Yes, Liza just left.' Her voice sounded sleepy still. 'Why don't you come over?'

For a moment, Arjun was tempted. But what she had said somehow didn't match the contriteness of her message to him the previous day. Suspicion reared its head once again.

'Are you still in bed?' he asked her.

'Still on the sofa,' she corrected him. 'How come you called?'

'I'm trying to find out why someone wants both of us dead, in case you've forgotten.'

'Both of us? Wait a minute, did someone—'

'Another hired killer, yes. I dealt with him though. But if they're looking for me, then you must be on their list as well.'

'Arjun, I was thinking last night. Maybe it's better that I go back to Mumbai.'

'And do what?' He realized he wasn't ready to say goodbye to her just yet.

'I don't know. Go and tell the police? I've caused you enough trouble.'

'Listen to me, Agnes, go to the police, and there's a good chance they'll lock both of us up. For the murders of Savitri Rao and the owner of the guest house in Manali. Yes, the old man was stabbed by the second hired killer. You stay put and give me a day or two, I'm fixing this.'

'Okay. I trust you, Arjun.'

'Everything will work out fine, believe me. I need to ask you something. Do you remember your grandmother ever mentioning anything about the Fanucci family?'

'I don't think so, no. Who are they?'

'The couple in the photograph. They were Italian. What about someone called Kailash Swami?'

'The fellow whose institute Munni went missing from? No, never heard her say anything about him.'

'I see. Anyway, like I said, hang in there.'

'You met Munni's mother, you said. What sort of a person is she?'

'Very interesting. Why don't you come see me later and I'll let you know?'

'All right, Arjun.'

He hung up, and then called Computer Baba, who was already at his office in Nehru Place. Baba had accessed Agnes's bank account: it had in it a few lakhs, a modest sum that was neither too small nor too big, and her transactions over the past three months involved salary transfers and small to medium withdrawals. He had also managed to access two accounts of Savitri Rao's, both in Mumbai branches: there had been a withdrawal of two thousand rupees from one account with a modest balance of about fifty thousand, while the day before that, there had been a cash deposit of Rs 25 lakh in the other account which had ten thousand or so prior to that. Arjun checked Baba's dates on the calendar: it was two and three days respectively before she had been killed. Had it been part of her migration money?

'And the money is still in her accounts?' Arjun asked.

'Yes, no one has touched it.'

'Any nominees?'

'That, I couldn't find out. Any other work for me, Arjun bhai?'

'Not at the moment. Why?'

'Let me know if there is. I'm off to Bangkok next week.'

Had the 25 lakhs Savitri Rao put into her account led to her being strangled? Money she might have swiped from Vishwanathan and his partners? Then why had the killer followed Agnes—to silence a possible witness? And could Vishwanathan access the dead girl's accounts? Arjun needed to find out about the nominees to her accounts.

After Computer Baba, he had one more person to call— Siddharth Biswas. The director's son said he would be at home in the evening but was going out for dinner, and asked Arjun to come over at 6 p.m. for a drink. Even as Arjun spoke to him, an unknown number called twice. After hanging up, he called the number.

'Good morning, Mr Ahuja!'

It took him a moment to figure out that it was Sunny Chadha.

'Good morning, Sunny. What's up?'

'Lovely weather, isn't it, raining and all that. Listen, do you want to meet up for lunch? There's this lovely new French place called Coq Au Vin on the way out to Gurgaon. I thought we could check it out and discuss the documentary? What say you?'

It was an unexpected invitation, and Arjun impulsively accepted. He might be able to ferret out something about Dinesh Chadha and the Fanuccis.

'Right-o. I'll see you at one then?'

'All right.'

Arjun went out to the balcony and lit a cigarette. The drizzle was persisting and it was slightly cold. He wondered what sort of food they served at Coq Au Vin.

62

HE LEFT THE FLAT AT half past twelve, after going through his notes on the case once more and taking a shower. Notwithstanding the information Mrs Smith had given him, he felt more at sea than ever. He decided to give Liza till that evening to dig up material on Riyaz Sheikh and his family, and then take a call on the case by tomorrow, Sunday. And maybe Poppy could help him again, with Savitri Rao's bank account nominees. Agnes Pereira would have to leave his secretary's place by Monday, and perhaps it was better she returned to Mumbai. The last resort: he would have to pay a visit to Commissioner Jha and try to explain things. As for the enigma that had been Munni, he felt he had been unable to capture the sort of person she had actually been, just as her disappearance had been unexplained so far.

The weather, as he drove towards Gurgaon, did nothing to improve his mood. Traffic everywhere, crowds waiting for buses, wet roads, the sky a sullen grey, and the persistent drizzle turning the air sticky and humid. It was the sort of weather which, if it lingered, would start giving everyone in this overcrowded city the flu and viral fever. Arjun tried listening to the FM station, but switched over to Kishore Kumar on the USB. *Aanewala kal, jaanewala hai*, sang his favourite Hindi playback singer as he crawled along Aurobindo Marg towards Andheria Modh.

The Coq Au Vin turned out to be a charming little place off the Sultanpur highway which headed into Gurgaon. He had to follow a dirt track flanked by the boundary walls of farmhouses before coming to a high hedge, with a hand-painted sign for 'Le Coq Au Vin' sticking out of it. There was an unpaved parking space with a couple of high-end cars in front of the slightly run-down white bungalow-like structure with French windows. The place had an unpretentious air about it, which appealed to Arjun. As he parked his car and got down, the front door of the bungalow opened, and out stepped Sunny Chadha in a pair of blue knee-length shorts holding what looked like a champagne flute in one hand.

'Mr Ahuja, welcome to the Coq Au Vin!' he shouted out.

Arjun waved at him and walked over. He wondered how Chadha had got there; the guard at the apartments had said he didn't have a car at the moment.

'You've already started, I see,' Arjun said with a smile as they shook hands.

'The weather, Ankit, the weather! May I call you Ankit, by the way? Come on in.'

'Of course,' said Arjun, stepping inside as Chadha held the door open for him.

'The weather reminds me of Goa. And my friend Charley who's just opened this place has a beautiful wife from over there, Tina. You'll meet both of them later.'

Inside was a sitting room of sorts, several settees with colourful cushions, and people in weekend casuals chatting, holding flutes of champagne. A tall girl in a pair of jeans and a white shirt was looking their way, and Chadha headed towards her. It seemed to Arjun that the late politician's grandson was wound up; could he be on pills or something of the sort?

'Roshni, this is the producer I was telling you about,' he said to the girl.

Chadha introduced both of them. A waiter came over with a tray with champagne. Arjun took one; Chadha drained his glass and took another.

'Champagne in the daytime,' he said. 'I love it! Cheers!'

The girl smiled nervously and looked around the room. There seemed to be something fragile and brittle about her, Arjun thought, noting her bright-red lipstick and pale skin.

'It's very good,' Arjun said. 'On the house?'

'Unlimited with today's brunch,' Chadha said. 'Roshni here doesn't drink though.'

'I don't take . . . alcohol,' she explained to Arjun, who nodded.

'So how's the screenplay progressing, Ankit?' Chadha asked him.

'Um, we're getting there. After all, your grandfather had a long and eventful life.'

'That's true,' Chadha said, nodding his head. 'The old man had his share of adventures.'

'Any incident in particular that you remember?'

'Well, he was mostly confined to the house when I was growing up . . . but I remember him telling me once about how they were travelling through somewhere in Madhya Pradesh and their jeep broke down at night. This was during the mid-1960s. A group of men on horseback came along, and when my grandfather requested them, they towed the jeep with their horses to the nearest town. Along the way, he noticed that two or three of them were carrying rifles and shotguns, and it was only afterwards that they found out that the men were part of a gang of dacoits known for kidnapping people. Amazing, isn't it?'

'Great story. But why didn't they kidnap him?'

'He wondered about that too. What he told me was, maybe they didn't harm him because he had requested them for help. So they had a sort of code, you see?'

Arjun nodded, and drank his champagne. He noticed the girl was still looking around distractedly. What was she doing there with Chadha?

'You've finished your champagne? Let's go to the dining area then. Roshni?'

Arjun followed them into an open courtyard with a moss-covered fountain in the centre with a trickle of water. There were tables and cane chairs on all four verandas, and a young couple tucking into their food. They sat down. A waiter appeared from behind a red curtain with menus.

'So there's no . . . buffet?' Arjun asked.

'No, not that sort of brunch, you have to order,' Chadha said. 'Charley's rules! So, what do you want to have?'

Arjun scanned the menu. He wasn't very familiar with French cuisine, but on a rainy day, the bourguignon seemed like a good bet.

'Excellent! I'll go for that as well.' He addressed the girl who was studying the menu with a frown, as though it were a difficult textbook. 'You better go for a salad, Roshni.'

She seemed relieved to have her choice made for her.

'Some more champagne, Ankit?'

'Do they have anything stronger?'

'My thoughts exactly!' Chadha said, and asked the waiter for a bottle of red wine.

Arjun lit a cigarette as they waited for their food. The girl crossed her legs and buried herself in her cell phone. Chadha made a call regarding some construction materials.

'I was wondering,' Arjun asked him when he had hung up, 'if your grandfather ever mentioned an Italian family in Bombay by the name of Fanucci?'

'Fanucci? I don't think so, no.' Chadha shook his head. 'Why?'

'It seems they were family friends, hence I thought you might have heard of them.'

'Not really. I'm sure if someone writes a book about him there'll be many things in it I have no clue about.'

The waiter returned with a bottle of wine and poured out two large glasses. When he left Arjun took a drink, and asked Chadha, 'And did your mother study interior designing in Italy, by the way?'

'No, that was her sister, my aunt.' He threw his head back and chuckled. 'This fellow has certainly done his homework on my family, Roshni.'

The girl looked up with a polite smile, and returned to her phone. The word that came to Arjun was 'distant'. Chadha hadn't hesitated while answering, he thought.

'Oh, we're trying to get a balanced portrait of Dinesh Chadha, that's all,' he said. 'You're an only child, aren't you?'

'Unfortunately, yes. A source of sadness in my life, really.'

'How many first cousins do you have?'

'Two. Both female. One elder than me, one younger than me.'

'Where are they now?'

'They're both abroad, in the UK. I don't know if you've heard, but some people have started this rumour that we're having a dispute over the property our grandfather left behind. All I can say is that it's complete nonsense. We've worked out our respective shares and are happy with it.'

The girl jerked her head up to look at Chadha as he said this, Arjun noticed. Just then Chadha's phone rang; he answered, leaning back in his chair, and listened. He seemed to stiffen, then said 'Theek hai,' and hung up.

'What about your grandfather's love life?' Arjun continued. 'Some people say he had a thing going with the actress Munni.'

'I find that hard to believe, because I never heard anything about it. It must have been just a rumour.'

'Didn't your parents have anything to say about her?'

'I remember my mother referring to Munni's mother, Sultana Begum, as a whore, if you're interested in that. Ah, there's Charley and Tina! How are you guys?'

The Frenchman and his Goanese wife had appeared from behind the curtain. They were both slim and stylishly dressed. The husband had a pencil moustache while the wife wore her hair short and cropped at the sides. The two of them came over to where the trio was seated, and introductions were made and hands were shaken.

'This wine is excellent, guys! Some more, Ankit?'

'I wouldn't mind,' Arjun said.

The drizzle, the laid-back decor and the wine had put him in a relaxed mood. I deserve a break, he thought, I've been working too hard.

Chadha asked the couple to join them but they declined, saying they had to get back to Delhi. Then he leaned towards the husband, Charley, and whispered something in his ear. Arjun could catch the word 'bill'. The Frenchman, looking uncomfortable now, nodded and held up a hand, as if to say that they would discuss it later.

'Thanks a ton, pal. I'm telling you, there aren't many people like you here in Delhi.'

'Who owns this building?' Arjun asked Chadha once the couple had left and a waiter had produced another bottle of red and refilled their glasses.

'An eccentric expat built and abandoned this villa, and then Charley took over.'

'So he started it with his own money?'

'Yes. A labour of love with his wife. Personally, I'm a bit sceptical of people coming out here to try authentic French food, but I hope I'm proved wrong.'

Again he found the girl looking at Chadha, as if she wanted to correct him. He asked her if she wanted to have anything to drink, coffee or juice, but she just shook her head.

'Must be dieting,' Chadha said, drinking some wine and looking at her.

She put her phone on the table and looked away. There was something he couldn't quite put his finger on, and the wine wasn't helping. Their food finally arrived, steaming hot and wonderfully aromatic. Arjun broke a piece of crusty bread, dipped it into his rich brown stew, and bit into it. The flavours were heartily sublime.

'Good, eh?' Chadha said. 'What about a last bottle of wine to go along with it?'

'I would be lying to myself if I said no,' Arjun said with a laugh.

He felt the wine giving him a gentle high. Chadha, like him, appeared to be someone who had trouble knowing when to stop drinking. The girl, meanwhile, pecked at her salad desultorily. They ate in silence for a while. The dining area was starting to fill up now. Arjun decided to ask his man a few more questions.

'You had mentioned Babul Biswas and Riyaz Sheikh as being good friends of your grandfather. Are you in touch with any of their family members?'

'No, not really. I know Siddharth Biswas,' Chadha gave a somewhat contemptuous snort, 'but I'm not in touch with him either.'

'Would you know if Riyaz Sheikh had a cottage up in Shimla?'

'He might have. He was a very rich man back then. It's only now that his family members are squabbling over what he left behind.'

The third bottle of wine was nearly over, and Chadha was high, with the stew dribbling down his chin which he kept wiping away with a napkin. The girl rose to go to the washroom, taking her phone along with her, Arjun noticed.

'Nice to have a bit of company now and then,' Chadha said to him, and winked.

The bill came, and Arjun wanted to split it, but Chadha had a word with the waiter and it was taken away. He said to Arjun, 'They're friends of mine.'

Finally they rose to leave. It was nearly half past three. The girl seemed to have been left exasperated by the slow pace of the lunch. Outside, Arjun thanked Chadha for the meal, and they shook hands.

'I'll put on a suit for the interview!' Chadha slurred, and looked towards the girl, but she had already gone towards a black Honda sedan.

He shook hands with Arjun, and walked unsteadily to the car. Arjun lit a cigarette, got into his modest Swift, and watched as Chadha exchanged what seemed to be angry words with the girl, holding up his left forearm and stabbing at his watch with his finger. There had been something off-kilter about the whole lunch, he reflected: the girl, the bill, Chadha himself. The monotonous drizzle continued to fall from a sullen grey sky.

63

ARJUN HEADED BACK INTO THE city. The traffic was moving slowly and it was already past 4 p.m. He had meant to go to the office for a while as he hadn't been there in the morning; now he thought it would be better to give his secretary a call. The landline phone on her desk rang for a while before she answered.

'I just got back to the office, sir!' she said breathlessly.

'Where had you gone?'

'Riyaz Sheikh's family, sir. I managed to speak to a cousin brother of his in Old Delhi. The family is divided, that's what I understood, and some of them don't speak to the others.'

That confirmed what Chadha had said to him at lunch.

'Well done, Liza. What else did you find out?'

'I got the addresses of his two wives and four children. One of his sons is in Mumbai where he runs a clinic in the Borivali West area.'

'He owns the clinic?'

'Yes, it belongs to him.'

'Is it a fertility clinic by any chance?'

'No, just a general health clinic. Why, sir?'

'Never mind. See what you can find out about this person and his clinic. I've been meeting some people regarding Agnes Pereira's case, so I guess I'll see you on Monday.'

'Sir, when will she . . . ?'

'I should be meeting her tomorrow. We'll work out something, okay? But she'll leave your place by Monday morning at the latest.'

'Thank you, sir!'

The relief in her voice was palpable. Was Agnes Pereira really such a bad house guest, he wondered after hanging up. He would have to figure out what to do with her by the next day, even if he hadn't managed to solve her mystery by then.

It took Arjun another hour to get to Sundar Nagar. The drizzle had turned to rain briefly before stopping, and the lights were coming on in the dusk. He parked in the market near the Biswas house and bought a cup of coffee at one of the shops. Then he came out and smoked a cigarette. It was still early for his appointment but he decided to go there anyway. He had a slight headache brought on by the wine at lunch; the only way to counter it was with a drink. He drove down to the three-storeyed dwelling beside the park. The press-wallah's flimsy establishment was still there, but the man himself seemed to have left for the day. He parked his car across from the gate and walked up to the guardhouse, where he told the bad-tempered old guard that he had an appointment with Mr Biswas's son. The guard made a call from a telephone to confirm, and then asked what his name was. Arjun told him, worried now that he might recall the name.

But the old guard appeared to have no memory of Arjun's first visit, and got down from his stool to open the gate. In the driveway, apart from the old Maruti, there now stood a black Mercedes saloon. He noticed an open door by the driveway which seemed to be a common entrance. The guard directed him to ring the bell at the front door. There was a small patch of lawn outside it with a few flowerpots. A middle-aged maid in a worn sari opened the door, and asked Arjun in Hindi to come in.

The spacious, old-fashioned sitting room had a musty smell. He perched on the edge of a wide sofa in a faded turquoise colour. The maid asked him if he wanted water or tea, and he chose the former. She informed him that Siddharth *babu* would come down to see him shortly, and left the room. Arjun checked his cell phone: he was nearly half an hour early.

He looked around the room. There was a bookcase in one corner, and several old rugs. A display case with various mementoes, trophies and souvenirs. Framed black-and-white photographs on the walls. Once again he felt the weight of history, the remnants of old lives. At the same time, there seemed to be no trace left of the actress who had lived here for three decades.

The maid returned with a glass of water and waited while he drank it. He declined her offer of more water, and asked her where Babul Biswas was. She replied that 'director *sahib*' was upstairs in his room, where he spent most of his time. He was very old, she went on, and never left the house. How long had she been working here? Arjun inquired. She had been looking after the house for almost fifteen years, she said, with noticeable pride in her voice. Did she know anything about the actress who had once lived here and had then disappeared? She frowned at this and told Arjun that it was before her time in this house. Picking up the empty glass she left the room.

Arjun sat there, taking in the atmosphere. The silence lay heavy; it seemed to say that everything important had happened in the past. Was that another factor which had attracted him to this case? He got up and walked around the room. In between the orange-spined Penguin paperbacks in the bookcase, Arjun spotted a biography of Field Marshall Cariappa. In the display case was a Filmfare Award statuette, for best director, for the year 1964. He went over to the photos hanging on the wall. They were mostly in black and white,

361

and depicted scenes from the director's life: on the set with his actors, at award ceremonies, on holiday. There were none with Munni or Sultana Begum though, or even with his wife and son, or so it seemed to Arjun. One picture in colour caught his eye, a middle-aged Babul Biswas and the playback singer Kishore Kumar smiling into the camera in what looked like a recording studio.

'At a recording session for the film *Black Market*,' a voice said behind him and Arjun turned to see Siddharth Biswas standing there, dressed incongruously in a red dressing gown. 'Ever listened to him?'

'One of my favourites actually,' Arjun said.

The eyebrows went up theatrically. 'Who would have guessed!'

He had the impression again of the man trying out someone else's lines, an older relative possibly. Someone still trying to fix the image that he wanted to project to the world.

'There are no pictures of Munni here. Or of you and your mother.'

'That was my late mother's decision. She wanted this room to be devoted to my father's career. As for that . . . actress . . . can't you guess for yourself?'

'Not really, no.'

Siddharth Biswas let out an exaggerated sigh. 'There was enough drama over her disappearance. Why remind people of her all over again?'

'Good riddance, you would say?'

'You're putting words into my mouth now. But I called you here for a drink. Come this way please, I have the spirits in my office.'

Arjun followed the dressing-gowned figure down a wide corridor and into a dimly lit room that had a desk with two computers in front of a bookcase that covered the entire wall, and on the other side a sofa set around a low table. In the corner beside it was a small liquor cabinet, open, and a table with a record player and a lamp with a paper-cut shade.

Siddharth Biswas asked Arjun to sit, and took a seat opposite him.

'So, Detective Arjun Arora,' Biswas said, pausing slightly between each word. He leaned back on the sofa. 'Are you making any progress with your case? Have you found the bad guys yet?'

'Things are moving forward,' Arjun said, glancing sideways at the liquor cabinet. He sorely needed a drink.

'What can I offer you?' Biswas asked, and went over to the cabinet. 'Single malt, Chardonnay, Ciroc—'

'Blenders Pride, if you have it.'

'Blenders Pride!' Biswas repeated in an amused tone. 'I do happen to have a bottle of that, believe it or not. Are you sure though?'

'Positive.'

'Very well then,' Biswas said, and turned his back to Arjun, thereby blocking his view of the liquor cabinet.

In the dim light of the room he couldn't really see what the director's son was doing, and a horrible thought went through his mind: was he going to be poisoned?

'Ice?' Biswas asked.

'Only water,' Arjun replied.

His host turned around with two glasses, a tumbler with Arjun's drink, and a wine glass filled with what looked like white wine. They said cheers, and Biswas sat down.

'Why do you drink Blenders Pride?' he asked. 'Indian whisky isn't real whisky, you know, it's full of spirit. Scotch whisky, on the other hand—'

'I know,' Arjun interrupted, 'but it's what I'm used to,' and took a sip.

It tasted as it had always done. But what if the poison was tasteless and odourless?

'You should venture out of your comfort zone,' Biswas said, swirling the wine around in his glass, sniffing it, and drinking. 'Nothing ventured, nothing gained.'

'Your philosophy in life?'

'My god, no, not a *philosophy*. More like a rule of thumb. You wouldn't be a good detective if all you did was follow a routine, would you?'

'I guess not,' Arjun said, and took another sip.

The remnants of the wine and now the whisky would start to give him a mild buzz; he would have to distinguish that from any other feelings of dizziness or nausea.

'So did you manage to find out what happened to Munni?' Biswas asked.

'I'm getting there,' Arjun said, 'just one or two more missing links.'

'I guess I'm a suspect too?'

'Maybe.'

'What's this case about, if you could give me a few details?'

Arjun decided to reveal a few details, just to see Biswas's reaction.

'There's a girl whose life is in danger. She's been accused of embezzlement by some people, but she's also discovered evidence that points to her being a descendant of Munni.'

'You mean a daughter?'

'Granddaughter. Before you ask, yes, Munni did have a daughter.'

'So where was the daughter all this while?'

'She was given away. By her mother.'

Biswas laughed out loud. 'What a sordid affair. And to believe my father was making movies on social realism with people like these!'

'I think they were just trying to survive.'

'Oh, they did more than survive—they thrived. Selling a fantasy to the public, Mr Arora, just like today. Only back then the directors and producers had more taste.'

Arjun drank some more whisky. He remembered an article he had once read in *National Geographic*, about people who ate the fugu or puffer fish in Japan, risking death.

'Wouldn't your father have known about the daughter? In fact, I was hoping I could talk to him.'

'That wouldn't help you in any way, he's too old and too infirm. And no, I don't think he knew about Munni's daughter.'

'What about Riyaz Sheikh and Dinesh Chadha, I believe they were great pals with your father?'

'Yes, they were. Don't tell me you think one of them is the father?'

'Maybe not. But I hear you keep in touch with their family members?'

'That's not a crime, is it? And I've had enough of Sunny Chadha, I can tell you.'

'Why is that?'

'Well, he just won't grow up.'

Biswas finished his wine with a large sip, and stood up. 'Give me your glass for a refill.'

Arjun drank up and handed the glass to his host. He couldn't be sure if he was just feeling slightly tipsy or if there was more to it. It struck him that it wouldn't be a bad way to go, being served poison in his whisky, like Socrates being given hemlock. He said, 'Just a small one for me, please.'

'As you wish. I need to leave in a while too, a friend's hosting a dinner at Olive, and I absolutely have to be there.'

'What do you know about the trust your father set up for Munni? Who controls that now?'

'I have no idea about that, sorry. As far as I'm concerned, the less I have to do with the affairs of that woman the better.'

The edge in his voice was unmistakeable. Arjun could feel a brief momentary disorientation. Was it the dim light, his old condition of hallucinations or something in the whisky? And he couldn't let Biswas suspect anything either. He took the glass to his lips and took a small sip, then put the glass down.

'I'm sorry, I forgot,' he said, 'but I need to go and pick up my daughter.'

'Finish your drink at least, Mr Arora.'

Arjun raised a hand. 'I'd already had a few before coming here.'

'The detective who drinks—is there any truth in that cliché?'

'No, most of us prefer tea,' he said. 'Would you mind if I made a move?'

'Not at all. Give my regards to your daughter and wife.'

He walked with Arjun to the gate.

'If I need to ask you any more questions?'

'Well, I'm going to Paris on Monday. I'll be back in about ten days. So you'll have to wait. Goodbye, Mr Arora.'

Once again, the guard didn't show any sign of recognizing Arjun. He got into his car, rolled down the window and lit a cigarette. Did he really feel a bit disoriented, or was he just tired, or being paranoid? He thought about what the director's son had said, about being away for ten days. Enough time for Arjun to try and convince Commissioner Jha to conduct a search of the premises, and failing that, to somehow enter the property himself to have a look. On his way out, he had noticed that the boundary wall at the rear wasn't very high, maybe about ten feet, and without any barbed wire or spikes on top as was usually the case.

64

ON THE WAY BACK HOME, in the middle of Saturday evening traffic, he was still wondering if Siddharth Biswas had tried to poison him or not. If there were any sudden severe symptoms he could enter Moolchand hospital on the way. But he passed the hospital without feeling different in any way, and took a left through Greater Kailash. Waiting in a long line of stagnant traffic at Nehru Place, the Intercontinental Hotel high above on the left, he considered once more his theory of the missing actress being buried in the one place no one would have thought to look—the director's house itself. The press-wallah had seen her walking out of the house, but she might have returned later at night, alone or with someone, and as for the couple working for her, well, money was always a consideration. But was it really a watertight theory?

He moved forward past a traffic light, the looming towers of Nehru Place to the left, and the flyover came into view. A young woman dressed in exhaust-darkened gypsy rags, a long skirt and a blouse in red and white, came up to his window, holding up a couple of bunches of flowers. He shook his head, and she moved on. Arjun had been thinking about a woman being buried, and suddenly a chain of connections appeared before him: flowers, a field, a box. They came together, and he had a sudden moment of insight, one based more on gut feeling than actual evidence, but one that he knew might be valid.

The traffic moved again, and he went under the flyover and right on to the Outer Ring Road, from where he carried on straight instead of turning left into CR Park. What had suggested itself to him was preposterous, but then it was a strange case he was dealing with. There was something he needed to pick up, and he thought he knew exactly where to find it.

He had last visited Savitri Nagar a couple of months back when he had been on the trail of the psychopathic butcher. Would this case also turn up a similar catalogue of horrors? Arjun came in from the Outer Ring Road and made his way through the narrow lane flanked by shops and buildings. He parked near the Malviya Nagar market, and walked to one of the iron fabrication shops which sold, among other implements, metal skewers. Arjun asked for six pieces, to avoid any suspicion, then mentioned he needed a longer one without a handle for clearing a drain outside his house. The owner, a short, muscular man with scarred hands, looked around at the back of his shop, then came up with what Arjun wanted, a slim rod about three feet long and with a pointed end. He wrapped up the skewers and the rod in a piece of sackcloth, and Arjun thanked him and left. Returning to his car, he reflected that the skewers wouldn't go to waste: he needed replacements for those he used on his welded grill, which was lying idle since the previous winter.

He headed towards the Qutb Minar, following the route he had taken earlier that day. The intuitive answer that had suggested itself to him, if correct, would mean that Kailash Swami was the one behind Munni's disappearance and the attempt on Agnes Pereira's life.

Before hitting the Mehrauli–Gurgaon stretch of the road, he turned right at the colourful, brightly lit flower sellers' market. He followed the smaller road that wound past a stretch of urban village with raw-brick buildings and buffaloes, heading towards the vast wooded area behind the Qutb Institutional Area known as Sanjay Van. When he got to the beginning of the scrubland he slowed down, and noted the reading on his odometer. Mostly stands of acacia trees amid boulders and dried mud; slowly that changed to greener trees, and when he wound down his window the air smelt of the vegetation and damp earth. He passed two or three anonymous gates. Then his headlights picked out a small path winding its way into the trees, with an electricity pole beside it.

Arjun went a little way ahead and stopped by the edge of the road. From the dashboard compartment he took out a map of Delhi and a torch. He looked at the Qutb Institutional Area and did a rough calculation based on how far he had come from the start of the wooded area. The Natural Life Studio wasn't marked on the map, but other nearby landmarks such as the Indian Institute of Foreign Trade were, and fixing his rough position on the road running through the woodland behind the Qutb Institutional Area, he could see that he wouldn't be far from the track that supposedly led to the rear of the studio, where Kailash Swami's residence was. The path he had seen leading into the trees could be it.

Arjun switched off the torch, and noticed a pair of headlights in the rear-view mirror. He had crossed a vehicle or two earlier, coming from the opposite direction, but could this be someone following him? The lights grew brighter in the night, till they passed him: a white Innova with just a driver inside, probably a taxi taking a shortcut. He put the guidebook and the torch back in the dashboard compartment, and picked up the compact binoculars he had stored inside. Getting down, he took out the oversized skewer from the dicky, and then locked the car.

There was just enough light for him to see the road and the outlines of the trees, spaced apart. What he was planning to do shouldn't take much time. If a police patrol car showed up later, he could pretend to have gone into the trees to take a leak.

He broke into an easy trot till he came to the path, and then walked along it. It was wide enough for a car—a way for Kailash Swami to go in and out of his compound without letting anyone know. The path sloped down and then up, before taking a turn. An owl hooted somewhere. He had been in forests in Assam and Arunachal Pradesh as a child, and then as an army man, and still remembered the thick, dense tree cover, dripping with moisture, and the smell of damp, rotting vegetation. You could run into tigers and elephants in those places. Here, in this dry, deciduous woodland, the most dangerous animal was man.

He could see lights up ahead and moved in among the trees. Crouching and making his way forward slowly, he could make out the gate that lay behind Kailash Swami's mansion, outside it a guard hut. Arjun stood behind the meagre cover of a twisted keekar tree and studied the area around the gate: two guards in uniforms in the hut, barbed wire on top of the wall that ran around the property and a solar-powered lamp post beside the gate. He cautiously moved forward till he was out in the open and behind the hut or cabin, then inched forward and stood with his back to the hut's pre-fab wall just beside the open door. He leaned the rod against the wall, picked up a stone and threw it at the gate. A loud, metallic noise rang through the night, and as the first guard stepped out, Arjun tripped him from behind and sent him crashing to the rough ground.

The second guard stepped out, saw Arjun and started to move back, but Arjun stepped forward and punched him hard in the jaw, sending him back into the hut. The back of his head hit the edge of a table, and he fell sideways and didn't get up. Arjun turned to the first guard, who had scrambled to his feet and produced a whistle from his shirt pocket. Bending quickly, Arjun picked up a handful of earth, and as he stood threw it in an underhand motion into the guard's face, forcing him to turn his face away. He punched the man twice in the stomach, knocking the wind out of him and sending him to the ground. Arjun punched him in the face and dragged him into the guard hut, where the second guard had begun to moan and stir.

It took him less than five minutes to find a length of plastic rope and a roll of brown tape, cut the rope into two lengths and truss up the guards on the floor with their feet and hands behind them and tied together. Then he taped their mouths to keep them from shouting when they woke up. He discovered he was sweating when he stood up, so he lit a cigarette to calm his nerves. Looking at the counter below the glass front of the hut, he saw at its corner a sort of switchboard with large switches labelled 'Light', 'Gate', 'Siren' and 'Video'. Peering out of the glass he could see a CCTV camera set on top of the far column of the gate, pointing down: that would be the video. He flicked down the switches marked 'Gate' and 'Video' and stepped out of the hut. Only now did he hear the cicadas in the trees, so focused had he been. But there was still more to come. Stepping out of the hut, he picked up his rod.

He approached the gates and gingerly pushed at one. It was now open, as he had hoped. Flicking his cigarette away, he stepped through the gap and quietly shut the gate behind him. Before him was the gravel driveway, half in darkness, that went towards the marble mansion and curved around to its front. To his right was the spacious lawn with the flower beds and the waist-high fence. He took two steps and leapt over the fence, then dropped on all fours and crawled across the freshly cut grass to the flower beds. Most of the lawn lay in darkness, except for the part at the front and the brick wall at the end. Arjun reached one of the flower beds and lowered his body behind the large flowers with their strange aroma. The length of the flower bed was slightly more than his height, about six feet he guessed. It was a sort of confirmation. The flower beds were in a row, two deep and five long. More beds could be added to take the flowers ahead. Arjun had the feeling that that was what Kailash Swami had planned.

Still lying on the ground, he propped himself up on his elbows, took out the binoculars from the back of his jeans, and trained them on the rear of the mansion. It took him a while to bring the lighted area into focus, but when he did he could see two men sitting where he himself had sat a few days ago, but facing each other, with one of them leaning forward and gesticulating while the other person, in white, sat back listening. The second person was Kailash Swami, while the first . . . Arjun turned the dial to zoom in closer . . . and involuntarily swore out loud. A thick mop of hair—unmistakeably a wig—covered a large, pale face. Mr Vikas! So this was where it had all started. It was time to dig further—literally.

He moved closer to the flower bed, lifted the rod and jammed it down among the flowers. Then he started moving the rod and pushing it down. It was slow work, and sweat trickled down his face. Lucky for him the entire lawn wasn't lit up at night. When the rod was about halfway in, he took a break. What if he was wrong though? Then he had better get away fast. In front of him, beyond the lawn, was the garage complex and the rooms where the carpenters had been working. The source of his hunch—Kailash Swami, the carpenter who had learnt how to make coffins for his victims. He pushed the rod down again.

A while later, with about a foot of the rod protruding out, it hit something solid and wouldn't go down further. Calm down, he told himself, it might just be a rock. He took out the rod, and then repeated the procedure a couple of feet away. His left arm was cramping up by now with the awkward effort, but he kept going. About ten minutes later the rod halted at the same length. There was something down there. He took out the rod and rested a while. When he took a look with the binoculars, the two men had disappeared from the back of the mansion.

He cursed himself for not having come with a spade or trowel. His hands would have to do. Uprooting a few of the flowers, and moving the micro-drip pipes aside, he crouched on his knees and started digging the soft earth. The dirt went into his fingernails and over his jeans. Down there was the answer to all the mysteries Agnes Pereira had unearthed.

A dog barked somewhere, and he paused to listen, turned to look at the gate. All quiet, all clear. He was so engrossed in getting the earth out that only at the last moment did he hear a soft whisper like someone running on the grass. He started to turn but a knee dug into his back and a muscular arm went around his neck, choking him. An acrid-smelling cloth was pressed into his face. He struggled, but his attacker had the advantage of being above him. The last thing that crossed Arjun's mind was his car in the woods. Then everything went black.

65

THAT ACRID SMELL AGAIN, AND he seemed to be lying on something hard. He opened his eyes and found himself on his right side on a marble floor in a large white room, facing a closed door. His first thought was that he was somewhere inside Kailash Swami's mansion. Arjun tried to move his hands, but found that someone had put a pair of handcuffs on him, and drawing his feet up he saw both his legs shackled to a thick chain that was attached to an iron ring set into the wall. He heard a man clearing his throat, and turned his head to look.

Behind him, seated on a low four-poster bed, were Kailash Swami, Mr Vikas and the feline-looking assistant with short hair. They were all dressed in white, as if for a film shoot: Kailash Swami in his white linen trousers and shirt, the assistant in a white kurta pyjama, and Mr Vikas in a white, short-sleeved safari suit.

'Ankit Ahuja the producer,' Kailash Swami said with a smile, 'or is it Arjun Arora the detective?'

There was the sound of a toilet being flushed from behind a door, and then, as if to complete the picture, the door opened and a tall blonde in a black dress stepped out.

'That depends,' Arjun replied, 'on who *you* are: Kailash Swami or Lalit Prasad.'

The smile faded, and Arjun could see the coldness in the man's gaze.

Mr Vikas spoke. 'You were supposed to have died in Manali, you motherfucker. A lot of problems you've caused us. Where is the girl?'

Arjun said, 'Take off your wig and I might tell you, you sisterfucker.'

Kailash Swami raised a hand. 'No foul language in my house, please.'

The blonde approached Arjun and stood over him, then knelt down and gripped his face in a surprisingly strong grip. She was lean and bony, and looking into her impersonal grey eyes, Arjun felt a twinge of fear.

'So this is the subject,' she said in harshly accented English, her eyes going down to his feet and then up again. 'About 5 feet 10 inches tall, 70 to 75 kilograms in weight.'

The growing fear he was feeling made him reckless. He said, 'Are you going to make me a suit?' but the joke seemed to escape her. She stood up and went over to a side table. Arjun pushed himself up with an elbow into a sitting position. He saw that the woman had taken an injection syringe and was filling it from a vial. What was to come next?

Kailash Swami said to her, in Hindi, 'Just wait a minute, I need to talk to him.' And then to his two henchmen, 'Go and get it now.'

They left the room. Arjun already had a hunch as to what they were going to come back with. Had he finally managed to push himself past a point of no return? He tried his best not to think of Rhea, and instead examined the room they were in, the high ceiling and the tall windows. Were they on the ground floor or on the first floor?

'You break into my compound at night and start digging up the flowers,' Kailash Swami said to him. 'What were you looking for?'

'You know the answer to that. All those people who disappeared, including the actress Munni.'

The blonde sat down in a chair beside the table and crossed her legs. Kailash Swami stared at him for a long time before asking, 'I'm curious as to how you found out.'

'I put two and two together. The fence around the lawn, the flower beds, your training in carpentry. So how many bodies are down there?'

Kailash Swami got to his feet, walked over to the side table, then looked down at him.

'A total of nine people. You're going to be the tenth.'

'You'll be caught,' Arjun said, though he sounded unconvincing even to himself. He fingered the links of the chain—solid iron. 'People know where I am.'

'I doubt anyone knows you're here. We just have to find your car now. Where is it?'

'Outside my flat. So who did you kill first, Lalit Prasad? Munni or your parents?'

'You've managed to find out quite a lot, haven't you?' Kailash Swami reached out and stroked the girl's blonde hair as one might pet a cat. 'But there are other things you know nothing about. After I left home when the Ganga swallowed up our village, I wandered about India for several years. I came to know what this country really was, something different from the newspaper articles and people's talk. In Lucknow I learnt carpentry from an ustad. One day he took me to a kotha to watch a mujra performance. Do you know who the woman was? Someone called Sultana Begum. I caught sight of a young girl there—the woman's daughter, my ustad told me—and I could never forget about her.'

'And then years later, that girl showed up at your meditation centre?'

'Yes. I didn't know it was her at first. Then I found out who her mother was. But I never said anything to her. One day, after many years, she came to talk to me. Said she was planning to leave India and go and live somewhere abroad.'

In spite of the situation he found himself in, Arjun listened attentively.

'The next day I told her that I remembered her from years before, and that if she wanted, she could stay in this compound. She . . . laughed at me when I said that.'

Kailash Swami went back to the bed and sat down heavily. Arjun could faintly hear voices now—the two men were returning. He didn't have much time left. He could have said something cruel, something that would have infuriated the other man, but all he asked was, 'What happened after that?'

Even the blonde was looking at Kailash Swami now. He said, 'I drugged her, and then I put her inside a box that I had made with my own hands, and I nailed it shut. When she woke up, I could hear her screaming and scratching inside the box. From time to time, I would tap on the box'—his finger tapped on a wooden poster of the bed—'just to let her know she wasn't alone. After a few days, when she went silent, I had a part of the lawn dug up at night and buried the box there. And above it I planted flowers in her memory.'

The matter-of-fact recounting of the story, along with the expression of polite interest on the girl's face—who was she anyway?—made Arjun feel a chill in his bones. This wasn't how he wanted to go out. The door opened, and Mr Vikas and the assistant entered carrying a coffin-like wooden box. They set it down on the floor near Arjun. The sides were made of single planks of wood, while the cover had three planks joined together.

'This is where you're going to go,' Mr Vikas told Arjun, then asked Kailash Swami, 'Did you find out where the girl is?'

'No, but does it matter? I want you to go to his office on Monday morning and pick up his secretary. She might know where the girl is. Otherwise they'll have to send another man.'

'What has she done?' Arjun asked. 'Why do you want her dead?'

'She found out things she shouldn't have,' Mr Vikas said. 'Will you tell us where she is?'

'Open these chains and I might tell you.'

Mr Vikas turned to Kailash Swami. 'There's no hope with this one. Bury him.'

Kailash Swami looked at the girl, and gave her a slight nod. She stood up, picked up the syringe and approached Arjun. Mr Vikas and the assistant knelt down and held his arms, while the girl gripped his left wrist, turned it around and jabbed the needle into his forearm. Watching the clear liquid entering his body, a part of him felt a curious indifference to it all. Maybe this really was the end.

'It'll take a few minutes to start working,' Kailash Swami said to him. 'But don't worry, you'll be aware of everything that's happening to you.'

'This should be a mental hospital instead of a meditation centre,' Arjun said, trying not to show the fear that he felt. He could make out a slight dizziness coming upon him.

The girl and the two men got up, and Kailash Swami came forward and knelt beside Arjun. He lay a heavy hand on Arjun's shoulder and looked into his eyes.

'I told you my father was in the army. Do you know what he used to do to me as a child? Throw me inside a trunk and lock it up. My mother wouldn't open it, even though I would be screaming and crying inside. I would be kept inside for a day, sometimes two. When I grew up, one day I dug a pit near our hut when my parents had both gone to the temple. Later at night, I called them out of the hut and pushed both of them into the pit and buried them alive. That was my first time. Then Munni. And now you.'

The man was a pure psychopath, Arjun realized. If anything, he wouldn't show any fear. Go out with his head held high.

'Do what you have to do, you sick bastard.'

He could feel the dizziness turning into numbness now, making it difficult for him to even sit up. Kailash Swami raised a hand, and the girl took a hammer from the table and handed it to him. He held the heavy wood-and-iron tool in front of Arjun's eyes.

'My one true friend in this world,' he said with a crooked smile.

Arjun felt as though he was losing his balance, and fell on to the floor. He was aware of the handcuffs being taken off and his hands being pulled ahead of him and placed palms down on the floor. He could guess what was coming next. At the same time, a more objective part of his mind thought: why did they want the girl dead? Because she might have found out about her real mother, who had been buried alive? Could that be it? He felt his head being pulled up, and watched as Kailash Swami swung the hammer down on the back of his hands.

There were several blows from the hammer. He felt it bounce off the back of his hands. Who knew what the damage would be? It was the psychopath's way of ensuring that Arjun couldn't force his way out of the coffin-like box. The real pain would come later, when whatever they had injected him with wore off. Then Arjun was turned around, and he could make out the chain fixed to his legs being taken off. Next he was lifted off the floor and placed inside the box. He could see the four faces looking down at him, a smile on the face of Mr Vikas.

'Goodbye, detective Arjun Arora,' Kailash Swami said.

He tried to move but his body wouldn't obey any of his commands. No longer could he keep the thought of his daughter Rhea out of his mind. Would she think he had abandoned her? He blinked, and tears ran down his eyes. The blonde girl touched the corner of his eyes and put the wet finger into her mouth. Then the cover was put into place and everything went dark. He could feel the box shaking as the top was nailed into place. Claustrophobia gripped him, and he felt a terrifying sense of abandonment and fright. I have seen evil, he thought. He tried to move his hands and scream but nothing happened. This was it, the end. The hammering stopped. In the darkness, he felt an immense wave of drowsiness come over him and surrendered to it. Let me sleep for a while, he thought, and maybe I won't get up after that. He said goodbye to his daughter and his parents, and then closed his eyes.

66

HE WAS WOKEN UP BY a throbbing sensation in his hands. The drug had started wearing off, making him start to feel the pain from his fractured hands. He opened his eyes in the darkness and smelt the resin in the planks of the box. He tried to fight the growing panic he felt by looking at the situation dispassionately. He had been nailed inside a box in Kailash Swami's mansion, destined to be buried underground within a day or two, or maybe even within a few hours. No one knew where he was, and even if the police found his car, and Bunty came to know, and somehow connected the dots, he could already be under the ground by then. How much time had elapsed since he had allowed himself to be captured? Where was his cell phone?

Arjun found he could move his hands now, but just drawing them up to his pockets sent spasms of pain shooting up his arms and he let out a cry of agony. With the palms of his hands he could ascertain that his pockets were empty, and by shifting his body he found out that his back pockets were empty as well. Here he was, trapped in a coffin, fated to die a slow, agonizing death. Was it the result of all the wrong choices he had made in his life? The temptation to give in to self-pity was strong, but he forced himself to remain in control. With the movement returning to his body, the throbbing pain from his hands was worsening. No way was he going to be stuck in there to die.

He took a few deep breaths. Where was the air coming in from? The cover was made of planks, and there were minute cracks between them, and also along the sides where the cover had been hammered in. Arjun lifted his hands to touch the cover, and cried out as pain shot through his fingers and hands. What had the bastard done to him? He lay still, focusing on the slivers of light coming in through the cracks. He was most probably in the same room as earlier. But there didn't seem to be anyone around. There were no tools for him to use. His hands were useless now. What did that leave him with?

It struck him that the planks of the cover that went down lengthwise were nailed together sideways, or maybe held together by horizontal slats on the inside. He turned his hands around and with his palms touched an upper and then a lower piece of wood running across the planks of the cover. There was something he could try . . . his legs . . . the not-so-strong cover planks. After all, hadn't he squatted ten times with Gogoi on his shoulders just a week ago?

Arjun lay motionless for a few minutes, breathing deeply and trying to block out the pain from his hands. He focused on his knees and thighs, flexing his quadriceps. Then he jammed his knees up against the cover, placed his palms on the bottom of the box and strained upward with all his might. He tried to channel every inch of his energy through his legs into his knees. Nothing happened. He dropped his knees down, rested a while, then tried again. This time there was a tiny creak; he pushed even harder, jamming the heels of his sneakers into the bottom and straining to get his knees up. A larger creak, and then a crack. One sliver of light widened.

'Come on, motherfucker, give way!'

He pushed with everything in his body, for his own sake, for the sake of his daughter. His hands were pressing down on the

382

bottom now but he ignored the stabs of pain. Even if he got out, he wouldn't be free, but it would be a beginning.

'Come on, argh!'

The wood cracked and splintered and broke, and his knees were through the box out in the open. He had done it. But there was no time to waste now. He used his knees and his feet to kick and break the remaining splinters, and even his palms to lift up the pieces still covering the upper part of the box. All thoughts of pain were now gone—he just had to get free. He pulled himself up into a sitting position—the searing pain in his hands was a fire of agony he had never felt before, but more than that he felt the elation of freedom. He wasn't going into a box again.

He noticed that the box was in the same room. He put his legs over the broken pieces of wood, placed his elbows on the sides of the box, and got to his feet unsteadily. What time was it? He got the answer at the side table, where to his relief he saw his cell phone and wallet and car keys along with the hammer, the empty syringe and injection vial. He checked his phone and saw that it was just past 1 a.m. Somehow, he managed to put the phone, the wallet and the car keys into his jeans pockets. He examined his hands: the backs were now swollen from the fractures—he only hoped the bastard hadn't broken all the bones—and the skin had turned a blotchy black and red. The moment he got out of this madhouse he would have to get to a hospital. The anaesthetic or narcotic—whatever they had injected him with—appeared to be wearing off. Maybe his body, habituated as it was to large doses of whisky, had been able to shake it off quickly. He had got out of the box; now how could he get out of the compound?

Arjun crossed the room and pushed aside one of the curtains behind the bed: he was on the first floor of the mansion, with the lawn where he had been captured slightly ahead to his right. It was hard to imagine those horrors buried beneath it. The gate at the rear, he could see, was closed. If he opened the window, he might be able to jump down to the ground, but how would he cross the walls? He turned to study the room once again. They could return at any moment, and with his broken hands he wouldn't be much of a threat. His eyes fell on the telephone by the bed and he suddenly knew what to do. Gingerly picking up the phone, he dialled 100, and when the control room came on, he gave them a short explanation: the lawn behind Kailash Swami's mansion in his Natural Life Studio, nine bodies buried in boxes there, including the missing actress Munni. He was asking them to send help soon, when, to his horror, he heard the door opening. Turning his head, he saw Mr Vikas enter, take a few steps and halt. For a moment, both men froze; then, as Mr Vikas turned to escape, Arjun dropped the receiver and sprinted across the room.

Mr Vikas had made it to the door when Arjun turned sideways and kicked him in his back, sending him smashing into the open door. He fell, and Arjun kicked him in the side and shut the door. No time to lose, there could be more people coming anytime. He pushed the latch of the door into place with one palm, and when he turned, he saw Mr Vikas rolling over on his back and taking out a switchblade from the pocket of his white trousers. His wig was somehow still in place.

'Do you use that knife when selling cinema tickets in black?' Arjun asked. 'I knew you were a cheapskate when I first saw you.'

He wanted to rile the other man, provoke him. Mr Vikas got to his feet with a grimace.

'So eager to go to Bombay, weren't you?' he taunted Arjun back. 'I just had to show you the photo of the girl and you were ready to go. Chutiya saala!'

He lunged forward and slashed with the knife, but Arjun managed to step back and dodge it. His hands were useless;

what could he do? Then he noticed a piece of broken wood with a splintered end lying beside the box. He moved towards the table, drawing Mr Vikas towards him, then darted away and picked up the piece of wood. The other man lunged again with the knife but missed.

'What's the matter, motherfucker, can't handle a man with broken hands?'

He came forward again and swung wildly. Arjun stuck out his foot and tripped Mr Vikas, ignoring the pain in his hands as he drove the piece of wood into the other man's midriff.

There was someone banging on the door. Arjun went to the window and opened it. He could hear loud voices in the night now, and a few security men were running towards the rear gate. The police were already here! Arjun allowed himself a tight smile. He was about to climb out of the window, but then ran back to the table and picked up a matchbox that was next to a candle stand. The banging on the door grew louder. He would have liked to face Kailash Swami, but there was no time now, and the psychopath wouldn't be as easy to tackle as Mr Vikas. On the other hand, it could even be the police.

Arjun whipped the bed sheet off the four-poster, flung it over the dead man and the box he had managed to break open, and lit a match and held it to a corner of the cloth. He ignored the shooting pain in his hands—what failed to kill you only made you stronger. The flame caught, and he turned and made for the open window. As he climbed out he turned back for one last look. The flames were rising now and the door burst open to show Kailash Swami standing there, a wild expression on his face. Arjun raised a hand in farewell, turned and jumped. He let his legs take the impact, then fell and rolled, holding his hands close to his body but still screaming out in pain as the fractured bones brushed the pavement. Somehow, he rose to his feet and started running towards the gravel driveway.

The gate was ajar. Two more security guards were running down the driveway behind him. He took one last look at the lawn and the mansion, where the flames were now visible through the open window. What would happen to Kailash Swami? He slipped out of the gate and saw a group of the studio's security men before the guard post, among them the two men he had tied up earlier.

'There, that's the fellow,' said one, pointing at Arjun.

He would have been in trouble, but for the two security guards who were behind him.

'Delhi Police all over the place!' one of them said.

Arjun took advantage of the hubbub to slip away down the path by which he had come. When he reached the road, he felt immensely relieved to see that his car was still where he had left it. It was time to get home. With the adrenaline still flooding his body, he felt no pain as he took out his keys, got into the car, started the engine and gripped the steering wheel. Only two broken hands, he told himself, it wasn't too much of a problem.

67

ARJUN GOT HOME AROUND 5 a.m. He stepped out of the car with both his hands covered in plaster till above the wrists. It was a Sunday. He was glad there was no one around to see him, except for some stray dogs in the park. For a moment he stood watching the sky to the west beyond the park as it changed colour to a pale orange. *Above all, man must endure*—which writer had said that? He trudged up the steps of the building and let himself into his flat, which had never seemed so welcoming. Sitting at the dining table, he wolfed down the two chicken hot dogs he had picked up from the 24/7 store in the GK-II market—where the staff and a group of college students back from a party had stared at him the whole time—and washed them down with a bottle of soft drink. Then he poured himself a large measure of Blenders Pride, without water, and lit a cigarette. They had injected him with painkillers after putting on the plaster, but he figured he could risk a peg before he crawled into bed.

He had driven all the way to the hospital in Saket and walked into the OPD and told them he had two fractured hands. The nurse and doctor on duty were worried that it might be something involving a police case, but Arjun explained to both women that a heavy cupboard had fallen on the back of his hands at home and that he needed immediate treatment. In the end they had X-rayed and plastered his hands before injecting him with a strong painkiller at his request. Even Arjun had been surprised at how lightly he had gotten off—three metacarpal fractures in his left hand and two fractures in his right—for at one point in the hospital the pain had been so bad that he had thought all eight of his palm bones had been shattered. The doctor had said that the breaks were clean and would, in all probability, heal well. 'I certainly hope so,' he had said, and then thanked them and walked out of the hospital.

Arjun sipped the whisky—it would help him sleep in his wired-up state—and thought back to what he had gone through. He had survived, and he had solved the mystery surrounding Agnes Pereira. But the horrors of the box; he tried not to think what might have happened had he not broken out of it. And Kailash Swami's account of how Munni had met her end, screaming and scratching inside a similar box. Had he been born a monster, or had he been turned into one by his father's cruelty? Whatever the explanation, the man would land up behind bars for a long time, maybe even climb the gallows. All that, he would catch up with on the television news later in the day. For the moment he needed to sleep for a long, long time.

He slowly typed out a reply to the text message—the tips of his fingers had been left free—sent by Agnes the previous evening. She had called him to ask if he was at home but he hadn't answered; he told her to come over in the evening. Then he finished his whisky and dragged himself to bed.

X

Arjun came awake once or twice as the plaster casts on both hands meant he couldn't sleep for long in his usual position on his side—he had to lie on his back instead, with his hands on his middle. It was going to be an absolutely tedious four weeks, he thought drowsily at one point. He was woken up by the doorbell, and stumbled out into the sitting room. The wall clock said 12.30 p.m. He had asked Agnes Pereira to come in the evening. Who could it be? There was no point in him even taking out his revolver.

But when he went and looked into the keyhole, he saw it was Agnes, dressed in a pair of jeans and a black track jacket. For a moment he just looked at her, and then opened the door.

'I told you to come in the evening, didn't I?'

'But I couldn't wait. My god, what happened to your hands, Arjun!'

'It's nothing. Let's go inside first.'

'Nothing? How can . . . wait, is your daughter here?'

'No. I was sleeping. Come in.'

'Your message in the morning said you knew what had happened. I couldn't wait till evening to find out, so I came over. And then I see your . . . hands. What the hell happened?'

'Go sit down. Let me just wash up.'

In the bathroom he wondered how to wash his face and brush his teeth. In the end he dipped the face towel into a bucket of water, squeezed it on the slab by the sink with his elbows and wiped his face with it. Not much pain now, but he knew that was the painkiller working. Next, he somehow brushed his teeth holding the toothbrush between his thumb and fourth finger. Four long weeks to go, he thought. He was in his boxers and vest, and he changed into a clean T-shirt before going out. It had taken him nearly twenty minutes.

'Have you watched the news?' he asked her.

'No, but I read the newspaper in the morning and there was nothing in it.'

'This happened late, it'll only be in the evening edition and tomorrow's papers.'

'What? And how for god's sake did you break both hands?'

389

'I'll tell you. First, will you make us some tea?'

She got to her feet. 'What about breakfast? Have you eaten?'

'You can make some toast and omelette.'

She busied herself in the kitchen while he sat down on the sofa and closed his eyes. To think a sudden spark of intuition had led him to the answer. Even with the broken hands, he felt quite pleased with himself. When she brought him his tea he held the cup between his hands and drank. She insisted on feeding him his toast and omelette, and asked him again about what had happened. He told her everything, starting from the call from Sunny Chadha the previous morning. It felt nice to have someone looking after him, he reflected, as she gave him another spoonful of omelette. He realized, of course, that he was in a naturally vulnerable state. She interrupted him when he got to the part where he parked on the woodland road and took the path behind the mansion.

'Why did you decide to go from the back, and with that rod?'

He had left out, for the sake of brevity, the revelation that had struck him when the flower seller had approached him at the traffic light. Now he told her about it.

'The pieces suddenly came together,' he said. 'And there was only one way to test if it was true.'

'Just like that number plate, remember?' she said, feeding him a piece of buttered toast. 'Go on.'

He chewed the bread, drank some tea and went on with his story of how he had entered the studio premises, how he had been captured, and what they had done to him. A teardrop ran down from her eye when he got to the part where his hands had been broken.

'You had to go through all this because of me.'

'It was my own choice, Agnes. But don't you want to know how I got away?'

Her face grew grim as she took in his escape from the box, the encounter with Mr Vikas and the getaway from the compound.

'He was the person who had approached you initially, wasn't he?'

'Yes, and now he's dead.'

'You really think all those people are buried down there?'

'It should be on the news now. Put on the television.'

Agnes Pereira came closer and hugged him, then kissed him on his cheek.

'Be careful of my hands,' he joked.

She drew back and smiled wanly at him. 'At least you're still alive, Arjun.'

The television news was showing scenes from the mansion, as he had expected: the burnt room, the dug-up lawn and the boxes, Kailash Swami being led away to a police vehicle. It was being called 'a house of horrors', and a reporter said nine boxes with human remains had been dug up from underneath the flower beds, one of which unconfirmed sources said belonged to the missing actress Munni.

Agnes Pereira put a hand over her mouth and leaned forward on the sofa, and Arjun patted her on her shoulder with his plastered hand—the most he could do. He felt an urge to pour himself a shot of whisky, but decided against it as long as she was there.

'And you think this is why they wanted me dead?' she asked after a while.

Arjun nodded. 'There must have been a link from the furniture store to Kailash Swami. Maybe the owners knew him and alerted him to the fact that someone was inquiring into an old matter.'

'And he wanted me dead because I might start looking into what had happened to my grandmother?'

'Exactly.'

'But the person who gave you my photo . . .'

'Vishwanathan, alias Kumar Sampath. The furniture store owners would have approached him after hearing from Kailash Swami, or maybe Kailash Swami contacted him personally.'

'I suppose you're right. How do you think Munni's mother would react to this?'

'I doubt she'll come to know about it. If Munni's remains are found there, we'll have to ask the police to do a DNA test— to link all three of you.'

'Yes, I suppose so,' she murmured. 'Do you have a cigarette?'

They watched the news, and she ordered pizza for lunch. She offered to stay and take care of him, but he urged her to get back to Mumbai and her job. He gave her Commissioner Jha's number, to call when the police came to talk to her, and said he would explain matters to the commissioner later in the evening.

As they ate, something occurred to him which he hadn't asked her before.

'Agnes, why did you stay at Bharat Lodge and not any other place?'

'I wanted a place that was slightly, I don't know, away from it all. And I remembered staying there twice with my mother when I was a child.'

'What was she doing in Mumbai?'

'I don't know. Meeting a boyfriend, I guess. You need to have your medicines now, don't you? Let me get them for you.'

She left at dusk, after giving him a kiss on the cheek again and urging him to take care of himself.

'I'll give my daughter a call later,' he told her, not wanting to appear forsaken.

He lit a cigarette with some effort out on the balcony and watched her disappear from his view. She had said she would come and say goodbye to him before she left, but he secretly hoped she wouldn't. Some things he didn't want to be reminded of. The fingers in his left hand suddenly spasmed, sending a bolt of pain up his hand and forearm.

The case appeared to be over. Why then did he still feel a sense of unease? Was it because he had never known that Agnes Pereira had stayed at Bharat Lodge earlier? But what did that prove? Forget it, he told himself. All the skeletons had been unearthed.

68

LATER, WHEN IT WAS DARK, he walked to the nearby wine store and bought a bottle of Blenders Pride. Both the store staff and then the paanwallah in Market No. 3 from whom he bought his cigarettes inquired about what had happened. Arjun told them the same story about the heavy cupboard having fallen on his hands. The paanwallah offered to send over, after four weeks had elapsed, a friend who gave massages with traditional oils for fractures and broken bones, but Arjun politely declined.

When he got home, he called Rhea. He wanted to see if she was free to come over, and at the same time didn't want to alarm her by telling her about his hands. She sounded busy and a bit hassled, and informed him that she was helping organize a party that Sonali was throwing.

He couldn't help but ask, 'What's the occasion?'

'You forgot? It's her birthday today. Why don't you come over, Papa?'

'I can't right now. Just wanted to tell you that I got you a present from Lucknow.'

'You did? Great. So come over and give it to me, and get a present for Mama.'

'I can't come now, Rhea.'

'Is that . . . girl with you again?'

Arjun sighed. 'No she's not. I can't come because . . . well, you'll know when you come here.'

394

'What's the matter, Papa?'

'I just want to see you.'

He heard her whispering to someone, then she said, 'Here, wish Mama at least,' and then Sonali was on the line, 'Hi, Arjun.'

'Happy birthday, Sonali.'

'Thanks, Arjun. Why don't you come over for the party? Please? Come and see us, and say hi to Rohit at least.'

'I would have liked to,' Arjun said, and he meant it, 'but there's something . . .' he faltered. 'Rhea will tell you after she comes to see me, okay?'

'Arjun, are you all right?'

'Bye, Sonali. Have a nice evening.'

He poured himself a drink and switched on the news again. The Kailash Swami case was still dominating most national channels, with some running profiles of the man himself and others looking into the lives of the people who had disappeared and were now suspected to be among those buried in the boxes. One channel was going over Munni's life and career, and had even managed to rope in Prakash Saxena for a short interview, while another was going through the presence of a female doctor from Ukraine in the 'house of horrors'.

Arjun put off the television, put on some Dire Straits and sat back on the sofa. All alone, with two broken hands—but he would pull through. He was a survivor. The sight of the hammer coming down on his hands returned to him. Other scenes followed: the underground chamber in Ramadi where the two Americans had been beheaded, the flat where he had been tied up by the butcher to be dismembered, and finally waking up in the blackness of the coffin's interior. He imagined Munni waking up in a similar fashion, and screaming and scratching at the lid with her nails, but all in vain. He drained his glass and poured another peg.

In the cycle that governed his drinking, this was definitely a low point, notwithstanding his success in solving Agnes's mystery, and he knew he would hit the bottle hard. The question now was where he would order his dinner from tonight. He got up and went to the dining table to pick up the stack of home-delivery menus. That was when he noticed it, and his blood ran cold. His laptop was missing from its usual place on the table.

But how could I not have noticed it when I got back home? he thought. When I was eating the hot dogs sitting at the table? Could Agnes Pereira have done something with it? But he had seen her leave empty-handed, and he had been with her in the room all along. He quickly searched through the rest of the house, including Rhea's old room, before concluding that someone had broken in and taken the laptop. He had simply been too tired to notice early in the morning. But was anything else missing? Again he went through the house, and checked his bedroom almirah and the locker in it with his fumbling fingers. There was nothing amiss with the lock on the front door either—if it had been picked, it was the job of a professional. In the end he sank back on the sofa and lit a cigarette. Just the laptop. What did that tell him? He had been out of the flat the whole day yesterday. But why just the laptop, unless someone was looking for something specific? Something to do with the case he had been on. Was that why Agnes Pereira came, to check on me, he thought, before remembering he had called her himself.

Fuck it, he thought, first my hands now the laptop. Let them have it. He would go and file an FIR tomorrow.

X

The hangover, as expected, was bad, especially considering he hadn't eaten anything at night. Arjun sat up on the sofa with a groan and reached with both hands for the bottle of water on the table. The restaurant menus were strewn on the table like playing cards—a result of his indecision last night—and there was only about a quarter left of the bottle of whisky. The thought of the missing laptop only worsened his mood.

He cleared up the table, and managed to take a shower by wrapping a pair of old shower caps around his hands. Next he changed and brushed his teeth. He already felt exhausted, and there was still breakfast to be made. Would it make sense to fix some sort of tiffin service for himself? Arjun made himself a cup of tea and brought in the newspapers from the balcony. The 'house of horrors' was on the front page, and Commissioner Jha was quoted as saying that an 'anonymous source' had tipped them off.

The maid had arrived by then, and the sight of Arjun's plastered hands brought out a sudden motherly devotion in her. He told her he had slipped and fallen down the steps at a friend's house and broken both hands. She asked him what he wanted for breakfast (aloo parathas, he said, and two soft-boiled eggs) and said she would cook enough for his lunch and dinner. As she swept the house, she finally asked how Sonali and Rhea were doing, then hearing the sabzi-wallah's cries asked him for money and ran down to buy vegetables. A bemused Arjun wondered if it would take two broken hands to bring about a change in her attitude towards him. He checked his phone but found that the battery had died during the night, so he connected it to the charger. The laptop worried him—he had case information there—and there was also the matter of Agnes Pereira leaving for Mumbai.

The phone pinged with notifications of missed calls, and when he checked he saw they were all from late last night. He recalled he had set the phone aside after talking to his daughter and ex-wife, thinking he would charge it, but had obviously forgotten. There were four calls: one from an unknown cell phone number, one from Bunty, one from Liza and one, to Arjun's surprise, from Commissioner Jha. It was still early, but he decided to call the police officer.

69

'DETECTIVE ARORA,' SAID THE COMMISSIONER, 'I was trying to get in touch with you.'

'What about? Sorry, my phone was switched off last night.'

'This business with Kailash Swami's Natural Life Studio, aren't you following it?'

'I've seen it on the news.'

'I thought you would be excited by the whole thing. Don't you know whose remains are supposed to be among those recovered from the boxes?'

'Munni, the actress. But without a DNA test . . .'

'I agree. However, given that she *was* at the place on the day she disappeared . . . it is significant, isn't it?'

'That's true, yes.'

'It's funny, the anonymous caller who tipped us off named her specifically.'

'Could you trace the caller's number?' Arjun asked innocently.

'It was from a landline phone in Kailash Swami's mansion. You visited him, didn't you, during the course of your investigation?'

'Yes, I did. Just some routine questions.'

'Would you know who might have tipped us off?'

'No idea. Maybe a disgruntled employee.'

'Where were you on Saturday night, Mr Arora?'

'Me? In bed. Asleep.' If they examined CCTV footage from around the locality they would see his car returning in the early hours of the morning, but there was no reason for them to do that, yet.

'Hmm. I was hoping you might have something to tell us.' When Arjun didn't volunteer any information, the commissioner asked, 'You traced Munni's mother in Lucknow, didn't you? Could you tell me where she can be found? For the DNA test.'

Arjun told him about Ashraf and his shop in the Chowk area.

'There was another matter I wanted to ask you about.'

'I'm flattered by this interest in me.'

'You do seem to be mixed up with some interesting people. You had mentioned a builder in Mumbai by the name of Vishwanathan, and I had asked you how long you had known him for, do you remember?'

'Yes. And I said about two weeks. Why?'

'I asked you because he's been a person of interest to us for some time now. As part of a cricket betting ring. Anyway, your name cropped up in his phone taps.'

'My name? Who was he talking to?'

'Someone overseas. This other person said that you had interfered in their business before, and asked Vishwanathan to take care of you. Vishwanathan then said that if you were a detective, he could use you for something before getting rid of you.'

'Why are you telling me this?'

'Because another person Vishwanathan was in touch with was a certain Vikas, most possibly the person found dead and half-burnt in Kailash Swami's mansion.'

'So they wanted me dead. Well, there was a match-fixing case I was involved with earlier in the year.'

'You'll be happy to know we're close to getting that person back to India. I was hoping you could shed more light on Kailash Swami's links to Vikas. And to Munni.'

'I don't know much, really,' Arjun said, his head starting to hurt, 'but I'll be happy to share whatever I do know.'

'Maybe I'll drop by for a chat one of these days.'

'You're most welcome.'

Arjun hung up and went out to the balcony from where he studied the streets below. The overseas betting connection was probably Dubai. To learn he had been targeted from that far away shook him. He went back inside. The maid told him she would get turmeric paste for him, which he should drink with warm milk at night for faster healing of his bones. He thanked her and said it would be helpful, and looked at the front page of the newspaper again.

Then it struck him: the other victims found in the boxes no doubt had their own stories. Munni had her story too. But had he been looking too closely at the link between Munni's disappearance and the threat to Agnes Pereira's life? What if there was something else to it? They must have meant to use him to find her, and then silence both of them. But something else such as what?

He stalked restlessly around the sitting room, then stopped before the bookcase. Picking up the diary, or the copy of the diary, that had been sold to him by Sultana Begum, he flipped through its pages. What was it that he had missed? An entry he had seen before came to his attention: *2 February 1962: Confusing times, there's so much happening. This is a beautiful place though, and so near to Bombay.* That made him pause, and he reached for the book which had been placed behind the diary, Dinesh Chadha's autobiography. He turned to 1963, the year the politician had got married, then went back a couple of pages to the previous year. There it was, as he remembered: a holiday to Matheran a few weeks after New Year's Day. Could *Matheran* be the beautiful place near Bombay? Which would mean that . . .

Arjun looked up, and a colourful spine among a row of books caught his eye: *A Guide to Bombay.* He faintly recalled having picked it up just after his marriage at a second-hand bookshop in Connaught Place. Pulling the guidebook out, he skimmed through its pages. It was something he should have done before. He came upon a boxed section on a page and stopped to look. The heading said: 'When Led Zeppelin stopped by Bombay'. It had a black-and-white photo of Robert Plant and Jimmy Page inside the Colaba pub where they had performed an impromptu jam one evening back in 1972. The opposite page had a subheading that went 'Politics in the City', and a sentence from under it caught his eye: '. . . nationalism reflected in a growing trend of wanting to rename cities and roads in order to reclaim the past from the taint of colonialism.' A rather heavy style for a guidebook, but it made him think.

As the bits of information settled, and linked with his earlier knowledge, all of a sudden it came to him: there was someone else who wanted Agnes Pereira dead, and for some other reason. Arjun had been sidetracked by Munni's disappearance and Kailash Swami. But the truth was elsewhere. And then it struck him: the fourth phone number, the unknown one. He suddenly felt very afraid. Fumbling with his phone, he called his secretary and asked her what time Agnes Pereira had got home the previous night.

'She didn't come home,' Liza said. 'I thought she might have stayed over at her friend's place because she was leaving today. That's why I had tried calling you.'

'I see, thanks,' he said, and hung up, then dialled the fourth number. 'Come on, come on, please.'

The voice at the other end sounded muffled and indistinct.

'I tried calling you last night, Mr Arora.'

'Who is this?'

'What sort of a detective keeps his phone switched off?'

'Who is this, and what do you want?'

'Here, talk to someone you know.'

401

Arjun heard a woman's scream, followed by a sobbing voice. 'Arjun, help me please. He has me tied up and he has a knife! No, please!'

The other voice came back on, harsher now. 'You heard the bitch, didn't you? Now wait for my next call, I'll tell you where you have to turn up.'

'What do you want?'

But the line had gone dead. Arjun put the phone down. He was shaken. In the kitchen the maid was cooking. And the girl who had spent a night here with him was about to be killed. The voice was indistinct, but he thought he knew who it might be. There was only one person he could call now—Bunty. But he had to make another call before that.

Though it was just past 8 a.m., there was already someone at the reception desk of McLoyd & Co. Or maybe the person had been there the whole night. He sounded tired.

'McLoyd & Company. How can I help you, sir?'

'Can you tell me if Siddharth Biswas will be in today? This is a client of his.'

'Siddharth Biswas . . . I'm sorry, sir, but he's on leave from today.'

'Oh . . . when does he get back?'

'He's back next Thursday sir.'

'Okay. On leave, or on company work?'

'On leave, sir.'

'Any idea where he's gone?'

'I'm sorry, but I can't comment on that, sir, against company rules.'

'All right, you have a nice day,' Arjun said, turning the usual sign-off around.

Next, he called Bunty.

'Drop everything you're doing and get to my place. Someone's life is in danger.'

70

ARJUN WAS AT HIS DINING table; before him was the Black Eagle device connected to an old laptop belonging to Rhea. He had asked his maid to bring them out before she had left. Now, on a grid map of Delhi and the NCR he saw on the laptop's screen, a faltering red dot across the Yamuna indicated where the kidnapper's phone was. Hopefully, Agnes Pereira was still with him, and in one piece. They must have had his place under watch, taking the laptop when he was out and then following her when she had left the flat after visiting him.

The doorbell rang. It turned out to be Bunty. Before anything, though, he wanted to know what had happened to Arjun's hands, even when the latter had said he would tell Bunty once they were in the car.

'I don't care who's about to die,' he said, 'first you tell me who did this to you.'

Arjun told him what had happened, keeping it as succinct as possible.

'Sisterfucker, you were mixed up with what they're showing on the news! So who's in trouble?'

When Arjun told him, Bunty slapped his left palm to his forehead.

'What did I tell you, Arjun? Anyway, what do I have to do?'

'Take that device and laptop and my gun down to your car. We're going for a drive.'

Twenty minutes later they were on the DND Flyway speeding across the Yamuna. Arjun sat in the back of the battered, grey Tata Safari that Bunty had turned up in, a car belonging to a friend, he had said vaguely. Arjun tweaked the dials and tried to zoom in on the area. The phone's signal seemed to be coming from somewhere in the direction of Greater Noida.

'Are you sure it's him?' his friend asked, slowing down as the toll gate approached.

'Not a hundred per cent, but I think it is him. Take the first left after the toll gate, we'll have to go down and drive up to the Greater Noida Expressway.'

'Not a hundred per cent? Well, we have your gun if anything goes wrong. What's your device saying?'

'I'm checking.'

Bunty paid at one of the tollbooths, then went ahead and took the first left that curved down like a racing track to the approach road to the Greater Noida Expressway. He stepped on the accelerator and asked Arjun, 'But how did you manage to find out?'

'Everything just seemed to . . . fall into place.'

'If only your life was like that, right?'

'My life is my life, Bunty, I wouldn't change it for anything in the world. All right, this thing's picking up a stronger signal now. From somewhere near the Carmel International School.'

'It won't take us fifteen minutes to get there,' Bunty said.

Most of the traffic in the extended Monday morning rush hour was headed the opposite way, into Delhi.

Bunty fiddled with the FM radio for a while before turning it off. He said, 'So it was all about the property, eh?'

'Yes. Some things never change.'

'That's the problem with us human beings. Someone should come up with a new model, what do you say?'

'Hopefully not in my lifetime.'

They were out on the expressway now, three lanes and a service lane on either side, headed straight down towards Greater Noida and, beyond that, Agra. Office complexes and apartment blocks rose out of what had been farmland till a few years ago, with giant cranes further back building yet more structures. The car surged ahead on the spacious road.

'Look at all this,' Bunty said, waving a hand. 'It's like China.'

Arjun's attention was fixed on the laptop screen: the red dot was constant now, but seemed to be drifting. Could the kidnapper be preparing to move out? Then the light settled itself.

'There's the school,' Bunty said, pointing ahead and to his right.

Across the divider, and some distance from the road, was a complex of cream-coloured buildings. In front of it was farmland, with what looked like huts or village houses in the distance. A few half-completed high-rises rose up in the middle of the fields. Who would come to a school over here? But obviously there were people staying around here. This was the future. He checked the laptop once more.

'There, those buildings ahead of the school,' he said.

Bunty kept going till he saw an elevated section of the expressway, and turned left before it on to the service lane and then under the track and out to the service lane on the other side. The under-construction buildings were nearer now, the two cranes amid them stationary.

'Looks like nobody's there,' he muttered.

There was a dirt track that led through the wheat fields to the site. Arjun put the laptop aside and looked through the front of the car. He had to agree with Bunty. What if only the phone had been left there somewhere to mislead them?

'Just drive around the place,' Arjun said.

At the outer corner of the site was a line of tin-and-bamboo workers' shacks, all deserted. Had the money run out for the project, or had the permissions been obtained fraudulently? A perfect place for hiding someone though. They turned the corner, and as Arjun looked out of the side window he saw it: a familiar black vehicle parked in one of the buildings, beside a dusty pickup.

'Go ahead around that building and stop.'

Bunty turned around one of the half-constructed shells and stopped the car.

'What do we do now?'

'Let's get down,' Arjun said, and opened the rear door with the tips of his fingers.

Bunty got down too, with the .32 revolver. There was a dusty silence in the middle of the fields, and Arjun could see cars speeding by on the expressway. Looking up at the cement columns of the high-rise before them he wondered if this was where it would all come to an end. Just then his phone started ringing. He fumbled for it in his jeans, and saw it was the same number. It was 11 a.m.

'So, Mr Arora,' the muffled voice said, 'want to see her one last time before I cut her throat?'

He could hear Agnes Pereira let out a scream somewhere in the background.

'I'll save you,' he said silently to her, and then, out loud, 'where?'

'Get to the Greater Noida Expressway and then call,' the voice said. 'I'll give you further instructions.'

'All right,' Arjun said. They didn't see or hear us, he thought, or, they saw us but took us to be someone else—they don't know about the phone tracker. But was it *they* or just that one person?

He beckoned Bunty to follow him and made his way through the empty parking lot of the building before them, an area of at least 5000 square feet. They passed through a rectangle of bare earth, no doubt to be planted with carpet grass later, and then reached the building under which the two vehicles were parked. Arjun ran across as fast as he could, his hands held in front of him. Once inside the building, he ducked behind a pillar out of sight of the stairwell beside the elevator shaft. Bunty came next, moving with a speed that belied his large frame, and took up position behind an adjoining pillar.

Arjun listened, but heard nothing. He pointed in the direction of the stairs and whispered to Bunty, 'You go first, I'll follow.'

He followed his friend to the elevator shaft and then up the raw concrete stairs, where it was surprisingly dark. On the first floor, they saw why: the doors to the flats had been fitted to the inner walls, and all of them were locked. The only light came in from the corridors that went off at three right angles and ended in open space.

The two of them moved slowly up: the third floor, the fourth, the fifth. Bunty was breathing heavily now, and paused.

'Why not just call and tell him that you've reached?' he hissed. 'They could be anywhere.'

'It'll be good if we can surprise them,' Arjun said. 'Let's go till the tenth floor and see.'

'As you say, boss.'

They went up one more floor: inner walls completed, and doors all locked, a diffused light coming down the corridors. Bunty was just about to go up one more floor when a man came trotting down the steps. He froze when he saw Bunty with his gun, and turned and sprinted up the steps. They could hear him shouting, and ran up after him and then down a corridor where one door stood open.

'Let me go in,' Bunty whispered, moving the gun from his right hand to his left and wiping his palm on his trousers.

Arjun nodded and looked around. With his two broken hands, he was more of a liability than an asset to his friend.

'Just stall them,' he whispered back, 'and I'll try and come from the back.'

Bunty nodded and gave a thumbs up. Arjun went back towards the stairwell and took one of the other corridors that went off at a right angle. It was now or never.

71

THE CORRIDORS CUTTING THROUGH EACH floor all ended in open rectangles—maybe the builder planned to fill the space with glass bricks, Arjun thought. He had noticed from below that each floor had an outer ledge running around its length, a projection of about a foot and a half, and it was on to this that he now stepped out. Looking down at a pile of bricks, he had a momentary feeling of dizziness. Eight floors up: a fall from here would end in death. He turned so that he was facing the building and inched to his left, shuffling his feet sideways. He held his plastered hands against the cement walls, and then on the low open window ledges, to keep his balance.

Then came one of the support pillars, where the ledge ran out. Arjun had to reach across with one hand and foot to the other side, then swing himself across. The pain shot through his unhealed hands again, bringing tears to his eyes, and he stayed where he was for a moment, catching his breath. Then a scream again, from somewhere nearby: Agnes! He moved sideways as fast as he could, and peeped in from the side of an open window.

The spacious, unfinished room where the three of them stood like actors on a set was probably meant to be a bedroom someday. The fourth person was Agnes Pereira, the jeans and track jacket she had worn the previous day dusty and dirty by now. She was tied to a wooden chair with thin nylon ropes, and behind her stood Sunny Chadha holding a knife to her throat. Bunty had Arjun's revolver

408

pointed at the politician's grandson, and to the side of them, his back to Arjun, was the other man, clutching a wooden plank. He ducked out of sight, trying to decide what to do.

So his deduction had been right after all: it was Sunny Chadha who had been behind the whole thing. But could Arjun still save her?

'I'm telling you again,' he heard Bunty say, 'let her go or I'll blow your head off.'

'Pull the trigger and I'll knock your head in,' the man with the plank said.

'Sisterfucker, don't tempt me, I'll put a bullet through your balls right now!'

'If you shoot,' Sunny Chadha drawled, 'the knife cuts her windpipe.'

'Please, no!' the girl shrieked, and her captor yelled at her to shut up.

Arjun decided to show himself. He moved into view, his plastered hands hidden below the window ledge.

'So there's the prodigal grandson,' he said, and all eyes turned towards him. 'What's the matter, don't you want to share some of your fortune with your second cousin?'

He saw Agnes Pereira's eyes widen further in surprise.

Arjun went on, 'Or has Platinum Court bled you of the entire family fortune?'

'The busybody detective,' Sunny Chadha sneered. 'What do you want now?'

'You think you're smarter than everyone else, don't you? That's the cause of all your problems. I have a gun here with me, and if you don't step away from her I'll shoot you.'

'Both his hands are in plaster!' the other man yelled out, his eyes moving between Bunty and Arjun. 'I saw it downstairs.'

Arjun recognized him now: he was the mali at Sunny Chadha's flats.

Sunny Chadha smiled. 'What was that you said about being smarter?' He motioned with his head for the other man, who came towards him.

'Take this knife and keep it on her throat,' he said to him, 'and give me that plank. Let me take care of this idiot first, then we'll handle the other one. If he tries shooting, stick the knife into her windpipe.'

Arjun saw Bunty lick his lips nervously. He shook his head at his friend, telling him not to shoot. The mali slipped behind Agnes Pereira now with the knife, while Sunny Chadha took the plank in his hands, lifted it up, and rushed towards Arjun. It happened so quickly Arjun reacted instinctively, without thinking. He raised his left hand and took the plank that Chadha swung down at him on his forearm. A white-hot flash of pain radiated up to his broken hand, but the adrenaline allowed him to ignore that. He swung his left leg over the window ledge, straddling it, and with that support brought his left arm down and around Chadha—who was raising the plank again—and pulled him forward. Chadha, who was unbalanced, toppled over the window ledge, landed on the outer ledge, then slipped down, holding on by his hands as his legs dangled in the air. Breathing heavily, he clawed at Arjun's right leg with his left hand.

'You wanted to kill me, didn't you?' he asked Sunny Chadha, who looked up at him with an expression of pained defiance. 'Take this, you bastard.'

He lifted his right foot and brought it forward and down hard on Chadha's other hand. There was a howl of pain, and the other man dropped. Arjun watched as he fell and was impaled on the iron rods sticking out of a cement column of a half-constructed room down below. He was dead instantly—the spine would have broken on impact—and a red stain blossomed around the iron rods protruding out of his stomach.

410

He swung his right leg inside the room and turned around. Both Bunty and the mali looked unsure of what to do now.

'Your boss is dead,' Arjun said to him. 'Put that knife down and we'll allow you to leave. If you kill her, you die too.'

'Arjun!' the girl cried out.

The knife in the mali's hand wavered. 'How do I know you're telling the truth?'

'You have nothing to do with this. Leave. Otherwise you die.'

The knife came down, and the mali walked slowly towards the open door.

'Let him go,' Arjun said. 'Put down the gun.'

Bunty did as he was asked. The mali came to the door. Suddenly he lunged forward with the knife, but Bunty managed to move away and the knife only slashed across his arm. Arjun watched as his friend raised his revolver and fired—the shot rang out in the closed confines, and the mali fell to his knees, a red patch spreading on his shirt as well. Arjun became aware that Agnes Pereira was screaming and he stumbled across to her and put his arms around her.

'It's all right. We're safe now.'

Bunty untied the ropes and they went down the staircase with Agnes crying and holding on to Arjun, the body left behind. At the parking area at the bottom Arjun went to have a look at Chadha's car and saw his laptop lying in the back seat. He asked Bunty to break the window and take it out. The car's alarm went off as Bunty smashed the butt of the gun into the glass.

They hurried to the Safari parked beside the next building. As they approached the vehicle, they saw two men and a woman, shabbily dressed, coming towards them from a tin-covered shelter at the edge of the property. They looked like labourers or caretakers. Bunty unlocked the car and asked Arjun and Agnes Pereira to climb in. He tore a length of cloth off a window-wiping

411

rag and wrapped it around his bleeding forearm, then walked over to the approaching threesome.

'You must be in terrible pain, Arjun,' Agnes said, wiping away her tears.

'Oh, it's nothing,' he said, putting an arm around her.

Bunty, meanwhile, was gesticulating and talking to the woman and two men, who were nodding in agreement. Arjun added, 'But you stand to gain quite a lot of money.'

She looked up at him. 'What do you mean?'

'The police are taking a DNA sample from your great-grandmother in Lucknow to match with Munni's DNA samples. If your sample matches theirs, then you get the money in Munni's trust. Then there's the property of your grandfather, Dinesh Chadha. You should get a third of that now that your cousin's out of the picture.'

'Is that why they tried to kill me?'

'Yes, Sunny Chadha was broke and in debt. The last thing he wanted was another person to share his grandfather's property with.'

'And how much money are we talking about?'

'With the trust money, around fifty to sixty crores.'

'Wow, that's a *lot* of money.'

'Agnes, where were you snatched last evening?'

'While I was walking out to the main road to get an auto. I was dragged into the back seat of that car by the fellow your friend just shot.' She looked out of the windows at the construction site. 'But why did he want to kill you as well?'

'Because he knew I would find out that it was him who took you.'

Bunty was walking back to the car now, and the woman and two men were going back to their shelter. When his friend had got in and started the car, Arjun asked him what had transpired between them.

'I told them to tell the police that they saw three sardars with black turbans in a big grey car, from a distance,' Bunty said as he reversed and cut left and then went out the way they had come in. 'And that if they didn't, I would pay them a visit one night.'

'That should work,' Arjun said.

They reached the dirt track that led to the service lane and the expressway. Arjun looked back—he could faintly make out the bent body stuck on top of the cement column, the arms and legs stuck out, and the half-completed buildings and construction cranes around it. He turned around and patted Agnes Pereira's head with his plastered left hand, and as he did, felt that something which had begun a long, long time ago had finally come to an end.

72

'SO HAVE THEY FOUND OUT whose remains those were?' Bunty asked.

'They're collecting DNA samples from next of kin to cross-check,' Arjun said. 'It'll take some time. But one of the boxes has Munni's remains in it, of that I'm sure.'

A waiter appeared bearing a tray with two chilled bottles of beer, two mugs and a bowl of salted peanuts. As he filled their glasses, Arjun took out a new packet of Gold Flake king-sizes and fumbled with the wrapper. Bunty watched with growing irritation, and when the waiter had left, leaned across the table and opened the packet, put a cigarette between Arjun's lips and lit it.

'When will you stop, kancha? You're poisoning both of us.'

Arjun grinned and blew out a stream of smoke upward. 'I doubt cigarettes will be what kills us.'

His comment made Bunty's expression turn grave. It was midday on a Friday, four days after they had rescued Agnes Pereira, and they were meeting for the first time since then, in the smoking section of a stylish and deserted GK-II pub which was now playing '80s pop hits.

'It was my first time, you know,' he said, looking down at his beer. 'I don't know what happened to me, I just lost my cool.'

'Try not to think about it too much.' Arjun lowered his voice. 'I had to kill three people. Cheers.' He lifted his glass

414

with both hands and took a drink. And someone died in Manali because of me, he thought.

Bunty nodded. 'Cheers. I guess we're safe though?'

'Yes. I think those workers stuck with the story you told them. The newspapers have said "unknown assailants" pushed Chadha to his death and shot his gardener, probably over some building dispute.' In fact, Arjun had been visited two days ago by Commissioner Jha himself, but he saw no reason to burden Bunty with that piece of information.

'But what about the bullet, Arjun? Can it be traced back to you?'

'No, it's a common enough calibre.'

'So you were right about Sunny Chadha being behind the whole thing. But how did you find out?'

'By making connections. I saw something in a diary, one copied out from the original written by Munni. It said she had gone on a holiday to a place near Bombay in early 1962. The second time I saw it, it reminded me of something in Dinesh Chadha's autobiography.'

'Wait, what do you mean copied out?'

Arjun explained. Bunty shook his head in wonder: 'What an idea to make money!'

'And what I had seen earlier in Chadha's book,' Arjun continued, 'was that he had been on holiday to Matheran in early 1962. This was the year before he got married. And it struck me that they just might have been together there, Munni and Dinesh Chadha! She says in her diary that she had visited a place near Bombay in early '62, and that she was confused at that point of time.'

'But you told me that he had been interested in her mother, yaar!'

'True. But from what I had heard of him, it would have been natural for him to have been interested in Munni as well.

415

Maybe they went up to Matheran together, or separately and then met up there. He was a ladies' man, she was a successful actress—only natural, right?'

'And nine months later, another natural occurrence took place?'

'Correct. By then, things would have cooled down between them, and Munni was being pursued again by another former admirer, Riyaz Sheikh.'

'No wonder she turned into a recluse,' Bunty said, sipping his beer.

'Only Munni and Dinesh Chadha knew who the real father was, which was why he arranged for the baby to be adopted by an Italian couple in Mumbai. If it wasn't his child, he wouldn't have bothered. But then the Italians had to return home, so they handed the baby over to a lady they had met at a fertility clinic, Agnes Carvalho. The child remained in India.'

'And that child was . . .'

'Agnes Pereira's mother. Even if Sultana Begum had gone looking for the baby after Munni stopped working and went off to Delhi, I don't think she would have found her. By then Agnes Carvalho must have taken the child back to Goa, and disappeared.'

'Why was Agnes Pereira in danger then?'

'Certain details had been provided by Dinesh Chadha for contact in an emergency; those and a pair of Munni's earrings went with the child. Agnes Carvalho put them away, but Agnes Pereira found them after she died. And when she went looking—'

'The contacts informed Sunny Chadha?'

'Not them, but the owner of the lodge where the bar dancer was murdered.'

'The lodge?'

'Yes, the third book to help me after the diary and the autobiography was an old guidebook to Bombay. It mentioned something about names of roads and cities from the colonial days being changed, and I realized that Bharat Lodge could in fact be the same as the New India Lodge. Before she was kidnapped, Agnes Pereira had come to my place, and she told me then that she remembered staying at the New India Lodge as a child with her mother. And the lodge had also been a meeting place for Dinesh Chadha, the director Babul Biswas and Riyaz Sheikh.'

'It was the same place. So?'

'Two workers,' Arjun said, 'at Sunny Chadha's apartments seemed to be Marathi Catholics, I saw one of them reading the *Loksatta*, and I had also seen a Catholic calendar at the lodge in Mumbai. It occurred to me that the owner of the lodge might have provided workers to his old friend Dinesh Chadha's grandson Sunny. And the owner or the manager of the lodge could have passed on word of Agnes Pereira snooping around to Sunny Chadha.'

'And he contacted the Mehtas and they contacted Vishwanathan aka Kumar Sampath, who then contacted Mr Vikas, who was known to Kailash Swami as well?'

'You got it. And Vishwanathan had links to the match-fixing kingpin in Dubai.'

'Well, if you worked all that out, it's not chance,' Bunty said. 'What about the lodge owner though?'

'His son has been picked up along with the lodge manager by the Mumbai Police on the advice of their Delhi counterparts.'

'And Agnes, where is she now, back in Mumbai?'

Arjun nodded, and took a drink from his glass.

'So she never stole any money from this Vishwanathan or Sampath fellow?'

'That was just an excuse. They needed to track her down after the killer got the wrong woman in the lodge. And I turned out to be a convenient person for the task.'

'Tell me, do you miss her?'

Arjun thought about it and shook his head. 'No. She has her own life.'

'That's what you always say.'

They sat quietly for a while, listening to A-Ha's 'Take on Me' and savouring the midday beer. Arjun's phone rang. It was Rhea, asking when he would be home.

'In a while.'

'Where are you?'

'Having a beer with Bunty.'

'Don't be long, lunch is ready. Soup and salad.'

Arjun told her he would back within half an hour. Bunty asked him who it was, and when Arjun told him, he laughed.

'She's grown up, hasn't she?'

'Yes. Seems like just yesterday that I was dropping her to school. Come on, drink up. I don't want her waiting for me.'

Bunty looked up at the clock on the wall, and opened the second bottle of beer.

X

Two days earlier, on Wednesday, the doorbell had rung at Arjun's flat at ten in the morning. He had opened the door thinking Rhea had dropped by early, and was surprised to see Commissioner Jha instead, standing there dressed in a dark-blue suit.

'Good morning! I was on my way to a meeting and decided to drop by. What happened to your hands?'

'My hands?' Arjun raised them up, momentarily at a loss. 'Oh. They got stuck under a cupboard while I was trying to shift it. Fractured a few bones.'

'Sorry to hear that.'

'I should be okay soon. Please, come in.'

The police official followed Arjun in, looking around the flat before taking a seat.

'Where's the cupboard?' he asked.

'In my bedroom,' Arjun said, still standing. 'It can't be arrested unfortunately.'

'Ha ha. Well, I'm not here for that. The grey Swift parked below is yours, isn't it?'

'Yes, it is.'

'I had a look before I came up. There's a dent behind the front fender. How did that happen?'

'How do you think? Another car banged into it at Nehru Place.'

'You know, a few days ago a man was killed in an accident in Siri Fort. We found a gun on him, and later identified him as a known criminal and sharpshooter from UP. There was a sole witness, a pavement dweller, and he says he saw a medium-sized grey car hit the motorcycle. The witness couldn't catch the number plate though.'

Arjun shrugged, even as his heartbeat went up. 'There must be thousands of such cars in the NCR.'

'True. But a lab analysis could clarify matters. Anyway, that's not what I'm here for.'

'Wait, how did you find out where I live and what car I drive?'

'Come on, Mr Arora, give the Delhi Police some credit. What I'm here for is to tell you that Kumar Sampath, aka Vishwanathan, has been picked up by us in Mumbai and is being brought to Delhi. We've also put in a request to have the person in Dubai arrested and extradited to India. They're not going to get off easily. Does that make you feel relieved?'

'Certainly. I guess I should thank you.'

'We're just doing our work. But Kailash Swami's arrest gave the whole thing an impetus, you know. Whoever tipped us off did us a big favour.'

'You never found out who it was?'

The commissioner shook his head, then pulled his nose and looked down at the table. 'Would you have any guesses?'

'Like I said, maybe a disgruntled employee. Were Munni's remains found there?'

'I've sent two men to Lucknow to collect a DNA sample from the mother.'

'And if it turns out to be her, your mind will be at rest?'

'Certainly. It would have been the one unsolved case of my career. So I'd like to thank whoever brought this whole thing to light.'

'I'm sure he must be hiding away somewhere, or he might have left the city.'

The commissioner looked at Arjun for a while. 'Maybe. Have you heard about the death of Sunny Chadha?'

'Not that I recall.'

'He was the grandson of Dinesh Chadha, who was around when Munni was a star.'

'Who killed him?'

'Unknown assailants. Mystery surrounds this case.'

'I'll let you know if I hear anything.'

'I'm sure you will.' The commissioner looked around and stood up. 'I'll be off.'

'Thanks for stopping by. I have a feeling those will be Munni's remains.'

'There must be some truth to that if you say so.'

The commissioner looked at him, a half-smile playing on his lips. Arjun realized at that moment that Jha knew, but that he wasn't going to do anything about it. Solving the mystery of Munni's disappearance was something of far greater importance to him.

Arjun watched from his balcony as the commissioner walked to his official car, parked on the other side of the park.

Vishwanathan and Kailash Swami behind bars, Sunny Chadha and Mr Vikas dead, and the don from Dubai being extradited—he felt as though a great weight had been lifted from his shoulders.

X

By the time Prakash Saxena's article on Munni and her unknown child appeared in Poppy Barua's newspaper after being edited by her, a month had already elapsed since Sunny Chadha's death. The retired professor had completed his article a week after the happenings at Kailash Swami's mansion, but Poppy had had to wait as the Delhi Police took their time to confirm the results of their DNA tests on Munni's remains and on her old mother in Lucknow. The article, featured in a Sunday issue, was mostly about Munni's life (which Saxena had told Arjun about), with the revelation that she had given birth to a child who had been put up for adoption and that the actress herself had met her end in a box in the grounds of the mansion. It also mentioned the scratch marks found on the inside of the lid of Munni's box. On Arjun's request, Saxena and Poppy Barua had not mentioned Agnes Pereira or her mother by name. As for the identity of Agnes Pereira's grandfather—Arjun had kept that to himself.

He read the article in the newspaper as he sat in a waiting room at Apollo hospital with his mother. His father had finally agreed to go for a check-up, and Arjun had waited till both his plaster casts were off before driving up to West Delhi one Sunday morning to pick them up.

'Can you drive?' his mother had kept asking him. 'Are your hands okay?'

'Of course I can,' he had replied, flexing his hands on the steering wheel.

All five fractures had healed cleanly, though one metacarpal in each palm had bent slightly. Arjun had been surprised himself

421

by the healing process. His body could still fight back. Maybe it was time he took better care of it. Diet. Exercise. No alcohol and cigarettes. Or maybe just a peg or two on the weekends. And who knew what might follow on from that? Agnes Pereira was out of his life now, but she had helped him regain some of his lost confidence. An added advantage of his broken hands had been that Rhea had spent two weeks in her old room, cooking and generally looking after him. The maid had been thrilled to see her back.

Agnes had called him two days before, when the news of the DNA tests had come through. She had filed a claim for control of Munni's trust through a lawyer in Mumbai. The issue of Savitri Rao's murder had been settled by the Mumbai Police after clarifications were made by the Delhi Police, on the instructions of Commissioner Jha.

'Looks like I'll be getting control of the trust after all,' she had told him. 'Guess how much I'm going to give you?'

'How much?'

The amount she mentioned had made him start coughing.

'But that's too much!' he had protested.

'You saved my life, Arjun. Then there's the share from my grandfather's property.'

'You'll have to come to Delhi to settle that.'

'In a couple of months. I'll look you up when I'm there. You have to take me to—'

'To meet the nurse, I remember. We'll go to her place.'

He had told Agnes about Stella Smith's wish to see her, and she had agreed. As for Sultana Begum, Arjun had advised her not to go and meet her great-grandmother, saying it would be traumatic for both of them.

Arjun went through the rest of the newspaper while his mother chatted with an elderly woman whose daughter-in-law had come in for an ultrasound and whose sons ran a garments shop in Karol Bagh. How effortlessly she had unearthed all that information, a part of him marvelled as he went through the city news. Maybe that was where his instincts came from. An item in the paper caught his eye: another death. A young girl from Nagaland had been found murdered in her single-room accommodation in south Delhi. The police had apparently detained and then released a friend of hers, a boy from Delhi, but already there were student groups from the north-east complaining about discrimination in the probe.

His father was approaching them, leaning heavily on his walking stick with its three-pronged end, and accompanied by a young lady doctor. She let Arjun know that there were reports to be collected later on, but that apart from the old man's blood pressure problem, he appeared to be in good health. He thanked her, and walked out of the hospital with his parents. Some forty-two years ago in distant Shillong they would have left the hospital with him in his mother's arms; now here he was with them. He thought of Rhea—the circle of life.

It was a pleasant day, and out in the sun he felt something close to happiness. When they had gotten into the car, his mother innocently wondered as to how old the lady doctor might have been.

'Too young for me, if that's what you mean,' he said, taking the car out of the parking lot and towards the gates.

'You should look for someone,' his father said gruffly. 'Your mother and I have been talking about it.'

'Yes, I will,' Arjun said, slightly embarrassed.

As he drove away from the hospital towards CR Park, his thoughts, however, weren't about the lady doctor or Agnes Pereira. Rather, he was thinking of the dead Naga girl he had read about in the newspaper. Arjun wondered who might have killed her, if it was indeed a case of murder.